Dear Reader,

This month we have four wonderful new *Scarlet* romances for you which we hope will help chase away those winter blues.

Share *That Cinderella Feeling* with Anne Styles's heroine and find out if 'Cinderella' Casey really does live happily ever after . . . When the lawyer meets the dancer, sparks are bound to fly – and they do in *The Marriage Dance*, as author Jillian James brings us a new slant on the old problem of reluctance to commit. We are delighted, too, to bring you *A Darker Shadow*, the latest long novel by Patricia Wilson, in which Luc Martell is forced to remain in England with computer buff Amy Scott – the bane of his life. And finally, *Slow Dancing* by Elizabeth Smith shows us that life in Hollywood isn't always the stuff of dreams.

As always it has been a pleasure *and* a challenge for me to select these latest *Scarlet* titles for you and I hope that you enjoy reading these books as much as I did.

Keep those letters and questionnaires flooding in, won't you? We are always happy to hear from you. And don't forget, if you want to write to a favourite *Scarlet* author, I'll be glad to pass on your letter.

Till next month,
Best wishes,

Sally Cooper

SALLY COOPER,
Editor-in-Chief – *Scarlet*

About the Author

Jillian James spent her childhood in Surrey, England where she compulsively read all of Enid Blyton's books. If she wasn't in the library she was to be found in the local bookstore, and on Wednesdays Jillian was on her cycle, picking up her reserved romance comics, unaware that she was sowing the seeds for her future career.

Later she moved to Winnipeg, Canada, and became as enthusiastic about reading romances as she had been about Enid Blyton and her comics. Jillian began to write stories, inserting extra romance and happy endings into her favourite TV programmes.

Writing became a compulsion and she wrote anywhere and everywhere that she could. The author met her husband, Jim, when they were both working for the Winnipeg Free Press. Eventually, Jillian attended a creative writing course where the instructor told her to stop writing for a week and submit one of the many completed manuscripts she had stored in a suitcase!

Now a multi-published romance author, Jillian lives in Southern Ontario, Canada, with her husband and 'pleasantly plump' grey cat Mao. When she isn't writing, she plays golf and enjoys gardening. Jillian is thrilled to be writing for *Scarlet* where she's 'able to write the long contemporary romance novels I never even dreamed of writing.'

Other *Scarlet* titles available this month:
SLOW DANCING – Elizabeth Smith
THAT CINDERELLA FEELING – Anne Styles
A DARKER SHADOW – Patricia Wilson

JILLIAN JAMES

THE MARRIAGE DANCE

SCARLET

Enquiries to:
Robinson Publishing Ltd
7 Kensington Church Court
London W8 4SP

First published in the UK by Scarlet, 1998

A copy of the British Library Cataloguing in
Publication data is available from the British Library

ISBN 1-85487-870-0

Printed and bound in the EC

10 9 8 7 6 5 4 3 2 1

CHAPTER 1

Dancers flittered about like butterflies on the pink tiles surrounding the sparkling blue swimming pool, their toned, athletic bodies briefly covered by brilliant swimwear. Anni Ross took another sip from her champagne glass and switched her gaze to a man standing in the midst of the colourful guests. He remained still, out of place in his dark shoes, black trousers, and silver-striped white dress shirt. His only concession to the strangling, humid July heat was his black silk tie loosened below his shirt collar.

Anni guessed he wasn't a dancer, even if his narrow waist and taut thighs indicated he was athletic. He was also good-looking. Eyebrows, slightly darker than his golden brown hair, drew together over a straight nose, while a sensitive, full mouth had a tendency to thin when he became fidgety, and a nerve in his clean-shaven jaw twitched.

Suddenly he looked right at Anni. She could have dropped her gaze, slipped away into the profusion of rose bushes close by, but she didn't. She had been

1

staring at him because he was such a handsome man and she wasn't ashamed of it. She stood with the line of a dancer, her spine erect, her chest tightening with her breath as his eyes raked her willowy, supple figure in its halter-style ivory silk jump-suit. He rested his attention on her face, then her pale blonde silvery hair. Her new hair. But he had no way of knowing she had recently chopped her waist-length hair into a shimmering shoulder-length bell.

He lifted his glass in a salute to her, then he drank, draining every drop. Turning his back on Anni, he placed the glass on a rocky wall and began to stride towards the side of the house that would take him down some steps to a gate that led to the front driveway.

Anni couldn't let him go. Feeling as if she were being pushed by a giant hand, she ran across the lawn. The slim heels of her backless cream leather shoes forced her to slow down on the paving stones but she managed to catch up with him at the gate. By now her fingers clasped the stem of her glass so tightly she was sure it would suddenly snap.

Anni didn't have to say a word. He sensed her behind him and turned around. His blue-grey gaze met hers and she felt a lurch inside her stomach. Mingling with the floral aromas of the hot, sultry night was the scent of a sharp masculine cologne. Up close he was taller, more than merely hand-some.

She was breathless because she had been run-ning. Breathless because his aura completely sur-rounded her. But she managed to say, 'Hi. I've never seen you at one of Ray Gifford's parties before.' All her words sounded as if they were spoken during a gust of wind.

'Possibly because I've never attended one of Ray Gifford's parties before.' The man's voice was deep, authoritative, abrupt. 'And I don't intend to be here much longer.' He rattled his car keys. 'Excuse me.'

Her breathlessness didn't abate. Anni said with obvious panic now, 'You're not leaving.'

One eyebrow raised ever so slightly. 'No, I'm merely walking around the house for my health. Yes. I'm leaving.'

'You can't leave until I know your name.' This was imperative information.

He changed his stance to a more relaxed version. 'It's Steve Hunter.'

To Anni's surprise he tucked his keys into his pocket and then reached politely for her hand. His fingers were warm, firm and very strong. She clung longer than necessary. 'I'm Anni Ross. You're not a dancer?'

He withdrew his hand first, even if it seemed with reluctance. 'Lord, no. I'm Ray's lawyer.'

'Which is why you're dressed like a corpse in this heat.'

Steve Hunter laughed, his teeth a flash of even white. 'I could prove I'm far from a corpse.'

His laughter was contagious. Anni felt the rumble right inside her and smiled herself. She realized now that her presence seemed to have eased his agitation and he might yet retreat from his former bid to leave.

3

'How would you do that?' She matched his flirtatious manner, even if she did feel as if she were jumping into something headfirst without much thought to consequences. Yet she had run after him to detain him; she had caused this meeting to happen. If she'd left him alone, he'd be gone by now.

Steve Hunter's blue gaze almost mirrored her own. Anni felt something deep down respond, something more spiritual than sexual. He reached for the hand that wasn't holding the glass and pressed her fingers against his chest. Beneath hard muscle his heartbeat was strong and vital.

He said in a low voice. 'That's how.'

Anni's breathing quickened, a warmth curled inside her. Her tongue flicked over the lips. Then she glanced away, seeing the party crowd surrounding her and Steve like a flash of bright birds in a tropical setting. And she drew her hand away from his.

'Very much alive, wouldn't you say?' Blue eyes twinkled.

'Very much.'

He chuckled. 'Well, then. Now we have established I'm a living, breathing human, we'll discuss something more objective. How was the tour?'

Feeling as if Steve Hunter had turned her brain to mush, Anni tried to think straight. 'How did you know I'd been on tour?'

'Ray told me that was the reason for this party. The tour's over. The grand finale. The big bash.'

Anni danced her fingers, the ones that had briefly touched Steve Hunter, around the rim of

4

her glass. 'Yes, that's the reason.' These parties after a tour or the finish of any big show were held to unwind. She set herself on 'high' at the start of each long performance and stayed that way until the end. If she burned out in the middle she pushed herself mercilessly. This party, for her, was the ladder down to solid ground. She realized Steve was waiting for her answer. 'I was in Europe. It was great. But exhausting. Luckily it's the last tour for some time. We're beginning rehearsals for *Wedding Bells* in two weeks' time.'

'The rock musical?'

'You know *Wedding Bells*?' Anni hadn't expected a lawyer to have heard of the show.

Steve pushed his hands into his pockets and stood back surveying her. 'Not intimately. I've never seen a performance, but it's one of those shows like *Phantom of the Opera* or *Cats*, that you can't help hearing about. I also have to admit that I happen to know Ray has a production coming up. Are you in the dance chorus?'

Anni could barely believe he could be so informed. 'It's great that you've heard about the show. I'm not in the chorus. I'm performing solo as Selena.'

'Sounds like a starring role. You must be one of the best dancers in the company.'

'I wouldn't say that, but I try hard.'

He shook his head ruefully. 'Oh? I bet that's an understatement.'

It was. Anni had put her entire life into dancing. She had also spent a great deal of her life explaining her passion and not being understood, so she deliberately changed the subject. 'What's Ray done that he needs a lawyer at his party?'

Steve took the switch with ease. 'There were some modifications to his will since the divorce. The papers have been sitting around my office while he was away, and I wanted to deliver them.'

'You handled his divorce from Patty?' Patty Gifford had been one of the artistic directors in the Gifford Dance Company until the divorce. Anni missed her brilliant presence.

'Yes, I handled it.'

Anni saw Steve's mouth thin the way it had when he'd been fidgety, but she noticed he didn't seem quite so eager to leave now. 'Is that what you do, divorces?' Each question she asked seemed designed to detain him.

'Yes. However, lately I've handled a number of messy ones. Ray's was one of the messiest, with the two kids involved.' His tone matched the thin set of his mouth.

'Ray was a creep. But Lucinda is very nice.' Anni didn't add *but she's not Patty*.

'She must be. Ray told me he wants to get married again. I can't understand that. Out of the frying pan, into the fire.' Steve grimaced as if he thought the entire situation was distasteful.

'You wouldn't want to be married, then?'

He spoke with no hesitation. 'No way. What about you?'

'Well . . .' Anni wasn't sure what to say. She viewed marriage as a union that would restrict her career. But if she was in love, really in love, then . . . she was much less adamant than Steve. His

6

attitude towards marriage seemed so definite. So black and white.

Steve continued. 'All that aside, Ray suggested I drop the papers off tonight. I came straight from the office, which is why I'm dressed like one of the walking dead. If I may return to our original topic of conversation.' He grinned.

Anni returned his grin. 'Then work is over for the day and it's time to party. Relax, let go, chill out, kick back. Get out of your lawyer's strait-jacket.'

He waved in the direction of the gate he'd been trying to leave from earlier. 'I did already. I left my jacket in the car.'

Anni let her eyes wander to the smooth, hard flesh moulding the material of his shirt-sleeves. Remembering the hot, pulsing feel of him, she had to stop herself from reaching out to touch his arm. Instead she flicked her glass high in the air. Champagne spilled on to the pathway in a glisten-ing spray. She felt it might have been her emotions spilling there before him.

He chuckled. 'I think you've had enough of that bubbly stuff, Anni.'

'You're right. It's gone to my head because I never ate dinner.' Even as she spoke, Anni knew it was more than champagne making her giddy. It was Steve Hunter. She'd felt his attraction from afar and come running. Now she actually felt a little bit silly about the way she'd run after him. 'Um – the buffet table is on the other side of the pool.'

'Then go have something to eat, Anni.' Steve withdrew his car keys from his pocket.

Seeing the keys once more plunged her stomach into despair. 'Aren't you coming with me?' She heard the anxiousness in her voice and hoped he didn't. She was making a real mess of this meeting. He'd think she was too forward. He might even tell Ray about it and they would have a laugh at her expense. *So let him go, Anni.* She stepped back from him.

Meanwhile, Steve Hunter took one step forward and placed his hand on the gate latch. He appeared as if he were steeling himself to perform an action he didn't really want to perform. 'I came to deliver papers, not to party.'

'Don't you know how to party?' Anni said, wondering if she should bother to find more ways to keep him here.

His fingers played with the latch as he gazed thoughtfully at her. 'If I'm in the mood.'

'Aren't you in the mood tonight?' *Stop it, Anni. Let him go.*

He made a face. 'Truthfully? Not particularly.'

'You must have had a bad day?'

'I did have a bad day, Anni. Please. Let me go.' The words were forced out of him.

Even though she heard a desperate plea in the way he spoke her name, she couldn't help the flash of pain that he didn't feel the same urgent need to be with her tonight as she did with him. And yet her mouth seemed to run away without her brain monitoring her words. 'Why not wind down? At least eat. Let's go find that food. No way should you get into a car and drive after drinking champagne; I saw you drain that glass.

I'm not the only one who might be tipsy. Stay a while. Ray probably hoped you would. And I bet you're hungry.'

Anni saw Steve look at her, that all-over thorough glance he'd given her from the patio, and she suspected his escape was more than a mere dislike of parties. He wanted to leave her. Yet she couldn't believe it was because he didn't like her; she sensed it was more likely the opposite. So she stood beneath his scrutiny, her heart hammering. She could feel the vibrations, the push and pull from within Steve, the need pulsing through her own body. She might regret this tomorrow, but this evening it seemed right.

Eventually his hand left the gate and cupped her shoulder. Even though his touch was gentle, his flesh burned hers and Anni felt warmth and liquidity glide through her body as he used his hand as a guide. 'You're right. I am hungry,' he said, making her believe he meant much more, and she felt as if she was on a swing, one moment low, one moment high.

He pocketed his keys in a final gesture and they walked across the patio and the lawn, between the dancers to the buffet tables. Occasionally people would call out to Anni and she waved, very aware of Steve's possession of her shoulder, and even more aware that her fellow dancers would notice the possession and she might never hear the end of it.

Two tables were piled high with food. Slices of smoked salmon, green and pasta salads, roast beef, chicken, warm and raw vegetables, cheeses,

9

breads. The amount of food overwhelmed Anni, whose stomach felt full with emotion.

Steve let go of Anni's shoulder, took her glass, and put it on a tray. Then he handed her a plate and forced her to fill it.

'Soak up that champagne,' he said. 'You look as if you live on your nerves.'

She thought she had never met a man she suddenly knew was so right, but she didn't continue into the realm of the problems these feelings entailed. She'd save reality for tomorrow. She enjoyed spinning out of control. It was like dancing when the elements – body and mind – felt together.

'Anni?' Steve pressed.

In jerky tones she said, 'I do live on my nerves. I need a break.' The phrase was a common one but her voice held a hint of desperation.

'Will you be getting a break?' He sounded genuinely concerned.

She smoothed the surface of the plate with her fingertips and she saw them quiver. There was a lot behind her impulsive actions tonight. Steve Hunter might be an open door for her to walk through, a means of escape. Although she knew she shouldn't think that way, couldn't think that way. She was contractually tied with the Gifford Dance Company until next June. She had a show to rehearse for, perform. Although she had two weeks ahead of her with nothing much happening, she knew what was looming and lately had had sudden apprehensions that she might not be able to cope.

'Well?' Steve prodded. 'You seem to have drifted into dreamland.'

Anni forced a bright smile. 'I was thinking about my break. It's this weekend and for the next two weeks, except for Monday when we're taping a TV segment. I'm free until the rehearsal begins for *Bells*. But I still have to keep up my practice, so I'll go to Ray's studio a few times.'

Steve was loading his plate with breast of chicken, pasta and bread. 'It doesn't sound like much of a break to me,' he said.

'But it is. It's time at home, which I haven't had for a couple of years.' Anni ate a cracker with cream cheese on top then licked the cheese from her finger. She dished some freshly tossed greens on to her plate. 'But that's how it's been for me since I was a little kid and first began dancing.' She rarely discussed her dancing with strangers. No one ever understood the time and dedication required, but she was beginning to feel Steve might.

Steve pushed a slice of lean beef on to a spare corner of his plate. 'Didn't you go to school?'

Anni forked a slice of smoked salmon. The pink meaty fish might not have made it to her plate if Steve hadn't intercepted it.

'Whoops,' he said. 'It's lively. So did you go to school?'

Anni made sure the salmon was safe. 'Sure I did. But I danced in all my spare time. I didn't do the usual things kids do. Or teenagers. Or even twenty-somethings. You have to, Steve, to get good.'

He laughed at her intensity. 'I understand. I admire your tenacity.'

'But you laugh?' Possibly the trend of this conversation was not a good idea. He probably didn't understand.

'I'm not laughing at what you do, Anni.'

Anni wasn't sure if she believed him or not. 'Well, it was easy because I love dancing. There's nothing else I'd rather do for a career. Isn't it that way with you, with law?'

He sobered. 'Sometimes. Other times, I'd rather be on my boat.'

'You have a boat? I didn't think you were a complete office type.' It was a relief to turn the subject from herself. Dancing was so entwined with who she was that she found it difficult to explain. Besides, she wanted to know all about him.

'So you were thinking about me?'

'Yes. Before I talked to you.' Anni felt her breath begin to gather like an electric charge.

'I was thinking about you as well.' He still spoke solemnly.

Anni swallowed hard. 'You didn't mind that I ran to you, then?'

'No. I didn't mind one bit.'

Anni felt the air between them grow tense. She didn't know where to go from there so she waved her plate. 'Shall we eat this on the benches in the rose garden?'

'Sounds good,' he said, but he cast a lingering glance at the table.

'What's the matter, Steve?'

'Seems like I can't get any more on my plate.'

Anni saw food piled on food. She chuckled. 'My mother always says, "Eat that first. Your eyes are bigger than your stomach." You've got everything there is, Steve. You can always come back for seconds.'

He smiled. 'Mothers must think alike. Mine says that as well. Let's go.'

Anni walked beside Steve, still drawing stares from her dance company. She knew she would have to explain Steve to them and wondered what she would say. *For one evening I felt this tremendous attraction to a man and couldn't stop myself from being with him . . .*

They reached a secluded part of the garden. An iron bench beckoned between two trellises cascading with roses, and they made themselves comfortable beside each other between the scented walls covered with the thorny bowers. Anni wondered if the roses were an omen: beautiful to look at but dangerous to touch. Just like Steve.

13

CHAPTER 2

Steve was pleased now that he hadn't rushed away from the party. Anni Ross captivated him. But then he'd known she would. His eyes had sought her out as if she were the brightest star in the sky and he'd almost walked over to her. Except, he'd told himself, these people are dancers, they're not from your world. The woman might be magic this evening but tomorrow would bring reality. Reality is your real life. Your vision of dysfunctional relationships, your heavy workload, your upcoming hoped-for promotion to partner in the law firm. A dream that turned slightly sour today when you learned you weren't a shoe-in, that Craig Firth was your contender. There is also Lydia, who dresses in business suits and talks law and is respected in your circle of friends. The woman who could be just the ticket to your becoming the respected 'family' man you suspect they want. Craig has a family, two children, a social-climber wife, a woman similar to Lydia in some ways. That's what they want, Steve. That's what they're telling you. That's reality.

But now his reality wasn't real at all. It was Anni Ross with the sparkle in her purple-blue eyes, the swing of her silvery hair, the sheen of taut, velvety flesh over her sleek dancer's muscles. He'd felt her satin skin briefly beneath his fingers and his palm still felt her. He had to glance away from her to make sure he was still on solid earth. Still breathing normally.

Anni made him aware again by asking, 'Are you going for seconds?'

'No. I think I'll leave it. I'd rather be slightly hungry than stuffed.' He stacked her plate with his and placed the cutlery on top. 'Let's get rid of this and look for coffee.' Coffee might bring him back to earth.

'I don't need coffee,' Anni said. 'How about dancing? The music's started.'

No. He wanted to retain a grip on sanity, not be drawn further into craziness. 'I haven't danced for ages, Anni. You'll outshine me.'

'It's just for fun.'

'Let's decide after we take the plates back.'

They deposited their plates on the table and Anni tucked her fingers into Steve's. 'Come and dance now.'

She dragged Steve to the tile floor of the patio beside the pool. Other couples were dancing to wild music pounding from several speakers. Steve liked the loud, throbbing sound but he wasn't sure about dancing to it. As Anni began to gyrate with practised body and foot movements, her hair swinging into a silver arc, he realized that dancing wasn't part of his lifestyle any more. He'd got

15

staid, spending a great deal of time at his office. This was emphasized by his suit pants and dress shirt among all the half-naked glistening bodies. He instinctively loosened his tie a little more. He knew he shouldn't have stayed. He didn't fit in here.

'Steve,' Anni shouted, shaking and shimmying. 'Give it your all.'

He noticed other people staring now, likely wondering who or what Anni had picked up for the evening. So he wouldn't embarrass her or himself too much, he began to imitate her dance steps. The action took him back a few years before he'd become more thoughtful and serious. He couldn't quite recall when that actual instant had occurred.

'That's it, Steve. Follow me.'

'Women are supposed to follow men.'

'Not in my life.' She clapped her hands above her head and twirled in an imitation of a Spanish dancer. 'I dance solo.'

Feeling she meant she was solo in much more than dancing, Steve watched her silk-swathed backside swivel, feeling arousal at the same time as knowing he'd never reach her precision of step or body movement.

He asked, 'If you dance solo, then why am I with you?' He needed the answer to clarify what seemed to him an evening that had taken on a rather bizarre twist and was completely out of character for him.

She tilted her head sideways. 'To dance along with me, Steve.'

He hadn't got his answer; likely he never would. The music flowed through him, his foot tapped time.

'Steve. Jerk out of it.'

He began dancing. Luckily he was in good shape. Anni didn't stop for a second when the tune changed to one with an even faster beat. His heart hammered and his shirt clung to his arms and his chest. If the partners of his law firm could see him now they'd think twice about his promotion and give it to Craig Firth. No question.

When the opening chords of the next tune indicated a slower beat, he used the opportunity to grasp Anni into his arms, feel her hot moist flesh beneath his fingers and the heat of her pulsing body against his body. She leaned her cheek on his chest, near his pounding heart, and he gathered her closer and she didn't seem to mind that he was aroused and hot and needy for her. She wrapped her arms around his waist and he could feel her heartbeat and the small puffs of her breath from her exertion.

She glanced up at him. 'You did really well.'

He couldn't stop himself from kissing her mouth, which was soft, warm, and responsive. He wanted to continue but lifted his head. 'For a staid office worker.'

She looked a little startled by the kiss. 'Is that how you think of yourself? Certainly you're not used to dancing and letting go.'

'I've always been a little uptight on the dance floor. You're right. But I am letting go now.'

'Mmmm.' Anni leaned on him again.

17

He let the ends of her hair trickle through his fingers, and for the first time he felt Anni wind down. But there was something different between them now. A promise of a hot night to come. If they were alone he was sure he could carry her in his arms to a soft bed and make love with her. That was what he wanted.

Someone called out that the music was taking a break for half an hour. Reluctantly they parted and Steve grasped Anni's hand and they walked on to the cool lawn. The lights turned the humid evening into a misty daylight.

'I'm beat,' Anni said.

'Ready to go home?' He wanted to take her home, to get invited in to wherever she lived. To love her all night if he could.

She ruffled her hair, making herself look sexy and wanton, and Steve's fingers tightened around her hand.

She glanced at him. 'Actually, I am. I'm sleepy all of a sudden. I'm going to call a cab.'

No. She couldn't escape from him so easily. 'Where do you live?'

'I have a lakefront condo. How about you?'

'Rosedale.' He mentioned a select, established area of Toronto. 'I have to pass your way. I'll see you home if you like. Save the cab fare.' After all, she had given him a number of come-on signals for a night of love. A specific one was that she'd actually run after him to stop him leaving the party. After delving into Ray Gifford's life via his divorce, he was under the impression that dancers were fairly loose with their favours. He didn't think he'd be let down tonight.

However, she hesitated for a second before saying, 'That would be nice.'

Her hesitation made Steve wonder if there was another man in her life. Surely a woman who looked like Anni had a boyfriend? Nevertheless, it was knowledge he didn't want to know this evening. Later, well, fine. A boyfriend would get Steve off the hook. Because he couldn't take a woman like Anni seriously. Not that she wasn't serious. He sensed she was extremely serious. It was just that, well, she was right, a lawyer, a dancer. They didn't mix.

'Steve,' she said, 'I'm going to tell Ray I'm leaving now.'

He nodded. 'All right. I should thank him as well, seeing as I ate his food.'

They walked over to a small crowd of dancers hanging around the artistic director, Ray Gifford. Ray was theatrical in a masculine way. Wavy grey hair brushed his neck, black leather pants clung to muscular dancer's thighs, and a gold chain hugged his throat above the neckline of a black T-shirt. He was the type of powerful man people wanted to be with, either as women who were turned on, or as dancers hoping he might be their window to fame. Each time he came up to the office, female eyes lingered upon him.

Steve discovered immediately that Anni was important to Ray. As soon as he spotted Anni, he dismissed the other dancers, who obeyed by drifting away into the hazy evening.

Ray raised an eyebrow at the duo. 'Hi, Steve. Anni, you've met my lawyer. Well, well.' He transferred his glass and ever-present cigar to one hand and slipped a long arm across Anni's naked shoulders. 'Anni had a good tour, didn't you, darling?'

Ray's possessive gesture jarred Steve's nerves. *Calm down. Anni isn't yours yet. Maybe later. But never really yours even if you do make love with her tonight.* He knew that deep down in his heart, which was probably why he'd tried to leave before he met her. It wasn't only because they were opposites, it was because he knew from her conversation that Anni's dancing was the most important thing in her life to her, that anything else, anyone else for that matter, would take second place. Ray only stressed it.

Steve said, his voice curt and irritated, caused by the strain of knowing what he didn't want to know, 'She told me.'

Ray's voice also held an edge. 'She's an excellent dancer. My star. She needs to be free.'

Ray's eyes met Steve's and Steve saw the warning in Ray's brilliant green gaze. *Hands off Anni Ross.* But what if Anni didn't want to keep her hands off Steve? Frustration kept his tone abrupt. 'From what I've seen of Anni tonight, she's definitely free.'

Ray's gaze still pinned him down. 'I'm speaking psychologically.'

'I'm including psychological freedom in my comment, Ray. I'm merely going to drive her home to save her taking a cab. We came to say goodnight. Thanks for the party. It was great.' His outline statement of his plans made him add, *No loving. Goodbye at the door.*

'You're going with him?' Ray asked Anni.

Steve saw her give Ray a teasing smile. 'Yes. I'm going with him.'

Steve and Anni walked towards the house. Ray had let her go physically but Steve didn't think the emotional tie was cut.

'Do you feel the same way as Ray?' Steve couldn't help himself from asking.

She swept back her silvery hair with her hand as if she were used to longer strands. 'About what?'

'That you need to be free from outside emotional entanglements to dance. I believe that's what he was getting at.' Among other things. Was Ray possessive of Anni because of her star quality, or was it something more intimate? He knew damn well Ray went for young women. He'd been messing around on Patty for years. Lucinda, his current love, was an example. She was only twenty-seven to Ray's over forty-something.

Anni tossed her head slightly. 'Yes, I feel that, but it isn't something I want to discuss tonight.'

'Then it's a real big problem?'

'Only a problem if you make it a problem, Steve.' She brushed at her hair again as if it were in the way of her face. 'Please, I'm feeling tired. My luggage is upstairs in the house.'

Steve told himself to forget it. After all, he was the one going home with Anni, not Ray. He forced a smile. 'I'll help you.'

They moved through the open patio doors into the spacious sunroom with its polished wicker furniture and indoor palms. All the floors of the home were hardwood and Anni's heels and Steve's

21

hard-soled shoes echoed in the chandelier-lit hall. Anni led Steve up the scarlet-carpeted stairs into a big bedroom with an oak four-poster bed standing on a thick white carpet. Anni touched the cream brocade curtain that was drawn back with a golden cord sash and tassel. 'Isn't it a great bed?' she said. 'It was Ray's great-grandfather's bed. I'm invited to sleep here if I can't make it home.'

Steve could hear a change of tone in her voice, as if her words were an attempt to smooth the strain that had developed between them. And yet he couldn't help himself from pouring on more tension. 'With him?'

Anni's eyes met his and he saw her gaze narrow. 'I don't sleep with Ray,' she said softly but firmly.

'No?' Keep digging, Steve. The grave will be deep enough to bury you by midnight. It's what you want. You want subconsciously to bury these burgeoning feelings, the passion growing in your gut.

'Don't you believe me?'

The hurt in her voice vibrated right through him. He raked his fingers through his hair, wishing he could let Ray go, but he couldn't. 'It was the way he touched you.'

Steve could tell Anni was getting agitated with him. But she explained carefully, 'He's a touchy-feely person. It's nothing. Believe me, Steve.'

He wanted to, he really did, but he couldn't breathe properly thinking about her with Ray. But he knew if he didn't leave it she was strong enough to walk out on him, and he had come so far he couldn't bear that. Everything he thought sanely was contradicted by reality. 'Where's your stuff?' he asked abruptly.

Bruised by his accusations and brusqueness, Anni said just as sharply, 'Here. Two suitcases and my jacket.' She picked up the purple silk hip-length jacket and rescued her small silver purse from the pocket. 'Do you want to wash? I feel wrecked after dancing. It's so hot tonight. You seem like you need a cool-down.' She wasn't sure why she added the last comment. Likely she'd never see Steve Hunter again, judging by the way he was acting.

But he seemed a little calmer as he said, 'That's a good idea. You first in the bathroom.'

Anni went into the bathroom, closed the door a little harder than necessary, and opened her purse. There was a mirror in the flap of the bag. Her eyes stared back at her. Dark, turbulent eyes – full of desire? Or dark because she was tired, worn out? Or because she was exasperated with Steve right at this moment for even presuming she would have anything going with Ray? Oh, yeah, other dancers had, but not Anni. She had kept her distance, her perspective, kept away from his clutches. If Ray ever became her lover, he would have even more control over her than he did now. Besides, she wasn't attracted in that way at all. He was far too old, jaded, and all that stuff. Steve was far more her type. Too much so, it seemed.

To help calm herself Anni splashed her exposed flesh with cold water and fixed her eye make-up. She ran her tongue across her top and bottom lips, remembering Steve's kiss. It hadn't been more than a butterfly kiss, but it had kindled a flame inside her. The same way as feeling his arousal had. Did he really want her or had he merely reacted to the music, the heat and atmosphere of the dance? Figuring she didn't want him to want her anyway, because it would definitely cause complications in her life, Anni tucked the purse strap over her shoulder and returned to the bedroom. She should be pleased he was acting like an ass about Ray.

Steve was sitting on the side of the bed, still looking tense. 'Don't let Ray upset you.'

'I'm not letting Ray upset me.'

'It seems that way, Steve.'

He spread his arms in despair. 'I just know his recent history, that's all.'

'Lucinda?'

Steve nodded. 'Among others.'

Anni told him a conclusion a lot of her fellow dancers had come to. 'Ray is a Peter Pan. A lot of men are. Now go and cool down. You'll feel fresher.'

They seemed to be alternately caring for one another. Anni's annoyance fizzled out and a huge weariness overcame her as Steve rose and walked into the bathroom. The door closed with a definite thud that matched her own display of temper.

Raising one eyebrow, Anni brushed her hair in front of the dresser mirror, trying not to think of what her impetuous dash across Ray's garden might have precipitated.

When Steve came out, he picked up her luggage. 'This is it?

'Yes. And this bag.' She swung her huge soft bag made of shiny green plastic on to her shoulder. 'Ready to leave.' Anni spoke pointedly.

Steve carried the two suitcases and they made their way down the stairs and out to the front steps. The solid wall of heat after icy air-conditioning hit them, doing nothing to help Anni's weariness. By now even her legs felt as if they might cave in as she followed Steve across the driveway and past a line of cars to his black Mercedes. He opened the trunk and placed her luggage inside.

'Do you want your green bag in the back?' he asked her.

'Sure. Why not?' She swung the bag his way. He tucked it in beside her other luggage. Then he opened the car doors.

Anni climbed into the luxurious interior of the car with a sense of relief that she could now sit down and relax. If Steve let her relax.

'Seatbelt on?' he asked as he slid in beside her.

'Yes.' She displayed her fastened seatbelt that strained over her taut dancer's breasts. 'I can still take a cab, Steve.'

'What brought that on?'

'Your attitude.'

Steve leaned over and kissed Anni's mouth. She wanted the kiss but she pushed back into the seat away from him anyway. She figured Ray had made him jealous. Jealousy meant feelings, possession. She wished she'd never dashed across the lawn, and if she couldn't retract that action she certainly should have gone with the cab and made sure she never saw him again.

'Problem?' he said softly, not removing his mouth far from hers. She could feel his lips on her cheekbone and wished his touch didn't make her emotions rage out of control. She had to force herself not to wrap her arms around him and draw him closer to her. She felt a sort of weary longing to snuggle up with him.

'I'm not ready for this,' she said; her words seemed in direct contrast to her feelings, but it was her brain that was doing the talking.

'Neither am I.'

Did he feel the same push and pull? The same highs and lows? The same confusion? 'Then why are we doing it?'

'Because I want to kiss you. I can't help it, Anni.'

His features appearing strained, he lifted his hand and stroked her hair from her face. He kissed her ear and trailed more kisses back to her mouth. Anni let out a little sigh and her lips parted. His tongue touched hers briefly, much like a moth fluttering towards a bright light. She felt his moist warmth create another moist warmth. She was about to reach for him when Steve forced himself to sit upright in his seat and start the engine.

'Where are we going again?' His voice sounded gruff, dissatisfied.

Anni's mouth felt bereft, her body thrumming with desire. She whispered, 'Lakefront.'

'Of course.' Steve drove out of the circular driveway. 'Do you want the air-conditioning on?'

26

'No. Thanks. It's fine. I like being warm. May I open the window?' She knew she wouldn't get cool air but with the window down she wouldn't feel so confined with Steve.

'Sure.' He pushed the power button and the windows slid down.

Heat, saturated with the aroma of plants and flowers, seeped inside the car. Anni leaned her neck on the head-rest and closed her eyes.

As he drove along the tree-lined road away from Ray's house, Steve raked his gaze over Anni's delicate features, feeling an intense pressure fill him. He had never wanted a woman so much, so soon. He'd never before been made as jealous as he had by Ray. Love at first sight? He wouldn't say he'd believed in it, but now he might. He'd always wondered in what form love would come to him. Not that he was actually saying this was love. More likely lust. But it felt painful and wonderful all at once. And he didn't want it. He didn't want to become one of those embittered, raging people he saw in his office.

He thought this over as he left the suburban setting of Ray's home and drove east into the core of the city of Toronto. Finally he knew he must be close to Anni's home. 'Tell me where you live,' he said, his voice sounding loud after the lengthy silence.

She directed him to a tall condominium block on the shore of Lake Ontario, not far from the marina where he docked his boat. He carried her luggage into the elevator and rode with her up to the penthouse. Anni flicked on the light and said, 'Home,' with relief.

She had painted all the walls white, adding splashes of colour in accessories and furniture. Her chairs were red leather. Her cushions black, green, purple and yellow, like candy drops scattered on the chairs and corners of the wood floor. Rugs were furry white, easily tossed aside for dance practice. A barre and mirror took up one wall.

The window overlooked the lake and the green patch of the Toronto Islands, the scene dark now with lights in the distance. A couple of wing-back red and white striped satin armchairs sat by the windows with a set of shelves stuffed with books and magazines.

Steve figured it was the corner where Anni relaxed. Yet it was difficult to imagine her relaxed. She was so vibrant. So intense. Right out to lunch as far as being a match for him. Although he wasn't exactly Mr Laid Back himself tonight. Intense might also describe him. Intense. Confused. Wanting to stay with her, but at the same time wanting to run from the heat. He should have insisted on leaving when he had the opportunity.

'Great view,' Steve said, hearing himself sound peculiarly normal.

'It's merely a place to park my bags,' Anni told him. 'I haven't been home much in the past two years since I moved in.'

'It should suit your lifestyle.'

'I think it does. Do you have an apartment?'

'No. I have a house. It a very traditional home. Bricks and roses.' Steve smiled ruefully. No use trying anything on with Anni Ross. She was far too different. And yet. 'You said you were free this weekend?'

'Well, I must see my mother on Saturday. I'm free Sunday.'

'Sunday's good. It's my sister Janet's twenty-first birthday party. A barbecue at my parents' home.' *Crazy, Steve, to go that far.*

She hesitated the way she had when he had issued the invitation to drive her home.

He couldn't help asking the inevitable. 'Do you have a boyfriend?'

'Oh, no, no,' she said. 'It's just . . .'

'It doesn't make sense, does it?' he said. 'But that's okay.'

'It's not okay. But I would like to go out with you. It sounds like fun, a barbecue.'

'Is that a yes?'

She nodded.

Relief flowed through him and he heard it reflect in his voice. 'Great.'

Anni swung her arms around as if she were beginning a dance. 'Do you want anything, Steve? Herbal tea or something? I have some type of tea that makes you relax. Tastes gross but it does work. Or iced tea? It's so hot.'

'I think I'll pass. But you have something. I want you to relax.'

She laughed.

'What's so funny?'

'Number one, even though I feel tired I don't relax very easily. Number two, you're not re-laxed one iota. And number three –' she twisted her finger through her halter tie '– there's you and me. Opposites. The reason this isn't okay.'

29

He observed her finger sliding beneath the tie, wishing his finger were there, lowering to stroke her breast. He had to have her. Oh, yes, in real life they might be career opposites, she might not be good for him, he might not be good for her. But in bed naked he saw them as male and female, excruciatingly passionate, and he closed the distance between them, the distance he knew he shouldn't close if he were of sane mind. But Anni had made sure sanity wasn't a factor tonight.

Anni was supple in his arms, their kiss a continuation of their dance, a performance of tongues and mouths, bodies straining against one another. Her arms clasped around his neck, her fingers urgently mussing his hair. There was no doubt she wanted him. But suddenly, as much as he wanted her, he didn't feel it fair, even if she did smell sweetly of perfume and salty perspiration and he was ready to carry her in his arms to the bedroom. She was hyped from exterior events and emotions. Breathing raggedly, Steve lifted her arm and pressed his mouth to the soft inner flesh. When he reached her wrist, she moaned softly, her thigh gently nudging his arousal. He almost went over the edge and felt it time to withdraw. In slow motion, he watched Anni collapse on to one of the satin chairs.

She ran her fingers through her hair, looking at him. 'You could stay,' she said quickly. 'Although I'm not much use when I'm first home from a tour. I mean, it might be all for me, the feelings. Nothing for you. There hasn't been anyone for a long time. My career doesn't allow for long-term relationships. And I can't handle short affairs.

One-night stands would drive me crazy. So that's why you shouldn't stay.'

'Shush,' he whispered, thinking he had been drastically out of turn to believe she would be one of Ray's women. Of course she wasn't. 'It's fine. I understand. I stopped for that very reason. But our date is still on for Sunday?' If he had no loving, he had to have that.

No hesitation this time. 'Absolutely.'

'Great. I'll get going. Bye, Anni. Loved meeting you.'

'*Loved meeting you as well*,' Anni whispered when he was gone in the elevator and she chained the door. She kicked off her shoes and walked into the bathroom. In the mirror she saw her eyes, still dark, stormy, tumultuous. She had needed Steve Hunter to stay tonight. First time she'd admitted that about a man for an eternity. But she didn't want to hurt him. He was too nice a guy. She didn't intentionally hurt men, but it was the nature of her career that she was taken away from them for long sojourns, either physically or spiritually. There just wasn't time for men. She'd learned that for sure with Troy about five years ago. Since then she'd dated a few times, but nothing serious.

Anni's fingers clenched around the edge of the marble vanity top. This wasn't serious either. They would be incompatible. A lawyer and a dancer. One date with Steve, and that was it. That was all she could allow, because in her heart this meeting with Steve felt so right, so serious.

CHAPTER 3

Beep. Beep. Beep.

Anni stuck her head beneath the duvet. Shut up, phone. Go away.

Beep. Beep. Beep.

Don't give up, will ya?

Beep. She stretched out her arm and by feel picked up the receiver, cutting off the next beep. Her head still on the pillow, she planted the receiver against her ear and forced a muffled, 'Yes?'

'It's Ray.'

'Ray, it's my first morning home. I'm hung over. I'm a mess.'

'That won't do if Hunter is in bed with you?'

Anni lifted herself from beneath the duvet, shivering. It must be another hot day; the air-conditioning was working overtime this morning. She looked at the smooth rose-pink pillow beside her, thought about the man she had kissed so passionately last night and was forced, because it was the truth, not what she had wanted, to say, 'No. Hunter is not with me. Is that what you phoned about, Ray?'

'He's a lawyer, Anni. A workaholic. He'd be a strait-jacket. He's not for you.'

'Did I say he was for me?'

'You both looked turned on.'

'We humped in the car, Ray, what the hell, we couldn't wait. After that we didn't bother sleeping together. I mean, we got what we wanted from one another. A good lay.' She slammed the receiver down and jumped out of bed. She slipped a pale grey T-shirt over her head and ran to the bathroom.

Icy droplets of water mixed with hot tears. Not for the first time in the past year Anni felt Ray Gifford's pressure on her. Ten years ago, when she first started with him, she had accepted his control because she wanted the success Ray offered. Well, she had that success. She'd danced to sell-out audiences this year. And now there was *Wedding Bells*. Solo performances and emotional duets with Moe Ellison, the brightest male light in dance. Her career desires had been fulfilled but Ray's overbearing attitude was stifling. She felt as if she were in shackles.

The tour had exhausted her. But Ray's grip on her had begun to exhaust her even more. He didn't want anyone near her. Especially not a man she might fall in love with. *Well, Ray, I don't think I'll fall in love with a lawyer, even if I did dream about him all night and want to make love with him. I know, without you telling me, that I'm not wife-and-kids material.*

And yet she'd often, lately, longed . . .

Anni splashed more cold water on her face to dilute the tears. She was lonely, that was the reason

33

for this passion for a baby. She'd been aching inside from loneliness. She didn't know why these feelings had come now. Her dancing had been enough for a long time. It was as if she suddenly woke up and saw a great big void behind her. She'd given up half of her life. The half that was a man, marriage, children, an intimate life. Stuff she'd denied herself for years. And would have to deny even longer, she decided as she prepared for her shower. She still had *Wedding Bells* to concentrate on and after that there might be something else. Then, when her contract with Ray came up for renewal in June next year, she'd make a decision. She sometimes wondered if she unconsciously saw this desire for a baby as a simpler way to assuage her loneliness than desire for a man. Which it wasn't. She wasn't that naïve. And she would never go for one without the other. Children needed fathers. Her own father's devotion had proved that to her.

Anni found herself giving way to more hot tears in the shower. Somewhere deep down inside she was desperately unhappy, but it was a weakness she would only show to herself. While she dressed in denim shorts and a white cotton top to go and visit her mother, she listened to upbeat music on the radio to put herself in a better mood. But one of the songs was the slow tune she'd danced to with Steve, and his golden good looks were foremost in her mind as she drove her red sports car over to her mother's small apartment block in a pleasant shady area of the city.

Marian Ross didn't approve of Anni's chosen

career. The entertainment business frightened her mother. Anni should have been a nurse or a teacher, something respectable. A girl who danced half-naked on stage was not Marian Ross's idea of the perfect daughter. Because of this, Anni suspected, her mother ushered her quickly into the apartment, as if petrified one of her elderly neighbours might see Anni's revealing shorts. 'How was the tour?'

'A great success.' Anni had always wished her mother would loosen up. Even in summer Marian wore a conservative black skirt with a beige cotton top and sturdy leather sandals on her feet. Her brown hair was set in tight little curls. All much too dowdy for such a lovely sunny day. Anni would have loved to make her mother over, set her hair looser so that it emphasized her high cheekbones and exquisitely smooth complexion. Anni saw where she had inherited her own features as she kissed her mom's cheek. 'How have you been?'

'Not bad. The heat's getting to me, but my air-conditioning's working all right, thank goodness.'

Pleased that was the only complaint, Anni said, 'Great. Do you have some coffee on?'

'Yes. I'll get some.' Her mother began to bustle to the kitchen. 'Sit down.'

Knowing the rule that no one interfered in her mother's kitchen, Anni plunged on to the green velvet sofa. She always felt out of place in the subdued antique decor of her mother's home. Her mother had no paintings and few ornaments. Anni had always seen herself in her

35

mother's home as a brilliant bird fighting to be free from a cage.

Marian returned with two glass mugs, part of a set Anni had given her a couple of years ago.

'Here you go. Put it on a coaster, it's hot.' Marian pushed a cork circle close to Anni.

'Thanks, Mom.' Anni picked up the mug and drank the strong hot liquid. Her mother made excellent coffee, and she said so.

Smiling at the compliment, Marian sat opposite Anni. 'It's good to see you back, I must say, but it must be nice to travel. You've seen so much of the world these past few years.'

'You could travel,' Anni told her. 'Dad didn't leave you that poor.' As she spoke, Anni looked at her father's picture in a silver frame on a side table. He had been a thin man, fragile in some ways, with long pale hair. But always with a ready smile. Philip had died in his prime when she was eighteen. His death had left Anni devastated. He'd been the one family member who had supported her dancing. Even other relatives were on her mother's side. Anni should get married like all her cousins. Anni was sure they thought she slept around with different men, which was so far from the truth that it made Anni almost hysterical.

'I couldn't go anywhere alone, Ann.'

Anni brought herself back to the present. Her mother had never given in to the 'theatrical i' added to Anni's name. 'You don't have to go alone. What about one of those group tours? Why don't I look into it for you? I'd even treat you. I'm doing really well financially.'

'That's good to hear, but you don't have to spend your money on me. I know how hard you've worked to earn it. But if you just looked into a trip, it might help. I can't do everything myself. It's so difficult without a man. I wish you'd get married and then we'd have a man in the family once more as well as some grandchildren.'

Marian lifted her cup to her lips with a gesture of longing and dissatisfaction and Anni knew her mother was looking for something to put meaning into her life again. That something had to come from Anni. Strange, Anni now understood that more than she ever had before.

Her mother continued without waiting for Anni to say a word. 'You must have boyfriends and one day you'll have to make a choice. You know you will. You can't dance forever. You're almost touching thirty now. The chance to have babies doesn't last forever either. When I had you I thought I was going to be able to give you a brother, but there were things wrong inside me that didn't allow it. So you were it.'

Anni had never heard this story before. Her mother rarely spoke of such intimate matters. While she was pleased her mother had confided in her, she also felt that Marian was disappointed in her only child. And what had gone wrong inside Marian? Was it something genetic Anni might have inherited? Maybe she couldn't even have a baby. What if she was one of those women who longed for children but was – what was the word these days – barren? Then she knew other women who couldn't care less whether they

37

really had a baby or not and they got pregnant easily.

'Ann?' her mother questioned.

'Oh, I was thinking just about what you said. Dancers can perform longer these days.'

'Maybe that's true. But you don't want to wear yourself out. You're so skinny. You live on your nerves.'

Exactly Steve's observation, Anni thought, finishing her coffee. Steve. Her mind quickly went through last evening. Their meeting. Their dance. They'd been turned on. He'd been so hot and throbbing to hold. She could barely wait until tomorrow when she saw him again. She even wanted to tell her mother about him, but thought she'd better not. Marian might jump to conclusions and build up hope. Hope that Anni was also building. She had to tell herself that just because she'd felt this yearning for a child, it didn't mean she should rush into the arms of the first man who attracted her. Even so, remembering Steve made her lips tremble and she had to swallow hard to contain her emotions.

'Are we going shopping?' her mother asked.

Pushing everything from her mind except what she had to do at that very moment, something she had trained herself to do successfully, Anni nodded. 'Anywhere you want to go. It's your day.'

After a shopping trip to a mall and dinner at a seafood restaurant Marian Ross always enjoyed, Anni drove her mother home about eight o'clock, stayed for a few moments and went to her own apartment.

Upon opening her door she saw the red light on her answering machine flashing. Steve? After the way she'd hung up on him this morning it was more likely to be Ray. However, she almost tripped over herself getting to the phone. It was Steve. His lovely deep tones came over the machine, into her home, through her body. She stood trembling, listening, the inside of her head feeling light, as if it were on an instant high.

'Anni, where are you? Speak to me. Phone me. I miss you already.'

I miss you as well, Anni thought as she quickly wrote down his number, then punched it on her phone. Steve's phone rang and rang. She pressed the redial. It rang and rang and rang once more. Steve, where are you? His answering machine clicked on. She spoke rapidly after the tone. 'It's Anni. I'm speaking to you, Steve. Phone me later. I won't be going out again today. I've missed you as well.' She was crazy getting so involved. *Wedding Bells* loomed, which she thought was a pretty ironical name, given what she yearned for lately.

Now she didn't know what to do until Steve phoned. If he phoned. What if he called another woman and went out with her and she was the recipient of his hot kisses and sexy demands?

Determined not to think that way, Anni turned on some music, poured herself a soda, undressed, and put on a fluffy terry robe. Curled up on one of the satin chairs, she began to read one of her favourite mystery novels. But with her ear attuned to the phone she couldn't concentrate on the book. If Steve cancelled Sunday, she might never see him again, and her stomach was in knots by the time the phone rang. Feeling almost physically sick, Anni placed the paperback over the arm of the chair and cupped the receiver in her hands. *Let it be Steve.*

'Anni?'

So much relief she felt nauseous and could barely speak. 'Yes, it's me.'

'Hi. You're difficult to get hold of,' Steve said in his abrupt, what Anni thought might be client voice. 'What did you do today?'

Anni wondered if Steve used that authoritative tone when he was emotionally rattled. It seemed that way. Then, if that was the case, they were both emotionally rattled. Her stomach not settling one bit, Anni explained about her day out with her mother. 'What about you?'

'I put in a few hours at the office.'

Anni fiddled with the edge of her book. 'Ray said you were a workaholic.'

'When did he tell you that?'

'Oh, he phoned me this morning.' The book slipped to the floor and she leaned over to pick it up.

'Specifically to tell you that?'

He sounded angry and Anni didn't like him angry. 'Actually, yes, I believe he did. More like warning me off you.' Why was she telling him this? Was it a way to put some space before her so she wouldn't be tempted to get involved?

Steve made an exasperated sound. 'What does he think I'm going to do to you?'

'Take me away from my dancing.' She retrieved the book and tossed it on the other chair. 'That's what he thinks, Steve. And he's right. It could happen.'

'That's bull. I don't understand. You can't take me away from my career.'

'It's different, Steve. Different for women. More of a fight. Men don't understand.'

'No. I don't. I hope this conversation doesn't mean you've changed your mind about tomorrow?'

His voice was even harsher now and Anni felt an ache begin inside her stomach and she wanted to cry. 'No. I haven't changed my mind. Ray doesn't run my life.' But Anni knew that was a lie. She let Ray run her life because she was frightened of a world out of dance. Or even a world sharing dance with another aspect of her life. She wanted to scream *I'm so confused*.

'That's good to hear. It'll be a younger crowd tomorrow. A lot of Janet's university friends will be there for her party. There's a swimming pool, so bring your gear.'

'I will,' Anni said, wondering at the seesaw of her emotions since she'd met Steve. Was it only last night? However, she knew seriously that she couldn't get involved with him. She'd have to tell him that tomorrow, and the thought of having to wreck her date with him made her shrivel inside.

'Are you still there, Anni?'

His voice was more tender now. Possibly he'd been afraid she wouldn't be going with him. 'Yes. I am. I'll see you tomorrow.'

Feeling more than relief that Anni hadn't cancelled their date, Steve made plans to drop by her apartment around three in the afternoon. After they said goodbye, instead of continuing to work, he tilted back his burgundy leather chair and imagined Anni in her spacious white penthouse room. He glanced around him, at the vertical dark panels on the walls, the glass-fronted bookshelves full of bound leather classics and law books, the tile fireplace and marble mantel, the french doors opening into a garden lush with roses and summer perennials. Traditional. He *was* traditional. Anni was modern, off the wall. His world seemed dark. Anni's so brilliant. They were like night and day, they were so different. Anni Ross isn't your type, Hunter, he thought, and she knows it, even if she did make the first move on you at the party. It might help if you get that through your head before tomorrow and make tomorrow the last time you'll see her. Before it gets hot and out of hand. Even if hot and out of hand was what he desired. Lord, did he ever.

Anni's summer clothes on the bed appeared like dancers heaped upon one another at the finale of a piece. She mussed her hair with frustration. Nothing seemed appropriate. She'd stuffed her bikini and towel into a huge black canvas bag with a red leather handle. Red. That gave her an idea. She had that skimpy black number she'd bought in London. With it she could wear her red high heels. It would look great. She'd push a pair of canvas rope-soled shoes and a lace wrap into her bag for comfortable after-swim wear.

She was dressed by the time the bell downstairs buzzed. She rushed to let Steve in. Her heart beat hard. Her body felt shaky. Everything about her movements seemed unreal, but it felt good to be so crazy about a guy. Even if tonight it would all be over. She had to make that decision. How could she accommodate these effervescent feelings in her day-to-day dancing life? She couldn't. Therefore she had to make the most of every minute. The trouble was, knowing it was only for the moment, that Steve would end with this day, would also make every minute sad.

But sad wasn't what Anni was when she opened the door and saw Steve. If she hadn't decided that caution was the name of the game, she would have flung herself into his arms. Wearing white slacks and a loose navy blue silk shirt, he looked gorgeous. Had he scoured his closet for something appropriate to wear the way she had?

'Why are you looking at me that way?' he asked with a smile.

'You don't look like a corpse today.'

'Well, thanks. What do I look like?'

'Lawyer on vacation,' she told him.

His forehead crinkled. 'Is that how you define everything, by a sort of character?'

'Yep.' Anni danced that way. She defined characters and acted them on stage. On long runs or tours she became those characters sometimes and it frightened her. She couldn't explain all that in a nutshell so she rushed to get her gear and they locked her front door and made for the elevator.

Steve said as the elevator shot to the ground floor, 'If we're characterizing one another. I'll put in my ten cents' worth. Last night you looked like a dancer; today you look like a fashion model.' He raised one eyebrow at her.

His raised eyebrow made Anni wonder if he was pleased about that or not. 'Do I look okay?' She never usually had to answer to anyone about the way she looked. Except her mother, of course, but long ago Marian had stopped criticizing aloud.

'Sure. You look great.'

But what? Anni thought as she slipped into his car downstairs. She snapped the seatbelt, thinking about last night and the way he'd kissed her outside Ray's house. Would he kiss her today? Would it be a farewell kiss?

They rode through local neighbourhoods with trendy restaurants, bustling crowds, shops with their wares displayed on the sidewalks. Anni loved the arrays of flowers cascading to the edge of the road.

Impulsively she touched Steve's arm. 'Stop.'

'I can't stop here, Anni, there's too much traffic.'

'Please. I want to take your mother some of those beautiful flowers.'

'Anni.' He gave her an exasperated look. 'You don't have to.'

'I want to. Hey, you can pull in over there. I'll only be a moment.' Already she had her wallet from her bag.

Steve eased the car into the space she indicated. Anni jumped out the car and hurried to the flower

stall. She picked out a mixed bouquet of fresh asters.
Then, remembering it was Steve's sister's birthday,
she chose a small bouquet of white sweetheart roses.
She paid for them and dashed back to the car.

Back in the car she saw Steve smile.

'Where do your parents live?' she asked when
they'd driven on.

'Next street,' he said.

They turned into a street divided by a grass
boulevard. All the houses were big, built of stone
or brick, all with overhanging mature trees and an
abundance of floral colour. Some even had rock
gardens, ponds, or swimming pools. Anni wasn't
surprised when Steve drove the car into the driveway of one of the larger homes on the street. It was
a sprawling stone house with a tower of rooms on
one side that appeared mysterious to Anni. The
garage had space for four cars and above there was
a complete intact apartment that Steve said his
grandmother stayed in when she came from Vancouver for a vacation. Which she did often. She
was his father's mother. His mother's parents had
been dead for a few years.

'Did they die together?' Anni asked as he turned
off the engine.

'Yeah. Car crash.'

'Oh, how terrible for your mother.'

'It was. Still is, I think. I remember they were on
their way back from Florida one spring. I was
sixteen. It's made her very jumpy about cars.'

'But she does drive?'

'Oh, yes.' He gave her a quizzical look. 'Are you
ready?'

Anni gathered her bouquets of flowers. 'I'm ready.'

They left the car and Steve led Anni around the house and through a gate to a red-tiled pool area where the Hunter family relaxed on loungers around a sunshine-yellow patio umbrella table covered with snacks and drinks.

'Steve!' A plump girl with long brown hair and a swimsuit peeking from beneath a tent-like white T-shirt came rushing over. She hugged him. 'I'm so pleased you're here. I adored your gift. Absolutely.'

Steve hugged his sister. 'I'm pleased it arrived on time.'

'It came to the apartment yesterday morning. I wondered what on earth, then I saw the card. You shouldn't have.'

'You'll need it for university,' Steve said and turned to Anni with his arm still around his sister. 'Anni Ross, this is Janet, my twenty-one-year-old-today sister. I sent her a laptop computer. That's what all the thanks are about.'

'Happy birthday, Janet,' Anni said. 'What a lovely gift.'

'Isn't it just?' Janet was giving Anni a thorough, rather surprised look.

'These are for you.' Anni handed over the white sweetheart roses. 'Happy twenty-first.'

Janet took the flowers. 'Thank you, Anni. I don't think anyone has ever given me flowers.'

'Well, then. Twenty-one and all sorts of new beginnings.'

Janet sniffed the flowers. 'They smell sweet. Thanks. Come and meet the rest of the family, Anni.'

Diane, Steve's mother, was just as thrilled with her flowers.

'It's sweet of you, Anni,' she said with a lovely white smile. She was a stunning blonde and Anni saw where Steve inherited his looks. Anni tried to imagine Diane in mourning when she lost her parents. How had she felt when she heard? Anni recalled how she had felt when her mother told her that her father was in hospital and then later had died. Her world hadn't ended but a bright light had left it.

Diane ushered Anni forward. 'This is Steve's father, Reg.'

Reg shook her hand solemnly. He was a thin, dark man with a moustache. Steve whispered, 'He's a judge.'

'Like, a court judge?'

Steve nodded.

'What does your mother do? She's beautiful.'

'She has her own clothes boutique. *Diane's*.'

'I know. Avenue Road.'

'Trust you to know all the clothes stores.' Steve kept his arm around her waist. 'And this is my older sister, Rachel.'

Rachel was the opposite of her mother. Tall and big-boned with an abundance of dark hair, she was what Anni would term statuesque.

'Pleased to meet you, Anni,' she said, and Anni didn't think she really meant it. Anni wished she'd also brought Rachel flowers but she hadn't known about her. Steve hadn't actually told her anything past its being Janet's birthday.

Anni smiled brightly. 'Pleased to meet you as well, Rachel.'

Rachel didn't return the smile. In a monotone, she said, 'Unfortunately my husband Ben isn't here. He has a pressing court case tomorrow. He's a partner in Steve's law firm.'

'Another lawyer,' Anni said.

'Yep. Another lawyer.'

'Do you have children?'

'Two boys,' Rachel seemed to relax more when she mentioned her children.

Anni pressed her. 'How old?'

'Jack is ten, Jason is fourteen. They aren't babies any more. They've gone to a camp for a few weeks this summer.'

'That'll be fun for them.'

'I hope so.' Rachel grimaced. 'Although with them away it gives me more time to work in mother's store.'

'You work at *Diane's*?'

'Yes, I do. Just part-time. Steve must have told you Mother runs a boutique?'

'He did.' Anni gave her another smile. Steve's older sister wasn't as personable as his younger one. Anni had the distinct impression Rachel disapproved of her.

She was pleased when Janet came over to introduce Anni to some of her friends who were playing with a striped beach ball in the pool.

They were all nice people, but . . . Anni knew the answer to *but what?* She felt out of place in her skimpy black dress and red heels. Everyone else was dressed in more conservative clothes, appearing terribly cotton trendy in their way, but not startling like Anni. She should have chosen cotton pants and a crop top or T-shirt. She had plenty of designer label sports clothes that would have looked appropriate. She couldn't quite understand why she had gone with the black dress and red high heels. Possibly to show Steve she was different. She'd done that. This is me. This is how I am. This is the package. Take it or leave it. On one hand she wanted him to take it, on the other to leave it so that her life could stay concentrated on her dance.

Steve pulled up one of the painted green wicker chairs for Anni to sit on.

'I'll get you a drink,' he said. 'Would a peach cooler do?'

'Lovely,' Anni said as she sat down.

Steve thought she seemed distracted. He could see his father watching Anni. While she wasn't wearing what Steve would have expected for an outdoor barbecue, any man would be hard pressed to say she didn't look stunning. She was a fantastic-looking woman and Steve was under her spell. He didn't really care what she wore. Hell, she was Anni.

He turned away and pushed open the patio door that led into a family room where there was a bar set up. It was cool in the room but Steve felt hot. He'd been burning up since he'd met Anni and he'd been sexually aroused the entire time.

He heard the click of the patio door closing and turned around to see his sister Rachel flicking her long dark hair off her shoulder. 'What is that, Steve?'

'I'm not sure what you're referring to, Rach.'

'Your date. Where did you pick her up?'

49

Steve's nerves were fragile. His instant reaction to the insult about Anni was to yell at Rachel, but he contained himself. 'I didn't pick her up. I met her at one of Ray Gifford's parties.'

Rachel's eyes looked innocent. 'And who is Ray Gifford?'

'A client. He runs a dance company. You should know that. You've probably got tickets to *Wedding Bells* already.'

'What's Anni got to do with *Wedding Bells*?'

'She's one of the star dancers.'

Rachel looked suitably disarmed.

Steve selected the bottles containing the drinks he'd come to pour.

'Even so, Steve, she's skinny. She's . . .'

'Gorgeous.'

'You're smitten?'

Steve added ice cubes to one glass and poured in a peach cooler. To the other he poured in the bottle of beer. 'She's a dancer, Rach. An entertainer. What do you expect?'

'You didn't answer my question.'

'It wasn't a question. It was a comment.'

'Whatever. Don't get hurt, little brother.'

'I've made thirty-five without being hurt. And I have no intention of getting hurt. I've seen what hurt can do, don't worry.'

'I hope that's the case. She makes me look like the Goodyear Blimp.'

Steve secretly agreed, but grinned. 'So that's it – you're jealous?'

'Possibly. She makes poor Janet look like two Goodyear Blimps. Luckily Mother's thin.'

'Since when did I compare my family to the women I take out? And since when do you have a say in the matter anyway?'

'When I see you with someone suitably inappropriate. You've a partnership in the works, and someone like her could damage you. And what about Lydia?'

Steve thought about the slim dark-haired woman he'd dated for about a year and a half on and off but he couldn't summon any deep feeling about her. 'Lydia's away in California for a few weeks.'

'So you two-time her?'

'It's not two-timing. Lydia's nothing to me.' He spoke the truth. He'd been waiting all his life to feel the sensations he was feeling for Anni.

'Then why do you date her? She's crazy about you.'

Steve shook his head. 'That's not true. We've talked our relationship over and it's convenient. Neither of us wants to get serious but it's handy to date.'

'Great relationship, Steve. But I suspect that Anni is different for you.'

'Shut up, Rach. Anni is my problem.'

'So she is a problem. Naturally you can see that. I mean, look at the gear. Dad's eyes popped out of his head. Steve, don't get involved. Get real.'

Steve picked up the two glasses. 'I've no intention of getting involved. You know how I feel about marriage.'

'I don't even think you should go as far as sleeping with her, Steve. For God's sake, use your head, not your appendage.'

51

Steve's smile was forced. 'I'm perfectly in control.'

He left Rachel looking as if she didn't believe him, which was possibly true, and went back outside to Anni. He handed her the drink. She half smiled, catching her pearly teeth in her lip. He already knew it was her apprehensive smile. His family could be snobs sometimes, he couldn't deny that. But he knew they didn't have to worry. Today was it. He'd made up his mind on that score. He had to leap from the fire before he became a statistic in his own files.

CHAPTER 4

Anni saw Rachel go inside the house with Steve and she could feel her ears burning, knowing she was being discussed. She wished she'd never accepted Steve's invitation. She didn't belong here. She belonged with her own kind. She'd known that since the day she started dancing. It had grown more and more obvious as she became older. Outside her sphere she was a star falling through the universe.

'So what type of dancing do you do, Anni?' Steve's mother asked her.

The question came unexpectedly, making Anni's hand jerk. Luckily the glass was tall and nothing spilled out. 'Oh, I'm a classically trained ballerina but I mostly do contemporary dance these days.'

'You don't miss the ballet?'

Anni had reached a point somewhere in her career when she just didn't want to talk about what she did for a living any more. Still, she had to answer to be polite. 'I dance ballet for my own enjoyment and for training. But I like contemporary. It's more experimental, more primal.'

Steve's mother nodded. Anni wasn't sure if she understood or not. She shouldn't have said 'primal'. It was often misconstrued into a sexual context.

'You're with a company. Ray Gifford, I understand?' Rachel now got into the act. She was stretched on a lounger, having removed her white pants and top to display a blue swimsuit with all sorts of tucks and gathers at the waist to hide her tummy.

It seemed Steve had told his sister this. Anni nodded. 'I've been with him for ten years. He's escalated my career no end.' It was the type of line she gave to interviewers. In a way, she supposed this was an interview. An interview to see if the family approved of Steve's date.

Rachel leaned over to pick up a glass of wine. She sipped it slowly. 'Steve also told me that you're going to be in *Wedding Bells*.'

'That's right. We begin rehearsals next Monday for an opening night September first.'

'I have tickets for the opening night,' Diane said. 'Isn't that wonderful, you'll be in it? Well, that's something.'

Rachel obviously thought of something that caused her to sit upright. 'Are you dancing with Moe Ellison? I saw him in New York. He's fantastic.'

'Yes. I am dancing with him,' Anni said, realizing as she often did that she knew some famous people. She had danced with Moe a number of times and never met any male dancer quite so dedicated to his dancing. Although he'd taken

54

time out a couple of years ago to marry and start a family.

'We have front-row seats,' Rachel said, sounding more friendly now.

'Then I'd better not fall,' Anni said with a chuckle. 'I hope you enjoy the show.'

The subject faded away. Rachel began a conversation about her children and her husband. After a few minutes of what was basically Rachel complaining, Steve's mother rose from her seat to go in to instruct the caterers to begin preparing the barbecue.

Steve, watching Anni while holding a desultory conversation about legal matters with his father, saw his mother leave and Rachel reluctantly follow. Anni was left alone with her long legs crossed, sipping her drink. But she didn't look awkward. Far from it. Anni appeared in command of her situation. He was rather pleased about this because in his mind it meant she was sure of herself.

'She's not the type you should leave alone for long,' his father said with a smile.

Despite Rachel's observation that Dad's eyes had popped out of his head, Steve was rather surprised his father had been so aware of Anni. 'You don't think she's out of the ordinary?'

'Nicely out of the ordinary. If I were a few years younger – well, more than a few – I'd go for her.'

Steve felt relieved his father liked Anni. 'She's pretty special to me. I only met her Friday but it seems I've always known her.'

'I'm aware of that, Steve. You don't bring home many gals. Go keep her company.'

Steve walked over to Anni, who was sitting in thoughtful silence sipping her drink. So much for all his planning. He couldn't ignore her even if he was heading to be a statistic.

Anni glanced at him. 'Hi.'

'Hi. Dump your drink. I'll show you the garden.' He wanted to be alone with her.

Anni placed her glass on the table and went with Steve. They passed through another gate from the pool into a designer-perfect garden. Grass pathways intertwined between evenly planted shrubs and flowers centred by a round pond with goldfish. A black and white cat sat on the edge of the pond flicking the water with its paw.

'Cindy, cut it out,' Steve said and turned to Anni. 'She won't get a fish because she's frightened of the water, but she likes to think there might be a chance.' As he spoke the words Steve thought how they applied to him with Anni. He was frightened of the water as well but he would like a chance to catch Anni.

'It's cute,' Anni said, slipping off her heels to walk barefoot on the grass. She carried the shoes by their spiky heels. 'I'd love to have a cat.'

'We always had one here. Janet's crazy about cats. She's a vet in training.'

'That's a demanding career.'

'It is. Long hours. But it's what she wants.'

'She's individual,' Anni said.

'Yes. Like you. Don't let my family bother you, Anni.'

She turned to face him. 'They don't bother me. I felt out of place in my own home after my father

56

died. He was the one who supported my dancing. My mother never did, but by the time he died I was into the dance scene. I couldn't be stopped.'

He thought her eyes appeared sad, almost resigned. 'You mean you always feel out of place?'

'Yes, except when my own kind are around. The way you felt out of place at Ray's on Friday.'

'I didn't really feel out of place. I just realized that I wasn't part of the dance scene. But you're part of regular life. This is different.' Steve could feel himself trying harder to catch the goldfish like the cat. Letting her go wasn't going to be the answer for him. He was going to have to risk the discomfort for the prize.

Anni juggled her shoes and caught each one in opposite hands. 'No. I'm not part of regular life. Long-term it wouldn't work between us.'

'You sound as if you can guarantee that?' He heard the anxiety in his voice.

'I can guarantee it.'

'I don't see how you can,' he argued. 'Just because life has had a certain pattern until now, there is always the possibility that this time will be different.' It had to be different. He couldn't let Anni go tonight or tomorrow or the next day. Yet he couldn't burden her with that knowledge now. She would construe that as pressure and run.

He changed the subject. 'You scored points with *Wedding Bells*. Rachel and my mother are addicted to stage musicals, especially those written by Carol Cornig.'

Anni stopped beside a bed of fiery lilies. 'You've heard of Carol Cornig?'

'I looked it up,' he admitted.

She smiled. 'That's really nice of you, Steve, to make an effort on my behalf. To find out what I'm doing.'

Steve noticed she spoke stiffly. 'What the hell do you mean by "nice"?'

'It's nice that you made the effort to connect with my dancing.'

'I like you, Anni.' The words sprang from somewhere down deep inside Steve that he hadn't known existed. 'Of course I'm going to make the effort.'

'My father was the last person who did that,' she said very softly.

Steve saw that if he loved Anni, if he was given the chance, he was going to have to live up to her father. Her father was her ideal man. Most likely all the other men in her life were failures because they hadn't mirrored her father. Now he had to ask himself the question, should he end this liaison with Anni tonight and go back to his safe life, or take the plunge into the scary waters where he actually wanted to be?

'I have to admit I feel the same.' She drew in a breath. 'I like you as well but I've decided that today is it. We can't go out again.'

The 'no' screamed in Steve's brain. 'Because I had to look up Carol Cornig's name?' he said harshly. 'Because I wasn't *into* dance before I met you on Friday?'

She touched his arm and he felt himself tense beneath her touch because he wanted her, not only sexually but in every way. He wanted her there in the mornings, in the evenings, at night beside him. He wanted her with him each time he came to this house for a family function. He wanted it all. So soon. So right. But so wrong for Anni. Or was it?

'Nothing like that, Steve. I'm just telling you what the situation is between us. Upfront before either of us gets hurt. That's all.'

He kept her eyes locked with his and played his original card in the game, the one that made the most sense. 'It's okay, Anni. I'd decided that as well.'

Anni felt for a moment as if Steve had stabbed her chest. Stunned. And yet exactly what she wanted to happen was going to happen. Today was *it*. And they'd both defined the parameters. It was a mutual decision. She should be overjoyed that they would part amicably.

'That's okay with you?' Steve asked, and she saw his jaw was tight with nerves.

'Of course. It's what I want, Steve.' But the words were as false as her smile. It wasn't what she wanted. She wanted to stay with this man forever and have his babies. She didn't know where those feelings exactly came from but they were there. This was *the* man.

He didn't say anything. She continued. 'We should get back to your family. That pool looks very inviting. I wouldn't mind a swim before dinner.'

'Sure. Let's go,' Steve said and he led the way, walking faster this time, back to the patio.

Anni thought, *Well, it's over. It's the way it has to be even if it feels as if my heart is breaking*.

When Anni said she needed to change, Janet elected to show Anni into the house. The decor was pastel, the furnishings quite modern but very tasteful. Janet led the way up heavily carpeted stairs to a bright big bedroom in eggshell white and willow pattern blue.

'Don't mind the folks,' Janet said after explaining that Anni could use the adjoining bathroom if she wanted.

Anni placed her bag on the bed. 'It's fine. Steve and I are just friends. We probably won't see one another after today as I'm pretty busy with my dancing.'

'Don't you like Steve?'

'Yes. I like him.' Anni had to be honest. 'He seems like a great brother.'

'He is. I love him to bits. He's always spoiled me because when I was a baby he was older. Rachel's different. She was always jealous when I got attention. She never likes any of Steve's girl-friends either. So don't worry.'

'I'm not worried, Janet. As I said, it's nothing between your brother and me.'

Janet tugged her T-shirt down around her thighs. 'I'm sorry about that. I really am. I would like to see Steve settled down. He's too good not to be a husband and a father.'

Anni drew her black bikini and towel from her bag. 'He'll find someone suitable.' The words almost ended on a sob. She had to clear her throat and search inside her bag for her sandals. She tossed them on the bed. 'I thought I'd forgotten these.'

'Well, you didn't,' Janet said and headed to the door. 'See you in the pool.' She sounded pleased about something.

Thinking that she liked Janet, Anni changed clothes, slipped on the lace top cover-up and returned downstairs. Everyone had left the pool and was clustered together talking, laughing, drinking, and munching on potato chips.

Steve was sitting on the pool edge splashing his feet and waiting for her. Observing him undressed, Anni felt his power. His sleek thick hair lay against his neck and she wanted to touch him there and run her fingers over his broad muscled shoulders. She sat down beside him and his eyes were as blue as the sky as he gazed at her. She'd noticed his eyes were more grey at night, more blue in daytime.

'I like that lacy thing,' he said softly. 'Not much beneath it either.'

Anni touched his chest and felt the velvety smoothness of his skin over muscle. If she ran her palm lower she would meet navy blue swim briefs that emphasized everything male about him, and then his long muscled legs. He captured her hand against his warm flesh. 'What are you doing?'

She had to be truthful. 'Touching you. Because you look so good. Stronger than I would have expected a lawyer to look.'

'I'm a sailor as well,' he said with a roguish grin. 'Ah, Anni, lass.'

He leaned over and kissed her mouth. Not softly, but demanding, as if he had a great deal of stored-up emotion and he was ridding himself of it in that one kiss. Anni responded for a moment then pulled away. He still held her hand hard against his ribs.

'What's so scary about me?' he asked.

'I never said you were scary.'

'You have. You want to end us today because going on would mean more commitment from you than you want to give.'

Anni tried to untangle her fingers but he held them firmly. 'Steve, please. I've made up my mind. I want to swim.'

'Then go swim.'

She was suddenly free and with shaking hands she tugged off the lacy top and slipped her shoes from her feet. Aware of Steve watching her every move, Anni walked to the end of the pool. Mischievously she wriggled her hips and leisurely strolled up the steps to the small diving board.

Aroused by Anni's wriggling, as well as amused by it because she didn't want him and yet he was sure she did, Steve watched Anni's body curve into an arc as she executed the dive. Then with an unaccustomed anxiousness watched the silver splash of water until she reappeared once more. Relieved, he stood up and went to the diving board.

'Out the way,' he called down.

Anni waved and swam to the shallow end. Steve performed his dive and joined her. He couldn't help running his hand up her thigh beneath the water. He couldn't help covering her squealing mouth with his own or feeling that she responded desperately this time before pulling away.

'You take liberties,' she said, but she was laughing.

He slicked back his hair with his hand. 'Do you know how alluring you look in that bikini? Of course you do. You're an entertainer. Is that what you're doing, Anni? Entertaining me?'

She ducked beneath the water, reappeared and wiped her face with both hands before answering. 'You ask so many questions. Can't you just accept today for today's sake?'

'Can you?'

Anni couldn't imagine never ever seeing him again. She wanted to be held forever in those strong arms, caressed by those blunt-nailed fingers, kissed by his lips, touched by his tongue, his body upon her, inside her. She wanted him. And instead she was sending him away because it was best. Best for him. Best for her. In the long run.

'Can you, Anni?'

She turned away from him. 'I feel like a witness on the stand,' she whispered.

'I want the truth. I'll tell you my truth. I did think I wouldn't see you again. But I can't go through with it. I'm scared of you, of what this might mean to me, but I have to go on, Anni. Please. Just a few more hours. Say a boat ride in the week.'

She'd made up her mind about Steve. 'No.'

He stroked her waist beneath the water. 'You have two weeks before you begin work again.'

His fingers made her sizzle despite the cool water lapping around her. 'Not entirely. I told you I'm taping the TV segment tomorrow and

I'm going to rehearse at the studio. I can't get rusty. I've got less than two months until opening night.'

'I'm busy as well, but I can make space for you.'

Maybe Steve was right. Maybe it would be better to see one another again. Tiring of him would be a natural progression. A chance to show him instead of merely telling him it wouldn't work. She wouldn't be left feeling so let down, so sad. She turned in the circle of his arm and placed her hands on his hips. 'How about I think about it?'

He kissed her short and hard. 'As long as you come up with the right answer.'

'That's not fair, Steve.'

'Everything's fair. Come on, you're starting to shiver.'

The call for food greeted them when they left the pool. Steve pulled a black T-shirt over his briefs and Anni left on her bikini to dry under the lace top. It was wonderful to feel the summer sun on her limbs and she realized she would be having a great time if it weren't for the problems Steve was initiating by being argumentative. Why couldn't he simply leave it be as they had decided?

She strolled over to Janet's friends, who were huddled into a corner. At once Anni saw the focus of their interest. One of Janet's girlfriends held a baby.

Anni looked at the small bundle in the young mother's arms – the woman was only about nineteen or twenty – and she felt a terrible sense of loss. She was nearly thirty and she hadn't been able to have this experience.

'Let me hold it,' Anni heard herself saying. It wasn't herself holding out her bare arms.

The mother looked surprised.

'This is my brother's girlfriend, Anni Ross. The lady who brought me the roses,' Janet explained. 'This is Paula, and her baby's name is Carmine.'

'Hi,' Paula said with a smile. 'The roses are lovely.'

But Anni's mind was on the baby. 'Let me hold your little girl,' Anni said.

'All right. But she's only four months, so be careful.'

The child was too small against her breasts, too fragile to hug. Cradling Carmine cautiously in her arms, Anni smiled into the tiny features. At first the baby sort of smiled back, but Anni soon saw the beginning of a frown and the signal of tears, so she handed her back to her mother. 'She wants you,' Anni told Paula, wondering what it was like to have someone want you so badly.

She turned around almost blindly into Steve.

'Dinner's ready,' he said softly.

'Fine,' she said, fighting the tears by straightening her top.

'Are you okay?'

She had herself under control now. She smiled brightly. 'Yep. Lead me to the food. I'm starved.'

Steve moved through the last part of the afternoon feeling as if he were in a dream. Anni was there in reality but he could tell she'd removed her mind for some reason. Had his pressure on her to prolong their relationship put her in this mood? Or was she as mixed up as he was? Her eyes behind a pair of round white-framed dark glasses told him nothing.

The strained atmosphere was no better by the time he drove her home. Anni, appearing relaxed from swimming and sun exposure, leaned her head back on the seat headrest and closed her eyes. But Steve knew she wasn't relaxed. The neon sign they were parked near at the traffic lights outlined her features. Steve watched the coloured patterns blink over her pale skin. As it was now dusk, the glasses no longer hid her expression; the darkness did.

Her eyes fluttered open. 'Why are you watching me?'

'Because you're beautiful. Why are you so silent?'

'I'm tired, Steve.'

'You should have eaten some steak.'

She turned her head, her hair like strands of silver in the half-darkness. 'I don't eat that type of meat. But I noticed you did.'

'I'm a growing boy.'

'From what I saw of you in the pool I'd say you've grown. It's not good to eat too much red meat.'

'I only eat it at my parents' house. They pay no attention to diet on the weekends, while all week they're into bran and fruit. I'm the same.'

Anni's laughter was soothing and hopeful to Steve. 'I don't believe you, but if you say so, fine. I just don't want you to be unhealthy.'

'You don't care. You won't be seeing much of me in the future.' It was imperative that he settle whether they would be seeing one another again before he left her tonight.

'Even so, I don't want to read a premature obituary.'

'Anni! What I'm really saying is, have you made up your mind about the boat ride?'

'Phone me tomorrow evening,' she said elusively.

'Keep me hanging, why don't you?'

'Either that or it's over tonight, Steve.'

Steve drove around her block to park the car in the visitor's spot. 'I think you should consider all aspects of the situation. We don't have to get serious. We can have some fun together.'

The car stopped. Anni placed her hand on her seatbelt to unclip it. 'What type of fun do you mean?'

He turned off the engine and withdrew the key. 'Male-female fun.'

'I thought that was what you meant. You want to go to bed with me? We can't, Steve. That's the problem. I don't want only a brief affair. I can't handle it. I know I can't. I've tried . . . it didn't work.'

He took her into his arms. He couldn't help it. He couldn't help anything with Anni. 'I'm not that guy, Anni. Dammit, I'm not asking for sex over this two weeks. I'm asking for your company. If, after two weeks, things weaken between us, then we'll call it quits. How's that?'

Anni was in his arms with her bag between them. Inside was her damp swimsuit and towel and Steve could smell the aroma of chlorine.

'I don't think it will work.' She spoke against his shirt. Steve tightened his arms. 'Why are you so damn sure?'

'Because I know how I feel about you.' He felt her quiver and he stroked her back. She was so muscular, so athletic, but so fragile in some ways.

'And how's that?' he asked softly.

'I know how serious it can get. And I'm . . . frightened.'

'I'm frightened as well, Anni, but I'm willing to go for the two weeks. If it's really bad then I'll play dead and go away. Please, Anni.'

'Can I tell you tomorrow?'

'Sure. Tomorrow's fine. But I'll be in agony until then. I really will.'

She tugged out of his arms and straightened her hair and gathered her things. He saw that her cheeks were streaked with tears. He was doing this to her, hurting her, causing her indecision, messing up her life. But she was also messing up his life. He'd been content. Or had he? Who knew what he'd been? He did know he'd never felt like this before. He didn't want to part from her. He wanted to be with her every minute, every hour, making love and being with her.

She opened her door and slipped out into the warm night air. Steve followed, hating the bright lights of the elevator that highlighted their apprehensions in the surrounding mirror, Anni's tear-streaked cheeks, his own features haggard.

'I didn't mean today to end like this,' he said as they walked to her penthouse door.

'I didn't either,' she said producing her key. 'I thought we could end it in a civilized manner.'

He took the key, inserting it far more firmly than she was trying to do. 'We are being civilized. We're discussing the circumstances of our situation.'

'Which aren't good,' she said with a small smile. 'Steve, we're going to have to leave it until tomorrow. I have to think.'

'Don't think too hard,' he said, and kissed her. He didn't make it a long, passionate kiss, just friendly. Then he backed away and returned to the elevator.

On his way home he cursed himself. He should have handled everything better. But at least he had tomorrow to put things right. She'd given him that option.

CHAPTER 5

The limo skulked through the steamy morning with Anni huddled in the back, gazing out of the window, feeling as if she had been dragged from her bed still half-asleep. Her eyelids felt as if someone had hung weights on them.

Ray Gifford wriggled his shoulders and stretched his long, muscular denim-clad legs beside her, the scent of his strong spicy aftershave bothering her delicate sinus structure. At least he didn't smoke his cigars in the limo. She sighed.

'I thought you were asleep,' Ray said.

Anni turned to look at him. Sometimes his hawk-like features appeared gaunt and she could see the ageing in him since she'd first met him a decade ago. She felt, she almost knew, that Ray would never be truly content or happy, and wondered if she was destined for the same future. 'Almost.'

'Did you have a good weekend?'

'Yes, I did. I went out with my mother on Saturday.'

'And Sunday?'

Anni returned her gaze to the window. It was after the rush hour but nobody wanted to rush in the summer. 'I – er – went out with Steve Hunter.'

'I thought so. Didn't I suggest you should give him a miss?'

She whipped her head around, silver hair floating in the air. 'Ray, don't give me orders. Steve's a nice guy. As it is, I recognize we wouldn't make it. I'd hurt him, he'd hurt me, one way or the other. We both know it. It's mutual.'

'So you called it quits?'

'Sort of.'

Ray reached into the inside pocket of his black leather jacket. He drew out a cigar as if he were handling something precious. His brilliant green gaze kept on Anni. 'You mean you're going to see him again?'

'I might. Don't light that thing in here.'

'I'm not. It's that hot between you, is it?'

Anni fingered the straps of her athletic bag. 'It's not hot. Well, it could be, I suppose, but it hasn't been yet. I went to his parents' house. His dad's a judge. All very proper. Not my scene.'

Ray stared at the cigar between his fingers. 'Then you get the picture.'

'I got the picture as soon as I saw Steve at your party. Corpses and free spirits don't mix.'

Eyebrow raised. 'Corpses?'

'You needed to have been there.' Anni sighed again and half laughed. Everything she said about Steve was a lie. She longed to see him again. She longed to make love with him. Eradicate him from her system, if that was what it took. It was the only

71

time in her life she'd thought of using sex for the purpose of denying herself a man. But then what of her other wishes? The small soft face of the baby she'd held yesterday remained indelible in her mind.

The limo drew up outside the TV studios. The trendy local station Anni always watched when she was home included the entire spectrum of the arts in their programme repertoire. Often there were dancers on that she knew. She'd been on twice herself.

It wasn't a station you had to dress up for. Like Ray, Anni wore jeans. Hers were slim and she wore a skimpy silver top and drop earrings. She wasn't nervous. She loved being interviewed, loved TV, loved performing. They touted *Wedding Bells* for all it was worth. She was asked to dance and she did so in her jeans and bare feet and everyone on the set applauded her performance. Ray was pleased with her. He treated her to a lunch of California greens and pasta, and the limo dropped her off at home in the late afternoon.

Ray said when she turned to say goodbye, 'Your friend is waiting for you.'

Anni looked. Outside her apartment block, Steve was sitting on the edge of one of the concrete planters that held an abundance of red and white petunias. He wasn't supposed to be here, but even so Anni's heart flipped. 'He was going to phone me tonight,' she said.

'Obviously his phone got disconnected.'

'Ray, give it a rest. It won't turn into anything.'

'I hope not. It's the same old story. Financial times are tough. *Wedding Bells* will drag us back from the brink. People come to a show to watch you dance, Anni. They expect your all. Moe Ellison will expect your all. He's coming to us for a price.'

For a second Anni closed her eyes. She'd been hearing the same spiel from Ray for nearly two years now. She said exactly what she always did. 'I'll do what's expected.' She touched Ray's arm. 'All right?'

He hesitated for a second before patting her hand. 'All right. Go enjoy yourself.'

Steve was standing up now, waiting for her. With the strap of her bag slung over her shoulder, Anni hurried from the limo thinking how wonderful he looked in faded denims and a blue polo shirt to match his daytime eyes. His burnished hair gleamed. He was not an easy man to forget. She smiled. 'Hi.'

'Hi.' He shoved his hands into his back pockets. 'Ray giving you another lecture on why I'm no good for you?'

Anni told the truth. 'He's worried about finances and doesn't want a dud show on his hands.'

Steve shook his head. 'Why should I make a difference to your performance?'

Anni decided to make the moment light. She affected a flirtatious accent. 'Because you turn my legs to jelly and my mind to mush, Steve Hunter.' She walked ahead of him to open the front door.

He caught her up. 'You mean that, Anni?'

She fluttered her lashes. 'That's for you to figure out.'

73

'Anni,' he said as they entered the air-conditioned foyer. 'You play-act. I know. I saw you on TV.'

'You watched?'

'Naturally I watched. I taped the show for posterity.'

Anni flushed with pleasure. Steve kept surprising her with his enthusiasm and interest for her career. 'I taped it as well, but I won't look at it for a few days.'

'Why not?'

''Cause I don't want to come down from the high of the performance. I'll see awful things I did. Like I lick my lips, or I screw up my nose. Or my hair looks funny.'

He laughed. 'All those things are cute. They're you.'

'Then I did them? No, don't tell me. And why were you watching TV? Aren't you supposed to be at work today?'

'I worked at home then dropped in to the office for an hour. I thought it was such a great day we should make the most of it and go for the boat ride.'

His hand was close to her hip. Anni tensed, wanting him to touch her but not wanting to give in to him so easily. 'I thought you were going to phone me about it tonight and we would go tomorrow?'

'I'm here in person instead. Besides, tomorrow might be rainy. And what the hell, Anni! At least we can have two weeks together. Why limit ourselves?'

She punched the 'up' elevator button. 'Would it be only the two weeks, though? Because anything longer won't work, Steve. It never does with me. Men like women available for them. I know. I've been there, done that.'

He shifted his shoulders. 'I'm talking about a few days out of two weeks. Nothing more. Two weeks from now you can go your own way, do your own thing. And I do know about hard work, all hours of the day and night. I took a law degree. What I'm saying now is that we should have some fun together. Like a vacation.'

Anni dropped her guard. It was what she wanted. Not only to be with Steve, but to relax for once. As he said, to have some fun, to not be working. She'd even like to get off her diet. Eat fast food. Pig out. Except she knew once she stopped the ritual, the pace, she might never be able to summon the strength and energy, emotional and physical, to return. She would become lazy. Or at least, that was what she was frightened of. As she got older she even saw becoming lazier about her career as the way she wanted to be. The space would leave her open to fulfil other dreams. She knew Ray saw this, hence his cautions to her. 'Come on up. I have to change clothes.'

They went into the elevator. Steve pushed the round 'P' penthouse button and asked, 'Is that a yes?'

She nodded. 'Yes. It's a yes. I give up. I'll have a vacation with you, but I'm still going in for rehearsals. I can't lose it, Steve.'

'*It* being?'

'What I do to make myself perform. Some inner strength. A sense of focus.' Anni couldn't believe she was actually unveiling her art to Steve.

75

'If anything, I would think a break would revitalize you.'

'Possibly.' The doors opened and they walked to her penthouse. 'Come in,' she offered. 'Sit down, take a load off.'

'All right. Go get ready,' Steve said, sitting down in one of the striped chairs and looking out over the lake. But as his fingers clasped around the smooth wood of the arms he didn't see the blueness of sky or water, or the white sails of all the yachts. He saw Anni. Anni at Ray Gifford's party in her halter jumpsuit, Anni dancing, Anni rumpled from being in his arms. Anni in the black dress and red shoes, in the black bikini and lace top, her hair damp and sleek. Anni on TV, dancing around in front of the camera in jeans and bare feet.

No. Not dancing around. That sounded like a put-down. Performing her art past her ability. She pushed herself into overdrive and became a smooth, agile, emotional dancer. She had been so beautiful on TV he'd felt tears burn his eyes. Oh, he understood her dedication to her craft. He understood her fear of losing *it*. He wished he didn't. Because then he would barge in and use his male dominance to make her do what he wanted. But he'd learned from two sisters, it didn't work that way. And it shouldn't. Many of his divorce cases were caused by a woman fleeing to find herself. At first, he hadn't understood what they meant, but after talking to the women he now appreciated how they needed a sense of self even within a relationship.

Something most men had so naturally they didn't question.

Anni appeared in denim shorts, a white T-shirt, and a pair of navy and white deck shoes. She'd tied her hair back with a white clip. She looked perfect for boating. He said so.

She gazed down her long legs. 'I bought these shoes and never knew why I did.'

'For me,' he said.

Nibbling on her bottom lip, she nodded. 'Yep. Possibly. Maybe I knew I was going to meet you. Subconsciously.'

'Maybe you did. How long ago was it you bought them?'

'At the end of last summer. They were on sale and were the only pair left and they were my size.'

'Well, then. They were meant to be.' Steve was having a difficult time staying apart from her. He wanted to take her into his arms at that moment and reassure her that they would be fine together. But he knew that might wreck what he was being offered now. 'Are you ready?'

She stuffed her hands into her shorts pockets. 'Yes. Are you?'

He stood up, knowing he'd never be ready for Anni. He hadn't been ready to meet her on Friday. He wasn't ready now. He felt as if he were on an out-of-control rollercoaster heading for a crash.

Steve's car was parked out in the visitor's parking lot and they drove to the private marina where his boat was docked. It wasn't far from Anni's apartment. She thought it strange that he'd always been so close to her apartment and was also Ray

Gifford's lawyer but she'd never crossed his path before. So maybe the time was right to meet him. Had she been heading down this path to meet Steve now, when she actually was at a point of making a career decision?

Anni could tell he was proud of his boat and she understood why. It was beautiful, with a hull of varnished mahogany offset by brass rails and lanterns. The mainsail was furled at the base of the tall mast and neatly covered for protection. The boat was called *Siesta*.

'Fantastic,' Anni said as Steve dumped a cooler of food and drink on the deck and put out his hand to help her in. 'Did you name it?'

'Absolutely. It's the place I rest. Even if I don't go out on the water, I potter around polishing brass and just lounging on deck.'

She imagined him doing that. Pottering. She liked the thought of just pottering and not being so intense about life. 'Mind if I explore the cabin?'

'Sure, go ahead.'

Anni eased down the wooden ladder, jumped off the bottom rung and turned into the cabin. The galley was U-shaped with a stove and refrigerator, a sink, and storage below the counter space. The dining table was surrounded by apple-green and peach bench seats that could be converted to single berths. All the trim around the cupboards and lockers and the ship's lanterns was shiny brass. A sliding door led to a comfortable king-size berth covered with a navy blue duvet. A shower and a toilet were compact but usable.

'It's great,' she told him enthusiastically. 'No wonder you wanted to show it off.'

'I also needed an excuse to see you again.'

Anni pushed back her hair from her forehead. 'Well, you're seeing me.'

Steve leaned against a counter and folded his arms. 'You must have had boyfriends.'

She found Steve large down here, and restlessly paced around the small cabin. 'Boyfriends, plural. Brief encounters. Fun dates, you know. Then I have to either go on tour or I'm tied up for a month or two doing something else and they fade away. That's why I want to be up-front with you, Steve. Two weeks and that's it. It has to be that way.' Anni felt as if she were forcing herself to speak these words.

'At least it's two weeks now and not just a date. Did you have a serious relationship that made you really desperate to think this way?'

Anni stared out from a brass-trimmed porthole. A man and a woman on a nearby boat were laughing and talking together. She wondered if she looked like that when she was with Steve. Sort of perfect together. One.

'Anni?'

She turned around. 'Yes. I did, and it didn't work, all because of me.'

He gave her a sceptical look. 'Have you ever thought it might have been him as well?'

'Possibly. He was a radio DJ. He's still a radio DJ. It was mostly me.' She dropped her gaze to her feet, unused to seeing them in the deck shoes. The shoes made her look practical and sturdy. More in charge than she felt.

79

'I can't see that. If he loved you, he would have let you be free to be yourself. Anni, look at me.'

She looked him straight in the eye. 'Yes. That's right. In theory. But I'd also have to compromise. I don't think I loved him, because I wasn't willing. At least at that time.'

He wouldn't drop her gaze. 'Are you willing now?'

In that moment Anni knew Steve was serious about their relationship. Two weeks wouldn't be enough for him. 'I don't know. That's the problem. I'm sort of at a crossroads in my career. This time at home with *Wedding Bells* will be good. I won't be away on tour. I'll have time to consider how things are.'

'You mean you're tired of touring?'

'Don't push me, Steve. Please. It's really nothing to do with you.'

'Yes, it is. It's all to do with me. Whatever decision you come up with has a bearing on whether I'll be able to see you again or not.'

Anni had known this would happen. One date and then another and another and another and she'd be in a net struggling to survive. She remembered back to when her relationship with Troy had been wavering. They'd gone to a lake up north, where Troy had a family cottage. They went fishing one day and Anni had seen the fish in the net and she'd said to Troy, *'That's me, Troy. I have to get out. We have to break up.'*

Remembering this, Anni felt desperate, shaky. 'Steve. You promised. Two weeks. That's it. Don't discuss it any more.'

Steve unfolded his arms and raised them in acquiescence. 'I'm talking two weeks. Nothing else.'

Anni crinkled her forehead. 'I could have sworn you were talking more.'

'Anni, let's get something straight. I've seen the backside of marriage. Divorce. I don't want to go as far as falling in love and marriage. But I like women. I like you. All I want is to be with you for your vacation.'

His words put into focus the problems she'd had with Steve's arguments from the beginning. 'You never want to get married?'

He shook his head. 'Every marriage I've seen has ended bitterly.'

'Not your parents'. They seemed fine.'

'That's different. My parents' marriage was my ideal when I was younger. I thought I was going to get married and live happily ever after. Then I didn't meet anyone I could fall in love with and my career took off on the divorce side of law. The worst side.'

'So now you're jaded and disillusioned?'

'You could put it that way. So you've got nothing to worry about, Anni. I'll be gone in two weeks. For my own protection as well as yours.' He unfolded his arms and his expression said their discussion was all over.

'Well, then. We've got all that straightened out,' she said brightly. Too brightly. Inside she wanted to scream. This was the second time he'd turned the tables on her. The first was when she was going to be the one to make Sunday their one and only date and he'd beat her to it. But it hadn't been their one and only date. She was here with him now, agreeing to another two weeks.

'Shall we go back on deck?' Steve asked.

Anni reached for the top rung to haul herself up, wondering if he knew what he was doing when he entered into these deep discussions and left her wandering around lost in her mind. After all, he was a lawyer. He'd learned all the tricks. Every word he spoke could be a carefully constructed plan for all she knew. Except when he kissed her. When he kissed her, pretences were abandoned.

Steve followed her up the steps, his body far too close, saying, 'We'll motor out on the lake a little way and then raid the cooler and have something to eat. There's a storm warning on the lake tonight. We can't go far.'

Anni glanced back at him, feeling the rise and fall of his breath against her back. 'It sounds fine. I know nothing about boating anyway, so I can't help you much. I'd be disastrous in a storm.'

'You are a storm, sweetie,' he said, and patted her bottom.

Anni shrieked and ran up the last steps. On deck Steve grinned and leaned down and gave her a hard kiss on the mouth before going to stand before the wheel.

He was fun, she thought as the boat chugged through the narrow channel of the marina and she leaned over the railing. Some people on the grass bank waved at them. She waved back, feeling as if she was setting off on a long voyage. Much the way she would feel if Steve and she decided to make a go of it. What would it be like to pledge her love to him, to marry him, have his children? Of course that wasn't what he wanted. She wished in some ways she didn't know about his negative feelings toward marriage. They put an end to any daydream, any hope. Not that she wanted that hope. She really was confused.

'All right?' Steve asked.

They'd anchored a little way out so that the Toronto skyline looked like a silver spaceship with the CN tower protruding above the white dome roof of the SkyDome.

He placed his hand on her shoulder and Anni touched his fingers and stroked them. 'I'm all right. This is fun.'

'Then why do you look so sad?'

She looked into his eyes. Their lips met. This shouldn't happen, but his fingers clenched around her shoulder and she placed her palm on to his chest, feeling his hard muscles bunched beneath the light cotton shirt. She brushed her palm over his chest in a caress and when she felt his heartbeat she pressed harder and let the strong rapid thump vibrate through her body.

Steve drew back from the kiss. 'I need you, Anni,' he whispered.

'Oh, Steve. No.' She didn't withdraw her hand from his heart. Instead, she leaned forward and kissed him once more and their lips clung with intensity. She was falling in love. She could feel herself slipping off the edge. She wrapped her arms around his neck and wouldn't let him stop kissing her.

Steve kissed her ear, her neck, and pushed aside her loose T-shirt until her bare shoulder was beneath his mouth. They stretched out together on deck, out of sight with their arms around one another, their kisses growing stronger and more urgent.

Steve finally pulled away. 'Anni.' His voice shook. He stroked her hair. 'Anni.'

She touched his cheek with her fingertips. 'It's not fair, is it?'

'We could make love. We're going to feel sorry we didn't when we split.'

'I don't know about that.' But his legs were still entwined with hers and he wouldn't have to do much to take her.

'You seem to want what I want.'

'Pleasure for pleasure's sake.' Anni eased away from him until there was at least a foot separating them. She tugged her shirt back over her shoulders and for a second closed her eyes to try and stop her head from spinning. 'I can't do that.'

'We'll be together until it is enough. It might take a month, maybe six. How about that?'

Anni opened her eyes to look at him. 'Not when I'm performing, Steve. I can't handle outside influences. Especially passion. I go on stage and stay there until it's over. I need all my passion. Even when it's over I won't be free. It takes enthusiasm over the next project to bring me back to normal.'

'I'd bear with all that.'

'I don't know if you would. If *I* could. Tonight. That's it.' Anni made the decision as she spoke.

'I hope this isn't a game, Anni. You saying, just this day, making me crave you, and then giving me another day. It's teasing. It's not fair. And you did say two weeks.'

'Two weeks is too long to go on like this, dithering around. I'm not doing it on purpose, Steve. I can't help what we feel between us. I told you I didn't want today. It was supposed to have been Tuesday anyway. You jumped the gun by not phoning this evening and dropping by instead. Sunday should have been it.'

He tried to reach for her. 'That's what I mean. Sunday wasn't it, was it? Here we are today in the same damn boat.'

Anni felt she should lighten the situation. They were heading into a full-blown argument. Or maybe that was the way they should go? Fight and be so angry with one another that it would be over anyway. She chose humour. 'I've never been in this boat before, Steve. It's not the same boat at all.'

He forced a laugh, sounding more like a grunt. 'You're mean.'

'Lighten up, Steve. I've told you my side. I've been honest. I'm not teasing you. I'm torn as well.' Anni brushed her fingers across her hot forehead. The inside of her head felt tight, a furnace of pain.

He frowned with concern. 'Are you all right?'

'No. I'm getting a headache. I need to eat.'

'I'm so sorry, Anni.'

'Don't be. It doesn't matter. Well, it does matter, but you've taken everything too far.

You're making me tell you things I don't tell people, things people don't understand.'

'I've understood everything you've said. I've empathized with everything you have said. I've had to work hard as well, Anni. I've had to push people aside to study, to focus, to get where I am.'

'All right. So you know what I'm going through. That makes it easier, does it?'

'No. It makes it harder. If I was ignorant I would plunge right in and force you to come to my side.'

'But I'm me,' she said.

'Yep.' He reached out and stroked away a stray silvery strand of hair from her cheek. 'You're you. And I want you to remain you.' He dropped his hand and rose to his feet. 'Okay, let's eat.'

Steve had packed chicken and salad and whole-wheat rolls. Anni ate the meal with him, asking him questions about his own work. Anything to keep away from their personal feelings. He also seemed to want to keep their conversation less intimate and told her about his imminent promotion to partner in his firm, Roberts, Smithson and Martin. He showed her the high-rise building in the Toronto downtown skyline where his office was located.

'Will it be Roberts, Smithson, Martin and Hunter, then?' Anni asked, wiping her fingers on a paper napkin.

'Yep.'

Anni thought he sounded less than sure. 'You will get the promotion?' She picked up her can of cola to take a drink.

'Oh, yeah. I'm pretty sure I will.'

Anni still didn't think he sounded that certain. 'Will you still handle divorces?'

'Among other things like wills and deeds. I have a huge client base.'

'That's good. It's nice to know your career is going in the direction you want it.'

'So is yours.'

'Sure it is.' Anni really didn't want to discuss her career any more with Steve. She had too many snags to work out.

Steve stretched out his legs and cradled his can of drink in his hand. 'You know what I think? I think you should go out on your own. Be your own Ray Gifford. Instead of having someone control your career, be in control yourself, control other dancers' careers. Anni Ross Dance Company. Sounds good.'

Anni had been thinking this, along with the baby, and all other aspects of escape. True, Gifford had guided her, but for his own fame and fortune. She'd figured that out lately. Her friend Joni, who was skidding through an intersection herself, had really made her see it.

'I agree, Steve. I think I should. I do have the qualifications but I don't know when, though. Not quite yet. I have my commitment to *Wedding Bells*. I'm under contract with Ray till next year. There will be something else, I'm sure. I haven't made up my mind.'

'I think you're at a point of change. You wouldn't be so angry about meeting me if you weren't.'

Anni met his clear gaze. 'Possibly not. But you're at a point of change as well and you have time for me. Men and women are different.'

'In the most wonderful ways,' Steve mused. 'I'm not rushing you into anything but I'd like to be around while we work on the chemistry between us.'

A rumble in the sky made both Steve and Anni glance upwards. The clouds were silver with charcoal puffs around them. Anni chuckled.

'What's the matter?'

'Speaking of chemistry, we're being warned.'

He laughed. 'Yeah, we're being warned it's stormy. We'd better go back.'

Anni got to her feet, brushing down her shorts. She placed the empty can in the picnic hamper and cleared up the food while Steve started the engine and they cruised back through the marina to his berth.

They sat on deck waiting for the storm to arrive but the thunder abated and the sky cleared. The setting sun left red streaks in the sky making the CN Tower glint in the sunset glow.

Anni wrapped her arms around her body. She wasn't cold but she felt she needed to protect herself. Life became so complicated sometimes, which was exactly why she kept herself free of relationships such as this one with Steve. He was easy to talk to, so easy to . . . love. She rose to her feet. 'Steve.'

He looked up at her. 'Yep.'

'I should go home. I've had a long, busy day. I'm bushed.'

Steve closed down the boat. They strolled back to his car. He packed the trunk with the cooler and drove her along the lake to her apartment. She would probably be able to see his marina berth from her window, Anni thought, her head now muzzy with tiredness. At least the headache had been alleviated with food.

'Can I call you from the office tomorrow?' Steve asked.

'After ten. I want to sleep in.'

'All right.'

He went with her to her apartment. She opened her door, invited him in, but he shook his head. 'I want to say one more thing, Anni.'

'Steve, I push you down and you keep jumping up again.' She smiled. 'What do you want to say?'

'I'll book some time off. I'm due about two months' vacation so I can take a few days.'

'You don't have to.'

'Yes. I do. I need time off and so do you. I believe you just want to live for the moment and not be pressured for once.'

'You're right. But I'm still not sure if it will work.'

'We'll see.'

Anni laughed. 'Oh, Steve. I'll only do it on one condition.'

'More conditions. What?'

'You take me for a burger and you don't say anything about me being off my diet and you just let me pig out?'

He impulsively caressed her cheek. 'You're on. Bye, then, Anni. I'll call you tomorrow at ten.'

Still aware of his gentle touch on her skin, she watched him go to the elevator. He waited, saluted when the doors opened and disappeared.

Steve didn't go home. Music played on a CD as he idly drove up and down residential streets, and along four-lane roads lined with fast food restaurants and large stores. Now even the golden arches made him think about Anni Ross. She was something to think about. All the women he'd known. All the women he'd liked. Never feelings like this. And then wham, he'd been banged on the head like a cartoon character. Now he'd made some silly arrangement to see her for two weeks for fun only. No sex. No relief.

He eventually drove home thinking about tomorrow and ten o'clock when he would phone Anni and hear her voice again, and he knew he was either heading for disaster or delirium.

CHAPTER 6

Anni had always thought that the building housing the Gifford Dance Company wasn't much to look at on the outside, merely an old brick structure with a wooden door and a brass sign overhead bearing the name. But because the building had once been a theatre the interior spawned an air of excitement in the concrete floors and cramped dressing rooms. The stage remained but the auditorium had been gutted, leaving one monstrous room painted in rainbow colours with wood floors and mirrored walls with barres.

Two dressing rooms at the back were shared by all the dancers, one for males, one for females. This was the first time Anni had seen any of her company since the party. They all gathered in the small space, clothes and bags tossed over chairs, women shoving one another aside for mirror-room and changing area.

Cassandra Morowski was the first to approach her. 'I loved your performance on TV yesterday, Anni. And the one at Ray's party. Who was that gorgeous guy?' Cassie's green eyes were enhanced by tinted contact lenses.

Anni gave the very dark woman in the jeans and tight top a mischievous look as she wriggled into black tights. 'Steve Hunter.'

'Ray's lawyer,' Veronica, lacing dance pumps, put everyone straight.

'Is he serious?' Tanya Lamont asked. Tanya was almost Anni's height with straight blonde hair down her back. She was in the chorus for *Wedding Bells* but she also knew Anni's dances, and was Anni's understudy.

'No. He's not serious,' Anni said. She knew Tanya was hungry for success, hungry for something to happen to Anni to drag her away from the stage show. She smiled. 'Sorry.'

Tanya shrugged her almost bony shoulders. 'You don't have to be sorry, Anni.'

Anni began brushing her hair. 'I thought you wanted me to be serious with Steve so I'd run away and marry him and leave you the part of Selena.'

Tanya's fine features flushed. 'I don't think you'd do that, Anni. So there is no point wishing, is there?'

Anni placed the brush on the dresser and knotted her hair upon her head. She smiled. 'No. No point.' She grabbed a towel and made for the door. Tanya's attitude had been grasping since Ray had first announced that she was to understudy Anni. Anni didn't want to be mean to the woman but she could only take so many of Tanya's digs without fighting back.

The other women and a couple of the male dancers joined her. For a long time they performed exercises and dance routines. Ray came in for a while and helped with the choreography on a couple of chorus dances. It was much later that Anni found herself alone in the studio, when she could put on the music she wanted to dance to. She swooped her arms gracefully above her head and watched her posture in the mirror. The black leotard and tights slimmed her to matchstick-thin but she knew the thinness was deceptive. She had built up a muscular structure over the years and she thought about her mother saying that she was almost thirty, almost past it. Her mother was right. This past year or so, aches and pains she'd never had before had begun to appear. Joni had gone for massage treatment and recommended the woman to Anni but Anni tried to be stoic. She felt she should be able to dance for another decade yet. But what if she couldn't? What could she do instead? Starting her own dance company seemed to be an alternative which she wouldn't mind; she had lots of great ideas for creative dances. She didn't let herself think of Steve, of marriage, of a child to care for that would be an addition to the teaching/choreography package.

The music, an intense rock number from *Wedding Bells*, took her mind off these problems and she danced freely to the fast, throbbing music until she was exhausted and panting. She picked up her towel and buried her perspiring face in the soft, soap-scented terry cloth.

As she lowered the towel, her friend, Joni Reed, as slim as Anni, but as dark-haired as Anni was light, waved a hand in front of Anni's face.

'A hundred bucks for them, Anni,' she said. 'I didn't think you were supposed to be here. You're supposed to be home taking it easy for two weeks.'

Joni had been Anni's friend since they started dancing at age three. Together they'd added the 'i's to their given names to make themselves sound more dramatic and theatrical. It had been Joni who had first joined Ray. After becoming enthusiastic about his avant-garde choreography, she had introduced Anni to his clan.

Anni smiled. 'I got restless at home.' Steve had phoned at ten as he'd promised and they were going somewhere tonight for dinner. Excitement had driven her to such a high pitch, she couldn't do anything today but dance until she was exhausted.

'Do you want to go for lunch?' Joni asked.

Anni let out a breath. 'Yes.'

They showered, changed into cotton shorts and Gifford Dance Company T-shirts, and went to a bright and airy vegetarian restaurant close by, appropriately named *Veggie Things*.

'I have something to say,' Joni said when they were sipping vegetable juice. 'I've made my decision. I'm going to marry Charlie.'

They'd made a pact once. No men. Career came first. Although Anni had known this was coming. 'I'm pleased you decided what to do.'

'Me too. I feel right about it. We both want at least two kids and as I'm thirty in a couple of months we should get started.'

'What about your dancing?' Anni asked. Her voice sounded far away as she thought of Steve. Of the baby she longed for — she had to admit that. But it might never be Steve's baby. He didn't want marriage and Anni was old-fashioned enough to want to be married before she had a child. Then who? Anni saw herself forever bound in Ray Gifford's chains with all sorts of longings inside her trying to claw their way to the surface.

'I've come up with that solution. I'm starting my own dance company. Think about it, Anni. You could come in with me as a partner. I have to do this. It's only fair to Charles not to have me working my butt off with no time for him. You and I have given up our personal life all our lives. We had no childhood, no teen years, not like other kids. No dating life. I missed that. Now I've got a chance to be normal for a while.'

Anni said, 'Running your own dance company will be hard work.'

'True. But it'll be hard work for me.'

'I understand that. So you're leaving Ray?'

Joni nodded. 'For sure. He's driving me crazy, Anni. He's a control freak. He wasn't at first, but lately, I've told you I can't stand it. I need to fly alone for a while. And I need to think of Charles. This last tour, he missed me so much that he flew over to Germany that weekend, remember. It was so good to see him. I've hurt him. Not intentionally, but just being the way I am when I come home. It came down to a decision.'

'Have you told Ray yet?'

Joni shook her head. 'Not yet. I'm going to give him a letter and tell him at the same time. Charlie's written one on his computer for me.'

'Charles doesn't mind about the dance company? You might have to tour with it.'

'That depends on what transpires, but Charles doesn't expect me barefoot and pregnant. He'll help me set up the dance school. He wants to sort of spread his wings in business for himself and this might be the vehicle we can both go for. And I'd love to have you on board, Anni. Your own choreography is way more creative than mine. You have a flair for teaching.'

Anni accepted the compliment because even Ray had commented once in a while that she had her own dance design. 'I have thought about it,' she said truthfully, adding the vision of Steve also suggesting she go out on her own. 'But I've got no one to marry.'

'Marrying isn't the point. But teaching might give you a chance to be free to find someone. Not that I'm saying marriage is everything, but you need a man in your life. A friend. It's lonely out there.'

'I know, Joni. But I never feel I have much to give a man. I've spent my life dancing.'

'You've got so much to give, Anni. You're such a bright, fun person. Ray pulls you down, you know. He makes you work too hard and doubt yourself, because he's a perfectionist. He's lost out on Patty for his goals. Is it worth it?'

Anni picked at the greens in her salad. 'You mean is dancing worth it?'

Joni shook her head. 'No. I don't mean dancing. I mean being so obsessed with dancing.' Then Joni's eyes twinkled. 'Come on, Anni, what gives? I saw you at the party on Friday with that hunk. The lawyer?'

'How did you know he was a lawyer?'

'Ray told me. We all know you went home with him. Steve, is that his name?'

'Yes. Steve. I saw him on Sunday and Monday as well. We're opposites, Joni. We're just plain opposites.' Anni went on to explain Sunday with Steve's family and then the boat trip last night. 'He's not for me. He's going to be a partner in a law firm. Can you imagine me married to that?'

'If you love him, yes,' Joni said seriously. 'Charlie is a financial adviser. Not exactly a non-nerd-like profession.'

'Charlie's a neat guy.'

'And Steve isn't?'

'Yeah, he's neat, but he's a divorce lawyer. He's seen marriage at its worst. He's not interested. And neither am I interested in getting real serious. We're just dating for a few days.'

'You are dating him?'

'We're going out again tonight.'

'That's great.'

Anni nodded, beginning to laugh. 'We're going out for the next two weeks to let go and have some fun. Be normal. Until my rehearsals begin. He might take some vacation time.'

'He's taking vacation especially for you?'

Anni nodded. 'That's what he said.'

'Then whatever he says about marriage, he must think you're special. Anni, you can still date when

97

you're rehearsing. I've been dating Charlie for three years. It worked fine.'

Anni put down her fork. 'You're different. You can handle the ups and downs. I can't handle relationships. I like my life uncluttered and it would be very cluttered with Steve, believe me. Things have to be upright for me.'

Joni chuckled. 'Isn't Steve upright for you, or haven't you found that out yet?'

'Joni!' Anni joined in the laughter. 'Yes, I have, but we haven't . . . yet, but . . . we can't. Why bother?'

'You'll deny yourself even a great affair?'

Anni nodded, but she didn't say a firm yes. On the way back to the studio for another workout, which she was sure would feel like punishment, she wasn't quite so sure about any of her answers as she was last Friday before she met Steve.

Ray was in his office. Anni could see his shape through the mottled glass door. He hated paperwork but he forced himself to do it. She knew he was worried about the financial state of his dance company. As everyone was worried about finances these days. Anni had been smart: as soon as she earned extra money she had invested it. Then she'd bought her penthouse. It was almost as if she were making everything secure so she could move on if she had to. She had enough to go into business with Joni.

The studio was clear. Anni put on a fresh black leotard with a clinging top. She punched on the tape for the 'Marriage Dance' from *Wedding Bells*. The music began to thrum through the studio. She stood in the middle of the floor doing leg and foot exercises. When she became Selena she began to dance to the primitive drum beats. Dance Steve Hunter right out of her system.

'What's two and two, Steve?'

Steve was rudely jerked out of his erotic thoughts about Anni. Alfred Smithson, his cousin, his mother's sister's son, his friend, his soon-to-be partner, had his hands in the pockets of his grey suit pants. The sleeves of his white shirt were rolled up. His striped tie was crooked. He'd been out for lunch and it was damn hot out there. Sweat beaded on his receding brow and slicked the thin waves of his black hair so Steve could see his scalp through the strands.

'So what's two and two?' Alf persisted, grinning now.

'Four.' Steve raised an eyebrow. 'Is this a test?'

'Yes. To see if you were here on earth with me this week. And to see if you still had a sense of humour, which you haven't. What *is* going on?'

Steve lied. 'The hot weather is draining me.'

'I can't believe that. You have an air-conditioned car, an air-conditioned house, a pool, an air-conditioned office . . . So what is it?'

Steve rested his shirt-sleeved arms on a clear section of his desk, despairing of all the files that a very capable, efficient legal assistant kept piling there. They loomed like a barrier to his taking a vacation during Anni's two weeks off. 'I met someone.'

'Ah,' Alf said.

'Anni Ross. She's a dancer,' Steve said.

'A dancer?' Alfred swayed on the heels of his black dress shoes. 'Steve, what do you have in common with a dancer, other than maybe very athletic sex?'

Steve let out a breath. 'Shut up, Alf. You're just like the rest of the family. Anni's a real smart woman and a terrific dancer with a great deal of talent. She's appearing in the Toronto production of *Wedding Bells*. And, well –' Steve leaned back in his chair and folded his arms across his chest ' – we do have quite a bit in common. I think we're pretty compatible.'

'You think? Doesn't she think the same way?'

Steve made a face. 'I believe she thinks the same way but she denies it.'

Alf frowned. 'Are you in this for the long haul?'

'Hell, no. You know what I think of marriage.'

'Not all marriages are from hell, Steve. Only the ones we see here in this office.'

'Tell me about the good ones?'

'My parents. Your parents. Me and Sandy. Ben and Rachel.'

Steve uncrossed his arms. 'Don't be so sure about Ben and Rachel, and you met Sandy in law school. You're alike. It was obviously going to work from the beginning. My parents, well, luck of the draw.'

Alf shook his head. 'You have to be more positive, Steve. Marriage is good. Take my word for it. You'll end up lonely and I know it would be a good move for your career. I'll mention that. Not that I'm recommending you marry this Anni.

Can't you just go to bed with her and get her out of your system?'

'It's more complex than that, Alf. Much more complex. She has very strong ideals. She's very dedicated to dancing. She sees outside influences as a detriment.'

'People can change. Does she like you?'

'I think so.' Steve felt ragged. He hadn't slept. Even in his air-conditioned bedroom he'd tossed and turned and sweated all night. He'd fallen asleep at last and woken up fully aroused.

'Go for lunch,' Alf said, more kindly now. 'Relax a little. It'll work out. Go on. Outta here for a while.'

Steve grabbed his jacket and flung it over his shoulder. He walked out of the building into the bright hot sunshine. He tugged his sunglasses from his pocket and covered his eyes with the dark lenses. He walked purposefully, too purposefully for the heat because he began to perspire. But he knew where he was heading. He was going to Ray Gifford's studio, where he hoped to find Anni.

When he reached the studio, the door from the street was jammed open. There was no air-conditioning in the building, except in the dance studio and Ray's office. Steve knew that from when he'd been here once before. Last summer, was it, when Ray first called him about his divorce? Before that he'd handled minor legal matters for Ray and never visited the studio. If he had, would he have met Anni long ago?

He found a gaggle of dancers in the foyer, chatting and laughing. He removed his sunglasses and asked for Anni Ross.

'She's in the studio,' a thin, dramatic woman said.

She had a cap of short black hair, the absolute opposite of Anni in colouring. A fantastic contrast on stage, Steve was sure.

'Are you Steve?'

He nodded.

'I'm Joni, Anni's friend. She mentioned you. I saw you at the party on Friday. Go on in. She's alone.'

'Thanks, Joni.' He smiled.

Aware of the interested stares from the other dancers, Steve walked away from them to the door marked 'Studio'. He tucked his glasses into his top shirt pocket and held his jacket loose between his fingers.

Through the doors he heard the wild drum-beat of music. Anni in there, dancing? Still aware of the stares, he pushed open the door and walked inside. The room was massive, with a high scrolled plaster ceiling. Some of the design from the former theatre was still on the ceiling. The walls were the colours of the rainbow and a rainbow was painted over the ceiling to flow down one wall. The mirrors on each wall reflected a number of visions of Anni in a skimpy black leotard. She didn't notice him. She was completely wrapped into her dance. She twirled and leapt, her arms, her body, her hair slicing tightly into the space around her. Each movement was in precise rhythm to the heavy drumming music.

It was a primitive ritual, and watching her agile body experience the convulsions of the dance aroused Steve. His breathing grew harsh in his chest. His groin ached. All she had to do was dance in front of him and he desired her with a sharp, poignant agony. Alf didn't know the half of it.

He tucked his jacket over the barre and leaned against a bare bit of wall without a mirror or a barre. He pushed his hands into his pockets, trying to make himself come under control, but his breathing was shallow.

Anni must have seen him in a mirror because suddenly, almost in mid-leap, she stopped dancing, drew in a deep shuddering breath, and let it out. Steve could tell her heart was pounding rapidly and she was panting as she padded over to the CD/tape player and tapped off the button.

Silence.

Without facing him, Anni flicked a pink towel from the barre and dropped her face into it. She rested her face in the soft terry for minutes, it seemed, then he saw her shoulders gradually loosen, and she raised her head and began to breathe normally. She turned around.

He forced a smile.

She didn't return the smile. She slung the towel around her neck and walked over to him with that straight-backed athletic dancer's walk of hers.

'Hi. What are you doing here?' Her voice was curt.

Steve's body was taut, but he pretended he was cool and remained leaning against the wall. 'I couldn't go much longer without seeing you.'

'That's the trouble, Steve. That's the whole damn trouble.'

Her face was flushed. Her skin was flushed. Steve understood her mood. Anni's heightened emotions from the dancing and her anger were what fuelled her to stay focused on her career. She'd had people try and stop her from dancing. She'd possibly created this anger to keep everyone away from her. It was her shield. Her guard against her own vulnerability.

'Don't be angry, Anni. I'm not here to hurt you.'

'I can't mix it. I told you that. I said we'd see one another tonight. I agreed to tonight. You have to give me my time and space between meetings.'

He needed to be truthful. 'I know all that in my brain, but physically I couldn't stay away.' He crossed the space between them and placed his arms around her damp, slight body. He felt her quiver. He looked into her eyes that were dark purple. 'That music,' he said. 'That dance. It was sexy.'

'It was the marriage dance from *Wedding Bells*,' she said, and then wrapped her arms around his neck, her fingers thrusting through his hair, and kissed him.

Steve released himself into the kiss. He was in pain from the need. He'd been in pain all weekend. All last night. Today was only Tuesday and the pain was severe to the point of desperation. His mouth ravished her soft lips. His hands slid down her damp back and over her hips. He could feel all the bones and flesh of her with his fingers and he pressed himself into her, rigid with his need.

During their kiss her thigh eased between his and he almost exploded. He slackened his hold slightly.

It was during this slackening that Anni pressed her hands to Steve's chest and pushed him away. 'That's how I feel when I finish dancing, Steve. That's how it is with me. And it's all for me.'

'I don't believe that,' he said raggedly. 'You want me.'

Anni closed her eyes and opened them. 'All right. That's true. I was thinking about you as I danced. Thinking about how it would be with you. Then you appeared. You were just there in the mirror. Real, and I wanted to kiss you so badly.'

'That must be why I walked here. I didn't mean to walk here. I meant to go for lunch at the deli downstairs in my building. Have you been for lunch?'

'Yes. I went earlier with Joni.'

'I met Joni outside. She's your opposite.'

Anni rubbed her neck with the towel. 'We created a dance called *Shades of Black and White* when we were little. We've been friends all our life.'

'Danced all your life?'

'Yep.' She smiled one of her cute white smiles.

Steve returned her smile with relief that she had relaxed. 'Hell, Anni, you dance well.'

She wriggled her hips provocatively. 'Turned you on, didn't it?'

'It was like you were making love.'

'That's what the dance is, Steve.'

'You'll have every man in the theatre going nuts.'

'Possibly. Although it's not all sex. Anyway, I'm bushed. Are you ready to go out now, Steve? This early?'

'Sure. Why not. I haven't had lunch. Do you want to come for a drink with me while I eat?'

'All right. I could do with a cold drink. Mind waiting?'

'No. Go ahead.'

Steve watched her collect her gear and walk across the floor to a door. The door swung shut. He picked up his jacket and strolled around the studio, looking at some of the framed photographs on the walls. Some were of Anni dancing. A younger Anni. There was a photo of the entire company. Anni and Joni in the middle with Ray Gifford's arms around their shoulders.

'Hi, Steve.'

It was Ray. He'd left his office door open and Steve wondered what he'd seen. Or couldn't he see through the mottled glass? 'Hi, Ray.'

Ray wore tight black jeans and a red check shirt. He pushed his hands into his back pockets. 'Did you drop by to see me? Or Anni?'

'Anni today, but I do have to see you. Don't forget you have to sign those papers and return them to me.'

'They're signed. I'll bring them into your office tomorrow morning.'

'Great.' Steve looked around for Anni, hoping she'd join him before Ray became personal and began to talk about why Steve shouldn't be dating Anni. He glanced impatiently at the door Anni had exited through.

'She's really got to you, hasn't she?' Ray said.

Steve pressed his lips together and nodded. 'But it's nothing serious.'

Ray didn't have a chance to comment further. Anni, showered and wearing shorts, T-shirt, a denim shirt over the outfit and flat white sandals, walked over to them. Her hair was still damp, her facial skin smooth, and she carried a large canvas bag over her shoulder.

Anni said a trifle curtly, 'Hi, Ray. Steve and I are going out.'

Ray gave her a tight look that said, *This isn't good for you, Anni*. And Anni thought, *I bet Ray doesn't know that Steve doesn't want marriage or anything really committed. So I'm quite safe.*

Steve was standing with his jacket over his shoulder. Anni tucked her hand through his arm. She felt his muscles contract beneath her hand and pressed her fingertips into his shirt-sleeved arm, then she looked at Ray. 'See you later, Ray.'

She steered Steve from the studio outside into the steamy air. The sun was blinding. Anni let go of Steve's arm and they both put on sunglasses.

'Ray's a real slave-driver, isn't he?' Steve said.

'He has his reasons. A long time before I knew him, he was a great dancer and then he broke his leg. He never really got back into his stride. So he pushes all his frustration and lost ambition on to his dancers.'

'I didn't know that about his leg.'

'Not many people do. But he told me once. So I can't be too angry with him. Except . . . he does control.' Anni clasped Steve's arm again. 'Let's not talk about him. Where are we going?'

'Somewhere to eat before I starve to death.'

107

'Poor Steve.'

Over drinks and a sandwich for Steve, in the shade of a patio restaurant, they traded stories about where they'd travelled and the adventures they'd encountered on their travels. They'd both been to London, Europe, south to the Caribbean, and many cities in North America. London and San Francisco were their mutual favourite cities. They spent all afternoon doing this and Steve finally called his office from a pay-phone to say he was tied up.

Anni, behind him, wound her arm around his waist. 'I've got you tied up all right,' she said.

Steve captured her arm as he hung up the phone. 'I wish you meant that, Anni.'

She grinned. 'Fun week, Steve. Seriousness at a limit. Please.'

He let go of her arm. 'All right. So what shall we do?'

'Let's walk,' Anni suggested.

They walked in a park, they sat on a bench and watched children feed ducks in a pond.

'Do you want kids?' Steve asked.

Anni felt her emotions heat up. This was a dangerous ground for her. Nevertheless she said honestly, 'Yes. I do. But I don't know when. How about you?'

Steve was silent for a while, thoughtful and then said, 'Yeah, I think I do.'

'But you don't want to get married,' she said. 'How will that work?'

He looked at her and smiled. 'Do you want me to demonstrate? We could go somewhere, Anni.'

Anni didn't answer. She left the bench and picked up her bag. She felt he'd got the message as he never mentioned going anywhere again during their early dinner. Afterwards Steve had to return to work to finish what he'd left earlier so he reluctantly said goodbye to Anni on the street. She ran to catch the subway home. Sitting in the underground train, swaying with the motion, she realized how much she'd enjoyed the interlude with Steve. If Steve acted civilized like this each time they met during her two weeks off, she'd be safe from hurt and pain. The thought made her almost happy.

CHAPTER 7

Steve had been in his office for an hour in the morning when Ray Gifford showed up to deliver the signed papers. Always casual, today Ray wore dark slacks and a black shirt with the sleeves rolled over his forearms. Steve saw the women in his office give him lingering glances, but he also recalled Anni telling him about Ray's leg injury that had caused his career to falter and never truly recover, and today he saw Ray in a different light. A man who had been disappointed in his own career goals, who now lived vicariously through his dancers' success.

Since Anni, their lawyer/client relationship seemed strained. Steve could feel the tension even when Ray was smiling.

'If you'd rather Alf handle your affairs from now on, you're welcome to change,' Steve told him, sitting behind his desk, keeping the authority in his corner.

Ray lounged in a chair. 'Because of Anni?'

'It's not helping, is it?'

'Don't date her. Simple as that.'

Steve shifted his pen in between his fingers. 'You really think I have the power to change Anni's mind about her career?'

'At this point I do. She's been in dance all her life. She's getting tired. She needs a change. You could be her way out. She'd use you as a stepping stone, and then move on to whatever she wants to do. She's full of talent. Dancing is her life. She won't quit. She'll do it, whatever form it takes.'

Steve didn't like the thought that he might just be a vehicle for Anni's way out of her situation with Gifford. Would Anni really use him? Was he going to have to be more alert to those signs? Of course two weeks didn't make a lifetime. What did it matter if she did have those intentions? He'd be gone. The possibility of any situation like that arising was pointless to even think about. Therefore, he said, 'You think I want her to quit?'

'It has been known to happen.'

Steve shook his head slowly and hooked his arm over the back of his chair. 'Anni's strong. I don't think you realize how strong. Whatever decision she makes will be true to herself and true to the man who will be lucky enough to eventually be her partner. You don't need to worry. She won't let you down in the immediate future.' That was Steve's impression anyway. He was sure he'd hit it right.

'Either you're talking off the top of your head, or you're beginning to understand her.'

'Understand? We never understand other people.'

Ray shook his head. 'True. Hell. I guess I can't always make people do what I want. It's enough that they dance my composed steps, and even then, Anni tends to invent some of her own.'

Steve nodded. 'That's how I think of Anni. Independent. I can't change that. No one has before me. Besides, it's short-term, Ray. A little fling. You know all about flings.'

Ray looked rueful. 'Unfortunately I do, otherwise I wouldn't be signing my life away to Patty. Not that I regret Lucinda. She's good for me.'

Steve felt like giving Ray a dig. 'She brings back your youth.'

'Sure she does,' Ray admitted. 'Who the hell wants to grow old?'

'We all do, though. Can't do anything about it.'

'Yeah, but not before our time.'

'Agreed,' Steve said. 'Grab the moments, eh?'

Ray seemed as if he were going to mention Anni again but stopped himself. 'I have to run over to the studio. Everything in order?'

'Looks it. If there's a problem, I'll call you.'

'Thanks, Steve.'

Some of the tension dispersed, the two men shook hands at the door. Steve was relieved. He had enough complications with Anni already without Ray making an issue of their relationship.

He returned to his desk and looked at his work for the day. He didn't feel in the least like tackling the paperwork, the problems, but his next meeting was with a woman who had left her husband and wanted to begin divorce proceedings.

Loretta Melrose was only thirty-one, a tall, pretty brown-haired woman who appeared as if she had her life in order. She worked in an office as an administrative assistant, had two children, one boy, ten. One girl, twelve. Her husband had had one affair after the other; he'd thought she'd never known about them. Eventually, recently, she confronted him and he went into a rage and beat her. She had to get out. She was living with a friend and going to work from there. The children were with her mother. Yet she still loved the man.

Steve went over the proceedings with the woman, wondering how she could still love this guy who had beaten her when they were dating when she was only fifteen. Why had she even married him? Because she loved him, she said simply.

After she left, Steve wondered if love was that blind. Was he being blind over Anni? Possibly he was, because he felt like phoning Anni to tell her that things were better between Ray and himself. Yet what good would that do? Anni would go her own direction. Or would she? Had Ray eased the tension between them because he knew that Anni wouldn't easily slip away from him? Did he know that Steve had no chance, no chance at all?

He couldn't immediately face the previous client's story and all the other stories that made up his work, so he picked up his jacket, told his assistant he'd be back after a coffee break and rode the elevator to the main floor. He left the building and walked through the morning tourists in the opposite direction to Ray Gifford's studio. He was going to have to defy Anni's magnetism if

113

he was to survive after their two weeks together. And he had to survive. He vowed never to wake up one morning ensnared in circumstances like most of his desperately unhappy clients. He would just enjoy the short time with Anni and then leave a free man with her forever in his memory.

He watched two children, a boy and a girl being herded by their mother and they didn't look unhappy. The boy hung on to his mother's hand, the girl skipped beside the other two. The woman's face was clean and bright and she smiled at her children. One of the people who would never be a client, he hoped; she reminded him of Anni holding the baby at Janet's party, and he remembered the question he'd asked her in the park yesterday about wanting kids. And she'd said she did.

Turning on his heel, Steve returned to his office. He had work to do and he had to put Anni into a separate compartment. *Whatever will be will be*.

The red light was flashing on Anni's answering machine when she returned from a grocery shopping trip. She'd enjoyed mooching through the supermarket picking out her favourite foods. Grocery shopping was an ordinary undertaking that had become extraordinary to Anni. She listened to the messages as she filled her cupboards and refrigerator full of her purchases.

'Ann, dear.' Her mother. 'I hate talking to machines. It's like talking to the wall. You feel embarrassed, as if a hundred people are watching or listening, which is so stupid. I know, for you, it's fine. You're the younger generation, brought up on these contraptions. You're also used to audiences. Are you still in town, dear? If so, I'd like to hear from you. I need to ask you something.'

Second message: 'Ray, Anni. Joni dropped a bombshell and told me for sure she's going to quit. Don't let her talk you into anything stupid. You've five times the talent she has.'

That's not true, Anni thought. Joni was full of talent, but Ray likely had his nose out of joint. He always found it difficult to accept that one of his dancers might want to move on.

Anni poured herself a glass of fizzy water and phoned her mother.

'Ann, there's some furniture that needs to be moved out of my apartment on Saturday morning. Old stuff I'm giving away to charity. I want it out in the corridor for the men to pick up. You know that friend of yours, Troy something, the big guy with the beard? Do you think he could help?'

'I broke up with him years ago,' Anni said. 'I can help you with the furniture.'

'We'll never move it ourselves. One of the pieces is that huge dresser of Granddad's. We need a man.'

Anni had to agree. The big oak dresser was way past her strength and the last thing she needed to do was strain a ligament. 'I'll see what I can do. Maybe Joni's Charles. I'll see.'

'I wish you had a boyfriend, Ann,' her mother said before Anni hung up.

Anni didn't phone Ray. She didn't feel it was necessary. His message was merely a reminder for Anni to stay focused on her career.

Anni called around some friends about the furniture moving but everyone was busy Saturday. She never gave a thought to asking Steve until he phoned to tell her he was taking Friday and Monday as a vacation around the weekend.

'I'm going to be busy on Saturday,' she told him, and mentioned the furniture-moving.

'I'll help. No problem,' he said. 'Afterwards, we can take your mother home to my place for a swim and go out for dinner.'

Steve was pulling her deeper into a pit by including her mother that way. Anni argued. 'She won't swim. I've never seen her in a swimsuit.'

'She can still come with us, and she eats dinner, doesn't she?'

'Steve. It's not necessary.'

'I spend time with your mother and then don't invite her to dinner? That's rude, Anni.'

She'd known from the beginning that Steve was so damn proper. Of course it would be rude. She wouldn't leave her mother out herself but this was different. This was a case of whether she should get so enmeshed in Steve's life.

'Anni?'

Anni sighed. 'Yes. All right. You can ask her.' Anni hoped her mother would say no.

Anni rehearsed at the studio all day Thursday. Friday she had a lunch date with Steve. Like the previous afternoon they spent together, their conversation was non-stop as they strolled the streets with other people enjoying the bright sunny day.

116

Later they impulsively slipped into a movie theatre to cool down in the air-conditioning.

The opening scenes of the film were light-hearted, a man and a woman meeting in an office situation. During this part, Steve and Anni shared buttered popcorn and laughed when the dialogue warranted a laugh. Then the screen relationship turned sexy. Burning naked love scenes pulsed on the screen. All that could be heard were cries of joy as two bodies pleasured one another.

Anni squirmed in her seat and Steve reached over to clasp her hand tightly. His flesh was hot and Anni knew he was feeling excited. She felt the same way.

Anni whispered to him, 'Is there more pop-corn?'

He let go of her hand to pass her the container. The last of the popcorn was cold but Anni forced herself to chew on the soggy buttered salty pieces until the couple finished making love and she was able to relax slightly. Then the screen lovers started again. Anni crushed the empty carton in her hands, unsure why she felt so agitated by a mere love scene in a movie. It was as if she had opened herself up and Steve could see all her secrets. She felt extremely vulnerable sitting there in the dark. More vulnerable than she'd ever felt in the spotlight on stage.

After the lovemaking the couple were split apart by some plot contrivance, but were brought together at the end with plans to marry. A happy ending. The credits ran. The lights came on. People shuffled blinking from the cinema. Anni placed her mangled popcorn package beneath the seat and walked out with Steve. He was close to her, his hand on her waist, and she fought the desire to melt into him.

It was still light outside on the street. Anni's legs felt unsteady as she moved away from Steve.

Steve cupped her elbow with his fingers. 'Do you want a cold drink?'

'Yes, that would be nice. The popcorn's made me thirsty.' Even her voice sounded unsteady.

He grinned. 'You shouldn't have pigged out in the love scenes.'

'They were graphic, weren't they?' This had to be discussed.

'Very graphic, much like your dance.'

'My dance is more subtle.' Or was it? Why was she so fearful of her feelings?

'Not with you dancing it.' He squeezed her elbow, reminding her of the heat and dampness of their embrace and kiss after her dance the other day.

'So where shall we go?'

Anni didn't want to be forced to think coherently about mundane things. 'You choose, Steve.'

He led her to a pub and they sat outside at a table beside a tub of red geraniums. Anni ordered a glass of white wine, Steve a beer.

Steve placed his arms on the table. He seemed amused. 'I wouldn't have thought that a movie love scene would disturb you so much.'

Anni turned away from his probing glance. 'It didn't disturb me.'

'Fibber. I'll admit it turned me on. But I also thought the film was artistically executed and we knew the couple were falling in love so the love-making was in its place and rather beautiful.'

Anni was relieved to see the waiter with their drinks. Steve paid for them. Anni sipped on the cold wine, hoping the drink would relax her. 'You see through me,' she said softly. 'And I didn't think you believed in love.'

'I don't disbelieve in love. I just don't know how it is that love ever ends in bitter divorces. Those people said "I love you" once and some still say it.'

Anni grabbed the opportunity to discuss Steve. 'When these people come to your office, are they really unhappy?'

'Tears throughout the whole interview at times. Mostly the man or the woman have found other people and they want out. But inevitably one still wants to hang on in some ways. Even abused women still seem to love their men.'

Anni saw Steve's expression turn dark. His jaw tensed. She could see how his work really had an emotional effect on him. She touched his hand and stroked the back of it. She wanted to crawl inside him somehow. 'You don't get jaded?'

He rested his eyes on her face. 'I guess in some ways I am. I'm just thinking about love more lately.'

Anni felt a blush begin to creep up her face and she knew Steve capitalized on her temporary vulnerability when he said earnestly, 'Anni, were you embarrassed about the movie lovemaking or was it because I was sitting beside you and you want to make love with me?'

She felt flustered. 'I thought we were talking about you?'

'This is connected to me.' He turned his hand around and captured hers on the table. 'Tell me.'

'It was a bit of both,' she admitted. 'But I've never been very comfortable with intimacy.'

'Is it easier for you to bury yourself in your dancing so you don't have to deal with the intimate side of yourself?'

Anni winced. That could possibly be true, but she'd never really admitted it. 'When I dance, I dance in character.'

Steve squeezed her fingers. 'Exactly. But when you're with me you're you. And I'm me, and it's getting more difficult for me each time we see one another. I walked out of the office the other day and purposely went in another direction from your studio so I wouldn't be drawn to you. I want you so badly.'

'We only have another week. It's not worth it.' Anni spoke the words, but she felt alarm that the time was so short even though they were clasping fingers just like the lovers in the film.

'You're saying I'm not worth it?'

'Nothing of the sort. You deserve better than a week. You're worth more.'

He made a sad face. 'I can't think of better right now.'

'You did say fun, Steve.' But she was clutching his hand as if she couldn't let go and never wanted to.

'I did, I admit. But reality keeps creeping in.'

'Reality will do more than creep if we go past the allotted time, Steve. Leave it. It's for the best.'

He loosened his grip and let her hand fall limply to the table. 'Finish your drink.'

Anni glanced at her hand. Her fingers lying there still warm from his firm grip seemed lonely and forlorn, the way she knew she would feel when this was all over with Steve.

Steve saw her up to her apartment but he didn't ask to come in. Anni was left with simmering frustration from the movie love scenes and their intense conversation afterwards in the pub. After a restless few moments, she rolled up her rugs, changed her clothes for a bodysuit, switched on some music, and began to dance. Dancing was what she handled best, not men. But even so, all their conversations spun in her brain, especially the one about intimacy. She thought Steve might have hit a huge nail on the head with that one. She was frightened of intimacy. It sort of went back to when her father died and she had purposely cut a little bit of feeling from her heart. It made life more simple when one didn't hurt. That was why Steve had to go.

On Saturday her mother and Steve hit it off like a house on fire, chatting away about this and that. Anni had never seen her mother react to anyone with such vigour as the way she reacted to Steve.

When Steve was absent from the apartment for a moment, Marian Ross grasped Anni's bare arm. 'He's gorgeous, Anni. Hold on to him. He's better than anyone you ever brought home. And a lawyer. Lawyers are wealthy, prestigious. Keep him. Don't do anything stupid.'

'Mother, please. I'm only dating him.' For one more week, she added silently. No more. Or was that fear speaking? By limiting their time together she was giving herself a gate to walk out of and lock behind her.

Steve returned, wiping sweat from his forehead. 'I think that's about it, Mrs Ross,' he said with one of his flashing white smiles that Anni found so sexy and devastating. He was the type of man women couldn't stop looking at. She'd noticed women in the street and restaurants giving him long glances.

Marian was the same. Captivated. 'I'm so grateful, Steve. Now, what do you want to drink?'

'I'll get him a beer,' Anni said, hurrying into the kitchen to break her rule of never interfering in her mother's kitchen. She knew there were a few cans of beer stored in the refrigerator in case any of her mother's friends brought their husbands to visit. She poured the beer into a glass and handed it to Steve.

Standing in the kitchen, he drank half the glass. 'Thank you, Anni. I asked your mother to my place and she said she'd love to come.'

Anni seemed extra aware of his vital masculinity in the small kitchen. 'I didn't expect her not to come.'

'No. But you would have preferred it if she hadn't agreed.' He laughed and leaned over and kissed her, tasting of the beer.

When he withdrew his lips Anni moved a step away from him touching her mouth. Even Steve's light, friendly kisses left a resonance.

122

Steve raised an eyebrow at her as if he knew what she was feeling, finished his drink, placed the glass by the sink and returned to help her mother.

Anni busied herself washing the few dishes that were left by the sink and drying them. Rarely did she perform such domestic tasks but today it was necessary to get some focus and calm down.

With the need to kiss more of Anni pumping through him, Steve helped Marian switch her furniture to accommodate the space left by the huge dresser that had been removed from the bedroom.

'That gives me more space, doesn't it, Steve?' Marian said.

'It sure does,' Steve agreed, but he was looking at a framed wedding photograph. He picked up the photo and looked closer.

'That was Anni's dad. Philip. My husband. He was young when he died. Only forty-six.'

Steve felt a lump rise in his throat. Philip had been a thin man with a rather fragile look about him. His hair was light blond, the same colour as Anni's.

'She looks like him, doesn't she?' he said.

'She does indeed. No mistaking whose child she was.'

Steve heard Marian's voice quiver with emotion and he replaced the photograph on the bedside table. He turned to Marian, who was twisting her hands together in front of her. Disregarding her dowdy clothes and insipid hairstyle, he could see sharp cheekbones and pretty eyes. 'I think she looks like you as well,' he said. 'A combination.'

Marian smiled sadly. 'Maybe. Do you like her?'

'Very much.' Steve spoke without really thinking. 'I'm enchanted with her, actually.'

'I thought so, but she might push you aside. She does that with people.'

'Only because of her dancing,' Steve said. 'Not because she doesn't care.'

'Possibly, but it feels as if she doesn't care.'

Anni came into the bedroom at that moment and Steve and Marian passed one another looks that would end their conversation.

'How's it going?' Anni asked.

'What do you think?' Marian said to her daughter. 'More space?'

'Yep. It's great. Now you can get a pretty chair for your bedroom and match a quilt and curtains. Cheer it up.'

'Oh, Ann.' Marian laughed and turned to Steve. 'She always thinks this place is dull. And I have to admit the furniture from my big house never fitted into my new homes.'

'Anni, give your mother a break,' Steve said. 'This is good solid furniture. Antiques.'

'I know,' Anni said. 'It's fine.'

But Steve knew it wasn't fine with Anni. She just let it be because she didn't want to use up her emotional energy in an argument. He was beginning to know her, and that excited him as much as having her standing beside him in her skimpy shorts and top.

Anni could see Marian Ross was delighted to ride in Steve's car. Her mother sat in the back seat of the Mercedes, her head held high. Anni expected her to wave at her subjects any moment. In some ways, though, Anni was pleased for her mother. Marian had always coveted luxury and, even left fairly comfortably off, had found life more difficult after her husband's death. She'd had to find a job, for a start. Now she was retired, Anni helped out financially by small deposits into Marian's bank account. She'd tried giving Marian cheques but they were never cashed. The direct deposit worked.

Anni wasn't surprised to find Steve's home as traditional as his parents' house. Nevertheless, she liked the red brick, the big shade trees, and the voluptuous flower garden. A kidney-shaped pool sparkled at the bottom of steps off the shaded deck. Steve placed Marian Ross in a lawn chair to sip her cool drink.

In the kitchen, where Steve poured their drinks, Anni said, 'My mother thinks she's died and gone to heaven.'

'Let her enjoy herself, Anni.'

'She likes you, Steve. She'll never let me forget you.'

He grinned and handed her an iced soda. 'Good.'

Anni curved her warm fingers around the cold glass. 'That's not the plan, though.'

'When we part, you can tell her it didn't work out.' Steve sipped his beer. 'But I think she'll be upset.'

'I think I was too hasty with this relationship,' Anni said.

'You're supposed to be relaxing and forgetting everything. It's fun, remember? I'm not putting any pressure on you. You're putting it on yourself.'

'Possibly, but you've learned how to manipulate people through your career and I'm suspicious.'

'I'm not manipulating you, Anni. Now chill out. We'll go for a swim.'

Anni wore a brief one-piece swimsuit today and Steve asked her where her bikini was as they slipped into the sun-sparkling water.

'Don't you like this one?'

'I love it. Leaves nothing to the imagination but the important parts of you.'

'I just feel that I should wear something proper in front of my mother.'

Steve slid his hand beneath the water and patted the top of her thigh that was exposed by the high cut. 'You call this proper?'

'It's the most proper suit I own. Now stop it. I don't paw you under the water.'

Still touching her, he dipped lower until his shoulders were beneath the water. 'Paw me,' he invited. 'I dare you.'

Anni ducked beneath the water to join him. She reached out with her arms and placed them around his waist. His legs immediately captured her and she felt everything about him hard and strong and vital.

'I'm not going to kiss you,' he whispered breathlessly, 'but I love what I'm feeling. Anni, you have wonderful long legs. Wrap them around me.'

She did as he asked, at the same time her glance moving to the deck, but she noticed her mother had nodded off into a doze.

126

'She's asleep,' he said his breathing shallow.

Her mother's presence must have made her reckless because she tightened her grip on Steve's hips and their lips met. Softly at first, then burning like the sun beating down upon them. When they drew apart, the sparkling before Anni's eyes wasn't only the sun. The water lapping around her felt hot like her insides. She wanted Steve to enter her, to make her his, to make her complete.

Steve drew her head to his shoulder, stroking her wet hair. 'We're giving all this up, Anni. Remember that when we say goodbye in a week's time.'

He let her go, making her feel cold and desperate. She began to swim, but she still wanted him, wanted him like the love scenes in the film. Wanted him all those ways and more. Wanted him the blazing hot way Selena was supposed to want Saul in the finale of *Wedding Bells* in the 'Marriage Dance'.

When she felt cooled down inside, she lifted herself from the pool. Steve was already out, now wearing a T-shirt over his swim briefs. He was sitting on the patio on a towel, chatting to her mother. *Had* her mother been dozing? Anni wondered as she dragged a towel around her and dried off.

'Have fun?' Marian asked.

'Yes. Great fun,' Anni said, sitting down and fluffing her hair in the light breeze. Steve might say he wasn't manipulating her but it sure felt as if he was. She should have escaped when she wanted to but she couldn't quite recall when that was now. Would she have seen Steve again if she really didn't want to in her heart? Her smartest move would have been to have taken a cab that very first night from Ray's party. But she hadn't, and here she was, doomed to a heartbreaking finale at the end of one more week with Steve.

Later, all three of them walked to an Italian restaurant. On the way there, Anni recalled the time Joni had first met Charles. Joni had pushed Charlie away at first, but Charlie was persistent. He kept coming around to the studio or phoning her. He brought her flowers, he wined and dined her, until Joni ended up sleeping with him on weekends, and then sometimes in the week. Joni was in love. She'd managed to keep Charlie for two years in that relationship, and then the pressure to marry him had begun. It took a year for Joni to capitulate. Was Steve trying the same type of pressure? Or did he mean what he said about never wanting to get married?

They entered the small restaurant made intimately dark by the stone walls. Anni waited for a comment from her mother about the dim lighting, but nothing was said. Marian even elected to have a glass of wine, and was soon animated, asking Steve about his law practice, about his interests, and his parents. Anni wished her mother wouldn't do this. It all felt so right to be here with Steve and her mother.

After dinner they walked back to Steve's house for a cup of coffee and then Steve drove her mother home.

'Tomorrow,' he said as they rode Anni's elevator later, 'we'll go out on the boat.'

'You mean right out into the water this time?'

'Yes.' Steve's gaze stayed locked with hers. 'We won't sail, as you're not used to it. We'll use the motor.'

Anni felt weak from his hot, passionate gaze. 'You could teach me to sail.'

'I'd teach you if we were still going to be together a week from now, but as it stands it's not worth the effort.'

Anni flung her arms in the air. 'I'm beginning to think none of this is worth the effort. Us spending some fun time together was a stupid idea in the first place. People can't suspend themselves from all feelings and reality. It doesn't work that way.'

He gave her a pointed look. 'Isn't that how you live your life?'

'That's not true. I use my feelings and emotions in my work. I need them to create. I can't squander them.'

'Especially on me?'

'Steve, that's not true. I like you. I really do. You know that. But I have a huge commitment coming up. And you've said yourself, you don't want more than an affair.'

The elevator doors opened and Steve followed Anni out. She unlocked her door and then stood with her back to it. She didn't want him to come in tonight. If he did she would make love with him.

'Why do I have to keep saying this over and over?' she said helplessly.

'To convince yourself,' Steve said. 'Would you go for more than an affair, then?'

'You don't want marriage, Steve.'

Without answering he leaned over to press a kiss on her mouth. It seemed as if he'd been storing the kiss for all the time since breaking the kiss in his swimming pool. Anni couldn't help returning the kiss, but at the same time she pushed him gently away.

'Goodnight, Steve. Thanks for all your help with Mother.'

He flicked his finger down her cheek. 'Goodnight. See you tomorrow.'

With Anni's presence inside and outside of him, Steve drove quickly home. He walked out on to the patio and saw the towels that he and Anni had used earlier. They were sprawled over the loungers on the patio to dry. He sat down heavily on one of the loungers, making it creak. He fingered the towel Anni had used. She was right. This two weeks of supposed fun wasn't going to work.

Steve raked his fingers through his hair. How would he survive without her? How would he go to the office with Anni a mere few feet down the street in Ray Gifford's studio? What if he saw her on the street? Would they speak?

He realized he couldn't put himself into that situation. He couldn't say goodbye to her, or know she was only a short distance from his office. He wouldn't make it without her.

To achieve anything past the next week with Anni, he needed to be patient. Complete the vacation on Anni's terms, then never give up. He would have to take the marriage risk as everyone else did. It was the only way he could ever see Anni in his life. And at the back of his mind were the hints he'd been hearing lately from his soon-to-be partners. *Steve, it would be more appropriate if you were married.* He didn't believe they would pass him over for Craig Firth if he wasn't married, but if he now had the chance to be married, there would be no question of his promotion. To be passed over for someone else would cripple Steve's ego. How could he face his brother-in-law Ben, or Alf, in the office or out of it, at family functions? He would have to move to another practice or set up his own. He didn't want to do that. He liked where he was.

He suspected Craig might have heard that Steve's promotion wasn't automatic. The other day the thin, rather surly man, in Steve's opinion, had actually passed a comment about family being a credential in the firm of Roberts, Smithson and Martin.

Steve had taken Craig's comment to mean that Steve was related to two of the partners, but afterwards he thought about the comment in depth and began to wonder if Craig had meant his own family, his wife Marie and his two children. Something Steve didn't have. Something Steve suddenly wanted desperately with Anni.

On Sunday, it rained so they couldn't go sailing. Instead they went shopping for a gift for Rachel's ten-year-old son's birthday. Anni didn't mind. She enjoyed shopping. Monday was a similar dreary day and they ended up having dinner and seeing another movie in the evening. This time a comedy with no erotic love scenes. Tuesday Steve returned to work. Anni went to the studio feeling out of practice. Next Monday the rehearsals for *Wedding Bells* started in earnest. Moe Ellison, who had been on the cover of a popular magazine this past week, would be dancing with her instead of Ray sometimes, being Saul to her Selena. She had to get her act together.

The second week of her vacation passed quickly. One afternoon Steve took her to a Blue Jays game at the SkyDome. Anni didn't understand baseball but the upbeat atmosphere in the huge domed stadium was fun and she found herself rooting for the home team with every other fan and screaming when they won.

Their final Sunday dawned sunny and bright. Perfect for boating. Steve decided to raise the sails as there was a nice brisk wind blowing away the humidity and giving them blue sky and bright sunshine. Anni endeavoured to follow Steve's orders as efficiently as possible. Booms, spinnakers, lanyards, halyards, winches, were all foreign terms to her. But he was a fair teacher and didn't expect miracles. However, she discovered he was a very able and exacting sailor. Every one of his moves was geared to safety and efficiency.

Sailing, she felt, when they were away from the shoreline, was rather like dancing. She felt free on the water. It was pleasant when Steve anchored and they were able to enjoy the silence and peace.

'You did well,' he told her, hunkering down beside her and handing her a cold canned drink. 'Are you warm enough?'

She gazed at him, enamoured of his ruffled hair and brilliant white smile. 'Yes, I'm fine. It's so much cooler out here on the water. But it's been so humid and hot lately that it's a pleasure to cool down.'

'I love it out here.'

She gazed into his eyes. 'I know you do. Thanks for bringing me and sharing it.'

'Our time together should be special. Precious.'

Anni's voice shook as she said, 'Yes, it should.' After today, if everything went as they'd planned, she'd never see him again. Or maybe she would. She might see him around the city now she knew who he was. She'd never paid attention to Ray's visitors before. Now she would. He might come to the studio to deliver more papers. How would they react to one another?

'Something the matter?' Steve asked.

'No. I'm fine.'

'No. You're not. And neither am I.' He took her drink from her and put it on the deck with his own. He placed his arms around her and kissed her mouth very gently. 'We have to say goodbye.'

'Later.' Anni didn't want this.

But Steve's expression was determined. 'No. Now. Here. While we're private.'

This time his mouth was more insistent. Anni felt her limbs grow weak and her veins flow with heat. She could never help herself with Steve, especially when the kisses had been few and far between as they had been this past week. She lifted her arms and placed them around his neck, keeping his mouth sealed to hers. His tongue thrust deep between her parted lips and she felt the centre of her curl with need and reach out to him. She wriggled against his body until his bare thighs were against hers. He moved on top of her, pressing her into the soft mattress they had been sitting on, and Anni's leg touched *his* leg, the crisp hairs brushing against her smoothness. She gasped from the effect of the sensations floating through her body.

Steve left her suddenly and returned to his drink.

Shakily Anni sat upright and picked up her own can. She sipped slowly. 'That wasn't fair, Steve.'

'It's not fair of you either. You don't want to get physically involved, so I stopped while I still could stop.'

Anni didn't say any more. She'd wanted to get carried away with him and make love with him, the decision swept away in passion so she would deal with the consequences later.

She gave him a puzzled look. Ever since Steve had picked her up today, she'd sensed something different about him. Something definite. Positive. It was as if he were on a mission. It could be that, as today was their last, he was being mentally strong about the situation. Hours difficult to endure summoned all his self-control.

'Problem, Anni?' he asked.

'You seem different.'

'No. I'm exactly the same. In agony wanting you, knowing that I can't have you. Precisely how it's been for me since Ray's party.'

But he wasn't the same. His words taunted her and jabbed her in vulnerable places. They made her feel guilty. He was being cynical, sarcastic, caustic. 'You've worked yourself into a snit about this, haven't you, Steve?'

He laughed harshly. 'A snit?'

'Yes. You're being mean because I'm making us break up.'

'How can you accuse me of being mean, when you're being even meaner by not allowing me to see you ever again? Besides, what are we breaking up? A few *fun* dates.'

Anni leaned towards him to prove her point. 'I am protecting myself, my career, my space, my time. You said you understood that. You agreed.'

'Yeah, I've got that message, Anni. I don't need it reiterated over and over *ad nauseam*.' He finished his drink, placed his can aside on the deck with a thump, and jumped to his feet. 'We're going to sail back now.'

'It's over?'

'Yes. It's over.'

Steve didn't come into her penthouse with her. He didn't even kiss her goodbye. Anni walked to her window to watch his car drive away from the visitor's parking. When the red tail-lights disappeared around the corner, she felt as if someone had actually pulled the ground right from underneath her. She had expected more. Maybe for Steve to be insistent, at least some kisses, some sort of farewell. She'd had a vision that they would cling to one another in a tearful goodbye. But nothing. It *was* over.

CHAPTER 8

An elderly man, puffing from the humid heat that had returned with a vengeance this week, stood in the doorway of Ray Gifford's studio. All the dancers stopped to look.

The man held up a long floral box. 'For Anni Ross.'

Anni grabbed her towel and hurried over to the man. 'That's me.'

'Great. Found you first time.' The man handed her the box, a slip of paper, and a pen. 'Sign here.'

Leaning on the box, she scrawled her name, handed back the paper and pen. 'Thank you.'

When she turned back to her fellow dancers, the box in her arms, everyone gathered around her.

'Who's it from?'

'Flowers. Great.'

'Anni, open them quick.'

Anni knelt on the floor with the box and lifted the lid to see three large-bloomed roses. Two peach and one red. Plus a card. '*For one perfect evening and two perfect weeks. Steve.*'

'Anni has an admirer.'

'I bet it's Ray's lawyer, the guy Anni was with at the party. Is that right, Anni?'

Anni closed the lid. Clutching the box, she jumped to her feet. 'Yep. That's who it is.' She was trembling. For three days she'd tried to forget Steve and now he'd made her remember him again. In a way, though, the roses were just a reminder that their time together had been close to perfect, so perfect it couldn't be repeated, or extended. Why mess up a wonderful interlude? But why remind her when they'd made a deal?

'Anni, are you okay?'

'Yes,' she lied. 'I'm going to put these in water in the dressing room.'

In the dressing room Anni had a fake crystal vase that had once held another bouquet. She filled the vase with water and arranged the three roses and the ferns that accompanied them. Two perfect weeks. One perfect evening. She hadn't forgotten. She couldn't forget. She barely slept or ate.

She stood back to survey the roses. The scent slipped to her nostrils and she inhaled deeply. She should thank Steve. She always compulsively thanked people for everything. She even sent thank you cards for Christmas cards, a habit her friends laughed over. But Anni always recalled her mother saying, 'Thank the lady now, Anni.'

Or maybe she could phone him. At least that way she would hear his voice. But she'd always felt the phone could be a coward's way out. And she wasn't a coward most of the time. Just over Steve.

Seeing him would be the better choice. When she saw him, she could judge what his motives were for sending the roses. Were they merely a thank you, a goodbye, or were they something more – a plea for a continuation?

She decided she would go to his office; it was only up the street. Quickly showering and then dressing in her long black skirt and white ribbed crop top, she picked up her big leather bag and ran from the studio. As she let the door swing behind her, she again felt the curious stares, almost as if everyone knew she was rushing to Steve.

Despite the heat, Anni dashed along the street. She couldn't really say she was consciously hurrying to Steve. She felt as if her actions came from another part of her that wasn't her brain. If she slowed down, stood back, thought seriously, she would stop herself going to Steve. She would ignore the roses as any kind of gesture and when all their petals fell and they died she'd throw out the stems and hips and forget Steve ever sent them.

Steve's building was cool, almost frosty inside. Anni found his firm's name listed with the number of his floor. She rode the elevator to the sixth floor with a plump man in a short-sleeved shirt and trousers. The man kept looking at her as if he wanted to speak but didn't know what to say. He made her feel self-conscious and she wondered if there was something wrong with her other than the goose bumps erupting on her bare arms.

She was pleased to leave the man's scrutiny. A mirror by the elevator door reassured her she looked respectable. At least in her mind. Inhaling a breath and letting it out slowly, she walked up the corridor. Roberts, Smithson, and Martin, declared a gold plate on double doors, and she imagined Steve's name with the others and thought she would be very proud to see it there. She pressed down the gold handle and pushed open one door.

The office was impeccably carpeted in a deep maroon and the furniture, including the two computer work-stations, was dark oak. Two women sat at the desks. The younger one had thick black hair piled up on her head and wore a navy suit with a frilly red blouse. She smiled at Anni. Anni asked for Steve.

'I think he's in with Alf,' the woman said.

'He is,' the older woman, who had perfectly coiffured blonde hair and wore a grey suit and white blouse, confirmed. She stared at Anni. 'Are you a client?'

'No. No. I'm a . . . friend of his.'

'Then I'll call him,' the younger woman said, giving the older woman a rather exasperated look. 'Sit down.' She waved to the row of charcoal leather armchairs. 'I'll have to tell him who is here.'

'Anni Ross.' Anni stepped away from the desks, her heart beating fast. She didn't bother sitting down. She knew she shouldn't be here. She'd once scolded Steve for arriving at her place of work with no notice. Now she had done the same thing to him.

It took a few seconds for Steve to come out of one of the offices. Something inside her collapsed when she saw him again. Had she really not wanted to see him, ever? He looked all proper, the way he had the night of the party, except his tie was knotted neatly beneath his shirt collar. He didn't meet her eyes with his.

'Hi, Anni,' he said in a smooth deep voice she was sure he reserved for clients, those bitter, tearful unhappy clients who did not deny their emotions, at least. Not like Anni, who pushed her own emotions into her art. But was that so wrong?

'Anni?' he said. 'Come on in.'

Anni walked between the desks and Steve ushered her into the office that had Alfred Smithson's name on the door. Behind the desk lounged a man with black receding hair. He stood up with brisk movements.

'You've gotta be Anni.'

Anni nodded. 'Good guess.' Had Steve told everyone about her? What had he said?

Steve pressed his hand to Anni's waist. Her top split from her skirt waistband and his fingers immediately encountered her soft flesh. Her breathing increased at the feel of his warm hand on her cool skin. She felt she should be wearing a neat suit and blouse like his legal assistants or whatever the titles of the two women were.

Steve cleared his throat. 'Anni, this is my cousin. Alf Smithson.'

Smiling, Anni left Steve's fever-invoking touch and went forward to shake Alf's hand. 'Pleased to meet you, Alf.'

Alf held her fingers in his. 'Pleased to meet you as well, Anni. Steve told me he'd met you. A dancer, isn't it?'

'Yes. I'm a dancer.'

Alf released Anni's hand and grabbed his grey suit jacket from the back of his chair. 'Have you come for lunch, Anni? Steve and I were just going downstairs to the patio.' Alf sounded very flustered.

'Actually, I just came . . .'

Steve interrupted. 'Have lunch with us, Anni. She doesn't eat much, Alf, so we might have to force-feed her.'

Anni gazed at him. 'That's not true.'

Steve smiled at her, a sort of mischievous all-encompassing smile, as if he'd planned this meeting. As if he'd known she'd come running after receiving the flowers. But how could he know that?

Alf's eyes were all over Anni. 'She looks fine to me, Steve. I wouldn't complain. Let's go.'

While Steve went to get his jacket, Alf introduced Anni to Jennifer and Pauline at the front desk. Pauline was the older woman, Jennifer the younger. He introduced the women as legal assistants and mentioned Anni was a dancer. They asked her a couple of questions and she told them about *Wedding Bells*. Alf wondered if she could get them some tickets and she said she'd try. She made a note to send a package of tickets to Steve's office.

In the elevator Anni stood between Steve and Alf. Her entire body pounded, as if her blood had heated to boiling point and was bubbling. She could still feel Steve's fingers on the skin at her waist. Her breathing didn't get any easier with Steve standing so close beside her. She wondered if he felt the same unreal sensations she was feeling. She had never felt this way with any man. She'd always had the upper hand which had enabled her to walk away. The way she'd run to him today, using the roses as an excuse, she certainly didn't have much power over herself where Steve was concerned. Remembering his views on marriage, she knew she might be in for a huge fall.

They chose a shaded table on the patio of the deli, which was right next to the street. Anni ordered a Greek salad and agreed to share Alf and Steve's basket of cheese garlic bread. The men ordered breast of chicken with salad. Alf asked Anni questions about her dancing and Anni was aware of Steve observe them talk, as if he were mesmerized at her interaction with another person. Even as she speared olives and feta cheese from her salad and drank iced club soda her blood still bubbled with excitement. Her pulse throbbed. She felt as if she was performing a frantic dance.

After Alf had eaten, he said he'd take care of the bill as he had a client to meet upstairs. Anni thanked Alf for lunch and stayed with Steve to finish their drinks.

'I like your cousin,' Anni told him, pushing the remains of her salad aside. She enjoyed the cheese, the olives, the first leaves of crisp greens, but hated the oil-soaked mass at the bottom.

'Everyone likes Alf. He's a good guy.'

'Happily married?' Anni asked finishing her drink.

Steve grinned. 'Happily married to his college sweetheart. Father of two rambunctious boys, and son to a couple who retired to Florida about two years ago.'

'An all-round good guy.' Anni twisted her straw around in the ice in her glass. 'And proof that all marriages don't end up in hell.'

Steve leaned forward. 'Are you proposing to me?'

'No. I'm just giving you a different viewpoint of your job.' Anni began to get restless. She could see this impetuous move taking her towards another brief involvement with and heartbreaking exit from Steve.

'So you haven't come here because you changed your mind and want to see me again?'

'The reason I'm here got lost in meeting Alf and having lunch. I came to thank you for the roses.' Anni reached down by her chair for her bag. 'So thank you, and now I'm leaving.' She stood up, shouldering her bag strap.

Steve also rose. 'I'm pleased you liked them.'

'I loved them, but I only came to thank you. Not to continue anything.'

'That's what I like about you, Anni. You're so outspoken. You tell it like it is. But I'll walk you back to the studio. For old times' sake.'

Anni shook her head. 'There's no need.'

He began to walk to her side and she waved her hand at him. 'Don't move. Stay.'

Steve placed some change on the table beneath his plate. 'I'm not a dog. I'll move if I want.'

Anni smiled, she couldn't help it. She supposed she had spoken that way.

Steve smiled as well. 'Although I expect if I do walk back with you we'll have another heart-rending goodbye at the studio door.'

'It's your fault. You sent the roses.' Anni became aware that a number of people were listening to their conversation.

Steve must have realized this as well, because he put his arm around her waist and escorted her through the patio gate on to the street. 'You didn't have to thank me in person. You didn't have to thank me at all,' he said when they were away from prying ears and eyes.

Anni tried to move out from beneath his arm but he wouldn't let her leave. 'I'm a compulsive thanker.'

He chuckled. 'I didn't know that, but I'm pleased you are. How are the rehearsals coming along?'

'Good.'

'Then you should return to the studio. Come on.' He herded her along the steamy street.

When they reached the studio Steve insisted on coming right through to her dressing room to make sure the roses that had been delivered were as ordered. Joni was in the dressing room waiting for Anni.

Anni saw that Joni appeared quite shocked to see Steve with his arm possessively around her waist.

Anni introduced them.

'We've met,' Steve said.

'Yes. We've met,' Joni agreed.

'Well, then,' Anni told them, 'that's great. Steve, you'd better get back to work.'

Joni picked up a perfume bottle on the dresser and replaced it. Steve didn't take Anni's hint.

Joni said, 'I came in to invite you to our

wedding. There's no time to send out invitations. It's a week Saturday.'

'Why so soon?' Anni asked.

'Because we're in a rush.' Joni was wearing a pair of very tight, slim jeans. She touched her stomach. 'I found out I'm pregnant.'

Anni felt a sharp pang of envy. For the marriage, for the baby? She wasn't sure. 'How could you be pregnant? You haven't been here.'

Joni chuckled. 'Germany. Remember?'

Anni remembered. Joni and Charles had holed up in Joni's hotel room for an entire weekend during a break in the tour.

'Congratulations,' Steve said before Anni could voice her own best wishes.

'Thank you,' Joni told him. 'We're so excited, but we really do want to be married before the baby comes, so here we go, head first. Also, I want to get the ceremony in before *Wedding Bells* opens, so everyone can come.'

'That's wonderful, Joni.' Anni clasped her friend in her arms. She really meant her words. But at the same time she was awfully jealous. She wanted so much, she hadn't realized how much, to be with a man she loved and to have his baby. But then, Joni didn't have *Wedding Bells* in her future. She'd never even been chosen for the chorus or signed a long contract with Ray. Two reasons that had probably precipitated her decision to marry Charles. She was free to walk out of the studio and go home to the house she'd shared with Charlie for the past year, marry her man, and have their baby. Anni was still tied up contractually until next year. And the man who wanted her didn't have marriage plans in his future anyway.

As if she knew what Anni was thinking, Joni whispered in her ear, 'It'll happen for you, Anni.' The two women parted. 'Steve, would you like to partner Anni to our wedding? It's going to be held in my parents' back garden. Nothing really elaborate?'

Steve stood with his hands in his pockets. 'I'd love to come, Joni. Thank you very much for inviting me.'

Anni could see herself sliding right back into a relationship with Steve. She could kick herself for responding so gullibly to his gift of roses. Yet it was what she secretly wanted. Steve's action had precipitated something Anni didn't have the guts to continue with if she allowed her brain any choice in the matter.

'Anyway, I must buzz,' Joni said. 'I have a doctor's appointment. Who gave you the roses, Anni?'

'Steve,' she said.

Joni grinned and said, 'See you guys. I'll be in touch, Anni.'

The door closed behind Joni and Anni sat down on a swivel chair in front of her make up mirror. She stared at herself. Her make up was pretty well shot from rushing around in the heat outside and her hair was tangled. Steve, behind her, still stood with his hands in his pockets. She felt his presence like an electronic force. He was so tall, big, handsome. So exactly her opposite. Or was he her opposite? Maybe when two people fell in love they became one. But were they in love?

'You don't have to go to the wedding if you don't want to,' Anni said.

'I want to go,' he told her firmly.

She picked up a brush and drew the bristles hard through her hair. 'It'll prolong everything.'

'If you didn't want anything prolonged, why did you even bother coming to my office today?'

'It wasn't me, it was someone else.' She slung down the brush.

Steve laughed wryly. 'That's good, Anni. Blame your other self.'

She twirled in the chair. 'I can't get involved, Steve.'

'Old age must be getting to you. You repeat yourself.' He strode over to her and placed his hands on the arms of the chair close to hers. His fingers covered hers. Then his mouth, warm and desperate, covered hers. Anni opened her lips and let his tongue plunge inside her mouth with deep hunger. Just as hungrily, she reached for him, sliding her hands down his hips and taut thighs. She could feel the pressure he was putting on his control. She wanted him to lose it the way she was losing it and she splayed her fingers towards his groin. She began thinking of where they could make love here. There was a small sofa in the corner.

Steve withdrew from her abruptly. 'Anni, no.'

'Isn't that what you want?' Her words sounded like a cry from her soul. She was denying her desperate physical needs. Her body wasn't her own any longer.

He adjusted his belt. 'Yes. It's what I want. But not here. Anyone could come in. Besides, I have a client to see in half an hour. I can't do that, feeling so aroused.'

Anni buried her face in her hands. 'I'm sorry, Steve.'

He crouched at her knees. 'No. Don't be sorry. I do want us to make love, really I do. Don't feel bad. But we've got to sort out something between us, something workable that doesn't interfere with your dancing.'

Unable to stop touching him, she placed her hands on his shoulders. 'What about your work? You've got a promotion coming up. You'll have to work hard for that.'

'I know, but I can do both. I mean I can work and have you. I can strike a balance. You'll have to do that as well, Anni.'

Anni nodded. 'I didn't want this to happen. We were supposed to have said goodbye on Sunday. Then you sent roses.'

Steve straightened and buttoned his jacket. 'And you used the roses as an excuse to see me. Admit it, Anni.'

Anni slumped her shoulders. 'All right. I'll admit it.'

He grinned. 'And seeing me has prompted another date, the wedding. I'll call you about it. I'm pretty busy myself for the rest of this week. I'll see myself out, Anni. Be good.'

'Thanks again for the roses.'

He left, looking smug. Anni closed her eyes, hearing the door shut rather than seeing it. She wanted to cry, but she knew she couldn't. She had too much to do this afternoon. Rehearsals began at the theatre. She needed her full concentration. But how was she ever going to concentrate with Steve's presence so engraved on her mind?

Feeling like a kid let out of school because the roses had worked and he had Anni in his life for longer, Steve hurried back to work. His client hadn't arrived yet. Alf called him into his office.

'She's something else, Steve. I really like her.'

'You do?' He didn't want to sound surprised. The rest of his family hadn't disliked Anni but there had been cautiousness underlying all their praise.

'I think she's great. Really good-looking. Wow!'

'I like her a lot,' Steve said, and he knew he meant more than *a lot*. He meant he loved her.

Then he realized there was someone standing at Alf's door. Someone who had probably heard their conversation. It was Craig Firth. Tall with a slim build and short clipped sandy hair, Craig always wore sharp, loose-cut suits and gold-rimmed glasses. He rarely smiled.

'Hi, Craig,' Alf said, looking around Steve. 'Help you?'

'There's someone here to see Steve. His client. Jen and Pauline are out for lunch.'

Steve gave him a smile. 'I'll be right with him, Craig. Thanks.'

Craig left the doorway.

Alf made a face and raised an eyebrow. Steve knew that Alf didn't care much for Craig.

Steve walked to his own office and used his own bathroom to wash before he saw his client. As he dried his hands he thought about Craig overhearing Alf's comments and his own about Anni. Craig was his opponent, although Alf would never willingly choose Craig over Steve for the partnership. Steve knew that. But pressure from the other two partners to keep the status quo, i.e. married, settled, family men or women, would keep Steve with one foot out of the door and Craig with one foot in. Steve couldn't stand for that. He knew that now. So what was he to do? He wanted to marry Anni. He was in no doubt about that. His feelings were intense. He loved her very deeply. Maybe, now he had Anni back in his life, he could persuade her to marry him. Although he couldn't very well tell her about the promotion condition. That would give her an excuse to turn away and he knew Anni would grab *any* excuse to run from him. But he'd have to come to some decision about the direction of his life soon.

His client was getting impatient now, but Steve managed to have the man chuckling by the time they sat down in his office. The meeting concerned paperwork for a will and it didn't take long to finalize the details.

Once alone, Steve sat in his chair and thought about his plan to marry Anni. It had to happen. He couldn't wait until he saw her again.

It was near the end of a busy afternoon when his brother-in-law Ben Martin walked into Steve's office and closed the door firmly behind him.

'Steve,' Ben acknowledged, and sat down in one of Steve's chairs, smoothing his chalk-stripe pants that he wore with braces over a striped shirt. Even the navy blue bow tie, Ben's trademark, didn't detract from his uptight image.

Steve gave his staid brother-in-law a quick glance. Rachel once told Steve that Ben used to wear one of those satin robes and sit in it to smoke a pipe. Although the pipe-smoking had now ended! 'How's it going, Ben?' he asked.

'Fine. How's it going with you?'

'Busy,' Steve said.

Ben cleared his throat. 'Steve, about your promotion . . .'

Steve put down his pen and placed his hands on the desk. He hoped at last he was going to be given a date. Damn the marriage condition. He felt his breath tighten in his chest cavity – as if his breathing *could* tighten any more! Or maybe his heart was giving way! Definitely his brain had been addled by his meeting with Anni. He was beginning to understand his clients' emotions more now. Sometimes you just couldn't help yourself.

Ben crossed his legs, stared down at the chalk stripes, glanced at Steve, held his braces with both hands and twitched them. 'You know that we really do want you as a partner.'

'Yes,' Steve said cautiously, sensing a mighty big 'but' in the air between them.

'Well, there's one drawback. You're single and we would prefer it if you were married. Actually, we would want you to be married.'

151

Just as he had believed. But he said, 'It's almost the twenty-first century, Ben! What the hell? I'm a home-owner and a taxpayer. I get the work done, more than done. I'm responsible.' *And I'm not a sulky sleaze like Craig.*

'We know, Steve. We know.' Ben let go of his braces and began to inspect his blunt fingernails. 'But we have another man here.'

'I know. Craig.'

'Yes. He's married and a family man. An excellent candidate for a promotion.'

'But he's younger than me with less experience. I mean, just because he's married doesn't make him eligible. There are such things as a work track record. And if you've got your heart set on Craig, why not both of us?'

'One at a time, Steve. You'll never be in the running if you stay a bachelor. I know it's old-fashioned but it's our policy. Always has been.'

'So you're telling me, Ben, that I'm out of the running right now? Craig's a sure thing?'

'I think we've mentioned this, yes. I'm just saying that we're coming down to the final decision and . . .' He stared at his knee before looking at Steve again. 'It's a family business here as well, Steve. I mean, there's me, there's Alf. But Paul doesn't want that to get in the way. We shouldn't make exceptions.'

Steve had to move fast on this. He was going to be dumped. He could see it now. He knew he might pay for this, but Steve said probably far too confidently, 'You don't have to worry. I've met someone and I'm planning on marrying her soon.'

Ben's entire demeanour switched to one of relief. 'Great. Even if you're just engaged, the promotion will be a sure thing.'

'I'm planning on an engagement,' Steve said. 'We'll likely get married this fall.' Now he would have to convince Anni to marry him after the *Wedding Bells* run. How he would do that he wasn't sure. He wasn't even sure he would see her after Joni and Charles' wedding.

'Lydia Cruikshank?' Ben inquired curiously. 'She's a nice smart lady.'

'No, not Lydia. We were never serious. This is someone I'm crazy about.'

'Not the dancer you took to the barbecue that Rachel and Alf, who met her today apparently, can't stop talking about?'

Steve saw acute male interest in Ben's expression and he'd bet the impetus for this discussion was precipitated by Alf's telling Ben about Anni. 'Yes. The dancer. Anni Ross.'

Ben relaxed in his chair and Steve suddenly saw the man he often saw at family gatherings. 'That's great, Steve. I mean, Rachel doesn't really approve but Alf liked her. Besides, you have to marry the woman you love, not the woman people think you should love.'

Steve was surprised to find this philosophy coming out of old Ben. 'Did you marry the woman you love?'

'You know I did,' Ben said and stood up, hands in pockets. 'I'm pleased. I'll mention it to Paul and your partnership should be secure by November of this year. Paul will be pleased too. He didn't want to pass you over.'

Steve also stood up. 'Sounds good to me. I'll hold you to November.'

'We'll look forward to the wedding and your promotion celebrations. Good. That's good. Is it safe to tell Rachel?'

'Sure,' Steve said, making a note to call his parents to warn them. He wasn't too sure what type of reaction Ben would receive from Rachel when she learned that Steve actually planned to marry Anni.

'Fine. See you later, Steve.' Ben backed out of Steve's office and left him alone.

Steve remained standing and walked to the window. He saw a roof garden with people sitting out in the sunshine in canvas deckchairs. Next to that was the slate roof of Ray Gifford's dance studio. Anni was in there. Anni who had given him no peace since he'd met her that Friday at the party, Anni who he now had to convince to marry him, otherwise his entire world could come crashing down. No Anni, no promotion either and he'd be out in the cold. How lucky that he'd met Anni and fallen in love in time to fulfil his obligations to his law firm and thus keep his career intact. After all, marriage to Anni would mean a family. To keep a family in the style he was accustomed to himself, he would need a steady career. But, all that aside, he would have Anni. He'd do anything in the world to have Anni. He'd even lose his promotion if it was decided that it wasn't attainable because of Anni. After all, law practices were easier to come by than another Anni.

The phone on his desk buzzed and, feeling full of emotion, Steve strode forward to pick it up. 'Hunter.'

'Steve.' Cool husky tones came over the line. 'It's Lydia. I'm home.'

CHAPTER 9

Steve glanced at his diary and saw that for today he'd marked '*Lydia returns*' in pencil. Naturally, with Anni on his mind, he'd forgotten.

'Hi,' he said, knowing he sounded impatient. He'd been introduced to Lydia by Rachel about a year and a half ago. His first impression was a savvy lawyer in a sexy body. They hit it off intellectually but physically sex had been a bust. Once was enough for Steve. He never really knew why. Just no chemistry, he guessed. However, Lydia insisted on keeping up the friendship, and occasionally they met for lunch or coffee or used one another as convenient dates. Her mother was remarried and lived in California, which was where Lydia had taken her vacation for the past three weeks.

'Aren't you going to ask, "How was your trip, Lydia?" It was great, Steve. Really great. Mother's fine.'

Not that he cared but he tried to sound enthusiastic. 'That's good.'

'You sound so thrilled that I'll issue the invitation I was going to issue. Do you want to meet for coffee?'

Steve winced at the sarcasm and glanced at his watch as well as the heap of files on his desk. The work piled up while he chased Anni Ross. Thoughts of Anni brought on a stab of guilt, although why he couldn't fathom. Maybe the guilt was telling him he should see Lydia and tell her about Anni. 'All right, I'll meet you,' he said. 'That bagel place near your office okay?'

'I'd like that. Half-hour?'

'I'll be there,' Steve said, and hung up the phone.

He shuffled the file folders until they were in a neater pile, remembering his impressions of Lydia the first time he met her. The short-skirted black suit, the long brown hair, the steady brown eyes. She worked for Tarkington and Landsdowne, two heavy-duty defence lawyers. She was becoming pretty heavy-duty herself. Rachel had figured they would be a fantastic match.

Which was probably why Rachel had disliked Anni on sight, Steve thought as he made his way through teeming pedestrians to the bagel café. He saw Lydia before she saw him. She was sitting in a booth in the little restaurant, dressed in a cream linen suit. Her fingers were restless on the table top. In front of her was a mug of coffee. Steve knew that she was probably longing for a cigarette. She'd quit six months ago and she hadn't handled the cessation very well. Part of his problem with her had been her smoking. Containing a deep sigh, he slid into the opposite seat.

'Hi.'

Lydia looked at him and smiled. 'Hi, Steve. Sorry if I dragged you away from work.'

'I'll go back later.'

He gave his order to the waiter, who scurried away and returned with another mug filled with thick aromatic coffee.

Both touching the handles of their mugs, they looked at one another across the table. The guilt over Anni reared once more and he quickly sipped his coffee. He had no reason to feel bad. There was nothing between him and Lydia. He knew that Lydia didn't want to get married or have a serious relationship. She'd told him so. That was half the reason he hung around with her: they both held the same values. Or had. Anni had changed everything he'd ever considered valid about his relationships with women.

'We're really talkative,' Lydia said. 'Something wrong?'

Steve decided to be forthright. 'No. Nothing's wrong. In fact a lot is right. I've met someone who I'm serious about.'

'A woman?'

'That is my persuasion,' he said with a smile. 'Her name is Anni.'

'Anni,' Lydia repeated. 'I was away for three weeks and you met another woman named Anni.'

He heard the caustic edge in her voice, but he continued evenly, 'Not *another* woman. You and I have been nothing but friends for over a year.'

She gritted her teeth at him. 'Because I thought being friends was a way to get you. I really liked you, Steve, from the beginning, but your heart wasn't in it. I didn't have any choice but to stay friends.'

He'd never known this before. He felt the guilt wash over him once again. He should never have told her about Anni. He should have put her off and dropped her from his life the easy way.

'You've got this warped idea of marriage, that's your problem,' she snapped, the way she snapped at witnesses in court. He'd seen her in action. She made people cower.

Steve could be just as hard-nosed. 'Lydia, I didn't come here to meet you for coffee to be told my hang-ups. I don't know if you've forgotten, but we didn't work out.'

'It means no more dates for you and me?'

'That's why I'm telling you,' Steve said.

She leaned across the table and said softly but succinctly, 'But I love you, Steve. I always did. I let you have your way over our loose relationship because I thought I could keep you. If you love me, say so and I won't leave.'

How could he say, *I never loved you*, and not hurt her? He couldn't. He had to try another way to say what he had to say. 'You should never have gone along with me if you felt that way about me. It was dishonest.'

'I thoroughly agree,' she said candidly, 'but we'd make a good couple. I'd be a perfect wife for you. Your promotion might even hinge on someone like me. An old-fashioned firm like the one you're in might require a married man.'

Steve moved the spoon he hadn't used. 'You're

right, of course. But it's not a problem. I'm serious about Anni.'

Lydia frowned. 'Are you telling me that you've met someone who's actually changed your idea of marriage?'

Steve nodded. 'Yep.'

'She must be something else to do that. I'd like to meet her.'

'You probably will one day.' Steve sipped the now cool coffee. 'I don't want to hurt you, Lydia, but that's the situation. You knew it really.'

'When were you going to throw this news to me?'

'When we saw one another again. You made it today.'

Lydia let out a sound of disgust. 'I can't believe it. All that rhetoric about not wanting ever to marry. Me going along with it and now this. *You've met someone.*' Her tone was imitative. 'And you're going to marry her. I can't believe it, I can't . . .

Anger rose inside Steve. 'Lydia, stop it. You've turned the tables on me with your confession. I didn't know anything about the way you felt. You always agreed that my philosophy was yours.'

Eyes flashing, entire demeanour extremely annoyed, she pushed her mug aside. 'Only because I loved you,' she said between her teeth, and stood up from the booth. She picked up her purse and briefcase. 'You can pay for my coffee. See you, Steve.'

Steve watched her walk from the café, high heels tapping on the tile floor. Pleased they were the only people in the restaurant except for the bored waiter, Steve placed a few coins on the table to cover the coffee and tip and left the restaurant himself. Lydia was gone from the street. He could see this story reaching Rachel.

Damn. He crossed the street to an entrance of the Eaton Centre. He often walked through the bustling mall to reach his office. He'd been honest in his relationship with Lydia but she hadn't. If he'd known she'd been harbouring such emotions he would have called it quits long ago. Instead he'd not really thought about their relationship much at all. It hadn't *been* a relationship. That was the truth. For a smart woman Lydia had been pretty dumb. Anni might be frustrating but at least she gave their relationship and the consequences some thought.

'Steve.'

He turned around to see Anni in the long black skirt and brief white top she'd worn at lunch. Her hair was upswept and she wore a pair of red-framed sunglasses. For a second he thought his mind had conjured her up.

'Are you okay, Steve?' she asked.

'Yeah. Hi,' he said. 'I didn't expect to see you.' He also hadn't expected to feel the thrill, the heightened, fevered emotions to fuel the desperation to have her by his side forever. He remembered lunchtime in her dressing room, the desire he'd felt for her, and the same desire boiled over again. 'What are you doing here?'

She lifted her plastic shopping bags. 'Ray's giving Joni her send-off next week. So I was shopping for her gift.'

161

'What did you get?'

'Oh, a big card and I think we'll settle on a stereo CD/tape player for her new studio. I didn't get that, obviously. I have to go back to the others and see if they agree and if I can raise enough money.'

'So what else did you buy?'

Anni held the bags against her body in a protective gesture. 'Nothing much.'

'You have four bags full of stuff, Anni. There has to be something inside.' For some reason whatever she had in the bags caused her a great deal of tension. Was it a gift for him? If it might be for him, he decided to let it go.

But Anni let the bags fall to her side. 'It's baby stuff.'

Steve felt a lurch in his stomach for no reason he could think of. 'Baby stuff?'

'Yep. For Joni.'

'Of course. Silly me.' Steve thrust his hands into his trouser pockets forcing relaxation. 'I was thinking all of a sudden that you ... No. It couldn't be. We haven't, have we?' Oh, but he wished they had and it was his baby and Anni would be tied to him for life. He recalled her cuddling Janet's friend's child the day of the barbecue. Anni had asked to hold the baby and Janet had mentioned to Steve when he talked to her a day or so later that Anni seemed to like babies. He had a sneaking suspicion Anni rather longed for a baby. After all, she was almost thirty. An age when a woman who hadn't had children might consider having a child. A biological urge. Even he, a confirmed bachelor up until this very summer, would like to have a child with Anni.

'Steve!'

She brought him back to their conversation. 'Well, we haven't. Even if you did try to seduce me today in your dressing room.'

'I didn't, Steve.'

He saw her high cheekbones flush. 'Oh, you did, Anni. You wanted to touch me *there*.'

'Shush, Steve.' Anni averted her glance. He stared at her perfect profile, the fall of her hair resting against her pale skin. To see her like this for the rest of his life beside him would be no hardship. No hardship at all. Steve remembered her fingers sliding towards him and what she might have felt had they found their destination. He let out a harsh breath. 'Admit it, Anni.'

She turned on him, bags swinging. 'All right, I admit it. I wanted you in the dressing room. We could have used the sofa. It's driving me crazy wanting you, Steve.'

Her emotion swayed him, rocked him. If they weren't in a shopping mall, if people weren't shoving past them, he would have hugged her. 'I feel the same way,' he said softly, and took her arm. 'Let's go somewhere quieter. Have you had anything to eat? Because I haven't.'

She didn't pull away from him. 'We're always eating, Steve.'

'That's all you'll allow me to do with you so far.'

'Moan, moan, moan,' she said, but smiled. 'All right. Come on. I was going for coffee when I saw you.'

He guided her through the throng of people until they found a quiet coffee bar. Steve ate a toasted club sandwich and Anni used a fork to eat bits of the chicken and salad filling, plus a couple of fries. He enjoyed sharing the food with her. It felt so intimate, the way things should feel with Anni. He couldn't forget her admission. She wanted him. She'd even planned that they might make love on the sofa in her dressing room. She'd been thinking that while he'd been kissing her. He couldn't believe he'd forced the admission from her.

'This isn't supposed to be happening, Steve?'

'But it is. We can't keep away from one another. We're like magnets.' It was the truth.

Anni turned her mug in a circle on the table. 'If we said we weren't going to see one another again, ever, we'd still see each other. I'm sure we would.'

'Which is about what we did.' She seemed to be changing her mind about him. This was great. The euphoria he felt was sexual and heady all at once. He wanted to ask her right then to marry him but he stopped himself. Anni was far too important to him to be rushed.

She shook her head emphatically. 'No. You sent roses. I'm a compulsive thanker, so I came to thank you.'

'And Joni invited us, as a couple, to her wedding.'

'I know.' Anni sighed deeply. 'I don't know what to do now.'

Steve wiped his fingers on a napkin. 'You know what I suggest?'

164

'What?'

'We'll see one another when it's convenient. It could work out. We'll be attending the wedding together. You'd be going anyway, so why not with me? If you're busy for anything I want to do with you, then say so. I'll do the same. We'll always have a date.' He'd said similar words to Lydia once but never with such desperation. Never with such need burning inside him. Never with his breath in his throat, his entire life feeling as if it was on hold, as he awaited her answer.

Anni wasn't sure if she quite trusted Steve at that moment. He'd lapsed into his smooth lawyer 'reserved for clients' tones. His manipulative 'I want you on my side and you'd better capitulate' voice. 'It would mean that neither one of us could get possessive,' she said. 'No tantrums. Or snits.' She gave him a pointed look, hoping to remind him of the Sunday afternoon on his boat when she was sure he'd been in a snit.

'No tantrums. No snits.' Steve stretched his hand out across the table. 'Shake on it?'

Anni supposed that what they were shaking on was an unemotional relationship, no strings. Could she handle it? Lovemaking one night, then nothing. Maybe never anything again. She would have to make sure she never got pregnant. But was that what she really wanted? What about being free to have a baby? For that she wanted the sanctity of marriage, nothing else. And she knew definitely she wanted a baby. All the longings and desires she'd tried to push aside had arisen today when she had found herself in the baby department. She had fed the yearning in her heart by compulsively buying gifts for Joni's expected baby.

'Anni, shake on it,' Steve said firmly.

She placed her fingers into his and he clasped them warmly. Immediately, Anni felt as if she were sinking into quicksand and she bit into her bottom lip to stop it from trembling.

'All right,' Steve said.

Anni didn't think it was a question, but an expression of triumph. Had he planned this move? Were the roses Move One? Had he anticipated her reaction to receiving them? 'All right. But just for a while. See how it goes. I'm not promising anything long-term.'

He withdrew his hand, his eyes narrowed so she couldn't see his true feelings. 'Trust me.'

'I'm not sure I do trust you.'

'You've had some bad tricks played on you in the past, haven't you?'

'I suppose I have. Three boyfriends who said they were going to respect my dancing and then got possessive. Troy, the D.J. – I thought with him it would be different.'

'How different?'

Anni brushed aside a wisp of hair. 'Just different, but he tried to get me to quit.'

'I wouldn't do that, Anni. That's disgraceful. I promise I'll give you space. Any time you want it to end, tell me.'

Did Anni imagine that Steve held his breath at that moment?

Steve shut himself up at that point. He wanted to give Anni an out and he felt he had, without letting her know he was in the process of snaring her. Anni was his soulmate. He'd found her at last. All the images of the bitter divorces he'd witnessed faded in the glow of Anni.

She reached for her purse at her feet and gathered her packages at the same time. 'I have to go home now, Steve. I'm tired.'

'Sure.' He slid off his stool.

She was on her feet, her big bulky bag over her shoulder, the parcels in her hand.

'Do you want a ride home?'

'No. I have my car in a parking lot up the street.'

'Then I'll walk you to it.'

He carried her parcels for her into the warm, scented night. He even liked walking beside her, he thought. Everything he did with her was an experience of the senses. She was right for him. However, he had to let her go at her car. Agreeing to contact her about Joni's wedding, he watched her drive out of the parking lot. Then he walked back to his office to pick up his briefcase. He noticed his rival, Craig Firth, was still in the office. He acknowledged Craig before walking into his own office. His voicemail message was flashing and he punched the codes to access the messages. Two of the messages were clients, another was Rachel.

The clients he would leave until tomorrow. Rachel he called in case there was a family emergency. She didn't often phone him.

'Ben told me,' she said.

Steve was standing. He kept the phone at his ear and at the same time filled his briefcase with papers to take home. 'Told you what?'

'That you're going to marry that dancer. Steve!'

Steve wished he'd never answered Rachel's call now. He hadn't expected this. Or maybe he should have. 'Her name is Anni. She's not *that dancer*. And I can't quite understand where you're coming from, Rachel. This is my choice. You should accept it.'

'We don't have divorces in the Hunter family.'

'I'm getting married, not divorced.' At least he hoped he was getting married. He had a long way to go to convince Anni yet. 'I suppose you've discussed this with the rest of the family?'

'No. Ben told me and I called you. I want to talk you out of it before you make a fool of yourself.'

'And toss my promotion out of the window at the same time?' Steve said in a harsh whisper. At the same time he castigated himself for making it sound as though he were using Anni. That was so far from the truth.

'If that's all you're getting married for, why can't you marry Lydia?'

'Because it's not all I'm getting married for. I love Anni, Rachel. That's the reason I'm marrying her. The promotion conditions are a coincidence. And if Anni won't marry me then I'll let them go, I suppose. I can't force her to marry me.'

'Does she know about these conditions?'

'No. I don't want to lay anything else into a fragile situation.'

His sister was silent for a while, then said, 'She's really shaken you up, hasn't she? You want her badly.'

'You're not kidding, Rach. I'm sorry, but I can't think of anything else at the moment but Anni.'

'All right. I suppose if you really love her and she loves you, then it might work.'

'Give me the benefit of the doubt,' he said.

'When do you want the announcement made to the family?'

'It's not official yet.'

'She hasn't said yes yet?'

'I haven't asked her. But don't tell Ben that. It will happen, Rachel. Believe me.'

Steve hung up after Rachel. Then he realized Craig was standing by his door. Did he listen in to everyone's conversation? Or was he merely out to haunt Steve? Steve placed another file in his briefcase. 'Yes, Craig.'

Craig raked his fingers across the top of his stubby hair. 'Someone phoned for you earlier. A Mrs Stoneguard. She didn't want to leave voice-mail. Doesn't like talking to a machine. She's one of your clients.'

'Yep. Thanks.' Steve leaned across his desk, dragged forward a pad and pen and wrote down the message. 'I have her number.'

Craig cleared his throat. Steve had noticed he did that often before he spoke.

Craig pushed his hands into the pockets of his loose suit pants. 'Seems like we're up for the same promotion,' he said.

Steve couldn't face more confrontation. 'Seems that way, Craig.'

'But I hear you'll probably win because you're

going to get married soon. The woman that was up here the other day? That dancer?'

Steve was sick and tired of people calling Anni *that dancer*. But he also thought he'd better stake his claim for his partnership. 'Yep. We're getting married.'

'That's not fair, Steve.' Craig was inside Steve's office now.

Steve jammed down the top of his case and clicked the clasps. 'Course it's fair. The partnership stipulates a married man. Just so happens I'm getting married soon.'

'Marie sees Rachel all the time and she told her you only just met her. It's something you've cooked up between you, isn't it? And then you'll split up after.'

Steve gave Craig a narrow-eyed look. 'You're not only way off base, you're also very much out of line. Marrying Anni has nothing whatsoever to do with the promotion. If she doesn't want to marry me then I guess I'll let it go. It just so happens the two incidents coincide.'

'Damn lucky for you,' Craig snapped, and walked out of Steve's office. Steve heard Craig's door slam.

Damn, he thought. But he'd put his cards on the table. Craig could relay *that* to his gossipy wife. And hopefully, after his conversation with Rachel earlier, she would have a change of heart. And hell, if Anni didn't marry him – well, it might be the end of his world emotionally but career-wise he could move on. He'd often had offers put to him to join other law practices.

Before he left Steve phoned Mrs Stoneguard, made the appointment she wanted, and then grabbed his full briefcase to head home. Even though it might kill him, he made up his mind that he should leave Anni alone for a few days. He had enough work to cover the weekend. It would give her space from him and time to think. He had to trust the cliché that absence really did make the heart grow fonder.

Anni couldn't quite understand why she hadn't heard from Steve. Hadn't they made an arrangement to date, to see one another? Or maybe he felt the wedding was soon enough to see her again. She knew he was busy. The same way she was busy and didn't have time to be thinking about any excess baggage. She had Joni's going-away party to plan.

Anni's suggestion for a compact disc and tape system for Joni to use in her new studio met with approval from the other dancers. She collected enough money to buy a good one and she had it professionally wrapped and delivered to the studio on the Thursday afternoon of the party.

Lucinda turned the studio into a party room with flowers and loaded tables of food. Anni and Lucinda placed the gift on the podium table from where Ray could present it.

'I'm jealous of Joni,' said Lucinda, pushing aside a lock of thick gold blonde hair.

'How's that?' Anni asked, giving the tablecloth a twitch to straighten it. Lucinda wasn't a dancer. She was a consultant for a marketing firm.

'Because she's having a baby. Ray and I have been trying for over a year now.'

'I didn't know that,' Anni said. Ray had two teenagers from his marriage. One boy, one girl. She'd thought he was satisfied with them. But then, maybe Lucinda wanted a baby of her own. Anni didn't think she'd want to be in Lucinda's precarious position. Even if Lucinda did get pregnant, Ray might not marry her.

'There's nothing wrong,' Lucinda went on. 'We've both been checked out. And I'm only twenty-seven. Still young.'

'Younger than me.' Anni smiled. 'I'm sure it'll happen, Lucinda. Ray was away for quite a long time this year so you can't count those months.'

Lucinda chuckled. 'True. I guess we have to make up for it.'

Anni nodded, but she felt hollow inside again. Pangs for the need for her own union with a man, for her own baby. She'd never felt such loneliness as she'd felt since she met Steve. He'd caused her to re-evaluate all her desires and goals and now he wanted a relationship she was rather suspicious of, but she felt she should go along with it. She had to eradicate him from her system somehow.

Ray came in and put his arms around his girlfriend and kissed her. Hands on the hips of her long flowered skirt. Anni watched them. Why did Ray put shackles on Anni when he wanted the exact things she wanted? Or did she put the restraints on herself and use Ray's possessiveness as an added excuse?

You have to be honest with yourself, Anni. Admit what you want. You want your dancing, but you also want your man and a family. It's time. She perfectly understood Joni's defection.

'Anni.'

Joni's voice shook her from her thoughts. 'Hi.' Anni hugged her friend. 'I'm going to miss you, Joni.'

Joni hugged Anni and then drew away. 'You don't have to miss me. Come and see my new studio after the party.'

Anni would go to see the studio. If she felt right there, as if it were her calling, then she might be able to begin making some decisions as to whether she could go into business with Joni. The idea was quite appealing. 'I'll come and see it,' she said.

'Bring Steve,' Joni said, and moved her head to indicate the door.

Steve stood there wearing jeans and a navy blue short-sleeved shirt. After not seeing or hearing from him for a week she wanted to run to him and hurl herself into his arms, but she contained herself. Years of dance training kept her in control. But she did wave.

He smiled and walked over to the two women. 'Hi, Joni,' he said. 'Anni.'

'What are you doing here, Steve?' Anni asked.

'Make me sound wanted!' He winked at Joni. 'Joni invited me. She wants me to meet Charles. They need a lawyer for their new business and they want me to see the location tonight. I believe you might be going there afterwards.'

Anni glanced at Joni, who merely shrugged her slim shoulders beneath her white T-shirt. Anni felt as if she had been set up. 'I would have appreciated being forewarned,' she said.

'I couldn't get hold of you this afternoon,' Steve said.

'There has been a weekend in between now and the last time we saw one another,' Anni told him as Joni went to greet Charles who had walked in the door.

His expression was innocent. 'Did you miss me?'

Anni didn't trust Steve's motives for ignoring her. 'Was that the intention?'

Steve placed his hand on his heart, his eyes teasing. 'You've caught me out.'

Anni took hold of his arm. 'Steve.' But she had no chance to question his motives. Joni was ready to introduce Charles to Steve.

Charles McKinnon was a large man with a shock of dark hair prematurely speckled with silver. He didn't look much like Anni thought a financial adviser should look. More like a retired football player. He adored Joni and acted rather like a cuddly bear around her. Joni introduced Steve and Charles and the two men shook hands and began a conversation.

Joni grinned at Anni and Anni felt as if she were being drawn into a circle against her will. Or *was* it against her will? She had been longing to be with Steve again and here he was.

After the party, Charles carried Joni's gift out to the car and Steve and Anni followed. She didn't have her car so she rode with Steve to the studio.

She had the route from Joni written down on a piece of paper and with the aid of a flashlight Steve handed her she guided their direction.

It began to rain lightly as Steve drove through a residential neighbourhood and the lights from the elegant brick homes streaked across the damp road surface.

'Give me the number, Anni,' Steve asked.

'Thirty-three. It's on the corner past the stores.'

Steve drove past a store displaying vegetables and fruits outside and a clothes store with racks of T-shirts, jeans and leggings. He pulled up across the road from thirty-three. 'Huge place,' he commented.

Anni leaned over him, looking at Joni's studio. 'It will make a fantastic studio.'

Steve placed his arm around her shoulders. 'It will. Joni and Charles haven't arrived yet. Do you want to neck?'

Anni laughed. 'Steve!' But she snuggled up with him and they kissed long and slow while the rain turned into huge heavy drops. All the humidity of the last weeks dripped from the sky.

Charles and Joni drew up in their little sports car behind them and Charles must have seen Steve and Anni embracing because he honked the horn.

Anni straightened her hair and slipped out of Steve's car. Joni gave her a perky grin. Anni shrugged her shoulders. It was becoming inevitable now that she and Steve were seen as a couple.

They walked across the road to the house. Almost jumping with excitement, Joni opened the door and clicked on the light switch with pride. The door opened first into a spacious foyer. Another door led into the studio, which was the entire downstairs of the house, except for a kitchen and another room that was going to be an office and looked out over the fenced back garden.

Anni really liked the room and saw the end result that hadn't yet been achieved. Peach paint stood in cans waiting to be put on the plain walls. Two barres needed to be erected. The wood floor was being finished to make it smooth and Joni had already ordered the mirrors for the walls. Upstairs Charles had his computer and other office machinery in place and they'd left one room overlooking the back as a sitting room.

Leaving Charles and Steve upstairs, Joni and Anni slipped back to the studio.

'So what do you think?' Joni asked, skipping around the spacious room.

Anni held up her skirt and danced a few steps. The floor was well sprung. 'I think it's going to be great. Really great. I mean it.'

'All my own,' Joni said. 'All *our* own. Come on board, Anni.'

'I wouldn't be able to join you until after *Wedding Bells*. And then I'm contracted with Ray up until the end of June.'

'He might not have anything lined up after *Bells*. Why did you ever sign one of his silly contracts, Anni?'

'I needed security and there was extra money involved.'

'I know, but . . . well, it makes him like your guardian or something. Anyway, June isn't far away. I'll have had my baby by then and be getting into things. We can still make plans. I want your input even if you're not physically here until later. Steve's agreed to do all the legal work.'

Anni fingered the scraped wall and imagined the pale peach walls. 'Giving up Gifford's won't be easy.'

'You'd be surprised,' Joni quipped.

'You have Charles and a baby to look forward to.'

'You have Steve,' her friend said quietly. 'Don't let him go, Anni.'

'That's exactly what my mother said.'

'She's right.'

'Steve doesn't want marriage.'

'Balderdash. He's mad about you. Any fool can see that.'

'*I* don't want marriage.' Anni danced some more steps away from her friend's eagle eye.

'Balderdash to that as well,' Joni said.

Anni made a face at Joni. 'Back to this studio, Joni. It's wonderful. So bright even when it's dark. I bet the sun just pours through that front window.'

'It sure does. I'll have to put up blinds.' Joni went over to her gift. 'Help me set up this sound system. We'll blast those guys back downstairs.'

Anni and Joni unpacked the system, set up the speakers, pushed the plug into the wall socket, and turned on the switch. Radio music pounded into the studio.

Joni grinned. 'Wow! Great speakers. This was a wonderful gift.'

The two men came down the stairs. Charles immediately went over to the sound system and fiddled with knobs and digital push buttons. 'Can't you ever get the tone right, Joni?'

Joni rolled her eyes at Anni. 'Can't men ever accept that sometimes women want things their way? It sounds fine to me.'

'It can't possibly sound fine. You had a tinny sound,' Charles retorted.

'If you say so, darling.'

Steve grinned. 'Anni, you have to learn some finesse from your friend.'

'What do you mean? Give in? No way.' Anni winked at Steve. It was fun with the four of them together. She imagined them all old, still friends. Their children friends.

Charles patted Joni's shoulder. 'Come on, love. You need to get home to sleep.'

'He's babying me about this child,' Joni said, but entwined her hand with Charles's. 'All right. I'm locking up. Turn off the sound, sweetie.'

Steve and Anni said goodnight and returned to his car. Mentally filing the business he had discussed with Charles, Steve drove in the direction of Anni's apartment. The rain had ended but the roads were still sleek and glittery. Steve felt relief at the end to the humidity. The cooler air charged him with energy and made him think about the autumn and the end of Anni's run with *Wedding Bells*.

'The studio is a great idea.' Steve said. 'Charles mentioned that Joni is asking you to be a partner in her dance company?'

'Yes, she is. But obviously it'll have to wait until next June.'

'That's when your contract with Ray expires?'

'Yes.'

'What if he doesn't have anything lined up for you after the run of *Wedding Bells*?'

'He'll have something.'

Steve glanced at her expression, but it was hidden by the darkness. Anni stared straight ahead. 'Do you want to go in with Joni?'

'I'm thinking about it.'

'Seriously?'

'Yes. Seriously. But I have *Wedding Bells* to do yet. There's no question which is most important.'

No question, he thought. *Wedding Bells* was erected like a barrier in Anni's life. She put it before everything. It was like a brick wall that kept everything else out. But he had needs, desperate needs. One of them was to be with Anni for the rest of his life. Other than marriage he couldn't see any other relationship with her. An affair wasn't good enough.

He stopped at a traffic light. 'I know you're putting off all life-and-death decisions, but if we got married, Anni, we could wait until after the show at the end of September.'

Steve felt Anni's abrupt turn of amazement move the car. 'Are you asking me to marry you?'

CHAPTER 10

Anni watched Steve drive through the green light. 'I didn't think you believed in marriage.'

'I've changed my mind. I'm willing to take a chance with you.' He glanced at her. 'I love you, Anni. I can't live without you. I've come to that conclusion.'

Anni's brain felt scrambled by the sudden announcement. Especially that he loved her. She'd known he lusted for her. But love? She also knew she wanted Steve, the love, the babies that would come from their union. She also wanted her dancing. *She wanted it all*. Buzz words that were so true but incredibly difficult to achieve in reality.

'We could get married in October,' he continued.

She cleared her throat. 'What if the show gets held over?'

'We could *what if* forever. Even so, I'm sure there will be an interlude that will give us time to get married. Please consider October.'

Anni stroked her long flowered skirt down over her knees. 'We never decided on marriage, Steve.

We said an on-again, off-again, loose, how-we-felt-that-day relationship.'

His hands clenched around the steering wheel. 'I know what we decided but I don't believe it would work. I don't know any other way we can go.'

'Steve, marriage is a huge step. We've only known each other a few weeks.'

'That's nothing to do with it. I know you're right for me.'

She shook her head. 'I don't think I am. That's the point. Think of all those divorces, Steve. You didn't want anything to do with marriage when I met you.'

'Obviously I hadn't met the right woman.' He smiled gently. 'I'm in love with you, Anni. No question.'

'If you want to make love with me, then we will as soon as we get to my place; we'll do what we wanted to do the first night we met and then maybe we can see sense.'

Steve shook his head. 'No. You give me a commitment first. I couldn't handle making love with you and splitting up and I know *you* can't.'

She reached for him blindly and held his arm. 'Everyone wants me to change direction without any thought. I can't just *leave* Ray. I can't just *get* married, Steve. You will have to give me time to think this out.'

'I am giving you time. I'm asking you to consider October. Hell, you can be married to me and still work with Ray. I don't understand why that's a problem unless you've got something going with him, which I know you haven't. All I want is for you to marry me in October.'

'Slow down, Steve. You're speeding along here.'

He slowed the car. 'Don't change the subject.'

'I'm not. I want more time. How about I tell you Saturday, after Joni and Charles's wedding?' Anni said. 'Please give me until then.'

'All right. Saturday evening you tell me for sure.'

They left it at that with a brief kiss at her front door. Anni knew she was in for some soul-searching before she formed an answer to Steve. What her heart wanted and what her brain suggested were in blatant contradiction.

Anni had to dash about on Friday to find something suitable to wear for Joni's wedding. She was standing up for Joni, who was wearing a long satin dress with a bolero jacket.

Finally Anni walked up the brick steps into *Diane's*, Steve's mother's boutique. Diane was working on a display in the elegant dress shop and smiled warmly when she saw Anni.

'Hi, Anni.'

Anni was surprised to be greeted with such warmth. 'Hi. I need to find something to wear for a wedding tomorrow. I'm standing up for the bride and I haven't got a thing at home that's suitable.'

Diane got to her feet. She wore silk pants and a loose white top and her hair was soft and bouncy. 'Do you always leave things until the last minute?'

'I haven't had time and Joni, my friend, suddenly up and decided she was getting married with barely two weeks' notice.'

182

'Steve did mention he was going to a wedding this weekend. Well, look around. I hope we have something. I can get alterations done right away if necessary but you look an off-the-rack size.'

'I am,' Anni said, already fingering a row of dresses. No. She didn't want a dress. 'Do you have any suits?'

'Over in the corner. That lilac one is silk and would look wonderful on you.'

The lilac suit did indeed look wonderful. Anni modelled the short skirt and snug jacket that was fitted into her slim waist. She lifted her hair on top of her head.

'Yes, it's lovely. Wear your hair up.' Diane suggested.

The suit was also expensive, but even though Anni could afford it Diane gave her the family discount.

'After all, you might be part of us soon, I hear.'

Anni picked up the garment bag the suit was in. 'Did Steve say something?'

'We've heard he's thinking marriage.' Diane smiled.

'He did ask me, yes. I haven't given him an answer yet, though.' Anni felt that Diane should be prepared for a let-down if Anni did decide not to marry her son. She wished Steve hadn't been so precipitate in telling his family.

'It wasn't Steve who told me,' his mother said quickly. 'Rachel mentioned something.'

'Oh,' Anni said, wondering how Rachel knew. Unless Steve had told his sister. Whatever. They knew.

'I want you to know we'll welcome you,' Diane told her, giving her the charge card receipt. 'I hope you enjoy the wedding, Anni. And that Steve has a good time as well.'

'I'll tell him where the outfit came from,' Anni told her. 'Thank you, Diane.'

Anni returned home, feeling she might be in a trap. If Steve's family expected marriage and would welcome her she wouldn't want to disappoint them. She wished Steve hadn't spread his marriage proposal around before she'd made her decision. But when he phoned later and she told him she'd purchased her dress from his mother's shop and questioned Diane's knowledge of his proposal, he denied mentioning it to his mother. Although, he admitted he had sort of hinted to Alf and Ben that he was serious about her.

'So Ben told your sister?'

'What are you worried about?' There was humour in his voice. 'Feel trapped into giving a yes answer?'

'You'll wait until after Joni's wedding,' Anni told him. 'You can't get to me by setting your family on me.'

'It wasn't intentional, Anni, but it might help my cause.'

As it was, she hung up smiling. Even though she felt manipulated.

On Saturday, Anni dressed, looped her hair into an upswept style, placed long silver earrings in her ears, and pushed her feet into silver heels. She was only just ready when Steve arrived. She hoped he wouldn't start pressing her for an answer to his

184

proposal right away. She wanted to enjoy the day for Joni and not have to brood.

However, when she saw Steve she almost flung herself into his arms to tell him she would be with him until the end of time. He wore a black suit, a crisp white shirt and a black silk tie. His burnished hair seemed a little longer than when she'd first met him and he looked so stunning she knew she wouldn't have been able to pick such a perfect man if she'd had a free choice. Was she stupid to be dithering? Other women would likely have said yes the other evening. And if she turned him down would she then go through life disillusioned and grow old without her desired children and no love in her life?

'You look wonderful,' he said as she scurried around making sure she had everything in her small purse. 'Mother said you bought an original.'

Anni added a lilac lipstick. 'It was the only suit like it there. I'd hate to see the same thing on someone else.'

'I doubt if you would recognize it on anyone else, but I also don't think you will see it again. It's great. Mother also said you didn't blink at the price tag but you got the family discount. So now you have to become family to make that legal.'

Anni stuffed in some tissues. 'I don't want to hear about this until after the wedding, Steve?'

He pushed his hands into his pockets. 'Okay. I can wait. Now let's go. Don't we have to pick up your mother?'

'Yes, we do. Do you want something to drink before we leave?'

'I'm fine. I'm sure we'll drink our share at the wedding. I know you're quite partial to champagne.'

Their eyes met and she knew he was also remembering their first night. Her race across Ray's lawn to stop him leaving. What had possessed her to run to him? If she hadn't felt that urge she wouldn't be here with Steve today. She'd be in her own car going to Joni's wedding alone.

Marian Ross, in a pale blue silk dress and white shoes that Anni had helped her shop for a year ago for another wedding, was ready to slip into the car when Steve climbed out to open the back door.

'Don't you look nice,' Marian told him as she stroked the arm of his expensive suit. 'Anni will be crazy to let you go.'

'I've asked her to marry me,' Steve said impetuously, thinking that maybe Anni's mother could have an influence.

Marian's eyes lit up. 'She *has* said yes, I hope.'

'She's thinking.' Steve gave a wry smile.

'She has nothing to think about. Steve, convince her. You'll be good for her.'

Driving on to Joni's parents' home through attractive residential streets with full summer floral gardens, Steve wondered what Anni's answer would be to his marriage proposal. Would he know at the end of this day? His future hung in limbo awaiting that answer.

It surprised Steve to discover that Joni's parents, George and Jean Reed, lived in a home similar to that of his own parents. Why he should be surprised, he wasn't sure, because he knew for a fact there had to be family money to start Joni into a dancing career. George, a slim, grey-haired, handsome man looking fit in his tuxedo, was a retired engineer. And Jean, a short blonde lady in pink, worked as a freelance accountant.

Marian seemed to be very close friends with the Reeds.

'We lived next door to one another when my Dad was alive,' Anni explained as they sipped drinks beneath a striped marquee where the reception was to be held after the ceremony. 'Joni's dad and my dad used to fish together.'

This information surprised, even shocked Steve. He'd thought Anni had come from circumstances so different from his that there would never be reconciliation. 'You lived around here?'

She swiped a strand of silvery hair from her face with the hand that wasn't holding her glass. 'Next door. My mother stayed for a while after my father died and then it just got too expensive to handle, so she moved into a bungalow. When she quit work, she moved into the apartment.'

'You know what this means, Anni?' He shouldn't sound excited but he did.

She didn't look at him. He'd noticed she was avoiding meeting his eyes today.

'What?' she asked curtly, her focus on a couple already munching on hors-d'oeuvres.

Anni's entire demeanour might mean that he was going to be tossed aside this evening. But he kept his cool. 'It means that we share a similar background.'

She took a gulp from her drink with an action so

forced that her long earrings swayed. 'Your parents' house is way bigger than this.'

'Bigger but similar. Traditional.'

She looked at him then. But she wasn't angry. She was confused, flustered. 'I'm not traditional. That's the point.'

'Anni.' He wanted to hold her, to kiss her, to tell her that everything would be fine between them, but there were too many people crunching in beside them. He said softly. 'You fight it. That's more to the point.'

'No, Steve, I don't fight it. I've removed myself from it. That is entirely different.'

'And you think I want to take you back to it?' He hadn't meant to discuss marriage with her, but hell, he couldn't help himself. Anni and their relationship was always foremost in his mind these days. 'That's not true. We'll be ourselves. Our own couple. We'll make our own family traditions. Anni, I'm not planning on capturing you and keeping you from living your own life. Can't you get that through your head?'

He saw tears flood her purple-blue eyes. 'Wait until after Joni and Charles are married. Please. I have to stand up for Joni. Don't make me feel bad. I want everything wonderful for Joni.'

He stopped himself from saying, *everything isn't always wonderful, though,* and instead placed his arm around her shoulders and drew her close to him until he could smell her sweet perfume and feel the cool silver of her earrings against his neck. 'Sorry. But please. I love you, Anni.'

'Anni.' It was Joni's mother. 'We're getting ready for the ceremony now. Do you want to go upstairs and join Joni while she's getting ready?'

'Yes. Love to,' Anni said slipping out of Steve's arm and handing him her glass. 'I'll see you later. Go keep my mother company. *She* loves you.'

Anni escaped Steve and walked into the cool house with Joni's mother. She wanted to go somewhere to wipe her eyes and regain her composure, but Jean was chattering on about something as they walked upstairs to Joni's parents' bedroom.

Joni was checking herself in the full-length mirror. Anni thought she looked beautiful in her wedding gown. Her extra-slim hips made the skirt hang in exquisite lines below the bolero jacket. Anni saw no sign of the expected baby in her figure. From her short dark hair hung a froth of net and a veil with which she would cover her face.

'Anni. I didn't think you were here,' Joni said. 'I'm in such a tizz. After all this time we've been together I feel like I'm jumping into hot water. And I threw up this morning and then I could barely fasten the dress. I feel like I'm pushed into the outfit. What am I doing?'

'Marrying Charles, who loves you,' Anni said softly. 'You're fine. It'll be fine. You'll have a great life. And the dress looks wonderful. I can't see a sign of the baby.' Anni meant all her words. Joni was capable of being herself within different situations. Anni had always found life awkward outside the dance world. But even so Steve's anguished '*I love you, Anni*' reverberated through her.

'Did you see Charles?'

'No. Not yet,' Anni said, smoothing Joni's veil so it didn't pucker at her collar. 'This is a lovely outfit.'

'What if he gets cold feet?'

'He won't. Don't be silly. Everything will go like clockwork. Now turn around. Let's see.'

Joni swished in a circle. 'Yeah, you're right. You look nice, Anni. Perfect, but then you always dress exactly perfect.'

'No. I don't. I wore a skimpy black dress and red high heels to Steve's parents' house the first time I went there. It was a barbecue.'

Joni chuckled. 'To a barbecue, Anni. Why?'

'I don't know why. Some subconscious way of showing Steve I was different, I suppose. And now that Steve has seen this house and knows I lived next door when I was a kid, he thinks we're the same.'

'Do you love him, Anni?'

The answer to that would truly be the foundation of her decision. The answer she hadn't thought about, didn't want to think about, wanted to deny until she had to make sense of her feelings. But she knew the answer. She knew it straight out and honestly.

'Yes. I love him,' she said succinctly. 'Right from the moment I first saw him. Do you believe in love at first sight?'

'Yep, 'cause that's how Charlie and I met. Across-a-crowded-room sort of thing.' Joni smiled. 'I really am so happy I could burst. Why was I worried?'

'I don't know. You have it all worked out.'

'The dancing bit, yeah. I have it all worked out. Who knows what will happen when the baby is born and we're married? Will Charlie get up in the night to see to the baby? Who knows? Go to the window, Anni, and see if he's here yet.'

Anni pushed open a couple of slats of the Venetian blinds and peered down at the colourful crowd in the garden. The wedding was to be held on the lawn and she saw Charles in front of a table set up like an altar and filled with flowers. His best man, Adrian Stokes, was there, so was Steve. The three men were all laughing about something and looked perfectly relaxed and having fun.

Anni turned away from the window. 'Don't look yourself, but he's there and he looks happy as anything. He looks like a man who really wants this, Joni.'

Joni hugged her. 'Come on. We have to go. I'm about to become Joan Elizabeth Reed-McKinnon.'

Steve sat with Marian Ross, who informed him who was who.

'Charles is such a nice man. So good-looking with all that curly dark hair. Joni's lucky. I think she knows it. Now we have to get Anni married. That's my dream.' Marian patted Steve's knee. 'I hope she says yes, Steve. I really do.'

'I hope so too,' he said.

'Anni needs someone like you in her life. Someone stable. She doesn't think she does but she does.'

Steve watched Charles and Joni exchange their

vows, then kiss one another. They drew apart, staring into one another's eyes. It was obvious they loved each other passionately. Steve saw Anni's gaze move from the couple to the bouquet of mauve and yellow daisies in her hands. He thought he saw her bite her lower lip. Did she want the same type of love for herself? Or was she forever going to deny it? And did he want the same kind of love for himself? And if their answers were yes, could they find happiness together? Steve already knew his answer. He loved Anni and he'd try.

Anni returned to Steve as the caterers buzzed in and out of the tent. She sipped more champagne. All through the wedding ceremony she'd felt so choked up, so happy for Joni and Charles. Joni had no other direction to go. She knew that.

'Emotional time for you,' Steve remarked.

Anni nodded. 'It was a lovely wedding.'

'Exactly what your mother said.'

'Did she really?' Anni made a face.

Steve placed his arm around her waist. 'Just a teeny bit jealous, were you?'

She looked him in the eye. Could she admit that to him? 'Not exactly jealous. Just thinking about all the changes Joni will be going through.'

'You're going to be Aunty Anni in another few months.'

'That's true.'

'Don't let similar happiness pass you by, Anni.'

She finished her champagne and moved away to place her empty glass on the table. Her head felt a little bit sore from too much emotion. She turned back to Steve. 'I think we should circulate.'

'I have been circulating. Your mother and I get on like a house on fire and she's introduced me to everyone she knows.'

'A real conflagration, huh?' Anni remarked.

'Ever since I've met you I feel like I've been thrown into a roaring fire.'

Me too, Anni thought. Me too.

The evening brought music and dancing to a band on the lawn. By then the champagne had done its work. Joni and Charles danced to the loud rhythm. Anni kicked off her shoes and stockings. Steve rolled up his shirt-sleeves and abandoned his tie. Like the first night they'd met, he danced with Anni to throbbing sound, realizing that if his plans materialized he would always dance with her, so he might as well perfect his act. When the music turned slow, he loved holding her hot, damp body close in his arms.

He realized now that Anni was very much a person ruled by emotion. Her arms wrapped around Steve's neck, her fingers stroked his hair. She stared into his eyes and he kissed her nose and then her mouth. She opened her lips for him and he had to control himself from dipping his tongue into the willing heat.

But he grew more and more aroused until he couldn't take much more. He grasped her hand and they slipped away to a silent, empty part of the Reeds' house.

They stopped in a hallway and shared hot, drugging kisses. It wouldn't take much to find a bedroom and make love, except that Steve didn't want it this way. He didn't want champagne-induced emotions or wedding-day-induced emotions. He was learning something about Anni. She used her emotions to carry her along to do things she didn't consciously want to do, but couldn't stop herself from doing. She probably danced that way. Not probably. Did. So she used the trick in real life. But not with him. Never with him. With him he wanted straight-up, honest emotions. She was going to come to him with a clear head.

Using all the control he'd ever had to muster, Steve took hold of her wrists and dragged them away from his neck. He held her hands between them, gazing into her purple, passion-glazed eyes. 'Not here, Anni. I know what you're doing. You want to get carried away, swept away, so you don't have to be liable for what happens between us. But I want to be liable and right at this moment I'm not carrying any condoms.'

He felt Anni's fingers convulse in his.

'I know you want a baby,' he said softly. 'But you're not having my baby until there's marriage between us. Okay?'

She let out a long, sobbing breath. 'Oh, Steve.'

He clasped her into his arms, this time for comfort not passion. 'I understand you're going through some changes and maybe I've precipitated some of them. But I think you should work through them systematically. First things first. We'll make definite plans to get married.'

Anni drew away from him, blinked tears back. 'You want my answer.'

His fingers convulsed on her shoulders. 'Yes. I

want your answer.'

'If it's no, will you let me take a cab home? Let it be?'

'No. I'll still see you home. And your mother.'

Suddenly words burst from her. 'I love you, Steve. I want you to know that. If ever I wanted to marry anyone it would be you.'

'Will you marry me, then?'

She closed her eyes.

Steve actually heard his heartbeat. If she said no he might die inside tonight.

'Anni,' he whispered.

She opened her eyes and gazed at him, nibbling on her lip for a second before she said, 'I do, Steve, want a family, and you'll be the only one I'll ever want that with. So . . .' Suddenly she flung herself at him and he immediately put his arms around her to hold her.

He barely heard her muffled. 'Yes, Steve, I'll marry you.'

CHAPTER 11

During the remainder of Joni's wedding all Anni could think about was Steve. She'd said yes to his proposal, yes to marrying him. And it was something she truly wanted. No question. But how was she ever going to make her own wedding bells ring when she had such a demanding schedule in her future? Two weeks until the opening night.

Of course Steve told her mother of their plans and Marian Ross was absolutely thrilled on the drive home from the wedding. She said she'd do a lot of the planning.

Steve wanted to tell his parents the following day, which was Sunday, but Anni wouldn't be able to accompany him because she was due at the Empire Theatre at seven the following morning.

'On a Sunday, Anni?' he said after they had dropped her mother off and they drove home through empty streets at two o'clock in the morning.

'I don't work normal nine to five, Steve,' she said. 'This is how it is. You'll have to accommodate me.'

'I have to tell my family.'

'Go ahead. And I'll see them as soon as I'm available.'

They hadn't parted particularly well. Their short goodnight, in direct contrast to the hot, passionate kisses earlier at Joni's wedding, bothered Anni all night. She tossed and turned until her bed was a tangled mess. She eventually got up, slipped into a light robe, poured a can of pop into a glass, and sat on one of the striped satin chairs to look at the night outside. Even in the middle of the night the city was alive. She wondered what Steve was doing and felt a potent desire to be with him. And she would be. When they were married.

Sleepy and heavy-limbed, Anni arrived next morning at the newly renovated Empire Theatre. She downed a huge mug of hot coffee instead of her usual glass of water, knowing today she was to dance with Moe. She felt nervous about this. Anni had danced with him in rehearsals at Ray's studio but never in the actual theatre before. When she saw him, tall, deadly lean with a heavy fall of jet-black hair surrounding his sharp, handsome features, she felt her heartbeat turn erratic. What if she couldn't pull off her three duets with Moe?

Moe, who had been talking to Ray, became aware of Anni's presence and walked to her with his arms outstretched, his hands offering to take hers. 'Anni. How are you doing? All prepared?'

She held his hands and smiled confidently. The coffee was doing its job and making her feel more alert and her voice was bright and cheerful. 'All prepared. Although I haven't danced here yet.'

'It's no different. Concentrate on your work, not the workplace.'

'True,' she said, and let go of his hands. She wondered why one man's touch – Steve's – could send her wild with longing, while that of another man, an equally attractive man, did nothing.

Ray moved away from them. 'All right. Let's get going. We have two weeks until opening night. I'll see Anni's solo first, then the duets, then Moe's solo. In that order.'

Anni went to change in the dressing room that she'd been assigned. She noticed there was a small shower and a large sofa that would suffice for a nap. For once she was alone, without a bunch of other women. She dressed in her practice clothes, fastened her slippers and returned to the stage. Moe was ready now, a tall, splendid figure women went nuts over. They didn't care that he already had a wife and a newly born baby.

Despite Moe's attitude Anni felt that dancing in the studio compared to dancing on stage was a different exercise. Especially when the seats were all empty except for Ray in the third row. Dancing in front of Ray was also not Anni's favourite workout. Anni could tell by his grunts whether or not she was achieving the dance he'd envisaged. Sometimes he'd leap on to the stage and take over, showing her the steps he wanted her to dance. If she didn't agree with certain steps she told him so. She wasn't frightened of Ray but he did impose his will and she could get angry with him. Although that anger usually died when she saw that his leg was stiff and then she felt compassion for him.

He'd never been able to fulfil the personal dreams she had fulfilled herself.

Surprisingly, her duets with Moe went off without a hitch. Ray did not grunt. Moe's solos were an athletic endeavour of grace and emotion. Anni applauded. He'd steal the show she was sure. Which was why she needed to make her own solos wonderful. More than wonderful. The best.

After Moe left, Anni stayed on to practise. She really would have appreciated Ray not watching but he did. When she stopped and grabbed a towel from the side, he said, 'Oh, well.'

'What's wrong now?' she called out.

Ray sat with his arms stretched along the back of two seats. 'Your heart's not in it.'

When she thought of hearts, Anni immediately thought of Steve.

Anni tossed aside the towel. 'I'll try again,' she told Ray.

'Please,' Ray said impatiently. 'You were fine with Moe. Now get back on that stage and hammer out that solo. You're supposed to be sad because you've seen your lover with another woman. Put some feeling into it.'

'All right.' She balled the towel and tossed it aside. Tony began the music once more. She focused her mind on Steve and what she might feel if she saw him with another woman, and the fierce emotion fuelled the dance and in the end Ray stopped grunting and stood and applauded.

'I knew you could do it,' he told her. 'Now go home. Get some rest. Refresh your spirit and come back tomorrow morning.'

Ray hadn't spoken to Anni like that since she was younger and less accomplished. She'd known this would happen as soon as she let herself slip outside her profession. Steve had done this to her. Ruined her. Or had she been on the road to ruin before she even met him? Something inside her must have wanted to meet him, to have an excuse to slow down, to end what was becoming difficult. Not quit dancing, but quit dancing as the only outlet in her life. It wasn't exactly ruin. More change. And she knew she had to accept the changes. She wanted to marry Steve. She had no doubts.

'Anni?' Ray prompted.

'I'll go home,' she said.

He walked up the aisle to her. 'You're not dancing badly, Anni. You'll come through for *Bells*, I know that. But you have some decisions you have to make.' He patted his shirt pocket for his cigar but he didn't extract it. 'I don't think I can hold you back. What is it?'

She took a deep breath and told him. 'I'm going to marry Steve.'

Anni didn't wait around for Ray's reaction. He had known marriage was the inevitable outcome of her meeting Steve. He'd sensed it at the party. That was why he'd been upset. She went to the dressing room, showered, and changed into her street clothes. She was using the subway today. She sat on the rumbling train, her bags clutched on her blue-jeaned knees, wondering how she was going to survive this funk. One day at a time, that was what she'd do. She'd go to rehearsals each day, she'd perform the show and in between she'd make time for *a life*. She hugged her bag, the words inside her head unable to keep her calm. Anxiety churned inside her stomach. Not only for the future with Steve, but the premiere of *Wedding Bells* was soon. She had exactly one more weekend and one week to get her act in gear.

Steve was waiting by her apartment block when she arrived home. She went into his arms for his warm passionate kiss.

'I thought you'd forgotten about me,' she said. 'I thought you were mad that I had rehearsals on a Sunday.'

'I get over things,' he said with a grin. 'Did you tell Ray we're getting married?'

'I told him,' she said holding his hand as they walked in through her door. 'Then I walked away and didn't wait for his reaction.'

'Chicken.'

'Have you told your parents it's for sure?'

'I went over today.'

'And?' Anni gave him a sideways look as they waited for the elevator. He was wearing jeans and a blue shirt that matched his eyes. Absolutely gorgeous. No wonder she was head over heels crazy about him.

'It's fine with them.'

'Are you sure?'

'Positive. Don't worry about them.'

They stepped on to the elevator.

'I marry you, I marry them,' Anni said.

'They realize you are my choice, Anni. I want you. I need you. I love you. All those things. I want to be with you forever. It's not their life. It's mine.'

His arms were around her, feeling warm and comforting. Anni stroked his thick, clean, shiny hair. 'I love you, Steve.'

He stood slightly apart from her and looked into her eyes. 'And I love you, Anni Ross. Don't worry about my family. They're excited to be attending your opening night.'

'Then I have to be better than excellent. They'll judge me.'

'I don't think so. Once we're married everything will be fine.'

Anni chalked an imaginary stroke through the air before opening her front door. 'You say that often, Steve. I have this feeling that marriage is very difficult, but I intend to do my best.'

'Ah, sweetheart.' Once inside her apartment his kiss was hot, full of promise. 'I want you, but I think we should wait until your show is finished.'

'I think so as well. Then I can really concentrate on you. Besides,' she gave him a grin, 'It'll be kind of fun to wait until our wedding night.'

'I'll be a basket case.'

She might be as well. But when *Wedding Bells* was over and she could really focus on him and have him for her lover, she would get pregnant and fulfil everything that needed to be fulfilled inside her. All the voids, all the emptiness and all the craziness that was her own mind and body. But all that would come after the stage show. She couldn't think about the future now. It had to be shelved.

But her love for Steve . . . his love for her couldn't be shelved. It was now, immediate. She hugged him, her hands upon his back, feeling him warm and vital through his shirt. She brushed her palms down his ribs to his waist and felt him tense while she fingered his belt. But she could feel him holding back from her. 'What's the matter, Steve?'

He gave her a hooded look. 'What do you think?'

'We don't have to wait.'

'We do. Now let's think of something practical. Like what you want for dinner?' His voice was rather strained.

'I'll cook you Anni's special spaghetti. It gives me energy.'

He smiled. 'All right. I'll help you. I can manage Steve's special garlic bread.'

Anni grasped his hand. 'Sounds great. My kitchen needs a workout.'

It was fun being with Steve. They cooked the meal together, then ate while watching TV at the same time. Watching TV was something Anni rarely did. There wouldn't be any free evenings for Anni after opening night. She made this one special. But when he was gone, leaving behind his scent and his presence in her apartment, she realized that Steve was now real to her and what she felt for him was real. Hadn't she always thought that love might change her mind about marriage?

Joni was on her honeymoon with Charles in the mountains near Calgary, and even though rehearsals for *Wedding Bells* were ruling Anni's life now, she hustled all their friends to put together a wedding/baby shower at her apartment upon Joni's return. When Ray's Lucinda heard about the shower, knowing how busy Anni was, she offered to help.

As soon as Joni returned it wasn't difficult to lure her to Anni's apartment on the pretext of planning Anni's wedding – an announcement Joni was overjoyed about. The joy on Joni's face alone was enough to make Anni pleased she'd made an effort. Joni received an abundance of gifts, from a toaster to baby clothes. While watching her friend stroke a baby jumpsuit, Anni felt a lump form in her throat and had to rise from her chair and dive into the kitchen. She wasn't alone there. Lucinda was making more tea.

'All right, Anni?' Lucinda asked.

Anni liked Lucinda more now that they had got to know one another. But she still didn't feel confident enough to confide her emotions. Joni was the only person who was ever privy to those truths and even then Anni had never divulged her need for a baby. In some ways she felt her need might be abnormally obsessive, as if she shouldn't experience such primitive desires.

'Anni?'

Lucinda was waiting for her to speak. She smiled brightly. 'I'm fine.'

'You're bound to be emotional with your friend moving on into a different life,' Lucinda said. 'It'll be okay.'

Anni hadn't expected Lucinda to dissect her feelings.

'You'll miss her,' Lucinda continued as she poured boiling water into a red ceramic teapot. 'But I hear you will be moving on yourself. Ray said you were marrying Steve Hunter?'

'Yes. I am,' Anni said. 'Call me crazy, but I fell in love.'

'I can understand that. Steve's drop-dead gorgeous. I think it's wonderful. You need to spread your wings. You can get narrow in one world.'

'Does Ray think that as well?' Anni asked.

'In his heart he does but he won't say it.' Lucinda smiled. 'Don't worry about Ray. He's intense at times but he means well. He wants stardom for you, that's all.'

'I might be giving it up. Although I feel I've come as far as possible with Ray. You know what I mean?'

'I know exactly what you mean. Marry Steve, go in new directions. Leave Ray to me.' Lucinda placed the pot on the tray and carried it into the living room. She seemed so much wiser than her young years. Maybe that was why Ray loved her. Anni swallowed hard and returned to the party.

Steve opened the programme of *Wedding Bells*. It was a booklet containing biographies of each dancer, interspersed with advertisements for some of the fine dining establishments and élite fashion stores around Toronto. His family had already noticed *Diane's* had a featured advertisement. The centre pages listed the evening's dance pieces. Anni was solo twice. Steve felt his breath gather in his chest in the hope that she would triumph. She didn't only have to dance this opening night but to continue every night until the end of September. And then it would be over and she would become his wife. What the future held for her dancing after that, he didn't know. Neither did Anni. If the show was successful it might even be held over. If it wasn't successful the run could be shortened. That prospect didn't bear thinking about. Anni would be upset and Ray Gifford might have to close his dance company.

Steve rolled the programme and held it between dampened fingers. Marian leaned over. 'I never thought Ann would amount to this,' she whispered. 'She was a skinny little girl. Her father pushed her too much, I always thought.'

'She pushes herself,' Steve said. 'And she has a tough streak.'

'I wish her father were here to see her. I wish he could meet you.'

Steve said what he felt was the truth. 'After seeing his photo at your place, I think I'm meeting your husband in parts of Anni.'

'Possibly,' Marian agreed. 'He was a very strong man inside.'

Steve glanced along the row to his own family. Despite what he told Anni he knew she was right in her assumption that they would judge her tonight. But he didn't think they would judge her unkindly. Except for Rachel, the rest of his family had accepted his decision to marry Anni. Even so, he wished they were already married, already joined. It would make the next weeks so much easier for him, but then he wasn't thinking of himself by waiting. He was thinking of Anni, of this show, which was her life and the culmination of a dedicated career.

Anni had been generous with complimentary tickets and in the row before him were Paul Roberts and his wife, Geraldine, and Alf and Sandy. Craig and Marie Firth had been offered tickets by Steve but Craig said they couldn't get a babysitter this evening, so instead Steve had given the tickets to Jennifer and Pauline.

The theatre darkened. Here goes, he thought. Good luck, Anni.

Many choruses made up the basis of the wedding-mating customs before Anni's first appearance. For some reason he hadn't expected to see her dance a duet. Possibly he hadn't looked closely enough at the programme. This dance was a meeting with a lover and the lover was a real good-looking guy. Had she told him this? Or had she omitted it on purpose? The dance was sensual and erotic. Anni so fair, so pale, against the man so dark, so masculine held the audience entranced. Steve knew this was the man who would be her husband by the end of the show. That was the story. Saul and Selena, their courtship, their passion, their marriage. Watching Anni touch him, spin away from him, glance at him, he wondered if she felt anything. Surely a dance so passionate affected a dancer? Steve could barely watch the interaction, especially when Moe held Anni and their flesh brushed together.

He was relieved when the chorus returned and then it was time for Anni's first solo. He saw her haloed in the spotlight before she danced 'Another Lover' and hoped she could feel his presence within her.

This dance was sad, unlike the frantic pounding of the finale that he had glimpsed the first time he'd watched her dance. Steve began to choke up inside. He moved restlessly in his seat. He wasn't used to feeling such deep emotion or reacting to a mere dance in a darkened theatre. He wasn't used to fierce jealousy, love, or being in love. He might have what he wanted, Anni in his life and marriage in his future, but he wasn't sure he knew how to deal with the relationship. This was most likely the problem with waiting until he was in his mid-thirties to marry. At twenty he wouldn't have worried about any of this. Arrangements with the women he met then were black or white, sex or no sex. Anni was much more than that, more complex. Life now had shades of grey. And his soon-to-be partners were sitting right in front of him watching his woman, his future wife, execute this sexual art on stage.

He was almost pleased when Anni left the stage to be replaced by some light-hearted pieces. He relaxed for a while.

Until 'Marriage Dance'.

Anni appeared dressed in pure flowing white silk. The dance began with her alone, almost like a classical ballet piece. Slow and graceful, the music harmonious to her movement, Anni was able to show off her ballet training. Gradually the pace grew until the piece heated into a fast-moving contemporary dance. Anni's fast dancing was furious and liquid. She seemed to have no awkward limbs like the rest of humanity. Steve noticed Alf turn around and smile and he knew his cousin was thinking about the sex Steve might have with Anni.

Anni was joined by the dark-haired man. Steve knew what 'Marriage Dance' was about now. This was the wedding night, the lovemaking. The finale to all the mating customs portrayed this evening throughout the show. While he wanted to watch Anni, he didn't care to see the man toying with her, loving her, making love with her. Their bodies curved together and Steve could almost feel himself sliding into Anni; the intensity of the moment left him throbbing. And still the music and dance built to a crescendo. The audience was silent with awe and Steve grew intensely edgy. He knew what was coming. Anni and another man acting out a climax. He held the programme rolled tight. He didn't want to watch but he did. He saw their bodies wrap together in the aching, pounding orgasmic dance. He gritted his teeth. Yet he could feel the tension run through the audience as well. He wasn't alone with these emotions. He reached a point where he wanted it to stop. And it did. A sigh of relaxation rustled through the audience before the raucous applause began. Steve sat there, feeling the exultant moment caused by the expression of the two dancers' expertise and emotions. He was also aroused, remembering the day in the studio when he'd first seen Anni dance part of the same piece. Each time he ever watched her dance he was sure he would want to make love with her. He felt shaken after her performances. Each had brought him new emotions and he probably felt the way Anni had the evening in the cinema when she'd been uncomfortable with the love scenes.

When the lights came on, Janet next to him said, 'She's something else, Steve. I can't believe she's going to be part of our family. Wow!'

'You like her?'

'I think she's the neatest. It takes guts to go on stage and perform like Anni.'

Yes. It did take guts. Steve didn't think he could declare his own innermost feelings so openly. Yet Anni, in real life, kept a lot to herself. Up there on the stage she was Selena, in Selena's character. He had to remember that. 'Look, Jan, I'm going to see if I can find Anni. There's a party or something after. We'll meet you all at the restaurant later.'

'All right. Do you want Dad to drive Mrs Ross?'

'If you would. You're all going to have to get to know one another.'

'Fine. Go tell Anni she's wonderful. Make sure you tell her from me as well. And if she can get me an introduction to that gorgeous Moe Ellison, I'll be forever grateful.'

'Is that the guy she danced solo with? You really think he's gorgeous?'

Jan smiled mischievously. 'You were jealous?'

'Don't you think I had reason?'

'No. It's only a dance. Come on, Steve. She loves you.'

Steve squeezed Janet's hand. 'Thanks. I hope you're right. Love gets very complex.'

Steve half rose in his seat to leave when Alf turned around. 'Something else, Steve! You picked yourself a live wire.'

Sandy, his wife, a plain, dark-haired woman, said, 'Oh, for heaven's sake. It was just a dance. But she's lovely, Steve. Congratulations.'

'Thanks. Are you all coming to the dinner?'

'Wouldn't miss it,' Alf said. 'Where are you going?'

'To see Anni. We might be a little late.'

'I bet!' Alf said.

'Go see her and tell her we thought she's wonderful,' Sandy said and gave her husband a nudge. 'Get your mind from the gutter, Smithson.'

Chuckling at their relationship, which had always remained teasing and loving, Steve relayed the news to Marian that his family would drive her to the restaurant where they'd all planned on a late dinner and then he slipped from his seat. Anni had shown him her dressing room a week ago so he thought he could just go to it. He hadn't bargained on the opening night security being tighter and the security guard not wanting to let him past the public areas.

'Go get Ray Gifford,' Steve told the guy. 'He'll vouch for me.'

The security guard called over someone named Frank and asked him to look for Mr Gifford.

Steve pounded his palm with the rolled programme in frustration. Was it often going to be like this when he wanted to reach Anni? She might become a huge star after this performance. He might end up in the background while she shone. Hell, she should have given him a pass. But she hadn't been thinking of anything past the performance lately. He'd been the one relaying messages to her mother. He'd even cooked Anni a few meals, otherwise she might never eat. She might even be infatuated with that guy Moe Ellison for all he knew.

Frank returned shaking his head. 'Can't locate Mr Gifford.'

Steve said firmly. 'Go to Anni Ross's dressing room and tell her to give you permission to let Steve Hunter in. Thank you.'

Frank made the sort of face that asked, *Who the hell does he think he is?* but he trotted off to do as bid. He returned nodding. 'Come on with me.'

Anni's dressing room looked like a flower garden. She was still dressed in her white silk, still full of emotion left over from the dance. She ran to Steve. 'It's good to see you. I didn't remember to give you a back-stage pass. I'm sorry.'

Steve pushed the programme into his pocket and took hold of her hand. He tugged her forward to him and leaned to kiss her. He half expected to be pushed away but instead she blended her body into his and wrapped her arms around his neck. Her mouth was supple and eager and Steve's arousal, never far away, roared into burning need.

He was hungry to touch her and she was just as ravenous to be touched. He loosened the top of her dress to display her breasts, his hands eager to stroke her soft flesh. He lowered his mouth to kiss the hardened buds of her nipples and felt Anni's body rise to meet his mouth.

Whether it was the after-affects of the dance or not, Steve didn't care at this moment. He lifted her in his arms and carried her to the sofa in the corner.

She murmured. 'Lock the door,' as she lay before him, and he went to the door and pushed the lock, then returned in a hurry, slipping out of his suit jacket. He sat on the edge of the sofa and Anni reached up and loosened his tie.

He kissed her once more, then caressed her perfectly shaped feet, her long, naked legs. The dress was only wrapped around her and when it came apart, except for brief silk panties, she was naked. Her skin was pale and smooth like the silk of her dress. Steve's blood raced in his head and his gut ached from weeks of needing her. He had this feeling that now the time might have come, he would disappoint her. Or was it the time? After all, she was hyped from a performance. She'd practically made love to another guy on stage. She could be feeling Moe's presence, not his.

'What's the matter?' Anni asked him, stroking his shoulders through his shirt.

He touched her hair that was dampened from her exertion and kissed her mouth. 'We were going to wait,' he said.

Anni entwined her arms around Steve's neck. 'I don't know if I can wait, Steve. Knowing you were out there this evening first of all made me nervous – I think that was your family – but knowing *you* were there made everything right somehow, and it was good. Was it good?'

'It was wonderful, darling. You were wonderful. I don't think Ray will have to worry about the show closing down early.' He stopped himself from mentioning Moe. 'Oh, Anni.'

Desperate hugs led to long, drugging kisses that were interrupted by loud raps on the door.

'Anni. It's Ray. Are you in there?'

'Shush,' Anni said placing two fingers upon Steve's mouth. 'I'm supposed to be going to the party.'

'Anni.' Ray knocked loudly.

'You should go to the party. You're the star,' Steve told her. 'Come on.' He straightened her dress and covered the woman he wanted so badly.

'Steve?' Her eyes were huge and dark, her face flushed.

He was in no doubt she wanted him. He kissed the tip of her nose. 'We'll wait until we can be completely alone. Right now there's too much going on.' Reluctantly he stood up, straightened his clothes and put on his jacket. He left his tie loose. He didn't feel like being that uptight.

When Anni was also standing, brushing her fingers through her hair, he went to the door.

'I should have known Hunter was in here,' Ray said, striding into the dressing room. 'Anni, come on, get dressed. There's a limo waiting outside to take you to the hotel for the party. You were superb, darling. Superb.'

Steve watched Ray take Anni in his arms and kiss her on the mouth. He controlled his jealousy and managed to say evenly, 'I'll take her.'

Anni extricated herself from Ray's embrace. 'Yes. Steve will take me, Ray.'

'He can go in the limo with you.'

'I'm not that much of a star, Ray. I'll go with Steve. We'll go to the party for a while and then I have to meet his family for dinner. All right?'

Steve saw that Ray looked quite put out. He didn't have much choice but to shrug. 'All right. See you there. Lucinda and I will take the limo. Congratulations. This will be a full run.'

When Ray was gone Anni placed her hand on Steve's arm. 'I'm going to get changed. You will come to the party with me for a while? Then I'll go to the restaurant with you.'

Steve pushed his hands into his pockets. 'I don't want to drag you away from your limelight.' And he meant it. He couldn't be sour.

Anni shook her head. 'I'd rather be with you tonight and really, Steve, I'm very tired. I need you to help me.'

'That's an admission.' He felt pleased.

She placed her hand around his neck and kissed him on the mouth. 'I love you. Now I desperately need a shower. I have black silk pants and a silver top hanging in that garment bag. Get them down for me?'

'I'll get them for you while you shower.'

When he heard the water pounding in the small shower room, he lifted the garment bag from the hook. He unzipped it and unloaded the black silk pants that were in a wide-legged retro seventies style. The top was small and most likely tight. Both garments were designer labels and probably expensive. They seemed small and probably would fit closely to every curve of Anni's body. Folded over the hanger was also a pair of silk panties and a tiny bra. Oh, Anni, he thought. Being your husband will be a wonderful experience. What had he been worrying about? If they loved one another, then their love would feed their relationship and make it work. It might be a naïve way of looking at their marriage but for Steve it was the only way at the moment. It was a sort of 'one step at a time' situation.

When Anni, wrapped in a terry robe, returned from her shower Steve had her clothes laid out for her and she quickly dressed in front of him. She was used to dressing and undressing in front of other people but they were women not men. She would need to get used to his eyes upon her. She stepped into silver sandals and moved to the mirror. She sat down and began repairing her make-up and hair.

Steve stood behind her, silently observing. 'I like watching you,' he said eventually. 'You look great, by the way.'

'I picked up a bunch of clothes in Europe,' she said.

'You seem to always be able to make time for shopping.'

She grinned. 'Yeah, I suppose. It's sort of a release, especially on tour. I love clothes and especially shoes.'

'I've noticed.'

She finished her make-up and packed her gear into a big black bag that Steve picked up to carry for her. Anni only had to manage a small purse. In his Mercedes she closed her eyes. She forced herself to be full of life when really she was bone-tired. But she would sleep most of tomorrow morning and rehearse all afternoon for the next performance. The thought of the next weeks seemed like an effort and her dancing had never been an effort before. After the run she was getting married and she would go on a honeymoon to England with Steve. They'd already planned that part of their first two weeks of marriage. These thoughts cascaded through her mind as the car droned through the neon-lit streets and she was jerked to full consciousness at the sound of Steve's voice.

'We're at the hotel for the party,' Steve said.

Anni didn't really want to be there. She would be quite content just continuing the drive to nowhere. But the show must go on. She always quoted that to herself when she felt herself slipping out of her persona. 'We'll just be a short time. What time are they eating dinner?'

'They'll have appetizers and drinks until we get there.'

'Drinks? My mother?'

'Your mother was proud of you tonight. She told me so. Now come on. Star!'

Anni's entrance was greeted with flowers, kisses and hugs from male and female dancers. Anni saw Steve's glower when this happened and felt pleased that he was jealous but knew he would have to get used to this affection, either false or real, in her world. Ray, now having imbibed too much champagne, came over and gave her an extra kiss. Moe introduced his wife, Janine, who was also a dancer, to Anni.

'This is Steve, my fiancé,' she said, thinking that very shortly she would be saying *my husband* instead.

Moe shook Steve's hand and Anni saw Steve giving Janine an assessing look. Janine was tall and pale-haired like Anni. A little larger in bone-structure but similar.

'She's like you,' Steve said when they were alone for a moment.

'Sort of, I suppose. They've danced together.'

'It was probably obvious that you should dance with Moe for this show.'

'Janine has just had a baby. She's off for a while.'

'Otherwise would she have had the part?'

'I'm not sure, Steve. They brought in Moe for me.' Anni noticed that Steve was really intense on the subject of Moe. She wondered if he'd found the dance that suggestive, as if the dancers had really been in love. 'Were we that good?' she asked slyly.

He hesitated. 'What do you mean?'

'If Moe and I were good enough for you to get jealous, then we must have projected well from the stage.'

'You projected well all right.' Steve held her elbow. 'Anni, you were both great. You looked as if you were in bed together, it was as if you both experienced orgasm. I felt it.'

Anni touched his cheek. 'Oh, Steve. That's great news. Absolutely great news. I didn't know whether I did well or not. I felt I did but who knows what the audience feels? It's fantastic to have you in the audience feeling something and letting me have feedback.'

'Of course, it was only acting.'

'Yes. That's what I do. Act. I feel what it might feel like on a personal level. Run little scenes through my head. Maybe how much I love you and how it's going to be, then I react in the dance. Moe's been with Janine for a long time, Steve. I mean, we might look as if we were turned on, it's natural. But it's nothing personal, if you know what I mean.'

He leaned over and kissed her mouth. Anni let her lips cling. She wanted to show him she was his. His alone.

It wasn't difficult for Anni and Steve to escape an hour later. Anni wasn't really looking forward to the family dinner but she felt it was necessary. A sort of rehearsal for the wedding and the years she would have to live with Steve's family.

CHAPTER 12

Everyone at the big oblong table stood up when Anni and Steve walked over to it. 'Congratulations,' Alf Smithson said to Anni, holding her hand. 'You were great.' He introduced Sandra and Sandy hugged Anni.

'Welcome to the clan.'

Janet gave Anni a big smile. 'Really great. Introduce me to Moe.'

Steve gave Janet a nudge. 'I found out he's married to another dancer named Janine.'

'Who cares? Our names are similar.'

Anni laughed. 'I'll introduce you, Janet.'

Her mother tapped her arm and Anni kissed her and felt Marian's reassuring hug around her waist. It was strange how Steve's appearance in their lives had made her mother come more alive. Or maybe it was Anni herself who was more aware of those around her.

Steve's father gave Anni a hearty handshake and Rachel and his mother told her she was great. Diane hugged her. 'Welcome to the family,' she said, and Anni felt she meant it. Steve's family were being very gracious.

'I enjoyed the entire production,' Rachel said. 'It was very refreshing, very musical.'

The other person Anni had never met was Ben Martin. Steve had told her he was stuffy and in some ways he was, except for his clothes. He wore a blue suit, a striped shirt and red bow tie and braces. He was a very stern type of man but he couldn't be very old, about forty Anni would say. His profile was handsome. She could understand what Rachel saw in him.

'You were good,' he said in a deep authoritative voice. 'Quite good.'

'That's about as much praise as you'll get from old Ben,' Steve whispered as they took their places at the family table.

'He seems quite wacky.'

'Wacky?'

'His clothes are kind of bizarre.'

'In some ways, yes.' Steve smiled and turned to address the table. 'I bet everyone is starving,' he said aloud.

Rachel lifted a huge glass of wine. 'I'm quite happy, Steve.'

Anni realized that the few drinks had loosened up the Hunter family. Even her mother was sipping red wine. 'Then let's order and eat,' Anni said. 'I'm starved.'

And she was. For once she felt she would be able to eat after a performance. She chose the same as Steve, steamed salmon and stir-fry vegetables, and then she relaxed and enjoyed herself. And she didn't even feel out of place. Maybe being in Steve's family wouldn't be so bad after all. She even wanted to pay for the affair but Steve's father wouldn't hear of it. He footed the bill.

She had to leave early because she was almost falling asleep. Before they left, she told them to contact Steve if they needed more tickets for themselves or friends.

Steve dropped her off at home with a sleepy kiss. It was all Anni could do to discard her clothes and tuck herself into bed.

Anni felt that *Wedding Bells* went well after the premiere. Typically some nights were more 'switched on' than others but usually it was only the performers who felt the perceptible changes. The audiences were raving about the show and it was booked for packed houses until its run finished at the end of September.

'I think it might be held over,' Ray told Anni one morning as they ate breakfast together in a café close to the theatre.

'I'm getting married in a couple of weeks,' she told him, still unused to the diamond and ruby ring, which had been Steve's great-grand-mother's, on her left hand. She hadn't wanted to accept a piece of jewellery so precious but Steve wanted her to have the ring. His grand-mother in Vancouver had given it to him to give to his bride.

Ray laughed. 'I can tell, Anni. You keep drifting into dreamland. But that's fine. We won't begin the new run until about December twentieth, to give everyone a rest and to cash in on the Christmas ticket-buying. How's that?'

She would be married and back from her honeymoon long before December twentieth. November was Steve's promotion so she would also be free for it. Late in December would be a perfect date to begin work again. Also, she wouldn't have to worry about what she was going to do once she arrived back. Ray had no plans after *Wedding Bells* finished. 'Great. I'll be there.'

Ray grinned over the rim of his coffee mug. 'You see, I do think of you, Anni. I'm slotting everything in here. I might even take the time to marry Lucinda in the interim as well.'

'Congratulations. She's really nice, Ray. This means you think marriage is okay?'

'I thought it was okay once before, but things didn't work out.'

Anni reached over and patted his hand. 'I hope it works out this time. Then we'll both be married.'

'We will, but don't get pregnant right away. I'll tuck a pack of condoms in your wedding gift.'

Anni felt her cheeks flush with colour. 'Ray, for heaven's sake!'

He grinned. 'Well, you can't dance pregnant. Especially in a show where your character is courting, not married. I'm only being practical.'

'As if unmarried people don't get pregnant – although it's something I wouldn't want.' Anni picked up her coffee mug and drank some of the hot liquid. 'Being married won't change anything for me, Ray. Promise. I've worked everything out and I'll manage. Steve is very understanding. He's been wonderful through this run.'

'He's left you alone. Is that what you mean?'

'He's busy with his own work.'

'It's good he's so understanding. Good.'

But Anni saw Ray's top lip curl, which indicated he was being sarcastic. Was it because Ray knew first-hand how a career like dance could wreck a marriage, or was it because he was cynical about Steve's 'understanding' nature? And yet he was going to be married again himself. Even so, Anni didn't want to stay around to find out Ray's theories. She stood up, reaching for her bag.

'I'm going to practise, Ray. See you later.'

'Four more nights,' he reminded her as she left him.

Anni saluted, smiled and walked out into the rain-washed street. Four more nights, two more weeks and she'd be Anni Ross Hunter.

Marian had already pitched in and sent prettily engraved invitations to their small circle of relatives. Both sets of grandparents had died long ago, and other relatives, like Marian's sister in Vancouver, couldn't attend the wedding at such short notice. However, they did send gifts. And Anni's cousin Trisha, who was her father's brother's daughter, accepted her invitation. Her father's brother, Dan, also accepted the honour of giving her away.

'I'm pleased you asked, Anni,' Dan said the night they were all at her mother's apartment discussing the plans. 'Your father did mention it once.'

Anni liked her Uncle Dan. He was a huge bear of a man who ran his own construction company and built elegant houses with a dedication similar to the intensity that Anni put into her dancing. He'd never said a word, but sometimes she thought he understood her calling. 'He didn't know he'd die before I got married, did he?' she said.

Dan's big face looked forlorn. 'I don't know, but Philip liked to have everything planned in his life. He just said once, "If I'm not around when my daughter gets married, take my place, Dan?" And I said, Sure, sure, but you'll be around. Not long after, he was dead. He must have been feeling ill.'

'Dan's had some practice,' his wife Pat inserted. 'Giving Trisha away two years ago.'

'It'll be great,' Anni said, meaning it. Her excitement over her wedding was real now. 'Really great.'

She took her mother shopping at *Diane's*. Steve's mother and Anni made sure Marian selected an outfit appropriate to the autumn time of year and that was prettier than her usual style of dress. A pale orange silk dress with a jacket looked wonderful with her dark brown hair, styled more casually in loose waves, at Anni's suggestion.

Marian couldn't believe it was her. She said so every time she looked in a mirror. If Anni was grateful to Steve's appearance in her life for anything, it was her mother's drastic change, her renewed self-confidence. Marian even helped Joni organize a shower where Anni raked in tons of loot to start her new home with Steve. Since her new home was going to be Steve's house, she took the gifts there to store them away.

He had given her a key and she was alone in the house. The rain outside pounded upon the roof and flew against the windows in a heavy downfall. She had to admit she much preferred modern spaces, but at least Steve didn't have the house cluttered with furniture. Each piece was very tasteful, even if Anni didn't think the furniture personal. She actually couldn't discern if Steve's taste was his own, or his perception of how a house should be furnished based on his family upbringing. Although in his study she discovered a beautiful teak desk, burgundy leather chair and bookshelves with glass doors that she loved, and she was pretty sure Steve's study had been his own selection. The other furniture might have been left-overs from his family because the Hunters' home was fairly modern, as if old had been replaced for very expensive new.

Anni heard the door open and she went to greet Steve.

'Hi.'

'Hi.' His black trenchcoat was damp, his hair sprinkled with raindrops. He put down his briefcase and began to shed the coat. 'Good to see you here. What's the occasion?'

Anni tucked her fingers into the front pockets of her jeans. 'Shower gifts. I put them in one of the spare bedrooms. I noticed there were some wedding gifts there.'

'I know. We'll have to open them one evening and make notes of who sent what so we can thank them.'

'More to do,' she said.

'Poor Anni.' Steve grinned. 'Real life is intruding in your dream life.'

'Is that how you think of me, Steve?'

He tucked his arms around her and kissed her nose. 'Yeah, but I like you anyway. Now, do you want to go out to dinner?'

'Sounds good.'

They put their coats on once more and walked through the rain to the Italian restaurant they had taken Marian to back in the summer. It seemed a long time ago now. At the time Anni had been trying to make up her mind whether she should see Steve for a few dates or not. Now she was his forever.

Anni felt that her own relatives were an easy matter compared to Steve's. Steve had a contingent from the West Coast, aunts and uncles who brought his grandmother with them, the one that had given him Anni's ring. Expecting someone old, Anni was surprised to find Skippy, as they called her, a sprightly seventy-year-old with blonde hair. Skippy Hunter reminded her a little of herself, Anni thought, and wondered if that was sort of a subconscious way Steve had of seeing her, because he was devoted to Skippy, whose real name was Arlene.

Her mother's acceptance into the fold, as well as getting along well with Skippy, kept Anni in the centre of the Hunter family instead of on the fringe as she had suspected she would be. Even if Rachel eyed her cautiously, Skippy kept Anni grounded. After meeting Skippy Anni felt proud to wear Steve's great-grandmother's ring.

'Seriously,' Skippy told her one day when they were alone, 'I'm pleased Steve has decided to

227

marry you. He could have been stuck with some-one stuffy. And Steve isn't really stuffy. He's really a free spirit but the family put him through law school and that's where he's ended up.'

'He likes law,' Anni said.

'No doubt, no doubt, but he also likes sailing and athletics and films and music. I think you've brought him back to where he should be. He seems more fully rounded as a person.'

'I hope so,' Anni told her. 'I really do hope so.'

She also invited Joni and Charles and the entire Gifford Dance Company to her wedding. She wanted to invite Patty as well but Patty said it would be better if she weren't there with Ray and Lucinda. She didn't want any bad feeling on Anni's day. She met Anni for lunch and gave Anni a little silver dancer on a chain and said she hoped it would bring her luck.

Anni felt unhappy after sharing coffee with Ray's ex-wife. Patty seemed so sad, her usual sparkling green eyes dull, unlike the vibrant wo-man she had been. She also looked older, with lines marring her previously smooth features, and Anni had spotted streaks of grey in her lush brunette hair.

'Why so sad?' Steve asked that evening, only a few nights before their Saturday wedding.

'I had coffee with Ray's Patty this afternoon. His ex-wife.'

'And she put you off getting married?' Steve asked.

Hearing the uncertainty in his voice, Anni reached over the table and covered Steve's hand with a reassuring pat. 'No. She just gave me this.' With her other hand she reached inside the neck-line of her black sweatshirt and produced the silver dancer. 'She won't come to the wedding.'

'That's pretty, Anni. But her decision is under-standable, with Ray being there.'

'It's not fair, though, is it? She should be able to attend.'

Steve squeezed her hand. 'Yes. She should. But people have such problems when they are di-vorced. Anyway, I don't want to discuss di-vorce. We're getting married. Divorce is something I've put far from my mind.'

'You've really changed,' Anni told him.

'Because I love you.'

For a brief second in that small restaurant over their glasses of wine, Anni hoped love was going to be enough to sustain them. It was fine now while she was away from dancing and they had all the time in the world between them. But after the honeymoon, when her second run of *Wedding Bells* was under way and she wasn't home in the evenings, when she slept late, practised late and was fully involved in the show . . . then what?

All those worries were pushed aside in the next few days. Anni was free to do as she wished for, as far as she could recall, the first time in her life. No rehearsals, no practice, no pressing engagements. She drove back and forth from her apartment to Steve's house with suitcases and boxes full of her stuff. She wouldn't have time to sell her apartment or do anything about the furniture, but she kind of felt it wouldn't be a bad idea to keep the condo. She could always use it to stay downtown if the weather was bad and she didn't want to drive the distance to Steve's house. She knew she had to stop thinking about the house as *Steve's*, but that was how she did think of the big brick home.

I'll get used to it, she thought as she carried her last box into the foyer and closed the door with her behind. She walked upstairs with the box and dumped it into the spare bedroom, which was now a mess of received wedding gifts, a green plastic bag of ripped gift wrap and a notebook open on the dresser with the list of gifts begun.

The only thing that wasn't here was her bridal gown. It was in her mother's closet – actually it was her mother's. Anni was going to be so proud wearing the dress that her mother had worn to marry her father in. Her father, she knew, would love it.

Thinking about her father made her feel so sad she wanted to cry, even though the actual tears had dried up years ago. She sat down on the bed and, with her hands on her denim-covered knees, looked around.

'Dad, I can't believe you left such a huge trust fund for my wedding. I have to live up to that, though. I have to stay married to Steve. I have to work hard at this. As hard as I've worked at my dancing. I hope I can do it.'

Anni had been shocked when her mother had produced the money for the wedding. Naturally Anni wouldn't use it all. Whatever was left she would give to her mother. In a way she was a little mad at her father, because her mother had gone without over the years and all that time there had been that small nest-egg accumulating.

But Marian insisted she would never have used it.

So Anni was going to get the wedding of her dreams. A ceremony in a country stone church and a reception at an élite hotel overlooking a lake, where the guests could stay and enjoy themselves at the reception and not have to worry about driving all the way home. Perfect.

'Thanks, Dad,' she said, and rose to her feet just as Steve came into the room. He had taken this last week off and he'd been on some errand that needed doing before the wedding.

'Who's in here?' he asked.

She went up to him and cuddled him, tucking her hands around his well-formed buttocks in his blue jeans. 'Me. Talking to my father.'

He leaned back, his eyes twinkling. 'Oh, yeah?'

'Yeah. I haven't talked to him for a long time, but every once in a while I do. He's pleased we're getting married.'

'That's good, sweetie.'

Anni bit into his shoulder through his T-shirt. 'You don't believe me.'

'Yes, I do, and if you keep that up, we'll be breaking our vow to wait.'

'I want you, Steve,' Anni said with longing. Her dreams were becoming decidedly sexual lately and right now she felt like molten liquid inside.

He leaned against her, making the sensations inside her even more exquisite. 'Me too. But I can wait.' He patted her bottom and eased away from her with a lecherous smile. 'We're going to be ravenous.'

'I'm ravenous now,' Anni said. 'Let's go down to that Italian restaurant. It's our last real night together as singles.'

'Sounds good. We'll grab our jackets.'

'I still don't think she'll help you in your career,' Rachel said to Steve during his wedding reception.

The weather was warm enough for everyone to be outside the hotel on the patio. The brilliant maple leaves of an Ontario autumn gave the entire sunny day a warm red glow. Beyond the flowing lawn of the hotel resort was a small lake where guests strolled on the shoreline to enjoy the romantic setting. Steve glanced around to see if his bride in her traditional white froth of lace and silk was going to rescue him from his sister.

'Steve. Answer me.'

He placed his hand on his sister's green silk arm. 'Everything will be fine. I love Anni. She loves me. Her career is going great. My career is going great. My promotion's in the bag and will be announced when I return from my honeymoon. I've never been happier. So don't wreck things.'

'I'm not wrecking things, Stevie. I just don't want you hurt. She might have an agenda. I mean, she didn't want you at first. She pushed you away. Then all of a sudden she thinks she can swing it.'

'I was just as indecisive. But we discovered we are in love. What more do we need?'

232

'Oh, a lot more for a good marriage, believe me,' Rachel said with years of wisdom.

'Why do this to me on my wedding day, Rachel? I'm married already.'

His sister's face turned contrite. 'I'm sorry. But I just . . .'

Steve saw Anni hurrying towards him, recalling the first time ever she ran across a lawn to greet him. Inevitable now that they should be together always because he didn't leave that party. Rachel was wrong. All wrong.

He smiled warmly and gave Anni a kiss. 'What's up?'

'Nothing. Everything's just fine.' Anni smiled at Rachel. 'Hi, Rachel. Have you had enough to eat and drink?'

'Everything's perfect, thanks, Anni. Your mother has put on a wonderful wedding and you chose a great setting. The little country stone church and now this beautiful hotel resort for the reception. Fantastic.'

'And Jason and Jack were awesome in the wedding ceremony, Rachel. Great kids.' Anni impulsively hugged her sister-in-law and Steve wondered if that type of action would help Rachel come to grips with his marriage and see that Anni, his wife, was a super person.

His wife. He couldn't believe he was actually married, something he'd never intended to do. But now it had happened it felt so right.

'You really think they were okay?' Rachel said, looking a little disarmed by the impulsive hug from her new sister-in-law.

'Perfect. If I was fourteen, Jason would be my hero,' Anni said.

'He's getting to that age, isn't he?' Rachel said with a frown. 'I thought they acted like little gentlemen. I wish it were always that way. But boys will be boys. You'll find that out with a husband, Anni.'

'I'm looking forward to it.'

Steve clasped Anni's hand. 'I'm longing to show you just how boyish I'm feeling.'

Anni smiled at him. 'I'm longing to find out.'

Rachel discreetly left them and he grasped Anni around the waist and they kissed softly. Her blue eyes were purple with happiness. She was now minus the veil and only the flowered headpiece held her silvery hair in place in its upswept style. With the back of his hand, he caressed some of the wispy strands of hair that lay against her delicate neck. His need to love her was a desperate longing that was a great deal more than mere sexual appetite.

'When can we leave?' he asked.

She held him around the waist, her fingers stroking his hips through his suit jacket as if she wanted him with the same hunger. 'Any time. That's what I came to tell you.'

'Then let's get outta here. I can't wait much longer.'

'Me neither.'

He wrapped his arms around her and, without holding back any desire, kissed her. He wanted to show her how much he needed her. Anni's kisses told him the same thing until she eventually slipped from his grasp. 'Later,' she said, and clasped his hand. 'Come on.'

Holding hands tightly, they made the rounds of all their friends and family. Joni, with a slightly rounder belly now, embraced Anni and Steve warmly. 'Be happy,' she told them. 'Have fun in England.'

'They will,' Charles added, and then with a chuckle, 'Make sure you leave your hotel room long enough to see some sights.'

'We're staying in a little cottage in south Cornwall,' Anni said. 'No hotel. We want to be alone and away from all pressures.'

'Sounds great,' Joni told them. 'But you will see London again?'

'Our last few days,' Steve added.

They drifted over to Ray and Lucinda.

Ray kissed Anni while Steve looked on, trying to shelve any jealous reaction. After all, Lucinda stood beside Ray, looking stunning in black and white, and they were going to be married by the time Anni and Steve returned from England. And Steve and Anni were at last married, matching gold circles on their fingers to prove it. Even so, he was pleased when they left Ray and Lucinda to greet other guests, such as his partners and especially his cousin Alf.

Alf shook his hand firmly. 'Congratulations, Steve. I'm in love with her as well.'

Steve grinned. His cousin just loved women. 'Thanks, Alf.'

Sandy hugged him and Anni and they moved on to other guests. Then family. Steve noticed how

Skippy seemed to love Anni and he felt warm about that. Skippy, he felt, was the best judge of character in the world.

Now all they had to do was change into more comfortable clothes, slip into the airport limousine that was picking them up from the hotel, and catch their flight. It would be Sunday before they made love but Steve had to keep his hunger in control. When it happened he knew it would be a beautiful union with his new wife.

Anni had been to England many times but always with the pressure of dancing upon her. This flight was far different. There were no pressures. Just Steve and herself having fun together. After dinner they snuggled up beneath a blanket and slept holding hands. Breakfast was eaten in daylight watching the sun rise over the silver surface of the Atlantic. Their rented car was waiting at Heathrow and Steve was quite competent driving on the left-hand side of the road as he'd visited England many times. He had relatives near Colchester, but they weren't going anywhere near there. They planned to stay in the cottage on the Cornwall coast for almost two weeks, then take a few days in London before heading home once more. Life for Anni at this moment was close to perfect.

The stone cottage was one of a cluster of cottages near a seaside port and had been advertised with all the mod cons. However, there was no central heating. Steve built a log fire while Anni turned on all the heaters she could find. Soon the living room, with its many newly inserted modern windows, low polished beams and hardwood floors, warmed up.

'Don't use up all the coins you have in that meter,' Steve warned her. 'You'll run out.'

'I'll go buy something or find a bank. I won't freeze.'

He laughed and wiped his hands together, pleased with his blazing fire. 'Come here. Warm up with me.'

They settled on the sheepskin rug together, kissed for a while, checked out their gold bands and then hugged.

'This is going to be so good, Anni,' Steve murmured, lifting her hair to touch her neck with his mouth. He slipped aside her loose knit sweater and rained more kisses over her shoulder.

Anni closed her eyes. This was it. Finally, she was going to be joined with Steve forever. She lay down on the rug and helped him undress her. She wasn't cold any more. An aroused glow lit her flesh and the fire poured heat over them. She moved sensuously, stretching her limbs to greet Steve.

His eyes were dark with passion and his mouth curved tenderly at he looked at her. 'One moment,' he said.

He returned with a package and Anni turned her head away. He was going to protect her from pregnancy. Just what Ray Gifford wanted – although his promise to tuck condoms into her wedding gift hadn't materialized, most likely because Lucinda had taken charge of it. Still she would be an unpregnant Anni. And that thought made her hollow inside and she felt the deep void that often rose in the pit of her stomach. But maybe later. Maybe at the end of January, when *Wedding Bells* was over once more. She had commitments first.

Steve quickly undressed. She watched him kneel down with her, naked, golden in the firelight and she reached up and stroked him with both her hands.

'Touch me,' he said huskily, his features strained.

She caressed him. 'This is what you wanted that day in my dressing room?'

'It's what I wanted the first night I saw you at Ray's party.'

She drew him into complete arousal and he pressed his hot, hungry flesh to hers. His need probed her and she found herself completely ready and taking him greedily. Oh, yes, she thought, the baby would come later. This pleasure, this pulsing loving need, her husband, Steve, was for her.

Steve closed his eyes as the climax he'd been waiting for racked his body, surrounded him in sheer, mind-wrenching pleasure, and then released him. Anni, already pleasured, cuddled up to him and he held her fiercely.

'It's going to work out fine,' Steve said softly. 'Really fine.'

Anni believed him. In this perfect place with Steve she couldn't see any clouds of discontent.

Their time in Cornwall passed far too rapidly for Anni. She'd visited England's westernmost county once before and had fallen in love with the sandy coves, steep cliffs and rocky outlets around the coastline, which was why she wanted Steve to agree with her at this very important time in their lives. She was so pleased when Steve declared he loved the scenery too. It was warm for autumn and they had little rain. They were able to hike the cliff paths or sit on the beach and eat picnic lunches while eagerly observing the sea life in the rock pools and listening to pounding surf. Each evening they drove to a different cosy little restaurant for dinner. Their last day was spent shopping in Truro for gifts Anni wanted to buy for her mother, Joni and Charles.

In the town centre, surrounded by all the latest stores, Steve helped her choose the gifts, and bought her any clothes she fell in love with.

'Save some shopping for London,' she told him, feeling overwhelmed by the purchases. She loved clothes but Steve wanted her to have many more than was practical.

'We'll do more shopping in London,' he told her. 'It's just that clothes look great on you.'

'But we won't have room in our suitcases.'

'We'll buy some more luggage, then. Anni, I thought you were the one who flew by the seat of her pants!'

Anni clung to his arm. 'I am. But you're being so extravagant, Steve.'

'I want you to have what you want and enjoy yourself.'

'I've always enjoyed myself but it's never been like this. Never.'

He glanced at her. 'We almost denied ourselves this, Anni.'

'Crazy, weren't we?' She snuggled closer to him. 'All those unhappy couples probably never had this.'

'Probably not,' he said, but he knew they had because they told him so. Sometimes he still felt as if he were on that roller-coaster, out of control

They returned to London feeling windblown, suntanned and rested. Steve had purchased tickets for a few shows. They spent the days in museums or shops and the evenings in the theatre. On their last night they went out for dinner and then on to the last show. It was a German dance company performing many of their famous pieces. The performances were very avant-garde and Anni loved each and every one of the pieces even if she wasn't sure if she wanted to be reminded of what was upcoming in her life: another run of *Wedding Bells*. She felt rested, but she was getting used to the limited pressure in her life and she wasn't sure if she would be able to climb the necessary mental ladder to perform at such an intense level once more. She didn't say anything about this to Steve, however. She didn't want to wreck the harmony they had developed over this holiday together.

But she lay in bed beside him later, wide awake, contemplating their life together when they returned to Toronto. She was due to move into Steve's house and was prepared to accept all the problems with it. While it was spacious there was no actual room for dancing practice. She would have to see what could be done about that when they returned, though Steve might not want to clear out a room for her.

She sighed deeply as she turned over on her side and cuddled up to her pillow. Why did real life have to intrude on their idyllic honeymoon like this?

'Anni?' Steve whispered. 'Are you awake?'

'Yes.'

He reached for her and she rolled over to snuggle against him instead of the pillow. He immediately thrust his hands into her hair and kissed her with heavy passion. Anni felt herself respond and she moved over on top of his aroused body without removing her mouth from his.

'Yes, Anni, yes,' Steve rasped hoarsely, helping her adjust her hips to meet his.

She closed her eyes as she slipped on to him, feeling him fill her. They weren't using protection and she didn't say a word. She wanted Steve's baby, and if this was the time, then this was the time.

CHAPTER 13

Anni and Steve arrived back in Toronto in cold, lashing rain heralding the beginning of November. Steve's house felt chilly until they turned up the furnace to let the warm air blast through the cavernous rooms. Steve had never used the master bedroom in the house but now he intended to share it with Anni. He felt they should begin afresh. He even wondered if they should buy another home together.

'Do you want to live here?' he asked her when she had placed her luggage in the room they were to share that night.

Anni moved gracefully, as she often did, appearing as if she were going to begin a dance. 'I'm not sure yet, Steve. It's a nice house. An expensive house.'

But he could hear the doubt in her voice and knew that she didn't really feel at home here. 'If we sold our combined property we could buy something great.'

She looked surprised. 'You would sell this house?'

'Sure. I only really purchased it as an investment. Why don't we look for something together?.'

'Then I could have a studio?'

'You can have a room here, you know. Any room.'

'I will definitely need space until we decide what to do.'

Steve recalled last night in bed in London. Anni astride him, her silver hair flowing – it had grown longer since he met her – her slight body riding his with desperate passion. He recalled his deep satisfaction. That moment suddenly seemed far away. Anni seemed to have removed herself from him one step. Nothing tangible, but there was an emotional wall between them that hadn't been there last night in bed.

'Anyway,' he said with a smile, 'whatever you want to do, do it. And we'll definitely look for a place.'

She bit into her bottom lip. 'All right.'

'Something wrong?'

'No. I'm merely tired. I . . . er . . . started my period today.'

Steve wasn't sure what he felt when she told him that. They hadn't used any protection last night. And he had to admit that if she got pregnant right away he wouldn't mind. But he wasn't sure if he wouldn't mind because he wanted a family right away or to tie her more firmly to him. 'Does that upset you?' he asked.

'No,' she said. 'Not at all. I can't get pregnant, can I?'

But he could hear in her voice that she wanted to, desperately. And he wondered if half her

243

desperation in her lovemaking last night had been for a baby and not for him. He pushed aside some strange surfacing emotions that he wasn't ready to analyze. 'Not yet, but it won't matter to me if you do, Anni. I want a family as much as you.'

He noticed she didn't quite meet his gaze. 'That's good. But it would matter, Steve. I have a second run to dance. It doesn't begin for six weeks. If I was pregnant now I'd be almost two months by Christmas.'

'Then it's a relief you're not.' He felt himself becoming irritable with her.

'Exactly. Tomorrow I'll have to go over to my place and pick up some stuff. I'll have to start rehearsals again. I'm probably out of shape.'

'Sure,' Steve said, feeling Anni closing up on him. She put up doors, windows you could only look through. She gave of herself when she had time but that was all. This past month she'd had time. Now time was fading and she was ready to move on to her next phase. 'Maybe you should lie down for a while and get some rest.'

'I think I will.'

'When you want something to eat, let me know.'

'Thanks.' She was already sitting on the bed, unbuttoning the jacket of her black pant suit.

'Don't be shy. Look in all the cupboards and drawers. Use anything you want.'

'Thanks, Steve.'

They looked at one another for a moment, then Anni began undressing and Steve felt dismissed. Clenching his fists, he left the bedroom and hastily went downstairs. Janet had looked in on the house while they'd been away. She'd put some food into the refrigerator. She'd left a note to say she hoped they had fun and she'd see them when they got back.

We had fun, he thought. So now what's going on? Was it just Anni's time of the month making her depressed? Or was she already on stage once more? Dammit, she had another few weeks before the run began, although he knew the time would be laden with hard work. Work that included dancing intimately with Moe Ellison. Married or not, the guy was good-looking.

Steve tried to busy himself. He made phone calls to his parents to let them know they had returned safely. He also called Marian Ross to let *her* know. He told her Anni was tired and sleeping and would call later.

He made a pot of tea, placed it on a tray with some fancy china cups they'd received as a wedding gift, and added some of the biscuits Anni had bought at the Heathrow duty-free shop. He carried the tray upstairs to find Anni lying under the duvet on the bed. She was wide awake.

He placed the tray on the bedside table. 'Did you have a snooze?' he asked, sitting on the bed beside her.

'A little bit.' She smiled and stroked his hand. 'The tea smells good.'

'I'll cook up some eggs. Janet filled the fridge with milk and eggs. I also phoned my parents and your mother, just to tell them we were back.'

'Thanks. You're thoughtful.' She sat up against the pillows.

Steve poured the tea and they sat and drank it and chatted about their holiday. He wondered if their honeymoon was going to be the one focal point of their lives that they could always refer to without unrest. He wished he wouldn't keep thinking negative thoughts but his mind seemed to be magnetically attracting them.

Anni replaced her cup and saucer on the tray. She brushed biscuit crumbs from the duvet. 'Steve, I think I do want to move eventually.'

'I want to move as well. This is strange, having you here. It won't work.'

'No. It won't work. We have to start from scratch. It has to be *ours*.'

Steve held her in his arms. First thing, when he returned to the office tomorrow, he'd call a real estate agent. Maybe the house was the problem he felt between them tonight.

'It's good to have you back but you're all over the place, Anni. Concentrate.'

'I am, Ray. I am.' Anni felt as if she were being forced beyond her limits to perform something she hadn't the wits to perform. She'd known this would happen when she gave in to Steve. But what other choice did she have? She was in love with Steve. She wanted the marriage, a family. There was no other course. Life with Steve filled the recent void in her life. Meanwhile she had obligations. She had to dance. That was what she did for a living. She doubted Steve was in the office today not doing his best lawyer routine. 'I'll try again,' she told Ray. 'Bear with me, please.

I had a month off. I'm off balance.'

'That's the trouble, Anni. You shouldn't have taken time off.'

'I needed a personal life, Ray. I was burning out. The vacation probably wasn't long enough. That's the whole point.'

Ray came closer to her. 'Are you saying you don't want to do this?'

Anni reached for a towel and slung it around her neck. She'd had enough for today. She needed a snack. 'You know that isn't true. I love dancing. Dancing is my life. All I'm saying is that I need to take it slowly my first day back and you're pushing me beyond what I'm capable of.'

'I know what you're capable of. It's better than this excuse for dancing.'

'Ray, please.' Anni felt tears burn the backs of her eyes. She'd become vulnerable, not the hard case she always tried to be. 'Let me take a break.'

'I want you here with Moe tomorrow morning.'

'Fine. I'll be here.'

Anni left Ray looking disgruntled and wondered what would happen if she did screw up the next run of *Wedding Bells*. Even so, Ray annoyed her no end. He'd married Lucinda near the end of October in an intimate civil ceremony. Why was he allowed to have his personal life while she wasn't?

Anni opened her bag and took out an apple and a bottle of cranberry juice she had found in the refrigerator this morning courtesy of Janet. Steve's younger sister really was a gem. Munching on the apple, Anni picked up her cellphone. Someone had given them 'his and hers' phones for a wedding present. She couldn't remember who it was and that fact reminded Anni that she had to write her thank-you cards from the list she'd made. She punched in Joni's number.

Joni was having the new studio decorated and didn't have much time to chat but she was pleased Anni was home and they arranged to get together soon for lunch. Anni phoned her mother to find that Marian was out. Steve's office told her Steve was in a meeting, but would she like him to call her? Anni said no and disconnected the phone. Everyone she wanted was too busy for her. But that was the way *she'd* been for years. Always too busy for anyone outside her dancing. Now she was standing partly outside her dancing she felt disorientated. She was like an animal outside its cage, not sure in what direction to roam. One way might lurk danger. Another way might be perfectly safe. But which way?

Anni returned to her safety net, dancing and the stage, to dance for Ray. He didn't criticize this time. She then drove to her apartment. The place smelled of the paint on the walls even though it was two years since it had been painted. Her footsteps echoed on the floors, giving her the impression of unused space. Her furniture had been hand-picked but she had never lived here in the sense of really living somewhere. While she had taken a lot of her belongings to the house before the wedding there were still clothes she would need shortly as winter descended. She had brought along two empty suitcases and she packed them full. Mostly there was heavy coats and jackets, scarves, gloves, and boots.

When she was ready, she lugged the cases downstairs, packed them into her car and drove to Steve's house. Their house, she corrected herself. Until they chose one between them. She'd decided that was the only course to take. A new life, a new home, a new beginning.

A small blue car stood in the wide driveway. Anni parked her red Nissan beside it and opened her trunk. She carried one of her suitcases to the house and found the front door unlocked. Cautiously she pushed open the door and placed the suitcase in the spacious foyer, thinking how dark it was. The small windows didn't seem to bring in much light.

She was wondering who was here when she heard a laugh and Steve's sister Janet ducked out of the kitchen carrying a black bundle of fur.

'Anni, hi. I always have Steve's key. I hope you didn't mind me coming in. But I brought you Dash.'

'Dash?' Anni said smiling. She liked Janet immensely. In her old jeans and sweatshirt she was refreshing and normal.

Janet produced the bundle of black fur who was struggling to leave her arms now. Claws dug into Janet's green sweatshirt and she let the kitten scramble away. 'It's part of my wedding present to you. Steve's always wanted a cat but he's never got around to it and I thought now the two of you were here it would liven up this mausoleum.'

'Mausoleum?' Anni repeated, and laughed merrily. 'I'm pleased I'm not the only person who feels this house is rather austere. A cat is fine, Janet, as long as you'll be around to take care of it if I'm away or whatever.'

'Sure I'll be around. I always check Steve's house for him when he's on vacation. Dash is a boy, by the way, neutered, shots all taken care of. There's a vet down the end of this street where I work part time between school and that's where you can take him with any problems or for his boosters in a year. Anyway, I'll give you all the information. I even bought you a litter box and put it down the bottom of the basement steps.'

Anni thought, no wonder we get along. We're alike. Impetuous. 'That's fine. Where is the little guy?'

'Probably chewing up Steve's drapes. You'll have to watch him.'

'Steve likes cats, doesn't he?' she asked as they went to search for Dash. 'I met Cindy when I was at your party.'

'Cindy is new to my parents. There were others when Steve was a kid. Where is that little devil? Dash? Dash? Dash?'

Anni dropped to her knees on the floor and looked beneath the bed. Round yellow eyes stared at her from the darkness. 'Come on, Dash,' she coerced. 'Come to Anni.'

To her surprise the kitten came to her out-stretched finger and rubbed his cheek on her hand. She picked up the kitten and cuddled it to her. She was going to enjoy Dash.

Steve arrived home, parked behind Anni's car next to Janet's and walked through his unlocked door into his house. He could hear the two women in the house. One of Anni's suitcases stood in the foyer.

Leaping down the stairs came a small black kitten. Anni rushed after it, calling out, 'Steve, shut the door tight. Don't let him out. We've only just found him again.'

The kitten skidded to a stop in front of him. 'What is this?' he asked.

Anni scooped the kitten into her arms. 'His name is Dash.'

'Appropriate,' Steve murmured. 'I suppose my little sister is responsible.'

Janet came down the stairs. 'Yeah, I'm responsible. I thought he would lighten up this place.'

Steve remarked. 'She always thinks this place is dull.'

Anni cuddled Dash. 'I agree.'

The cat seemed to love being in Anni's arms, a position Steve loved as well. 'Have you got time to look after a kitten?'

'I'll do my best. You can help as well.'

'And I'll look in if you're away,' Janet said.

Steve spread his arms. 'All right. I suppose. It's up to Anni really. She's the one who doesn't like complications in her life.' He didn't want that to sound accusing but it did. However, Anni didn't seem to notice.

'It's fine with me,' Anni said, and grinned at Janet. 'What about food?'

'Come into the kitchen. I bought you some supplies and I'll explain everything.'

Anni glanced over her shoulder. 'Steve, there is another suitcase in my car. Would you mind bringing it in?'

'Sure, I'll bring it in,' he said and went to the hook where she always left her car keys. He walked out of his house feeling as if his life had truly changed. He had a wife, a kitten, a sister who loved his wife. His quiet existence had been replaced by the beginning of what he could safely call hectic. And he liked it.

And to think, he thought, carrying Anni's tremendously heavy suitcase into the house, this house was where he used to come for some peace and quiet. *Siesta* might be the only place to go now. But he'd have to wait for summer for that. *Siesta* was safely in her winter dock. And even then he wouldn't be alone. Anni would be with him.

'Janet's staying for dinner,' Anni told him when he'd finally hung up his trenchcoat and changed from his suit to jeans and a sweater and joined the two women in the kitchen.

'What are we having for dinner?'

'I don't know yet, Steve. I can't plan that stuff.'

Janet was checking the cupboards. 'You have enough spaghetti to feed the millions.'

'Anni does great spaghetti. It's the only thing she can cook,' Steve remarked, still hearing an edge to his words. He wasn't quite sure what was wrong with him.

She glared at him and he wondered if it was a real glare or acting. 'That was a cheap shot, Steve. I seem to recall garlic bread is your main specialty.'

'And scrambled eggs,' he added.

'All right, you two. Referee time.' Janet stood in the middle of them holding a package of spaghetti. 'Spaghetti and garlic bread. Steve, if you don't mind.' She handed Anni the spaghetti package. 'I'll do the sauce and a salad. You see, I'm used to

252

living with other people. I've shared with friends for years.'

Dash jumped up on the table and began to rub against Steve's arm. Steve stroked the tiny head. 'I'm not,' he said.

Janet shook her head. 'You're used to eating out in expensive restaurants every night and I bet Anni's not much better. Anyway, spaghetti it is. Snap to it.'

Janet left after dinner and Steve was enjoying another cup of coffee while he read that day's newspaper. Anni was running around the house with a piece of string and Dash was chasing the end. 'I thought you were this dedicated dancer who didn't do anything but dance,' he said when she entered the kitchen and Dash flopped into the basket Janet had provided for him and promptly fell asleep.

She poured herself a glass of water and sipped it, her denim-clad hips leaning against the counter. 'I am, Steve, but I seem to be coming apart at the seams a little. Ray's not pleased. But I'll be okay by opening night.'

'I hope so. I mean, if the kitten is too much, I'll tell Janet.'

Anni's gaze softened on the tiny bundle of curled black fur. 'No. The kitten's fine. I love him already. Is he okay with you?'

'He's okay with me. As long as he doesn't claw the place to pieces.'

Anni tossed her head. 'I'll watch him.'

'Sure you will. You'll never be here.'

'Then you watch him. He'll be fine, Steve.'

'Anyway.' He pushed aside the paper. 'We

253

might not be in this house much longer. I talked to a real estate agent today.'

She held her water close to her lips. 'And?'

'We have an appointment with her tomorrow afternoon, if that's okay with you.'

'I can't, Steve. Moe's in tomorrow.'

Moe. Immediate jealousy over seeing Anni and Moe dancing reared it's head. Steve closed the newspaper and folded it neatly. 'Are you dancing with him?'

'Naturally. We have to rehearse.'

'You did well in the last run.'

'I know, but there's always something to perfect. Besides, I'm rusty.'

Feeling even more tension knot his insides, Steve got up from the table and rinsed out his mug. He wanted to kiss her yet he also wanted to punish her and make her want him by not touching her. He began to leave the kitchen.

'Where are you going?'

'My study. I have some work to do.'

'I thought we were talking about the house sale.'

'I'll change the appointment. You give me a good time and day. All right?'

'All right. I have to unpack some of this stuff. Could you carry the cases up to the spare bedroom before you begin working?'

'Sure I will.'

Anni watched him go, finished her water, then went to supervise the placement of the suitcases in the spare bedroom which was still stacked with gifts. When she was alone, she clicked open the first clasps, but she wasn't interested in unpacking the heavy winter clothes inside. Maybe she was imagining things but Steve seemed distant tonight. He hadn't even kissed her hello. Of course, Janet had been here with Dash. They'd been distracted. But still . . . He was mad about the real estate agent having to be postponed, she could tell that, but that was the way things were. Dance came first.

Dash came upstairs to find out what she was doing and jumped in one of her cases to rummage through her clothes. Anni picked him out and they played while Steve was in his study. Occasionally she looked at the closed door and wondered if she should interrupt him, then thought about her own career, how she needed to be separate and uninterrupted, so she went to bed alone. He came up and crawled in with her but he didn't touch her. After a while she felt a whiskery kiss on her cheek and realized it was Dash. He cuddled up with her and they went to sleep. She woke up to the sound of Dash's determined clawing of the expensive rug on the floor and Steve in the shower.

Anni flew out of bed and slipped into a fleece robe. She rescued the carpet from Dash and wondered what marriage was supposed to be about. Two people, she thought. Then, eventually, a family. But the two people had to have something going for them before the family. Had they rushed into marriage? No. She loved Steve. But did Steve still love her? Once satisfied sexually, was he now wishing they hadn't been so hasty to tie the knot? Men could get sex anywhere without being tied to the same woman for the rest of their life.

She took Dash downstairs and fed him the required amount of food as Janet had instructed. Steve came down in his navy blue terry robe a while later.

'What's going on?'

'Feeding time. You never put the coffee on this morning, Steve.'

'I only just got up.' He began to prepare the coffee.

'Why did you work so late?'

'I have two clients coming into the office today and I had to do a lot of preparation. Lots of reading and notes. That's what I was doing last night. I was preoccupied. The way you're always preoccupied.'

Anni realized that her robe had gaped open and for a moment Steve's glance seemed hot with desire. Then he switched his attention to the coffee. 'Is this working out, Steve?'

He measured ground coffee into the filter. 'I don't know, Anni. I don't know. It'll take time, I'm sure. Are you sure you don't have time to come with me to meet the real estate agent?'

Anni raked her fingers through her hair and let it fall in place. Maybe she could fit it in later. 'I won't take my car; you can drop me off and pick me up about three o'clock. I've usually had enough by then.'

'That'll be fine,' he said, and turned on the switch. The coffee began brewing. Then he walked over to her and put his arms around her and Anni dropped her face to his shoulder.

'Oh, Steve.'

'It's difficult, sweetheart, I know. It's like, you go without a kiss and then it's awkward to kiss again. We build a gulf between us. After the real estate agent tonight, we'll go out for a quiet dinner and then come home and go to bed.'

Anni hugged him. 'All right. Sounds good.' She drew away and poured herself a big mug of coffee. With Dash following her around, she showered, dressed and Steve dropped her off at the theatre.

Their real estate agent's name was Winnie Dersken, a bubbly, plump lady, who seemed to be very successful in the rural property business. She was excited. The amount received from both the sale of Steve's house and Anni's condo would give them enough to buy a home with land attached. Steve and Anni took home a number of interesting listings that they might like to view, but Anni knew that house-hunting right now was out of the question. When she had danced with Moe today Ray had made some changes to their duets to make them more fluid. They would need every possible hour of the next month and half before *Wedding Bells* began again. Ray had mentioned they were to be dancing matinees on Thursday through to Sunday plus the evening show the week before and during Christmas. Double the work. Double the exertion. She would have no chance to be home. No chance to cook meals, to be a wife.

Anni thought about this on the car ride home and she could sense Steve occasionally looking at her wondering why she was so silent.

'Didn't you like any of these houses?' he asked.

'I haven't looked at the literature properly yet, Steve.'

'You don't want this, do you?'

She turned to look at him. 'Seriously, darling, I can't. Ray wants to change some of the pieces we're dancing. I have to rehearse them with Moe and we're also going to be doing weekend matinees as soon as the show begins again. I think we should wait until spring – until I'm finished.'

'This damn show,' Steve said. 'It always gets in the way. It's like a blockade to what we want to do.'

Anni swallowed back a flood of words. He knew what her career entailed. She had once tried to stop the momentum of their becoming a couple, and then tried to avoid marriage, but it had happened. They had to make the best of it. 'I'm not saying I told you so, Steve.'

'Well, you did and I didn't believe you. Oh, yes, I believed you but I didn't figure it would be quite so much of a problem.'

'You only make it a problem if you want me to live some kind of normal life. I can't be the little wife at home for you. At least not right now. After the show I'll probably have a long vacation.'

'All right.' Steve gave her a smile. 'It's okay. I don't think I'm ready to move right away either. But these properties will give us an idea of where we can go when spring comes and we have more time.'

Anni was relieved he understood. 'Thank you.'

He reached out for her hand. 'What were we going to do, have a meal and then go to bed?'

'Yep. We'll have something at home *in* bed. How's that?'

'Sounds good. Dessert before main course?'

Anni squeezed his strong fingers. 'You've got it.'

CHAPTER 14

Steve went to work the following morning to discover his promotion was a sure thing and the celebratory party would be held the next week. He phoned Anni's cellphone to tell her but got no answer. The phone most likely lay on her dresser or inside her athletic bag at the theatre. He hung up, feeling down. Anni was always the first person he wanted to tell anything to, and if she wasn't available he felt lost. It was terrible to be so in love, he thought, so dependent. He'd vowed never to get into this situation and here he was. Last night in bed he'd lost himself in Anni's arms. Then she was up this morning and out of the house early before he even saw her. The house had been quiet without her and yet he'd lived a number of years there alone. When Anni wasn't around Dash meowed a lot and jumped up on tables and counters. Anni was missed; it was as if a light went out when she wasn't around.

He wondered if he should distance himself and not always be so available for Anni. He felt as if he was setting himself up to be hurt badly and if he didn't change his mind-set soon he would be heading for that crash he always felt was imminent within their relationship. And yet why he felt that way, he really couldn't say. She had been loving and willing last night. She was a great lover. His dream lover.

Steve raked his fingers through his hair that had grown long against the back of his neck over the summer and during his honeymoon. Anni loved to run her fingers through his hair. But he knew he'd need a trim before his promotion party. At least he had his promotion. Even if, heaven forbid, something happened in the future with Anni, he was now a partner in the firm of Roberts, Smithson, Martin and now Hunter. Wow! A dream come true. Yet it didn't feel so great. It felt matter-of-fact. Shouldn't he be leaping over walls for joy that his career was at a peak instead of worrying about the direction of his marriage? Yet it was all related. If a family came along in the future he'd be well able to support his children. What he had to do was find a balance for his life, the type of balance he'd never found the need for in the past.

His promotion was also soured by Craig Firth, who at lunchtime, in the elevator, wished him congratulations in a voice that was obviously full of venom.

'You'll be next, Craig,' Steve said.

'I'm not so sure. This is a family gig.'

'That's not true. Paul isn't family.'

'He might as well be.' Craig pushed one hand into his suit jacket pocket and used the other one make his point. 'Anyway, you did well, Steve, rushing into a marriage just in time for your promotion. Very well indeed. You're lucky you found someone willing to go along with you.'

The elevator doors opened then. They both walked on to the street. Steve didn't ask, Are you going for lunch? Instead he went to find a sandwich on his own. While he ate he wondered if Craig had been partly right. Had he used his feelings for Anni to rush her into marriage purely for the sake of his promotion? If the promotion hadn't been an option, would he have waited until after she really had finished *Wedding Bells* to marry her? Anni probably would have preferred that. She would have had more freedom to begin their life together. Maybe he'd screwed things up forever by being desperate for his partnership as well as desperate for Anni.

Anni didn't arrive home until nearly ten that evening. Steve heard her car drive up and park and he went to the front door to greet her.

'I'm worn out,' she said after a brief kiss. 'How was your day?'

'Fine.' He didn't mention the promotion. She didn't seem in the mood to be particularly receptive to the news. Or if she was receptive, maybe too tired to take in the importance of the news. That was more like it. His thoughts over lunch resurfaced. He should have thought of their unfolding relationship more than the promotion. He should have waited. But he hadn't been able to wait. He'd needed Anni. He felt that need as he followed Anni indoors. She went straight upstairs to the bedroom. He didn't follow her there. Instead he went into his study and sat down at his desk and continued working on the papers he'd brought home.

About eleven he went upstairs to find Anni slumped on the bed and sleeping soundly, still wearing jeans and a sweater.

He sat down on the side of the bed and reached over to her and stroked her hair. 'Anni. Sweetheart.'

She mumbled something and barely opened her eyes. 'What?'

'You need to get undressed. I'm coming to bed now. I'll undress you.'

Feeling aroused at the mere thought of undressing her, he slipped the button of her jeans and drew down the zipper. She wriggled her hips to let him slip off the jeans. He tugged off her white socks. Unable to help himself, he pressed a kiss against her brief white satin panties and heard her groan with aching need. He helped her with her sweater and bra and hurriedly undressed himself. Before he lay down with her he reached in the drawer of the bedside cabinet.

Her arms around him, he positioned himself over her. He touched his mouth to hers as he joined with her and she eagerly opened to him, bringing him into the circle of her body. It was always a dance with Anni, he thought, trying desperately to cling on to sanity. Always a dance with a mad rushing climactic finale.

'Know something?' he said afterwards, when they were calm and sated. 'My partnership is confirmed.'

'Oh, Steve.' She rained kisses all over his face and she was smiling. 'Wonderful, wonderful news. Why didn't you tell me earlier? You must have been bursting.'

He folded his hands behind his head on the pillow. 'Yeah, I suppose. I think I've waited so long for it to happen that it doesn't seem real, or maybe it's because of everything else that has happened, like meeting you and getting married. It's been overshadowed.'

She heaved herself up on her elbow. 'It won't be overshadowed. It's great. Is there going to be a party?'

'Wine and cheese at the office, followed by dinner at a restaurant next Friday evening.'

'I'm pleased it's soon. I'll be able to come.'

He hadn't even thought of her not being able to attend his promotion celebration, but if it had been a week or so later she might not have been there. In that case everyone would have been giving him the *I told you so* treatment. He reached up and stroked her fall of hair away from her forehead. 'I never thought otherwise.'

She seemed to shelve something she was going to say and he knew it was the same as his thoughts. A couple of weeks later and she wouldn't have been able to attend. She smiled brightly. 'I'll be there for you, Steve. For sure.'

Anni kept Steve's promotion party in mind as she rushed through the week. She managed to make time for lunch with Diane and her mother, who came downtown together in Diane's car. The mothers wanted to be filled in on the English

263

vacation and Anni had plenty to tell them about the wonderful time she'd spent with Steve. On Friday afternoon Anni had an appointment at her beauty salon. Her hair had become straggly and far too unmanageable for her hectic lifestyle. She had her usual stylist shape it once more into the geometric bell that suited her high-cheekboned features. She then drove home to change into clothes suitable for Steve's promotion party.

By the time Anni rode the elevator to Steve's office she felt secure that she looked great. High-heeled black suede shoes to match her suit, tiny matching purse hanging from a long strap over her shoulder, smooth hose, slim calf-length skirt, hip-length jacket, cream silk top with lace edges peeking beneath her lapels, make-up as perfect as she could manage, and her silvery hair a freshly cut sleek bell. She felt she looked like a female lawyer ready for a court case and realized that she would never, ever stop being theatrical. She dressed for occasions the way an actor would dress for dramatic parts. But she knew in her heart that this time she was dressed for Steve, for his partners, for his family, for his career. She wanted to be a credit to him. And she realized that the woman who had worn the black dress and red heels to the barbecue wasn't entirely her any more. By meeting and marrying Steve she had added other dimensions to her life.

The elevator doors opened and Anni heard voices and laughter down the hall coming from Roberts, Smithson and Martin's open office door. When she arrived at the door she saw Steve immediately. He stood out in the mingling crowd as he had that night at Ray's party. His black suit, white shirt and black tie emphasized his golden hair. He saw her, saluted with his drink, and wound his way over to her.

He took hold of Anni's hand and squeezed her fingers extra tight. 'So glad you made it. I was beginning to wonder where you were.'

'I went to the beauty salon first. I wanted to look good.'

He moved away from her still holding her hand and observed her. 'You always look good,' he told her. 'And you really *do* look good today. Your hair is back to normal.'

'Tell you a secret,' she said, tucking her fingers through his arm in a proprietorial gesture, a fact of being his wife that always delighted her. 'The way my hair was this morning was my usual style. When I met you I'd just tried this style out. I never could bear the thought of having my hair cut at all before that.'

He gave her a grin. 'I love your long wild hair but I like this. It's . . . nice.'

Anni heard the hesitation and wondered what he'd been about to say. She felt it might have been *suitable*. Yes. This haircut was suitable for this gathering. Her other hairstyle was untamed, not very lawyerly, if there was such a word. But she didn't intend to make an issue of the subject. They both knew the circumstances and Anni was changing herself slightly to help Steve because she loved him. 'Who are all these people?' she asked as he handed her a glass of white wine.

'I have to admit I don't know all of them by name.' Anni laughed. 'That's good, Steve.'

'Ah. Some of them are from other offices who've heard there was free wine and cheese.' He placed his hand on the small of her back. 'We'll go meet someone we do know.' He urged her through the chatting people to where Alf and Sandy stood talking to Rachel and Ben.

'Anni,' Alf said with a smile and a half-bow. 'How are you? I must say you look good. Extremely good.'

'Thank you,' she said graciously, and acknowledged the others, always uneasy with Rachel, who she knew might never approve of her as Steve's wife.

They talked to the other two couples for a while and then somehow they got separated. Anni was left with Paul Roberts, Steve's balding, extrovert senior partner, and his wife, Geraldine. She had met the couple briefly at their wedding and had liked them immensely.

Today Geraldine wore her blonde hair twisted into a sophisticated knot and Anni thought she had the grace of a dancer. Anni could tell the couple liked her too. When Paul left them to talk to his other partners, Geraldine stayed with Anni. Anni sipped on the same glass of wine while listening to Geraldine's stories of their family, which included two girls and two boys, all grown up and married. Between them they had produced seven grandchildren. She wondered if one day she'd be here talking to a younger partner's wife about the same things. Her children and Steve's.

'Now I want to hear about your dancing,' Geraldine said. 'I always had a hankering to dance. My mother put me through a few lessons when I was very young and my daughter liked to dance as well.'

'I thought you looked like a dancer,' Anni said.

'Nothing compared to you, but Paul and I do some ballroom dancing now and again. We enter competitions.'

'That's wonderful.'

Geraldine touched her slim neck with equally slim graceful fingers. 'It's something we can do together. Being married to a lawyer doesn't always lend itself to togetherness. But you have a solid career yourself. I'm sure Steve won't see much of you.'

'It's not too bad now but when the show begins I'll be very tied up,' Anni admitted.

'We're all looking forward to your next opening night. I thought the first was magic.'

Geraldine then introduced Anni to some other people but eventually she found herself alone, still hugging her first glass of wine. She didn't want to let Steve down in any way so she didn't take a refill from the tray. Certainly a different Anni from the one at the tour party when she'd been giddy from the bubbly stuff. A different Anni from the one who had gone to Steve's parents' barbecue wanting to show the world she wasn't Steve's type. An Anni who was now a married woman and wanted to stay that way, despite all the problems being married entailed.

She looked into the crowd and found Steve watching her. He came over immediately. 'All right?' he asked.

267

She nodded. 'Fine. Just taking a breather. Geraldine is a lovely woman.'

'She certainly is. I met Paul when I was going for the bar and he took me home for dinner with him. Possibly I looked like a starving student, I don't know. They had kids at home then. Their family life was pretty chaotic. When I was qualified to enter a firm, he approached me right away and made sure I came in with him.'

Anni eagerly listened to Steve's story. He rarely told her much about his past. He only offered information, such as his mother's parents both dying in a car crash, when she asked. In fact, she didn't know much at all, she thought. Nothing about past girlfriends or lovers. She supposed one day she would have to ask. 'Well,' she said with a smile, 'now you're a partner in Paul's firm. That's wonderful, Steve.'

'It is.' He grinned. 'And it's beginning to sink in now. I'm happy. Happy with you. Happy with my career. I hope you feel the same way, Anni?'

'So far,' she said, easing closer to him. 'But there's one thing.'

'What?' He looked worried.

Anni chuckled. 'Where is the powder room?'

Steve looked relieved. 'That's it? You can use the one in my office instead of going down the hallway.'

'You have your own bathroom?'

'All the offices do.'

'You're still in the same office, are you?'

'No. I'm in the one the other side of Alf now. The bigger one with the view over the lake.'

Anni handed Steve her empty glass, which he promptly placed on a corner of a desk, and she walked into his new office. The leather armchairs were heaped with coats and his desk had been cleared of papers. Instead, used glasses and napkins were now strewn there. The view from the window was of twinkling lights and Anni was sure she could see her condo block.

Anni spotted a small alcove, turned the corner and found the door to the washroom. She took a few moments to tidy her hair and make-up before peeking into the cabinet behind the mirror. Steve had a toothbrush and paste there, plus a battery-operated razor. More things this woman doesn't know about her husband, Anni thought. There was so much to discover over her new lifetime with Steve.

Thinking about this, she felt a thrill flutter through her stomach and clench at her throat. She glanced at her wide gold band which this evening she wore with her diamond and ruby engagement ring. She couldn't believe she had actually taken the step and married Steve. The last few months seemed like a dream.

She supposed she should return to her husband, and after clicking the clasp on her purse she turned to leave. She had opened the door part-way before she realized there was someone in Steve's office. More than one person. Two. One was Rachel. The other was a woman Anni had never met. She had a cap of gold hair and well-defined features, and she was secretly sneaking a cigarette and depositing the ashes into Steve's empty wastebasket. Anni knew that Steve would be furious if he knew. His office was strictly non-smoking, as were all offices nowadays.

'So what happened about Lydia?' the gold-haired woman asked Steve's sister as she surreptitiously puffed.

Rachel perched on the edge of the desk, surveying her best feature – long legs in dark hose and black leather high-heeled sandals below a short black silk dress. 'According to Lydia, whom I saw at some do Ben took me to the other weekend, she turned down his proposal.'

'Then how long has he known this dancer?'

'Not long. He met her at a party back in July and they were married by October.'

The woman puffed harshly. 'Of course he knew the promotion would have gone to Craig if he hadn't been married, so he had to move quickly. I suppose he panicked when Lydia turned him down. Poor Craig, he's devastated. It's difficult living with a man when his career aspirations go down the drain.'

'He'll be the next partner,' Rachel said. 'He's younger than Steve.'

'I hope you're right.' The golden-haired woman leaned into the wastebasket and stubbed out her cigarette. 'Do you think I should hose that butt down?'

'You don't want to start a fire.'

The woman tossed in the remains of a glass from the desk. 'How's that?' She laughed as the butt sizzled. 'So do you think your brother loves this Anni – is that her name?'

'He says he does but I think he's in lust and the lust will eventually wear off, but she's got him what he wanted. The big P – Promotion. I mean, the practice really wanted Steve, you have to admit that, Marie, but they have this thing about their partners being solid family men.'

'Solid – with her?'

Rachel laughed and straightened, picking up her black velvet purse from the table. 'Yeah, well. She does have some attributes. She is a fab dancer and my little sister Janet thinks she's great. She's very nice, very polite. Good-looking. Steve has his feelings in a knot over her, that's for sure.'

'Something I wouldn't mind,' the other woman said. 'Your brother is really gorgeous, Rach. When Craig pouts and sulks I think about Steve and I realize that he really is their man. Although I'd never tell Craig that. Craig might not have made it to partner yet anyway. Personally I think they used him as ammunition against Steve to give him competition and probably impetus to get his personal life in order. And he did. I have to admit that I thought Anni was stunning. So tall and graceful. I bet she is great on stage.'

'She is. Magnificent. *Wedding Bells* is really sexy and Moe Ellison, well, you'd like *him* in bed, Marie, I'll tell you. I can probably get you tickets. Anni is able to get us complimentary passes.'

'I'd love that. Those type of shows are *soooo* expensive these days.'

The two women left Steve's office. Anni, for a moment, remained behind the door, stunned. Too stunned to burst into childish tears. Too stunned actually to walk through Steve's office door into the party once more. She closed the washroom door and turned back to the mirror. Her eyes were huge, purply blue, shocked.

Steve looked around the office. Everyone was going to eat at a restaurant called *Le Soup* and he wanted to tell Anni. He wasn't sure if she'd returned from the powder room. He hoped she was all right. She hadn't looked ill but she worked hard. He sometimes forgot how strenuously she *did* work. Most of the time all he did was sit in an office. Anni was constantly pouring out all her energy and emotions. Maybe he hadn't understood that enough.

Steve put down his glass and went into his office. What a mess his desk was, and he sniffed the air. Some idiot had been smoking. Hadn't they heard of non-smoking bye-laws in office buildings? His washroom door was closed but not unlocked. Anni was in there, leaning against the basin.

She looked very pale and he noticed her eyes didn't meet his. 'Are you okay?' he asked.

She surveyed the tips of her suede shoes. 'I'm fine. I just needed a little rest from the party.'

'That's not like you.'

'I'm not like me, am I?' She now looked at him and spoke sharply. 'I've changed from who I was when you first met me.'

Steve's head was buzzing from too much wine and excitement and not enough food. He was starving hungry. 'Anni, what the hell? Come along, we're going to *Le Soup*. You like *Le Soup*.'

272

'Yes. I like *Le Soup*.' Her purse hung over a hook by the cabinet. She lifted it and placed it over her suede-clad shoulder. 'I'm ready.'

'You'll have to drive,' he said. 'I've over-indulged.'

'Fine. Give me the keys.'

Steve handed her the keys to the Mercedes and after closing his office door, hoping the cleaners would have it back in order by morning, went with Anni in the elevator with a number of other people. Luckily there was no one he knew intimately. He was sure someone like Alf or Ben would notice the tension between himself and Anni. Newlyweds and they weren't even standing close to one another. And she'd been so normal when she'd first arrived. He didn't understand what had happened to change her mood.

His car was parked underground so he took her arm and directed her there. She drove competently for the two blocks necessary to reach the restaurant. Her excellent driving made Steve aware that Anni had lived as a single woman for a long time. She was almost thirty. She knew her way around. He was going to direct her to a parking lot but she obviously knew the area because she parked in the lot across the road and they hurried to the restaurant entrance in the chilly night air. He wondered how many other times she'd come to *Le Soup* and who with.

The restaurant was extremely expensive and catered to a trendy, wealthy crowd. Located in an old house, the walls were stone and decorated with paintings by local artists. An advertisement for *Wedding Bells* was pinned on the bulletin board in the foyer and Anni's black and white photograph was beside Moe Ellison's on the poster. Everyone shuffling through remarked on this, and Anni had to make some promises to provide tickets to the law office for the second run.

Steve noticed she did this with a stiffness that wasn't his familiar Anni. Anni could get uptight about things, mainly pressure on her time, but she was never stiff. She seemed to be containing anger or hurt.

Steve placed his arm around her shoulder. 'Are you feeling well, sweetie?'

'I'm absolutely fine,' she retorted.

Steve removed his arm abruptly. 'What the hell, Anni? What's wrong?' He wondered if, after having seen his place of employment again, circulated with the people he worked with, she felt she didn't belong? But she seemed to belong. She'd talked to Geraldine Roberts for ages and Geraldine had mentioned to Steve once again, as she had many times, that she thought Anni charming.

She didn't have time to answer because they were hustled over to their tables.

The law practice party had three big tables placed together. Steve was asked to sit at one end with Anni beside him. Menus were slim cards, the names of the dishes mixed up French and English to keep in style with the name of the restaurant. Red wine was chosen and a few bottles appeared on the table with large glasses. Steve saw Anni take a few sips and place her glass down. He knew she liked wine and always drank a glass with a special dinner.

'Are you sure you're all right?'

She tossed her head so her hair shimmered. Steve could see people surreptitiously watching Anni. She had a definite presence. A star quality. Ray was so right. 'I'm fine. I'm hungry. I think. Besides, I can't drink. I have to drive.'

'You should have eaten more munchies at the cocktail party.'

She glared at him. 'I don't eat junk. I'm working.'

'Excuse me!'

'You know that, Steve.' She gave him a warning look.

He flung aside the menu. 'I'm going to have the steak,' he said. 'To hell with all this health stuff.'

He noticed Anni's mouth tighten. She put down her menu. 'I'm going to have the stuffed grilled sole.'

'Aren't you just the epitome of sparkling health?'

As he spoke he realized that he was heading for a blow-out argument with his wife at the table. Luckily no one had noticed. Everyone was too busy checking out menus, discussing food choices and generally having a good time. Except him. Anni was wrecking his promotion celebration. Why?

He turned aside from her and struck up a conversation with Alf. The meal passed swiftly in a whirl of animated conversation, good food and wine. Steve was toasted a number of times and all the women gave him a kiss and a hug outside the restaurant door. Then he was alone on the sidewalk with Anni. She still had his car keys.

He looked at her. 'Are you driving?'

Instead of looking at him she peered up at the clear crisp starry sky. 'Yes. I'm driving. *I* didn't drink anything.'

'I don't understand why you didn't?'

'I didn't feel like it.'

'What *you* feel like is important. Always, isn't it?' He strode across the road towards the car. 'Thanks for wrecking my evening, Anni. Thanks loads.'

He heard her heels clicking behind him. 'I didn't wreck your evening, Steve. I behaved myself admirably. In the circumstances.'

He stopped walking. 'What circumstances?'

'You don't have to ask me that, Steve.' She kept walking to the car, opened the doors and slid into the driver's seat. Steve slid in beside her, cursing because he'd had one drink too many to pass the breathalyzer test. He wasn't drunk but he didn't want to get pulled over or chance losing his license. Especially when he wasn't and never had been a drinker.

Anni strapped on her seatbelt, started the engine and began to drive towards his house. Their house, he corrected. Although he barely felt married at this moment.

'I want to know what you mean by circumstances?' he repeated finally. 'Don't you like me having the limelight for once?'

She turned to look at him in the dark. 'If you think that, then you're way off base. I'm talking about something different.'

'Maybe you're talking about it, sweetie, but I'm sure not. I haven't got a clue what's going on in that ditsy head of yours.'

She made a sound like a little cry. 'I am not ditsy, thank you very much. I'm perfectly lucid. In fact I've never seen everything quite so clearly as I'm seeing it right now.' Anni concentrated on traffic lights and a left-hand turn.

'I shouldn't have said ditsy, I'm sorry. But, hell, I don't know what's happened to make you like this. You weren't like this when you first arrived at my office. What happened in the bathroom?'

'I had an out-of-body experience,' she said.

'I'm beginning to believe that. Look, Anni, I'm not a mind-reader. Tell me.'

She glanced at him, her eyes not really on him. 'It's complex. I don't know how to begin. It's humiliating.'

'I don't know what the hell you're talking about. What happened that was humiliating?'

'All right. I'll begin by asking you – who's Lydia?'

Steve was stunned into silence. He hadn't expected Lydia's name to surface. He hadn't even told Anni about Lydia. She hadn't been at the party.

'Do you know a Lydia?' she prodded when he didn't respond immediately.

'Yes, I do, but she wasn't there.'

'Obviously. You asked her to marry you and she turned you down. She's hardly going to be at your promotion party.'

For the first time since she'd left his office after the party, Steve heard emotion at the edges of Anni's voice. Even though she lived by her emotions she knew exactly how to contain those same emotions so she didn't overuse them or squander them. They had to be saved for her stage performances. This evening she had used that control against him. What she actually said took a moment to sink in. So did the injustice of her remark. Even so, his denial sounded false, because he recalled a time about a year ago when his partnership was being tossed around and deep down in his heart he knew the qualifications needed. He'd sort of suggested to Lydia that they might as well get married as they were both of the same mind and didn't really believe in romantic marriages. It would be convenient. At that time he hadn't known how Lydia felt about him. But he'd never actually *asked* her. 'I didn't ask her to marry me.'

Anni still drove expertly, as if she wasn't bothered by their conversation, but he noticed her long-boned, slim fingers were restless around the steering wheel. Her rings shone in patches of light that also lit up the dashboard of the car. Her face was half in shadow but he could see her features were tense with pain. When she spoke he heard pain. 'Why would Rachel say you did, then?'

Steve placed his hand along the back of their two seats so he could look at her. 'Rachel actually told you this?' He'd kill his sister when he next saw her. He really would. Was this Rachel's way of turning Anni against him? He knew she didn't believe in this marriage for him. Unlike the rest of his family, who had accepted Anni once his decision to marry her was made. Even Ben didn't seem to worry about who his wife was once Steve had filled the criteria and they were safe from having to admit

278

Craig Firth into their midst. Steve had found out just a couple of days ago that they really hadn't wanted Craig but he had been the natural choice if Steve hadn't fitted the bill.

'She didn't actually tell me to my face,' Anni broke into his thoughts. 'When I was in your washroom she was in your office with a blonde woman, whose name was Marie, and I overheard them talking. They mentioned you'd been turned down by Lydia. So, needing a wife for your promotion, you chose me.' She stared straight ahead and drove, swallowing back tears. 'I think this woman was the wife of some other guy who was up for the promotion as well. She was quite generous to you in the circumstances, seeing that her husband lost out. She felt that you were truly the flavour of the month if you fulfilled the requirements. Which you promptly did by marrying me.'

Steve saw silver droplets on her cheeks. 'Anni. None of that is true. Well, maybe the bit about Craig Firth being in contention for the partnership is true.'

'Of course it's true, Steve. Why would his wife lie?'

When she spoke the word lie she put enough emphasis on it to make Steve wince. 'All right. I did need to be married for the partnership, but I'd met you before I found out for sure I might lose it. I wanted to marry you before that. I have never asked any other woman to marry me but you. You have to believe me, Anni.'

Anni tightened her grip on the steering wheel. 'Why would your friend Lydia tell Rachel that, then?'

'I don't know. Unless she was hurt. Wounded pride. As far as the promotion goes, it was coincidence, Anni. Pure coincidence that we met at that time.'

'But *so* convenient.'

The words were biting. He felt his heart shrivel. 'No, Anni. Believe me, not those women.'

Anni's eyes appeared black when she turned to him. 'Can I believe you, Steve? You haven't told me much about anything, certainly never anything about Lydia.'

'Because she wasn't important. We dated on and off for about a year and half, that was all.'

'A year and a half!' Her voice was high-pitched now. 'I've never dated anyone for more than three months. A year and a half I would have considered important. Extremely important.'

'It wasn't intimate. We were just good friends.' Steve collapsed back in his seat and ran his fingers roughly through his hair. 'Rachel introduced me to Lydia. We hit it off. We . . .'

'Went to bed,' Anni added.

'Yes. But not at first and then only once. It was awkward, Anni, and we realized there was no lasting passion there. Then we decided, as we were quite good friends and neither of us had a significant other, that we could call on one another for dates. Which we did. But not lately. Not since I've met you.'

'Then you haven't seen her since you met me?' Anni's voice sounded stern, as if she were interrogating him.

He didn't lie. 'Yes, I did. Once. When I met you

she was away in California on a vacation and when she returned she phoned me. We met and I told her our arrangement was off. I'd met you.'

Anni laughed harshly. 'Was she pleased about that?'

'No. She wasn't pleased. She was angry. Apparently I got her feelings for me all wrong. But she'd never said how she felt. If she had, I'd never have continued the friendship as long as I did.'

'Then she was in love with you?'

'So she says. I haven't seen her since. I haven't wanted to.'

Anni wrenched the car around the corner. 'However, you did see her after you met me?'

'Yes.'

Anni gunned the Mercedes and they swished down his street. Their street. He'd have to begin thinking of them more as a couple. But right at this very moment they were definitely separate, more separate than the evening he'd first met Anni at Ray's party.

CHAPTER 15

Free weekends were to be a thing of the past with the second run of *Wedding Bells* about to open. Anni rose early on Saturday morning after a restless night beside Steve. Her mind kept re-running the scene with Rachel and Marie Firth in Steve's office. She couldn't believe Rachel had lied to Marie Firth. She also didn't believe Steve had lied. If anyone had lied it was probably Lydia, to save face after dating Steve for so long. However, that was exactly the point that Anni couldn't come to terms with. Why hadn't Steve ever told her about Lydia? While Steve probably wouldn't lie, Anni thought he might be holding back some of the details.

She was amazed he could actually sleep after the problems that had arisen the night before. Anni knew they should talk more but she wasn't sure what she wanted to hear from Steve. Maybe that was why he slept. He had nothing else to say. Rachel's comments were the truth. Lydia existed and he had asked her to marry him and she had turned him down. Anni was second choice. A convenient choice because she fell in love with him right at the very time he needed a wife.

After feeding Dash and drinking some hot coffee Anni left the house before Steve even woke up. Because the Mercedes was the first car in the driveway and she still had the keys in her purse, she took it downtown to the Empire Theatre. She parked and ran into the theatre to immediately change into her dancing gear. Neither Ray nor Moe were there yet and she needed to dance. She turned the tape player up loud and lost herself in her dancing. She certainly didn't want to think.

'Another Lover' would come easily now with Lydia on her mind. Who was Lydia? What did she look like? Anni imagined a woman with looks and bearing somewhere between Marie Firth and Rachel. They were a type. Women larger than herself, more capable of down-to-earth living. It might be true that Steve and Lydia had only made love once in the relationship but that once was enough to set Anni's mind into overdrive. She couldn't bear the thought of Steve's naked flesh buried inside another woman.

Ray, Moe and other dancers arrived. Anni vowed this second opening night would be even better than the last. Dancing was the only way she was going to deal with Steve. Dancing was only the way she knew how to deal with anything. Putting herself on the outside for a while hadn't done her any good. All she got was hurt. Enfolding herself in her art was like wearing a cloak of protection against the world.

Steve woke up to find Anni absent. He'd had a terrible night and finally fallen into a deep strange sleep with horrifying, Technicolor dreams. He sat up, rubbing his face. Wasn't Saturday morning a time when most couples managed a little fun? So much for having a wife in the entertainment business. But he'd been warned. He couldn't say he hadn't. Anni had warned him and he'd warned himself as well. But mostly he remembered last night. He wasn't in Anni's good books. She was probably pleased to leave the house today and not have to face him.

Hearing Dash meowing at the bottom of the stairs, he put on his terry robe and, tying the belt, walked downstairs barefoot. Dash wanted to play so he flung a few of his wool toys around, and while the kitten scrabbled with the toys, Steve read a note from Anni to say she'd be home later. If that was the case he might as well go to the office and finish the work he'd never had a chance to complete yesterday because of his promotion party.

There was still some coffee in the pot so he filled a mug, found it cool, re-heated it in the microwave and then went back upstairs. After a shower, he dressed in jeans and sweater, perfectly acceptable weekend gear at the office, and returned to the kitchen. He made himself some toast, ate it and placed the dishes in the dishwasher. Every movement he made seemed pedantic, every sound too loud. What was wrong with this house since he'd been married? Janet's description of it as a mausoleum seemed apt when he was alone these days.

284

Silent and eerie. If it wasn't for Dash the place wouldn't seem alive.

He grabbed his leather jacket and went outside. Patting his pockets, he realized he hadn't got his car keys and was about to go back indoors when he noticed the Mercedes was gone. For a second he panicked and then he realized that Anni must have taken it as it was the first car in the driveway and she probably still had the keys from last night. Her car was sitting snugly in the garage. He thought of taking the low-slung red car but recalled he'd hit his head the first time he'd driven it. Besides, he needed an excuse to talk to Anni. He didn't know how she felt this morning after last night. His explanations hadn't gone over very well. Maybe he wasn't really sure what everything was about. What were the rumours his sister was circulating among her friends? Especially to Craig's wife. Steve had to work with Craig day in and day out and it was a strained enough relationship as it was. They should both have been given partnerships to make life easier.

Returning to the house, he phoned Anni's cellphone and got her first time. Surprised to hear her voice, he was silent for a second, then he said, 'Do you have my car?

She breathed in his ear. 'Yes. I have your car.'

She still sounded upset with him. And he hadn't done anything to deserve it. Or had he? Omitting to tell her about Lydia was stupid. If he'd mentioned Lydia at the beginning everything would be fine now. 'Well, I need it, he said.

'Use mine.'

'It's too low. My head hits the roof.' He wasn't sure what he was asking of her. Did he want her to jump in his car and drive home right away with it?

'I'm sorry, Steve. I have to be here for another few hours. Just take my car and mind your head. The keys are on that hook in the kitchen.'

He slammed the phone down. He'd take her damn car! He had to admit he enjoyed driving the low-slung Nissan. He sped through the city streets, parked underground, and went up the elevator. His name was already on a gold strip on one of the double doors. He touched it. At least he had his partnership. Marriage to Anni had given him that goal. Maybe he had been thinking too much of the promotion when he'd rushed their wedding. They never had enough time to get to know one another before they'd been flung back into hectic everyday life.

Alf was in, feet on his desk, dictating into a machine. Steve stopped at Alf's door and Alf saluted him and turned off the machine.

'Survived last night, Pardner?' Alf asked with a big grin.

Steve nodded. 'I survived. Now I feel official.' He also smiled but the smile felt forced.

'Paul and Geraldine are really impressed with Anni. Loved her even more than they did the other times they met her.'

'That's great, Alf.'

'What's the matter? Aren't you one step into heaven this morning?'

Steve shook his head. 'Everything seems unreal.'

286

'Well, it's not. Your name's on the door, the letterhead is printed, so get to work.'

Steve saluted Alf. 'Thanks.'

Alf returned to dictating. Steve went into his own office. It had been cleaned up from last night and a lemon air freshener sprayed to mask the tobacco smoke. Marie Firth really was a witch. Smoking in his office and gathering all the dirt from Rachel. As if Marie was such a faithful wife herself. Steve recalled her coming on to him last Christmas at the staff party. She'd cornered him out by the coat rack in the hotel foyer and actually touched his zipper. He'd eased away from her as politely as possible and put her actions down to too much to drink, but she still left a bad feeling in his mind.

And Steve was furious with Rachel. She should be more discreet. Steve was married to Anni and it was his choice. Lydia was history.

He removed his jacket and scarf and hung them on his coat rack. Smoothing his hair with a rather agitated gesture, he walked to the window and surveyed the view. He could see Anni's condo from this office. Her spacious penthouse was perched at the top of the big block. It kind of grated on him that she still owned the condo apartment. He knew she hadn't had the time to begin to sell it yet, but he also wondered if by keeping it she was retaining her escape route. By not telling her about Lydia upfront – he'd truly forgotten or not thought it important, he supposed – she now had a reason for that escape. And if she needed an escape, then was she truly dedicated to this marriage?

His stomach feeling as if he'd eaten lead, he sat down at his desk and tugged the mail file folder in front of him. All the time Steve marked notes on some correspondence and placed other letters aside for answering he could hear Alf's voice droning into the machine in his office. He couldn't concentrate. Staring into space, he wondered if Lydia had actually told Rachel that he'd proposed? Maybe she had presumed his silly idea that a marriage of convenience might work was a proposal. Or was Rachel lying? He couldn't see that, because Rachel didn't lie. Rachel was forthright. Besides she was his sister. She should be on his side. She shouldn't listen to gossip, let alone spread it.

Almost without thinking, but knowing he had to solve this dilemma, Steve walked his fingers through his phone directory on his desk. He passed Rachel's and Lydia's phone numbers. Should he confront them? But what good would that do? Did he expect Rachel or Lydia to apologize to Anni? Anni didn't even know Lydia. And Rachel? Did he really want to show his sister that his marriage could so easily be brought to the edge of disaster? Rachel would only say, I told you so. He closed the phone directory. *To hell with it, Steve. Get on with your work and talk to Anni later. It'll work out.*

Anni was finished at three-thirty. She changed into street clothes and drove home. She opened the garage with the automatic control, found her car wasn't there and drove Steve's into the right-hand spot. So Steve had taken her car to the office. She hoped he'd be careful. The first time he'd driven her car he'd driven it extra fast. Men saw the Nissan as a car they could speed in. A fun toy.

After changing into navy blue leggings and a huge fleece sweatshirt, Anni poured herself some juice and sat at the kitchen table with Dash poking his nose into her work. She finished off her wedding thank-you cards, thinking that the next batch of cards would be for Christmas. She would have to take time off from rehearsals for her Christmas shopping and make sure her purchases were complete before the Christmas run began about a week before Christmas. The matinees would be tiring. She wouldn't have much of a Christmas either. But it would be a very different Christmas this year, celebrated with Steve's family. Somewhere in between *Wedding Bells* performances she would find a few hours for family moments.

Usually on Saturdays, when she was single, if she wasn't performing that evening or seeing her mother, she'd call out for pizza. Being married, she felt she should cook a meal. Wearing a wedding gift apron, Anni perused the freezer. She found a package of chicken breasts and decided to make a casserole with them. If she shared a long leisurely meal with Steve, maybe they could talk and work things out between them. Even if it meant making a firm decision as to what to do in the future. Scrawling her name with Steve's on a thank you card, she felt like a fraud. Their future didn't look very bright.

The casserole was ready to serve by six-thirty but Steve hadn't arrived home. Anni left the covered dish in the oven on low heat. The house was full of the delicious aroma of cooking food and she was beginning to feel hungry after not having eaten much last night and only munching on a bran muffin for lunch.

Anni went to check the meal once more at half-past seven and decided she'd better eat her part of the meal. She sat alone at the kitchen table and ate her portion even if she didn't taste much. All the while Dash played beneath the table with a ball containing a bell inside that jingled merrily in contrast to Anni's feelings.

By eight Steve still wasn't home. She turned off the oven and placed the dish in the refrigerator. She was half dozing on the sofa in the living room with the TV playing softly and Dash on her lap when she heard the engine of her car. She waited until the front door opened and then got up and went to the hall.

She didn't mean to be harsh but as soon as she saw Steve, she said, 'Where have you been?' Dash ran to see Steve.

Steve placed his briefcase on the floor by the door and acknowledged the little cat with a pat. 'At the office. I told you earlier.'

'I cooked you a meal.'

He shrugged out of his leather jacket. 'I didn't expect that.'

All Anni's frustration boiled over. 'What the hell do you mean by that? We haven't been married very long. I haven't had time to begin cooking and I don't *have* time most of the time. I cooked you a chicken casserole and now it's cold mush in the refrigerator. Help yourself.'

Steve hung his jacket in the closet. 'I can use a microwave.'

'Then do so.' Anni grabbed Dash and made for the stairs. So much for her plans to talk things out. It seemed obvious by his actions that Steve had married her solely for his promotion. Now he had that, he didn't give a damn about her. She recalled how he'd sounded on the phone when he called about the car. He'd been distant, snappy. She swallowed back painful tears.

Steve let her go. He'd wanted to come home earlier but instead he had stayed at the office and attacked his work. Alf had looked in on his way home. 'Give it a miss, Steve. You have a wife now. It's Saturday night.'

'Who might not be home,' Steve said, and had heard the bitterness which he was sure his cousin must have detected.

'Yeah, well.' Alf buttoned his overcoat. 'That's to be expected with her career. When I first married Sandy she was very busy with a number of high-profile court cases. It's only since the kids, her part-time work, and me not over-doing it here that we've had a smoother life. Your partnership is to help us all out. We'll be distributing the cases more evenly so that none of us has to do so many long hours.'

'But Anni's hours are going to be longer soon,' Steve said. 'She has matinees over Christmas. I have to do something with my time during the winter months when I can't go boating or play tennis or golf.'

Alf scratched his ear. 'I think she'll probably want you to be there for her, though. Sort it out soon. It can get bad if you let it fester. See you Monday.'

Fester. That was what was happening. Things were festering between them. Steve walked into the kitchen

291

where the aroma of food still hung. His stomach rumbled. He hadn't eaten dinner. All he'd done was pop down to the coffee shop for a muffin. He took the casserole from the refrigerator, spooned chicken and sauce on to a plate and reheated the meal in the microwave. He ate quickly, very impressed with the taste, and decided he'd tell Anni so. He noticed her small pile of thank-you cards and read a few. *Thank you for the lace table cloth or the dishes or the vase.* Signed *Anni and Steve*. Still a couple on paper at least.

He went upstairs to find Anni practising dancing in the spare room she'd set up. He observed her from the door for a while. She was barefoot in her leggings and sweatshirt, her hair knotted up on her head. She was working slowly at some intricate steps, nothing to make him flush with heat but enough to make him aware of her awesome dancing techniques. He couldn't see that she would have ever been anything but a dancer and he felt uncharitable about any thoughts he'd had otherwise. He had to let her be free to dance. In a way, his promise when he married her had been just that. He had no intention of changing her.

After a while she sensed him there, stopped, and turned around. She held her hands folded at her waist, her feet posed, her back straight. Her eyes were like mysterious black pools in her pale face as she looked at him.

He spoke quickly. 'I reheated the meal. It was really good. Very good. Excellent. I finished it off.'

'That's good, Steve.'

He took a breath. 'We have a lot to talk about,' he said.

'I know, but I won't have time to give the discussion justice over the next few weeks. We'll have to postpone our chat. In the meantime –' she smiled slightly ' – you can dream up some good excuses.'

He rubbed the doorknob with his fingers. 'I don't have excuses, Anni. You know the truth now.'

She raised one eyebrow. 'Do I?'

He had the feeling she was acting, toying with him.

'Don't believe what you heard.' Steve let go of the doorknob and placed his hands into his back pockets.

She began to dance again. 'Another time, Steve. I'm forgetting all that now. I need my mind clear.' Then she stopped suddenly. 'You know what else Rachel said, Steve?'

'What?' He felt as if he were in pain. His chest hurt.

'That you had your feelings in a knot over me. Maybe that's all it was, Steve. Lust. Not love. Perhaps you can't distinguish between them.'

She began to dance more earnestly, dismissing him. He left the room. Was she right? Were his feelings for her merely lust? No. He loved her. He fell in love with her the moment he saw her in Ray's garden. All he wanted was honesty between them. But he was a fine one to preach honesty when he hadn't told her about Lydia in the first place. Or any other girlfriend for that matter. As if he'd spent thirty-five years of his life without any women while waiting for Anni. But that was the way he'd felt. This was it. Anything else had been merely biding time.

He went back downstairs and cleaned up his used dishes. Then he went into the living room, sat down on the sofa and idly pressed the TV remote control. He watched snatches of programmes and commercials. Eventually Anni joined him.

'What are you watching?'

'Nothing.' He snapped off the switch. 'Come here.'

She sat beside him and he placed his arms around her and pressed his mouth to hers, but he could feel the hesitation in her. She didn't compulsively wrap her arms around him as usual so he let his own arms drop. Anni jumped up and went to find Dash. She came back with the kitten in her arms. Hugging the kitten instead of him. He had to overcome this silliness. Then they'd get their marriage properly under way and show the world they were a unit.

'It's time we held some dinner parties,' Steve said at breakfast on Tuesday morning. 'My partners and our parents for a start.'

Anni was digging into a half-grapefruit and nibbling dry toast. They hadn't spoken much since Saturday night. Well, they'd exchanged pleasantries. They'd even shared a bed. But during the evenings Steve hid himself in his study and Anni danced, so they went their separate ways as soon as they could. Now she had to respond. This sounded important. Demanding of her time. The way a conversation with Steve about the truth would be demanding of her time. And her emotions. She couldn't spare either. 'Dinner parties, Steve?'

'Yes. Dinner parties. Before you begin this new run in December. It's expected, and I doubt if you will be around much over Christmas.'

'Like marriage was expected. So now I'm expected to provide dinner parties?' Anni left the table and began fitting dishes into the dishwasher. 'I think you're asking too much, Steve.'

'We can't let everyone know we've failed, Anni. It's too soon. We'll work things out eventually but right now we have to get through a tough time. When you're ready to hear explanations and believe me, then things will be fine.'

She looked at him. He was dressed in his dark trousers, white shirt, conservative tie, appropriate law office wear. His hair was burnished gold and his skin smooth-shaven. So handsome he made her heart ache.

'Anni,' he said. 'Please answer me.'

'I think for our own self-respect we should tough it out,' she said. 'I'll do the meals. If you think that casserole was okay?'

'It was fantastic. We could just add some pasta and a salad and good wine.'

'All right.' Anni closed the dishwasher door. Tears burned at the backs of her eyes. Hurt ached down so deep inside her she thought she might keel over from the pain. But she managed to say quite calmly, 'Set the dates, then. I'll be here and do my thing.'

Steve left for work but his entire day was overshadowed by his discord with Anni. What he had

295

to do was show Anni that she was the only woman he wanted. He also had to show his family, especially Rachel, that Anni was his choice because he loved her and not for any other reason. Because of this Steve made arrangements to have his family over for dinner first. There was also another reason. Marian Ross was leaving on a two-week cruise to the Caribbean soon and he wanted to make sure she could attend. Steve did the inviting and then solicited Anni's participation in ordering chicken from the local butcher at the end of their street. A grocery store in the same row of shops sold fresh vegetables. They went out on the Saturday morning together, not in the car as usual, but walking. Steve found it fun to shop together. Even Anni loosened up as they strolled home in the damp November air with their bags of fresh vegetables and fruit, delicious hot baked bread, and a selection of cheeses.

As they worked around the kitchen together on that Saturday afternoon preparing pasta and Anni's now favourite chicken casserole, Steve saw her slip back into the Anni she'd been before she'd overheard Rachel and Marie talking at his promotion party. In those brief minutes Steve tried to recapture some of their lighter moments. He even touched and kissed her with promise of more passion later. But even though there was laughter, he could feel the undercurrents. Between him and Anni the atmosphere was now like the calm before a storm.

CHAPTER 16

As usual, after fixing her hair and make-up, Anni hunted in her closet for something to wear that would be appropriate when she was seeing Steve's family. Everything was on the bed when Steve came in to change.

He began tugging his sweatshirt over his head. 'What's this?'

'Me. Choosing something to wear.'

He tossed the sweatshirt aside and unbuckled the belt of his jeans. Observing his muscular torso, desire bubbled up inside her like a warm fountain and Anni had to stop herself from going over to him and sliding her hands up his chest. He slipped out of his jeans, tossed them aside. All he wore now was a pair of black briefs.

Anni's breath was on hold in her chest and she ached inside. She could see Steve was aroused and she wanted to reach out and beckon him to her.

'Do you always go through such chaos?' he asked.

'Yes.'

He gave her that all-over thorough look that he'd given her their first night. 'I kind of like you in panties and that little lace top.'

'We haven't got time, Steve.'

'I know. So what are you going to wear?'

Anni almost blindly picked up her loose, silky black pants. 'I'll wear these and that scarlet shirt I bought in London. Do you think?'

He walked into the closet and began hunting for his own clothes. 'You always look great to me, Anni.'

Anni presumed that to mean he didn't really care how she appeared before his family. Remembering the black dress and red shoes of her initial appearance, Anni changed the scarlet shirt to white silk.

Steve came out of the closet with his trousers and shirt. 'I'll take a shower,' he said. 'That looks nice.'

'Thanks.' After covering her outfit with a white lace apron Anni went downstairs to check on the meal.

Steve's parents arrived with Marian Ross. Janet came with Rachel and Ben. Everyone was dressed nicely. Marian, Diane and Rachel in wool dresses, Janet in black trousers and a white sweater, the men in trousers and shirts. Jason and Jack, also in their best pants and shirts, both took to Dash and gave the kitten some playtime he was being deprived of. Steve served drinks in the living room and Anni remained in the kitchen.

Anni looked up from the stove where she was stirring the pasta to see her mother in the kitchen.

Marian's dress was maroon wool and she looked very nice. She told her mother so.

'I bought this at *Diane's*. It's expensive but she gave me a discount and it was on sale. We were just saying we haven't seen you for a long time, Ann. You haven't called.'

Anni forced a bright smile. 'We've been so busy since we came back from England. Having a husband is extra work. And I know you're busy getting ready for your vacation. Are you looking forward to it?' Anni tried to change the subject.

'Very much. It's exciting. I'm trying to decide what to pack. I've never been on a cruise. You should come over and help me. You always choose the right clothes for the right occasion.'

Anni was truly surprised by that statement. 'I do?'

Marian smiled. 'You always stand out.'

'That's different.' Anni made a face.

'I think it's a sign of your individuality. I know I've never said any of this before but I think it should be said. And I do understand that you must be busy as life is different for you now with a husband. And you have this home to run. It's very big – I never realized how large it was the first time I came last summer.'

'We have someone come in once a week to clean. Steve kept the lady on. But we might move next year.' Anni felt she was babbling.

'Move? Where to?'

Anni heard the anxiety in her mother's voice. Marian's life was turning outwards and becoming interesting now with her daughter married to a man Marian loved. She wanted everything kept normal. Anni understood that. 'Oh, only to a different house. Maybe with some land around it. I wouldn't mind moving from the city.' Anni chattered about the dreams she'd had when her relationship with Steve had been more secure. At the moment she felt she was lying. She should be saying, *We've messed up, Mom. We might both have to bail out some time in the future.*

Marian looked relieved. 'A house with some land would be good if you start a family.'

Anni resumed stirring the pasta with a fork. She hadn't let herself think about the family she had longed for. She hadn't made love with Steve since his party. Even if earlier the sexual tension between them had still been apparent it didn't seem likely there would be any further lovemaking. They were building a gulf between them. But if there was no lovemaking, there would be no babies, and that thought made the old painful void open up like a pit inside her. She panicked when she thought of life without Steve, without ever having his child. She wasn't sure she could survive any more on her own. Dreams of him would always be in her mind.

'You will have a family?' Marian prodded her.

'When we're ready,' Anni fibbed with a bright smile.

'That's wonderful. I'm so pleased.'

Steve poked his head in the door. 'Hi, Marian. Need any help, sweetie?'

Anni kept her smile bright, a smile forced by necessity but also one of relief that she had been able to keep her mother ignorant of her problems with Steve. 'No, darling. Everything's fine. Mom will help me carry things out to the table.'

Anni was quite proud of her table. The classic lace tablecloth, the crystal wine glasses, the polished silver and the contemporary white bone china her mother had given them as a wedding present. She saw herself reflected in the mirror over the sideboard. There she was, a hostess giving a dinner party, dressed in black and silky white with her silvery table before her.

Play-acting again, Anni, she told herself. This isn't you on stage. This is real life. *Your* life. And it's going downhill fast!

Anni held her breath while everyone cut their first piece of chicken from the casserole. She let the breath out when they all tucked into the food with relish. She tried some herself. The chicken fell tenderly off the bones and the sauce was tasty. Thank goodness!

'You're a good cook, Anni,' Steve's dad said. 'How about it, boys?'

Jason was eating heartily, like most fourteen-year-olds. 'It's awesome.'

'It must be,' Rachel said. 'They don't usually like this kind of meal.'

'This tastes more like pizza,' Jack said. 'Your stuff tastes funny. And I like the pasta. You never cook pasta, Mom.'

'She did once but it stuck together like a lump and Dad said he could glue the furniture with it,' Jason remarked.

'Did I say that?' Ben muttered with a grin.

Rachel glared at her husband. 'I'm sure you did. And thank you very much, my lovely sons.' Rachel looked put out. But a moment later she smiled at Anni. 'Boys!' she said. 'Let's hope you have girls when you begin your family. Mother had two girls and I expected girls, but maybe females will be Steve's contribution to the family.'

'I won't mind,' Anni said. 'Boys or girls.' In front of Rachel she had to act her most content in her marriage, because it was Rachel who would probably spot any unrest and know why it existed. She wondered what went on in Rachel's mind. Knowing what Lydia had told her, did she wonder if it was the truth that Steve had married Anni to get his promotion? Or did she believe it was a convenient coincidence that Steve had met Anni and fallen into lust?

'What about you, Stevie?' Rachel said. 'Boys or girls?'

'Doesn't matter to me,' Steve said, glancing at Anni with a loving smile she knew must be as much acting as one of her own bright smiles. 'Whatever she produces will be beautiful. Another Anni might be nice to start off with.'

'They should have blonde children,' Diane said. 'Both being light-haired.'

'Is your hair natural silver?' Jack asked bluntly. Anni had noticed him staring at her a great deal.

Rachel glared at her younger son. 'Don't be rude.'

'It's not rude,' Anni said. 'Lots of people think I colour my hair. Yes, it's natural, Jack.'

'Wow!'

Anni had not noticed until then that Jack actually liked her. His eyes were like Ben's but more playful and they followed her around as she rose from the table and began clearing dishes. Rachel, Diane and her mother helped. They all followed behind her with piles of dishes which Anni directed them to put on the counter by the dishwasher.

'Jack's smitten with you,' Rachel told her. 'He wants to come to your next opening night. Is that all right? Personally I think *Wedding Bells* is too adult for a ten-year-old. But I don't like to put the kids off. I like them to explore life on their own. And it will be a Christmas treat.'

This was a side of Rachel Anni hadn't expected. She'd assumed Rachel would dictate her own likes and dislikes to her children. 'I agree. He should explore his own nature. Sure. If he wants to come, I'll get you extra tickets,' Anni told her sister-in-law. 'I think the show is an education in love and relationships, so he'll understand what he's ready to understand.' *Exactly like me*, Anni thought. *I understand about relationships. But only what I'm ready to understand. I can't cope with adversity.*

'If you put it that way,' Rachel said, peeking into the trifle. 'Doesn't this look good? Did you make this, Anni?'

'Yes, I did. Didn't you think I could cook?' Anni laughed merrily, naturally.

Rachel shrugged her dark blue wool-clad shoulders. Today she wore her long hair upswept and looked very regal. 'I have to admit I didn't think you were up to this.'

'I never cooked much when I was single,' Anni admitted. 'But I find if I use my creative juices, I can put things together and *voilà*.'

'You cook the way you dance, in other words?' Rachel's eyes were upon her, not scornful but admiring.

'Yes. You could say that. I treat it like a dance piece. A beginning, a middle, a finale. The trifle is my finale.'

Rachel chuckled. 'That's great. I'm a plodder in the kitchen, as you heard from my kids. Now they'll be comparing me to Aunty Anni.'

Aunty Anni. She knew she would think of herself that way to Joni's child when it arrived but never to Jack and Jason. She carried the dessert into the dining room and offered pie and ice-cream to the boys if they would prefer it.

'Naw, this looks great.' Jack bounced up and down until his father told him to sit still or he'd break the chair.

After the trifle was a mere scrape of cream in the bottom of the crystal dish, Steve let the women choose a handful of CDs and he slipped one into the player in the living room. The boys already knew about Steve's pool table in the panelled basement room and went downstairs for a game. Steve, Ben and Steve's dad finally followed and the women were left alone.

'More coffee?' Anni asked everyone.

'No, thank you. I'm full. It was all lovely, Anni,' Diane told her enthusiastically. 'You know, it's so wonderful to have Steve settled down.'

'I'll second that,' Marian said. 'It makes so

much difference to me to know Ann has a husband. And for me to have this extended family. I admit I'm being a bit selfish.'

'It's as if we women can't survive in this world without men,' Rachel commented, and gave Anni a strange little look.

What did Rachel believe about her? Anni wondered. That she hadn't been able to survive without a husband? And that now Anni was second choice for Steve. Well, she'd show Rachel. She'd stick with Steve. They didn't have to see one another often. Steve had his engrossing profession; Anni had hers. They could live in the same house, come and go as they pleased, and put on a great act for their families. They were doing just fine.

At work Steve found his partnership gained him new respect. His client base expanded. Paul, Alf and Ben included him in all their meetings and luncheons at their club and he was accepted as a member. He was also offered a membership at their golf course and he looked forward to next spring when he could play golf again. Events had unfolded the way Steve wanted. Even Craig seemed to accept the promotion and got back to doing his job.

Steve began to find that being at the office was a relief from his arid home life. Anni was barely at the house and when she did appear she scurried around preparing for Christmas. She furiously wrote Christmas cards and wrapped gifts. She hung big red velvet bows and sprigs of holly over the living room mantelpiece, where she also strung the cards they had received. Steve knew she was paring down her chores so they would be completed by her opening night but he also gained the impression she was avoiding long discussions with him. Still, his house had never looked so festive at Christmas before and that lightened his spirit slightly. Anni's presence was felt in some way.

'I've invited my partners and their wives for dinner Saturday,' Steve told her one early morning when he cornered her in the kitchen. She was dressed. He was still wearing his robe. 'We have to do it before you begin the run and the Christmas rush.'

'Right,' Anni said to him as she stacked dishes into the dishwasher. 'Shall I cook the same food as I did for our families?'

'Sure. I'll help you and I'll pick up the wine.'

'Fine. Whatever, Steve. Now I have to run.'

Anni gathered her dancing gear, stuffed the last of her Christmas cards waiting to be mailed into the front pocket of her athletic bag, grabbed her black leather jacket and left the house.

Feeling heavy of heart, Steve watched her back her car from the driveway and leave him once again. This wasn't right, he thought. He loved her. What he had to do was convince her that was true.

She truly was preoccupied, Anni thought as she punched on the car radio and let a popular Celine Dion tune keep her mind from straying to Steve and their jerky relationship. Except the song was about love and she began to listen to the lyrics and felt despair. Why had she ever allowed herself to fall in love? Everything she had to fit into her life, including her love for Steve, seemed to gather in her chest and made it burn with anxiety. For the first time in her life she would like to forgo the dancing, stay at home, and deal with the rest of her life. The rest of her life had never seemed so important before.

As he had when the family came to dinner, Steve helped her prepare for the evening with his partners. Anni set the table the same way with lace and crystal, except in the centre she placed a Christmas decoration that had been hand-made by Lucinda.

Anni had been surprised when Lucinda had given it to her the other day.

'Craft is one of my hobbies,' Lucinda said. 'To prove I have some creative bones in my body, I suppose.'

Anni had accepted the pretty centrepiece of petite pine cones iced with silver. 'This is lovely, Lucinda. Thank you so much.' Then afterwards she wondered if Lucinda had to prove her creativity in the shadow of Ray's mighty ego, and came to the conclusion that no relationship was simple.

For the dinner party, feeling as it was so near Christmas she should appear festive, Anni dressed in a long black velvet skirt, silver top and her special silver earrings. As she had already forged a relationship with Geraldine and she also liked Sandy Smithson, she wasn't too worried about the evening. Rachel was her only problem, but she'd have to deal with Rachel for a long time so she couldn't waste time bothering about her sister-in-law and what she thought or didn't think.

Later, after dinner, when the men were in the basement playing billiards, the women sat in the low-lit living room over more glasses of wine. Anni relaxed as the dinner and evening seemed to be proving a success.

'I like your decorations, Anni,' Sandy told her. 'It's all very subtle but you can tell the season.'

'It's subtle because I haven't got time for more than a few sprigs of holly and red velvet bows,' Anni said with a smile, and stroked the kitten sleeping on her lap. Dash blended in with her velvet skirt.

'I think the place looks cosier since you've lived here,' Rachel commented. 'Steve never did much. He went out and bought a bunch of expensive antiques and thought that was decorating!'

Anni laughed, mainly because that was exactly what she had suspected. 'Is that what he really did?'

'That's what he really did,' Rachel confirmed with a smile.

'That's probably all he had time for. He's always working,' Geraldine said wryly.

'Aren't they all?' Sandy said. 'If you need any guidance on how to live with a lawyer, Anni, ask me. I've been through it all. I know how lawyers think.'

'Because you're a lawyer yourself,' Anni quipped.

'I suppose that helps, but Alf and I have had some pretty tense moments over our chosen careers. I wasn't around for him much when we first got married. I know that's probably happening between you and Steve.'

'I'm really busy,' Anni admitted, wondering if it was obvious she and Steve were at odds with one another. It must be. Otherwise why would Sandy mention the subject? Or maybe Alf had said something?' Steve might even have confided in his cousin. She tried to sound casual, as if it were only a temporary problem and their entire marriage didn't hinge on it. 'And, naturally, Steve's workload has increased since his partnership.'

'Exactly. Even though his partnership was supposed to equalize the work more. Alf and I eventually decided to make dates to see each other. We'd meet on a Friday evening and go out to dinner or something.'

'I don't have many free evenings coming up.'

'That is a problem, I agree. Meet for breakfast maybe. Or lunch? You have to eat.'

'Possibly,' Anni agreed.

Rachel said. 'Ben was never around for the children at first. We had to work at it. But I was at least home. And who can go for dates when you have kids?'

'Very true,' Geraldine said. 'However, I did have to slow Paul down so he would actually get to know his children. We have a friend who never spent any time with his kids when they were young. All of a sudden he was paying for them to go through university and then they left home. The realization was a slap in the face to him.'

Anni sipped her wine and admitted to herself that a balance always had to be struck. They probably weren't the first couple to have marital adjustment problems. Overhearing that she might be second best for Steve was probably a microscopic blip in a much larger spectrum of problems they would encounter. Compromise was likely the answer, but Anni knew she wouldn't have any time to even consider how to go about that or discuss it with Steve until after the second run ended. At that point she was definitely going to have to stop and take stock.

The second opening night quickly approached. Anni made sure all her family had tickets, including Jason and Jack. For Jack Martin, Anni was a heroine and she had to take him backstage and introduce him to all the dancers and show him how a theatre worked. Interacting with Jack made Anni realize how well she got along with children and she began to long for some of her own once more. But somehow this deep-rooted dissatisfaction fed her art and her dancing became more dazzling than ever.

Ray was excited. With Moe and Anni, he had a hit on his hands. Even before the show opened once more the tickets were sold out until the end of January, and the run then extended until the end of March. Anni and the cast of *Wedding Bells* danced a preview for charity and became media darlings. Anni was called for newspaper, radio and television interviews either with Moe or alone. A TV station came to the theatre and followed them around for a week for a behind-the-scenes documentary which would be aired in January. Anni had never been so busy. She felt that this part of her life was wonderful, and the other part was falling apart. If she did indeed have time to think.

Steve was often greeted by pre-folded newspapers

in his office with Anni's face staring up at him. This morning it was Anni and Moe together. Knowing it was only a fit of jealousy, he tossed the paper into the blue recycle bin anyway.

Although the family and partners' dinner parties had been wildly successful, and now everyone thought Anni was wonderful, he wasn't satisfied. He slept badly, his nights often full of dreadful violent dreams that had no relationship whatsoever to his life. He was also building up a charge of sexual energy. He wanted Anni, yet he dared not wake her up from her sound, exhausted sleeps. She was dancing matinees and evening previews. She was the star of an extravaganza show this Christmas and needed that sleep. He also couldn't bear it if she turned him down. Yet he knew he had to see her more than he did. Otherwise they were headed for separate rooms and that had to be his worst nightmare.

By lunchtime he had pulled the paper from the recycle bin, read the article, clipped it, and placed it in his drawer with all the other articles. He knew she kept big scrapbooks which were updated in occasional bursts of energy.

He had to see her.

Barely even thinking, he grabbed his coat, went downstairs and out through the swing doors into the crisp winter air. Christmas shoppers crushed around him on the sidewalk. For an instant Steve found himself drawn into the intense crowd as they rushed, glazed of eye, on to the next store, the next purchase. He struggled free from the milling shoppers and headed for the Empire Theatre.

CHAPTER 17

Steve felt much the same as he had the first day he'd gone to Ray's studio to see Anni. Except that July day had been hot and humid. Today the sky was silver, the air crisp with the promised snow. He walked into the theatre to find Anni and Moe rehearsing one of their duets. Ray was watching; so was Lucinda.

Steve took a seat on the end of a row to watch. Moe and Anni were a man and woman enraptured with one another, dancing a primitive mating ritual, two beautiful bodies ebbing and flowing back and forth. Moe never touched Anni but he might as well have embraced her. Anni never touched Moe but she seemed to eat him with her eyes with her portrayal of her feelings for him. Some of this was new to him. Ray had changed their dances slightly. Now they were even more erotic, more enticing for the audience.

Rachel had taken the boys to the charity performance and Steve wondered if it were appropriate for them to see their aunt dancing such sexual scenes. He had to dismiss this attitude as

312

being prudish. After all, Anni was sexy even when she was serving dinner. He knew the boys adored her already. They'd see nothing more on stage than they probably already fantasized about. He knew Anni had taken Jack backstage. Jack hadn't stopped talking about the experience. Maybe there was a dancer or actor in the making in Jack. Who knew?

It was himself he had to worry about, Steve thought, as he felt sickness rising in his gut. He wasn't able to accept Anni's dancing. And yet he knew he'd have to face it for the rest of his life. What had he thought would happen when they married? Had he thought all these strange jealousies and obsessions would leave him? Of course he hadn't bargained on Rachel and her big mouth. Why hadn't he told Anni about Lydia? He could shoot himself for that stupid omission.

He cleared his throat on the bad taste of his thoughts. He wanted to creep away and return when the dancers were separate again. But he knew that Ray had seen him and he knew Ray was perceptive enough to realize why if Steve left so abruptly. So he stayed, forcing himself to be objective as he watched the pounding climax of the dance. It's Selena and Saul, his informed mind told him. Not Anni and Moe. But that didn't help. It *was* Anni and Moe and he knew how emotionally Anni entered into her dance pieces. He also knew how emotionally she made love and he became immediately hard and needed her desperately.

The music died, silence reigned for a few seconds, then Ray spoke. 'Great. Thanks. Both of you. Get some rest during the next couple of days and then we're on.'

Steve saw Anni glow. She glanced at Moe, who gave her a triumphant smile and raised her hand clasped in his. Ray's praise was praise indeed for both of them; Steve knew that as he let out a huge breath.

Ray and Lucinda came by to speak to Steve. Anni had mentioned that the couple had married and as it was the first time he'd seen them since he congratulated them. By this time Anni had disappeared but he knew she would be in her dressing room.

He walked along the narrow corridor, wondering if she'd seen him in the audience. He didn't know what she could see from the stage. She told him she tried not to think about the audience. She knew how to turn her mind off. He wished he'd learned to do the same. Or maybe he had once but not any more. Not while he was living amid such discontent. Not since he'd met Anni. Yes. That had been the turning point in his contentment: Ray's party. He'd looked across the lawn, seen the captivating creature in ivory silk and the flowing silvery, very unusual-coloured hair, and he hadn't been satisfied mentally or physically since.

He knocked and walked into her dressing room just as she was saying, 'Wait a minute.'

He saw why she wanted him to wait. She had already stripped her practice gear. She stood naked, about to put on a pink terry robe. She grasped the robe to her throat so that it hung down her body and partly covered her. 'Steve,

314

you frightened me. I saw you in the auditorium but I wasn't sure if you were going to come along to see me.'

'You should lock the door, Anni.'

'I thought I had. Sorry.'

'Anyway, I needed to see you.' And he certainly was seeing her. Her hair was piled on her head with a clip and lay in glinting wisps against her swan-like neck. Her naked limbs were pale against her pink robe that now covered even less of her. He felt the returned heat of arousal burn in his veins. His breathing quickened and he was the one who reached back and locked the door.

'Nothing's wrong, is it?'

She probably meant with their families. 'No. Nothing's wrong.' Except everything was wrong. But he was going to make it right.

'Well, then, I'll just take my shower. You can wait if you want.'

Steve wanted to show her that he loved her. That everything she had heard was lies, that this relationship was now becoming a lie. They weren't meant to be this way with each other. They were destined for happiness.

He followed her and reached out to place his hand on her shoulder. He felt her body stiffen but she twisted around and raised her face. He could see by the expression in her dark eyes that she wanted what he wanted, and he pressed his hand firmly around the back of her neck and his mouth sought hers desperately.

Anni tried not to submit but the desire for Steve to love her had been kept in check too long. The

315

feel of his mouth on hers, the stroke of his hands down her hips and thighs, made the robe tumble to the floor and she wrapped her arms around his neck to let his kisses take her beyond herself. For a moment he let her go and removed his coat and jacket, and by that time Anni had his belt unbuckled and she was stroking him into rigid arousal.

Steve tugged Anni around him, her legs supported by his hips, and he was soon inside her, his breath and the beat of his blood pounding in his ears. Only the wall supported them as they drove each other to wild satisfaction.

'Oh,' Anni whispered, crumbling into his arms. He stroked her damp hot body and kept her close to him. This was his wildest fantasy with Anni. A recurring dream generated by her dancing.

'I'll wreck your suit,' she whispered, still holding him around the neck.

'To hell with my suit,' he muttered hoarsely, feeling her sweet breath on his skin, and he tightened his grip on her and began a slow thrusting movement.

'Again?' she said softly, but she began to respond, clinging to him as if her life depended on him.

After a moment of delicious ecstasy he carried her to the sofa and lay her down. He quickly undressed and lay down with her. She cuddled up to him, stroking his hair, and when he joined with her she was moist and eager once again. This time their climax was aching, and so sweet. By the time Anni slipped from Steve's arms to go for her shower he felt something profound had passed between them. Hopefully something to change their relationship and make it more harmonious.

He washed at the basin and was fully dressed when she came out of the shower. He watched her slip into black silk undies and then pull on a black wool skirt, long white sweater, and high black leather boots. She blow-dried her hair quickly, using her brush. From a fluff of hair and blast of air she glanced at him. 'Why did you really come?'

'Because I was inside you,' he said with a grin, trying to loosen the tension. He wasn't satisfied with one explosive orgasm or with a slow, aching one. He wanted her again. All night. All day. Like their honeymoon. He wanted her wound around him to warm his mornings, not flying off into the cold dawn.

She made a face. 'Not that come, silly. Why come here to the theatre if there's nothing wrong?'

'Can't I visit you?' He heard himself becoming defensive again. He'd thought everything would be all right by making love with her but it wasn't. All they'd done was release tension in another area.

'I suppose. But I'd appreciate some warning in future maybe.'

'Why? Because that might not have been me making love to you after your dance? What you gave me was for him, wasn't it? That's why you left your door open.' By the time he'd finished, Steve didn't know why he'd spoken those words. But in his mind he saw the newspaper article. Moe and Anni's photo on the front page. They looked so right together. Both dancers, both understanding one another's moods and emotions. He didn't bother to remind himself that Moe had a beautiful wife and baby. And now he could see that his accusations had annoyed Anni. Maybe even hurt her. He hadn't meant to do that.

Anni tossed her hairbrush into her open athletic bag and turned to look at him, her eyes blazing so that they appeared purple. 'Who is "him"?'

Steve felt like a fool now. 'Moe Ellison.'

She rolled her eyes. 'That's not true, Steve. Not true at all. It's your imagination and that's fine because that's exactly what Moe and I want to portray on stage.' She strode to the door to take her black leather jacket from the hook. She shrugged it on, stuffed the rest of her gear into her bag and shouldered the strap. 'And you're a fine one to talk. What about Lydia? I haven't come to a satisfactory conclusion about her yet.'

'I've told you the truth,' he said. 'But I believe this is about much more than Lydia or Moe. It's about us and our disinclination to face up to what we may have or may not have together.' He felt he'd made a step to correcting something deadly wrong between them.

She pulled on a pair of leather gloves. 'I don't have time for this now, Steve. I have an opening night on Saturday. So please, we'll have to wait for a while before we dissect our problems.'

'You warned me about this, didn't you?' he said with an almost fatalistic feeling inside him.

'I did.' She turned away from him, brushing back her hair. 'Now, I was going to have something to eat.'

'I'll go with you. I sort of had that in mind.'
Nothing of the sort. What he'd had in mind was
exactly what had transpired. Release from his sexual
hunger. But he'd also hoped that the sex would bring
them together. All it seemed to do was illuminate
their predicaments even more. His profound feeling
must have been a fleeting post-sexual euphoria.
They needed a spiritual closeness as well as physical, which wasn't to be found over a rushed lunch.

Anni took him to Veggie Things, where they
were forced to join Moe and Janine and their little
boy, whose name was Craddock.

As Steve ate a tasty vegetable dish and pasta he
noticed that the entire focus was on Crad. Anni sat
the little boy on her knee and gave him some of her
sourdough bread. She was absolutely enthralled
with the child. As she had been the day of Janet's
barbecue with the baby. And she was so patient
with Jack. All this made Steve realize how much
Anni loved children and how well she treated them
so they loved her in return.

When the women had to take Crad to the washroom, Moe said to Steve, 'I think you'll be starting a
family soon, the way Anni is reacting to Crad.'

Steve glanced at the man. He had love shining in
his eyes for his small son. Or was it admiration of
Anni? No. Moe loved Janine. All it was on stage
was two people acting. Get that through your
skull, Hunter. 'I hope so,' Steve said, and he
really meant it. He wanted to be in a situation
that bound him close to Anni.

The women returned, fussing with Crad who
seemed cranky now.

319

'Come on, baby,' Anni said to the little boy. 'Why don't I take him outside for a while? I'm not very hungry. You guys finish up.'

'If it's okay with Steve,' Janine said, looking flustered. Her usually pale cheeks were flushed.

'Fine,' Steve said, and nodded to Anni, who crouched down to help Crad into his snowsuit. Knowing he was going out, the child began to cheer up.

Anni got into her own jacket. 'Bring my bag, Steve?'

'Yep,' he told her. 'Have fun.'

'We'll go across to the park. Come on, Crad.'

Janine sat down again and drank some of her coffee. 'I'm so pleased Anni can help. I'm pregnant again and I'm having a hard time coping.'

Moe put his hand on top of his wife's. 'Relax. Anni loves to play with the boy.'

Janine nodded. 'She's so suited for motherhood. I can see inside she's longing for a baby.'

'You think?' Steve said.

'I don't have to think,' Janine said. 'I know.'

After finishing their lunch, Steve decided to foot the bill, and then they all went outside to find Anni and Crad. The two were across the street at the little park having a walk.

'Mummy,' Crad yelled when he saw his mother. 'Daddy.'

'His two words,' Moe said, scooping up his son into his arms. 'Ready to go home, big boy?'

'He should be tired,' Anni said, standing close to Steve. 'Did you bring my bag?'

'Yep. I'll carry it to your car.'

320

'All right. I was going right home anyway.'

They said goodbye to the Ellison family and Steve walked with her to the parking lot where her red car sat. He put the bag in the trunk for her, reminding himself of the first night when he put her luggage in the back of his car.

'He's a cute kid,' he said as Anni tucked herself into the driver's seat.

'He's getting so big and he's so interested in everything, even a blade of grass,' Anni said with a soft smile.

'He's neat,' Steve held her door. 'So you're going home?'

'Yes. I'm going to relax for two days.'

'Okay. I'm going back to the office. Drop me back there?'

'Sure. Hop in.'

After letting Steve out at the kerb outside his office block, Anni drove home, planning on having a long slow soak in a bubble bath. She would make sure these next two days were restful. She still felt the pressure of Steve's body making love with her. Physically she felt fulfilled but mentally she felt as if her mind wouldn't stop spinning. What were they going to do about their marriage? It wasn't a question Anni felt up to answering at this moment. Especially after her little sojourn with Craddock Ellison. What a cute little boy. She would love to have a child like Moe and Janine's, but she didn't think it would happen now. Not with Steve anyway, and she couldn't even imagine bearing any other man's child.

At home Dash had thrown up a hairball on the front rug. She cleaned up and then was amazed at the way he began to play again, as if he hadn't been sick.

'You little terror,' she told him lovingly. 'Come up and watch me have my bath.'

Dash liked to sit on the rim of the marble tub but he was frightened of the bubbles. After fear grew too much for him, he hopped off and left her. Anni soaked until the water grew cold, then tucked herself beneath the quilt on the bed. If she could sleep for a while she might come up with a solution as to what to do about her relationship with Steve. He was right in one respect. This didn't really have much to do with Lydia, or any of Steve's jealous reactions to the men on the periphery of her life. It was something else. Anni suspected it was because neither of them knew how to correct what had become a mess.

Another opening night. Parents, family, workmates all showed up to make a party. This time Steve had a backstage pass to see Anni. When he got to her dressing room he found she had company. Ray, Lucinda, Moe, Janine, and Joni and Charles. The roses he had sent her were centre stage on her make-up dresser, his card beside them. Steve went over to Anni and kissed her mouth. Unsure whether she was acting for her friends and colleagues or not, he let Anni wrap one arm around his neck and hold the kiss a little longer. 'Thank you for the roses,' she whispered. Then aloud, 'We're all going to a hotel to party. All right?'

'All right with me,' he said, her kiss burning his mouth and a lingering longing branding his gut.

He helped her with her leather jacket and watched her slip into her high boots. He always found her so tall and graceful, so wonderful on stage, so wonderful in bed as his wife. He wanted her so badly that he wished everyone would leave so he could make long, slow love with her on the sofa as they had – was it only a couple of days ago? But this time they wouldn't get up and leave afterwards. They would talk and reach some sort of consensus. But he couldn't see that happening in the near future, if ever. And he drove Anni to the party feeling as if someone had trapped him in a cage.

The party was an added festive affair with Christmas decorations all over the hotel. Luckily with Charles and Joni there Steve didn't feel as if he was hanging on to Anni all evening and he was able to put on a semblance of enjoying himself. He could see Anni was holding herself on reserve emotions. At times, to him at least, she appeared brittle, as if she might snap. They were both so unhappy that his heart broke for them both.

Anni slept beside him in the car on the way home through soft crystalline snow. Their first Christmas together should be joyous, Steve thought.

He helped her out of the car to go into the house and she didn't seem to mind that he put his arm around her. He even helped her take off her outdoor clothes.

Then she forced a smile and brushed her fingers through her hair. 'Thank you. I'm really tired. I'm going up to bed.'

Steve let her go.

Christmas came and went, with Anni appearing when she had a moment. Christmas dinner at his parents' house was cooked around her hours. Sometimes Steve drove Anni to the theatre or picked her up. Other times he drove Marian Ross back and forth and spent the rest of the time at his parents' home. He took Jason and Jack sledding after a Boxing Day snowfall and he realized how much he wanted a family. He yearned for a family. He wanted himself, Anni, Dash, his kids . . . a unit. Or was he being too fanciful? Maybe it didn't work that way any more. Some of his clients certainly didn't think so. Although he'd just had a couple who had divorced two years ago come into tell him they were remarrying. They'd been so excited, like young lovers, and yet they were well over fifty. So maybe there was something enduring to love.

Wedding Bells was fully booked now until the end of April. Ray's choreography was receiving rave reviews and his financial position was much improved. Steve continued going through the motions of pleasure in Anni's success, knowing he was proud of her but unable to actually show her how proud. She ran on high, on another level from him.

That day in her dressing room when they'd made love so passionately . . . who had that been for? Anni? Her male co-star? Nothing good had come out of that passionate coupling. They were still stiff and unsure with one another. Steve was now convinced by his own conclusion. It wasn't Lydia or any of that outside stuff. It was stuff inside Anni, inside Steve, stuff that they'd have to work out in time. He thought about all this as he worked late at the office and went home evenings to an empty house. If it weren't for Dash for company, he wouldn't have survived.

After Christmas the weather turned colder and the snow began to fall. When the weather was bad Anni stayed at her apartment, which was closer to the theatre. The only time Steve saw her was when he taped and watched the TV documentary *Ringing the Bells*, a behind-the-scenes look at *Wedding Bells*. He felt her disappearing from his world, even his house. A lot of her clothes were gone from the closet and returned to her apartment. He knew she exercised and practised there. Eventually she would shift her life back there and she'd be gone.

Anni made no moves to repair their breakdown, although he had to tell himself this was because she didn't have time. She'd warned him about this situation; he hadn't taken the warning. What he hated the most was that she didn't seem to care about him any more. Had she loved him? He wondered now if that had been the case. Had he rushed her into something she hadn't been ready for? Obviously he hadn't been ready himself. He didn't know how to deal with the situation as it careened out of control.

January was freezing cold and it snowed almost every day so the roads were icy. Anni didn't want to drive very much, so she used sunny clear mornings to return home to see Steve and Dash. She'd known it was going to be like this, with no time to spare when she worked, but she hadn't bargained on all the other problems between them to make it worse. It was better just to stay away and pretend nothing existed but her dancing and the dancing world. Then she wondered if she'd always lived her life that way. Maybe she had, especially after her father died. She hadn't been able to cope with her mother's grief and loneliness or her own, so she'd gone away, if not always physically, certainly spiritually. But this time she wanted to be braver. After the show she was definitely going to face Steve and their problems and hopefully come to some satisfactory conclusion. Even if it was divorce. They'd just have to put aside their pride and their families' disappointment in them both.

Making up her mind to do that seemed to make her more peaceful inside, even if frightened of the outcome after so many long weeks of strain. Her best times now seemed to be with Joni. With Joni she could return to a point in her life when she didn't have any emotional problems. Like the one looming now because she was two weeks overdue and worrying about the fact that she might have become pregnant the day in her dressing room, when Steve appeared and took her so suddenly. They'd made love twice and used no precautions. Not that she didn't want to become pregnant. She did. She'd be happy as anything if her marriage was secure. She might have to cut short her run with *Wedding Bells* but for a baby she would do that. Her life would be full circle, all her desires fulfilled.

Today Joni was waiting for Anni in Veggie Things. She patted her swollen stomach. 'Look at me.'

'It's strange to see you with a big stomach,' Anni said as they sat down. 'How are you?'

'Healthy as a pig.' Joni grinned as she slipped out of her thick leather coat and let it hang over the back of the chair. 'What about yourself?'

Anni took off her own jacket. 'I'm fine.'

Joni frowned. 'Just fine? I thought you'd be head over heels about the success of the show. Ray's getting so much publicity. The documentary was really good. You were great, especially when you danced that improvisation. I realized how great you were. It's wonderful. I'm really pleased.'

Anni fluffed her hair with her hands. 'All that's great, Joni. Moe is fantastic to dance with. He's so full of natural talent he sometimes makes me feel like a clod.'

Joni picked up the menu, even if she did know it by heart. 'That's not true. So how is Steve?'

'I don't see him as much as I should.' Anni couldn't be dishonest with her long-time friend. 'I warned him, Joni.'

'I'm sure you did. He's not happy about it, obviously. On opening night he looked very sad.'

'Did he?'

'Yes, he did. I could see things weren't the same between you two. Charles noticed it and that's saying something. Charles rarely notices stuff like that.'

Anni stared at her unopened menu. 'There are things I can't deal with until after this run. We need to sit down and talk.'

327

'What things?' Joni asked bluntly.

'Things like: he had a girlfriend when he met me that he never told me about.'

'He did?'

'Yep. And he's seen her since we met. According to his sister he even asked this woman to marry him but she turned him down. You know he had to be married to receive his promotion?'

Joni's eyes were wide now. 'What are you saying, Anni?'

'I'm not sure really. Steve says he didn't ask Lydia to marry him. I suppose I have to believe him. But he had to be married for his promotion and I was it, I suppose.'

'But he does love you?'

'He lusts after me, Joni.' And that was where Anni had got to in her thinking now. Steve was in lust for her entire persona. 'It might all be superficial. You know, because of what I am, what I do, how I look.'

'Has he told you this?'

'No. But it's a conclusion I've come to.'

'This other woman? He's not having an affair with her now?'

'I don't think so. I believe it was merely a business relationship. You know, they used one another for dates because neither one wanted a serious relationship.'

'You believe that kind of stuff?' Joni asked.

'With Steve, yes. He was really anti-marriage when I met him.'

'And you changed his mind, Anni. Don't you see how romantic that is?'

Anni wasn't impressed. Too much water under the bridge, she presumed. 'Well, there are other problems. We haven't got a solid base. We met, we married, we honeymooned, we came home and everything at home was the same as when we left it when we were single. We haven't sorted any of that out. And it was Steve's house. I haven't had a chance to change anything about it. I haven't even had a moment to put my condo on the market. And I've been back there a lot because it's handy for the theatre and Ray's studio, which is why I purchased it in the first place.'

'All you seem to need is a good talk between you,' Joni concluded. 'I like you guys as a couple so much.'

Suddenly thirsty, Anni picked up the water glass and sipped the iced water. 'Now there's something else,' she said. 'I might be pregnant. Only might. I've never been particularly regular because of my strenuous dancing. But since Steve I've been pretty regular, and I'm two weeks out right now.'

Joni smiled. 'Anni, you're telling me on one hand that you two are washed up and now you're saying you're going to have a baby.'

'Might be having a baby,' Anni corrected.

Joni reached across the table and touched her arm. 'Anni, I don't know what to suggest. Wait until after the run and then take a vacation with Steve. You'll have to force some decision, especially if there is a baby on the way. You'll want Steve, believe me. I couldn't do this –' she patted her stomach ' – without Charles. I don't know how those women who have children by themselves manage, emotionally or physically.'

'I don't either,' Anni admitted. 'I'm a firm believer in fathers. Anyway, it might be a false alarm.' Anni picked up the menu. 'Let's order, why not?'

'I thought you'd never get to it,' Joni said. 'I'm starved. I think I'm eating for an army. This kid is going to come out hungry and eat me out of house and home just like his father.'

Relieved to have the subject fully on Joni, Anni said with a smile, 'You know it's a boy?'

'Yes. We decided to find out. I didn't want to at first but then I did. Jonathan Charles.'

'You've already named him.'

'We'd argue for days and the child would be an *it* if we didn't,' Joni said chuckling.

'You argue with Charles?'

'Of course. He's a stubborn dominating prig.'

'And here's me thinking you had the perfect relationship,' Anni said with the first genuine laughter she'd experienced for weeks.

'We've had longer than you and Steve to figure things out. Give it time. Now let's eat otherwise I'll shrivel away.'

Two weeks later Charles phoned Steve early one morning. Joni had given birth to an eight-pound boy.

It was one of the nights Anni had spent at home. She had woken up to the sound of the phone, groggy from her late night.

Excited about the news, Steve didn't think about their awkward relationship. He relayed Charles's message.

'Wonderful! Great!' Anni leapt out of bed and

began rushing around. She disappeared into the walk-in closet. 'Can we go to the hospital, Steve?'

Steve walked to the closet door, holding a piece of paper. 'Sure we can go to the hospital. Charles gave me the information. I'll drive. It's pretty snowy.'

She poked her head through a grey wool turtleneck. 'If you would. I'll take flowers. I know where we can pick some up early in the morning.'

They bundled into warm clothes and into Steve's car that he had thoughtfully warmed up so it was toasty inside. Anni directed Steve to the corner variety store that sold huge bouquets of mixed flowers. She bought three bouquets and spent the rest of the journey fixing them into one.

'Sure you have enough flowers?' Steve asked, his hand on her back so she wouldn't slip on the icy driveway as they rushed through the driving snow into the hospital. 'What a terrible day. We'll always remember the day Jonathan Charles was born.' *But would they be together like this?*

Charles met them downstairs. He'd made special arrangements for them to be here at this time. The special arrangements had been made with a promise that the staff would get to meet one of the stars of *Wedding Bells* in the flesh.

'Thanks, Charles,' Anni said jovially as they went into Joni's private ward.

'It's not official visiting time,' Charles told her. 'So I bribed everyone. Joni's just finished feeding the baby.'

Plumped up on pillows, Joni looked radiant but tired, her new son in her arms.

'He's just finished feeding,' Joni said. 'Here's

331

your Uncle Steve and Aunty Anni, Jonathan. They're your godparents.'

Charles sat on the bed and took Joni's hand. 'Only five hours' labour but I feel as if I've been through it all.'

Joni squeezed his hand. 'You're a pet, Charles.'

Anni held Jonathan, who was wrapped in a white lace shawl Anni had given Joni. She immediately saw Charles and Joni in the puckered face. Joni's dark eyes, Charles's cheeky grin. Anni glanced at Steve, who was standing behind her, while Charles went for water for the flowers. Would part of both of them be in their child?

Steve touched the little guy's hand and the fingers clutched him. 'A baby suits you,' he said softly. 'I remember thinking that the day of Janet's party.'

A long time ago. Yet he remembered. Maybe there was hope for them somewhere in this muddle. Anni handed Jonathan back to his mother. 'He's gorgeous. Are we really godparents?'

'Definitely,' Charles said. 'But we'll have to be bestowed with the same offer.'

'I'll keep it in mind,' Anni teased, thinking that the honour might only be about seven months away. She had an appointment booked with the doctor at the end of the week.

Steve drove her downtown to the theatre before he went to work. In his pocket was a cigar from Charles which he would never smoke himself so he handed it to Ben, who liked the odd puff once in a while when Rachel wasn't around.

'Anni's friend Joni had a baby,' Steve said in

explanation, and then went to his office feeling dissatisfied. Charles now had what he wanted. The beginning of a family. He picked up his day timer book and checked the dates. *Wedding Bells* had a few more weeks to go yet and then he was going to arrange some vacation time with Anni. They had to scrape away the bad and begin again.

In the meantime life went on. Anni working. Steve working until he kind of lulled himself into believing that maybe his existence wasn't so bad after all. He spent a great deal of time with his partners at the club, discovering that he could have an evening meal there before he returned to the empty house. On those occasions Janet would drop by to feed Dash. In fact, he saw his younger sister more than he saw his wife.

One evening he was putting on his overcoat to leave the office when Craig Firth walked in.

'Going to the club?' Craig asked.

Steve nodded. 'They do good meals.'

'Doesn't your wife cook for you?'

'She's busy evenings.'

'Oh, yes, she's a star, isn't she?' Craig pushed his hands into his pockets. 'Handy, Steve. A marriage you don't have to nurture but you get what you want.'

Steve knew what Craig meant. And he'd actually thought the animosity over the promotion had been forgotten. Yet it was something he hadn't the energy to pursue. All he did was stand up and begin to gather papers in his briefcase.

'I needed that partnership, Steve. I have a wife and two kids, who both want more out of life than I can afford financially at the moment. A partnership would have sealed their livelihood.'

Steve looked at Craig. 'I'm sure you'll be up for the next one,' he said, thinking that Craig would definitely have to change his attitude.

'It might be too late.'

Steve clasped his briefcase and held it at his side. 'I'm not sure what you mean?'

'Marie isn't pleased I didn't get the partnership so I might lose everything.'

'That's not my fault, Craig.'

'It bloody well is. If you hadn't picked up with that dancer at the appropriate time, I would be in this office.'

'I didn't pick up with her, Craig. I met her and I was planning to marry her before I really knew marriage was part of the promotion deal. So you can tell that to your wife and anyone she cares to gossip to.'

Craig hadn't been expecting Steve's wrath, especially spoken with a steel-grey gaze upon him. 'I don't know what . . .'

'You bloody well do, to use your phrase. You know that Marie gossips and social-climbs. You wouldn't be in such a twist about the promotion if she wasn't that way. Craig. I'll see about a raise for you, okay? But you have to make sure you keep yourself under control. We can't have this tension in the office.'

Craig nodded. 'You're right about Marie. She wants so much. I would appreciate your word to the other partners, Steve.'

'All right. But I don't want to hear any more

about the idea that I married because of the promotion. I love, Anni. That's the only reason.'

Craig nodded. 'I know that you were first choice. They might have skipped the requirements anyway. At least, I was told that.'

'That's possible,' Steve said, although he wished Alf or Ben had mentioned that at the time. He might have given Anni her space to finish her show before they married.

'Anyway.' Craig shrugged his shoulders. 'Thanks.'

'Take it easy, Craig.'

The phone rang as Craig turned and left Steve's office.

Steve said, 'Roberts, Smithson, Martin and Hunter.'

'It's Ray Gifford, Steve. Could you come down and pick up Anni from the theatre? She won't be dancing tonight. Tanya, her understudy, will do the show.'

Ray hung up before Steve could get any details. His heart racing with fear that Anni was hurt, he grabbed overcoat, scarf and car keys, locked up behind him, and spent a freaked out moment pacing for the elevator. The early March night was below freezing, the snow like crystals falling from the sky. It might have been romantic if he wasn't trying to make time through left-over rush-hour downtown traffic. What had happened to Anni?

He eventually reached the theatre. Anni was waiting in the foyer with Janine Ellison.

Anni looked small and pale wrapped in her

oversized black wool coat and scarf. Nothing like the vibrant star of the current stage show.

Steve rushed to her and took hold of her ice-cold hands that she held up for him. 'What's wrong, Anni?'

Janine said, 'Nothing's wrong. She just needs a rest. She's pregnant, Steve.'

CHAPTER 18

Anni saw that Steve felt embarrassed in front of an accusing Janine. She knew he felt he should have known Anni was pregnant. If he'd been a normal husband, if she'd been a normal wife, he would have known. To save Janine discovering that all wasn't right between them, she touched Janine's arm. 'I only just found out for sure from the doctor myself,' she said softly. 'I haven't had a chance to tell Steve.' Which was completely true.

'All right,' Janine said, but she seemed sceptical as she passed Anni to Steve. 'Take her home and look after her.'

Anni took the support of Steve's arm as he walked with her to the car. She wasn't exactly ill but she'd become very dizzy on stage during a brief rehearsal. She had wanted to go on this evening but Ray wouldn't hear of it. Anni had expected to feel terribly disappointed, but in fact she felt relieved. Almost a sense of release.

'How long?' Steve asked, speaking for the first time and sounding loud in the silence made by the new snowfall in the city.

337

'Ten weeks,' Anni said. 'It was that time in the dressing room.'

'Naturally. It was the only time.'

Anni winced at his bitter tone and then wondered at his gentleness as he made sure she was comfortable in the front seat. She wasn't really sick, but she'd worn herself out during a time when she should have been taking more care physically and emotionally. What she really wanted to do was crawl into the comfort of Steve's arms and stay there. But he was already walking around the car and getting in his side. He slammed the door, checked his safety belt, his mirrors, started the engine. Every movement mechanical, but also typically Steve. He drove a car the way he navigated his boat. With safety in mind.

Steve paid for the parking and drove into the slushy street. The traffic was still choked up. They sat behind a line-up at a green light that should have been moving.

Anni saw Steve's hands grip the steering wheel.

'So I guess you're unhappy that your understudy is dancing tonight?' he said.

Anni slipped the scarf from around her neck and loosened her coat collar. 'I thought I would be but I'm not. The baby is the most important thing in my life now.' All true.

Steve gunned the engine and the rear of the car swerved in the snow. Anni tensed, noticing Steve's features were set tight.

'Careful, Steve. The baby.'

'I know what I'm doing,' he said moodily. 'The roads are slippery tonight, that's all. And what the hell have you been doing to help the baby? All that dancing can't be good for it. Didn't you know?'

'I had a feeling but I didn't know for certain until I got the results from the doctor. Now it's a fact, I'll be careful. But the doctor said dancing wasn't a problem. I have to exercise.'

He stopped for another red light. 'When did you go to the doctor?'

'Friday morning.'

'You never even told me you suspected anything?'

'I was going to come and tell you tomorrow morning.'

'Sure you were.'

'Believe me, Steve. I was. I have to get used to the idea myself. Although . . .' she touched her stomach as she'd done surreptitiously for the past few weeks '. . . it's what I want.'

'I can tell that. Everything else goes to hell because of your dancing. But a baby – hell, we're up for a baby, aren't we?'

Anni turned in her seat and observed his set profile. 'I don't quite get your drift.'

'My drift? We have barely spoken for weeks and she can't get what I'm saying.' He glanced at her and then returned his eyes to the road.

'Are you angry about the baby?'

'How can I be angry about a baby I created?'

At least he wasn't unhappy about the baby. Which meant to Anni that he would love the child. It must be Anni he was angry with. Anger caused by disappointment because she wasn't Lydia? Anni didn't even want to think about the evening of Steve's promotion when she had discovered Lydia existed, and that Steve had needed to be married to acquire the promotion. It was that evening when the gulf between them had truly been created.

They eventually reached home. Exhausted, more from the tense drive with Steve than anything else, Anni let Steve hang up her coat and take her boots. She went upstairs to their bedroom and into the bathroom. She turned on the taps in the big bathtub. It seemed strange to feel that someone else was dancing Selena tonight while she ran hot water into a bathtub. Strange also to think there was a potential person living inside her body.

Steve came in. He'd removed his suit jacket and tie and was rolling up his shirt-sleeves. 'Let me do that. Do you want bubbles?' He picked up a huge jar of bath crystals.

The jar came with a little spoon. Anni had received the bath crystals as a gift for Christmas but she hadn't been here to use them. It made her realize how much of a stranger she had become to this house. And Steve.

Anni left him to tend to her bath and slipped out of her clothes in the bedroom. Curiously she wasn't shy with Steve about her body, despite all the tension between them. Before she tied the cord of her flowered terry robe she glanced at her belly. It was still quite flat and muscular but she did notice a little thickening around her waist. A slight roundness. A baby. She had known in her heart but the confirmation made it real.

Steve watched Anni observe herself. He wanted to touch her stomach, to feel if there was a roundness, any indication of his child inside her. But he wasn't sure she would appreciate his doing so. He wasn't sure of anything any more. More than anything he wasn't sure about her love. Had she seen him solely as a vehicle for the baby she desired? He'd heard of women who just wanted a child and used men for the sex act only. After all, her dancing hadn't been tossed aside just like that for him. But for a baby she didn't seem to care that she had just lost a starring role to a mediocre dancer. He also remembered what she had said when he asked her to marry him. Her acceptance speech: *I do, Steve, want a family, and you are the only man I'd want that with.* After the agony of the past few months, during which he'd barely seen her and she'd barely seemed to care, he now wondered if Anni had married him because he'd been her chance for a child. Maybe her only chance, because she was thirty later this year and time was running out. And all this discord between them had nothing to do with Lydia or his promotion, but all to do with Anni wanting and waiting to get pregnant. And now she was. To hide his roiling emotions, he leaned over the bath and felt the water temperature. 'Your bath is ready,' he said.

Anni looked up and her eyes were sparkling for the first time for a long time, but he knew they weren't sparkling for him. They were sparkling for the life growing inside her. She had what she wanted. 'Thank you, Steve.'

'Thank you for giving you the baby,' he snapped, unable to stop himself.

A shadow dulled the sparkle. 'What?'

'You wanted a baby, didn't you? You've wanted

341

a baby for a long time. You've had some kind of absurd obsession about having a baby. I could sense it way back when you went out and bought all those baby things for Joni in the summer. Well, now you have one. I was convenient, wasn't I? Lucky I was able to provide the service.'

He saw Anni's face flush to deep red and he presumed it was guilt. But she said, her voice wavering with tears, 'You're not innocent in this, Steve Hunter. We've both got what we wanted. I was convenient for you for your promotion and now you've given me a baby. So we're even.'

She kept her eyes riveted to his. They were both breathing heavily. Steve didn't know where to go from there. She still believed the gossip she had heard and it made him angry and hurt enough to inflict violence, but not on Anni. Besides that, he hadn't physically hurt a person in his life. So he finally turned around and left the bedroom to roam moodily through the house while Anni took her bath.

Was she pleased he'd walked out of the room? Did she find him irritating in her life the way she'd intimated in the beginning that she might? He should have listened to her. She'd warned him that in the long run they wouldn't work. Her personality wasn't conditioned to keeping a marriage together. Neither was his, apparently. He should have listened to his common sense instead of his heart and what Rachel termed his *appendage*.

Rachel. She'd caused part of this problem, but mostly it was Anni. Anni had latched on to

Rachel's untruth and capitalized on it. Now she had her dancing and her baby. He wondered if she expected him to participate as a father for this child. They had a lot to talk about but they couldn't talk. They only argued with one another. They'd built a huge wall and it was going to take a long time to dislodge it brick by brick.

After staring out of the window for a long while Steve decided he couldn't remain inactive while their marriage dissolved. He should try to tear down the wall and reconstruct what they once had. He could begin in small ways by trying to show Anni that he loved her. He checked out the boxes containing her favourite teas and selected a blackberry flavour. He boiled the kettle, warmed the glass pot and the glass cup. Anni had a thing about drinking out of glass. Something to do with traces of lead found in pottery glazes. Now she was pregnant he was pleased she was so fussy about her diet and her habits. He definitely wanted a healthy child.

He placed some biscuits on a plate, put everything on a tray and walked upstairs. The door to their bedroom was still closed. He put the tray on a table in the hall and opened the door. Anni lay on the bed wearing a pink cotton nightshirt. Her skin looked flushed from the bath. She appeared much more healthy than she had earlier in the foyer of the Empire Theatre.

He picked up the tray and placed it on the bedside table.

'Anni.'

She turned her head and looked at him. Or right

through him? He wasn't sure.

'Tea,' he said.

She pulled herself up against the pillow and began to sort out her tea. She poured herself a cup and sniffed. 'My favourite, blackberry. Thank you, Steve.' She picked up her cup, cradled the warm glass, and sipped the steaming liquid.

Steve placed his hands into his pockets, much the same way as he would if he walked into Alf or Ben's office for a discussion. 'We can't postpone talking much longer, Anni,' he said.

'I know. Once I've made arrangements with Ray for Tanya to take over I'll be free. We can decide what we're going to do then.'

He frowned. 'You mean you're going back to dance?'

'Probably for a week or so. I told you the doctor says it's fine.'

'I don't think it's fine.'

'It won't be longer than a couple of weeks, Steve. It might not even be that long. I have to sort things out. I can't just leave the show stranded.'

He understood her commitment and dedication. He couldn't argue with a person who sat there before him knowing exactly what course of action she was going to take. She was stubborn when it came to her career. He'd known that from night one. She had her reasons. Reasonably he understood them. Unreasonably he wanted to tear all her reasons to shreds.

'All right. That's fine. When you're free, come and see me.' He sounded as if he were making arrangements with a client. But he couldn't think of anything else that needed to be said so he left Anni to finish her tea and sleep. He went to his study and sat over a pile of files full of letters and reports that needed writing. He dug out the tape recorder and began dictating, until eventually his mind became captured by his work.

Anni wanted to call after Steve as he left but she didn't have the energy. In the hot steamy water of her bath all her anger and despair had abated. Despite Steve calling her yearning for a child an absurd obsession, confirming her own deepest fears, she still had something precious inside her that she wasn't going to let go of. Something she wanted so badly she hurt. But she also wanted Steve. She wanted his love and the intimacy they had shared on their honeymoon. How long ago the cottage in Cornwall seemed now, how long ago the wild lovemaking in her dressing room that had made their child.

'The doctor said I could dance for a few more weeks, Ray.'

Ray rubbed the side of his face as if inspecting whether or not he had shaved today. 'I don't think that's practical. Tanya should take over immediately. The run is indefinite, with no end in sight before the summer, so she needs audience acceptance. The only problem I see, Anni, is that you are still under contract with me until June. This means you will be breaking that contract.'

'You make me sound as if I'll be doing something wrong.' At the time she had signed the contract, Anni suspected he'd wanted her for two years because that was about the time her seeds of restlessness had been sown.

'You did do something wrong. You didn't hold up your end of the bargain.' Ray had a snarl in his voice that made Anni realize Ray was angry with her. Very angry with her.

'I can't help getting pregnant, Ray.'

'Yes, you damn well can. You don't have to get pregnant. But you wanted this, Anni. You wanted a way out. I could see you looking around for that way out when we were in Europe last year. Then you met Steve, but he wasn't the way out, was he? No. You managed to juggle marriage and your work. But a baby is a way out. A baby changes you physically, it puts demands on you to care for it. It means you can leave me high and dry.'

Anni's face flushed hotly. She'd always known Ray hoarded a lot of hurt and pain but she'd never actually had his bitterness spill over to her. 'I'm not leaving you high and dry. I'm dancing for another couple of weeks, then Tanya will take over. I didn't expect the run to go this long. I thought I'd be finished by now. All I am is a commodity to you, aren't I? I'm making you money and that's all you care about.'

Ray's brilliant green eyes narrowed the way they always did when he didn't want his emotions to show through. 'That's not true. I've cultivated you because you're a great dancer. I don't like to see talent go to waste.'

Anni shook her head. 'I'm not going to waste. I've used a great number of valuable years of my

346

life. But I'll soon be thirty. I'm beginning to feel the aches and pains. I've tried not to admit it, but they're there. It is time to move on. I've seen it for a while and here's my chance. I appreciate everything that you've done for me. Your brilliant choreography, your patience, and the chance to go around the world with your company. I don't want to quit dancing, hell, it's the job I do for a living, but I'm ready to change in some way. I'm being honest, Ray. I'm admitting –' she felt tears clog her throat ' – admitting what I didn't want to admit to myself.'

Ray sighed, a signal that his anger was abating. 'I know. I guess what scares me is that I don't see anyone coming up to equal you. And I really care about the dance company, Anni. I know things have picked up now, but if it ever died . . .' He fumbled for his cigar in his shirt pocket and glanced at the object that was always his soother.

'Because of your leg,' she said softly. She was used to up-and-down emotions with Ray. Adding today's display, they'd run the gamut over the years.

'That's no reason.'

'Yes, it is, Ray. It's the reason you run us all ragged trying to prove something to yourself. I'm sorry I got pregnant so soon. But it happened. I wanted it to happen.' She told the truth. 'Not because I want to leave you –' half the truth ' – but because I need more in my life than dance for a change. You have Lucinda. You must understand?'

He put the cigar in his mouth and scoured the pockets of his tan leather jacket for his lighter.

'Dance has always been my ambition. I've had a wife and two children and they didn't give me what I needed. Dancing did. I know my injured knee ruined my chances to be a solo success, but I regained that with the choreography success.'

'What about Lucinda?' Anni said.

'I never expect anyone to supply my happiness, Anni. It's what I do myself that counts. But she is a solid supporter behind me. She understands.'

'I'm pleased, Ray.'

He located his gold engraved lighter but, responding to Anni's frown, didn't light the cigar. 'You have to realize, Anni, something maybe you never did, that Patty and I were both in the same business. We were competitive. There were ego problems years before the kids came. We tried but eventually we lost communication with one another.'

Communication was exactly what she'd lost with Steve. 'You never tried to talk?'

'Every time we met we fought like cat and dog. We were both miserable. Then I met Lucinda and my world became a better place. Sometimes the person you love isn't always the person you need to be with, Anni.'

Anni thought about this as she shrugged into her black leather jacket and slipped her bag strap over her shoulder. But she had no doubts. Steve was the person she loved and the person she needed to be with. 'I'll see you this evening,' she said to Ray.

'No, you won't,' he said,

Anni felt her stomach knot up. 'I'll be here. I'm fine now.'

'No. I told you. Tanya's going to take over now. What the hell, Anni. You're finished.'

Anni felt tears burn her eyes. 'That's not fair, Ray. I'm perfectly healthy.'

'You might be healthy but you're still pregnant. I can't have you collapsing on stage the way you did in rehearsal last night.'

'It won't happen again.'

'It might. It could. Anni, accept it, you're finished with me.'

Anni couldn't think of any more retorts and left Ray's office. Other than a visit to tie up her loose contractual ends, this might be the last time she walked out of his studio, she thought as she hurried to her car. She drove home barely noticing her surroundings. She had what she really wanted, didn't she? She had a baby growing inside her. What did it matter that Ray and Steve had both discarded her? She was only home a few minutes when Steve phoned from the office.

'What are you doing home?' he asked.

'Oh, I'm not dancing tonight.'

'Not feeling well?'

Anni heard concern in his voice. For the baby. Not for her. 'That's it. I decided it was a risk. Tanya's dancing.'

'At least you know your limits,' Steve remarked. 'I called to leave a message to say I was meeting a client at the club and will be eating there.'

'Okay, fine,' Anni told him. 'See you later.'

Anni couldn't stay in the house alone. As she hadn't told her mother about the baby, Anni decided to go and see Marian. After a phone call she got herself invited for supper.

Marian was delighted to hear the news and fussed with her daughter. She gave Anni a healthy menu list, food which Anni ate anyway to keep healthy for dancing, but she tucked the menu in her bag and kissed her mother to thank her. There was one thing, however, something that hung around her mind, frightened her, gave her doubts. 'You know you told me you couldn't have another baby . . . was it because of something genetic?'

Marian looked slightly startled by the question.

Anni continued, 'I'd just like to know if there's anything wrong that I have to watch for.'

'I don't think so, Ann. You were a perfect birth. I was in an accident and had some internal injuries.'

Anni had never heard this. But she was aware that her mother told stories in bits and pieces. Eventually the bits and pieces made a whole, even if the last bit was told a few years later. Anni had the feeling Marian might go to her grave with pieces of stories untold. But she wanted all the facts of this story. 'What type of accident?'

Marian made a comical face. 'I've never told you this, but I loved horses. I rode a lot before I met your father. I quit when I married him and we had you, then one day someone asked me if I'd like to ride again and I did. I began doing it secretly. I didn't think your father would like it. He always said it was a dangerous sport and it made him worry. Anyway, he found out because a horse threw me and I was quite badly injured and he had to come to the hospital to fetch me. I recovered but it put an end to having any more children. I think it's also a factor in my arthritis.'

'Why didn't you ever tell me this, Mother?'

'I don't know. We never really talked like this before, did we? You were always so busy.'

'I'm busy now, Mom.'

'I know, but you've changed. You see yourself differently. Steve's helped. And besides, you're going to be a mother yourself.'

Anni hugged that thrill to herself and she didn't add anything about Steve. She didn't want her mother to know there were problems between them, especially with the baby coming.

She went home after visiting her mother to an empty house and went to bed alone. This wasn't how she had envisaged her marriage to Steve but it might have to do. She couldn't bear the thought of having their failure exposed to their families.

CHAPTER 19

Anni came downstairs in the morning to find Steve already in his suit. 'You came home late,' she commented neutrally, tying the belt of her robe firmly around her waist.

He kept his attention on the coffee dripping into the glass carafe. 'I crashed on the sofa in the family room. I didn't want to disturb you.'

'Oh.' Anni heard her voice sound like a sob. 'That's fine. I'm not dancing any more, by the way. Ray's finished with me. I just have some contractual business to attend with and I'm outta the Gifford Dance Company.'

He looked at her then and she saw his features were taut with strain. His eyes seemed blank. 'Are you pleased with that arrangement?'

'I would have liked to continue for another couple of weeks,' she said honestly, 'but that's fine. The baby is my first consideration.'

'Of course.' The coffee finished dripping and he poured himself a mug, drank some of it briskly, then went to the front door where his briefcase and coat were already awaiting his departure.

Hugging her arms around herself, Anni watched his car leave the driveway. Feeling at a loose end, she went upstairs to dress in leggings and a sweater. What did women who stayed home do all day? She cleaned up the kitchen, then decided she would choose the room she wanted to use as a nursery. She would decorate the brightest room with baby wallpaper and special furniture. It would have to be the room next door to hers. She might even have the baby sleep in the same room. She might not be able to bear its absence.

Anni stopped herself in the big square foyer, wondering what she was considering. She might not even be here to do any decorating or make changes to the house. She might be back in her apartment, where she had been most of the winter, and have to bring up her child there.

The phone rang and it was Diane, saying that Steve had called to tell the family about the baby and she was delighted. She was going to bring Anni's mother over that afternoon and they would take Anni shopping. Anni really wasn't in the mood to face both mothers and have to act happy, but she didn't have much choice but to go along with their enthusiasm. Each mother wanted to buy Anni a smart maternity outfit. They bent to Anni's taste. One pair of black leggings and a thigh-length pale ivory sweater, and one long-skirted full dress in navy blue covered with flowers of all different colours of blue. When they arrived home, Anni invited the mothers to dinner. Steve usually didn't come home anyway.

* * *

353

Steve parked beside his mother's white Cadillac in the driveway of his house. He'd had a difficult day at the office and he really didn't feel like facing his mother and pretending everything was fine with himself and Anni. In fact, he was getting pretty weary of the entire situation. Anni wasn't dancing any more. Her time was free. It was time to make changes even if they weren't to his liking.

He sat for a second in his car, exhaled a huge breath, got out, grabbed his briefcase from the trunk and walked into his house. Marian was also there and all three women were in the kitchen preparing a meal.

Anni, wearing a pair of black leggings and white sweater with her hair knotted upon her head, glanced at him. He thought she appeared pale and a little startled to see him. Had she expected him to stay at the club again?

His mother said gaily, 'Hi, Steve. We've taken over your wife for the afternoon.'

Thinking, no one could take over his wife, Anni had her own agenda, he forced a smile. 'That's fine.'

Steve felt a desperate need to walk over to Anni and kiss her soft lips but he couldn't make himself do it. There was far too big a gulf between them.

'Dinner's ready,' Anni said. 'The moms are staying.'

He said abruptly, 'Good.'

'The table is all set in the dining room,' Marian told him.

'Then I'll stay a while.' He returned to the hallway to discard his coat. He dumped his briefcase on his desk in the study but didn't stay there. It was probably the first evening for weeks that he wouldn't bury himself in his study. He saw now that by doing this he had a ploy to avoid facing reality. He was going to have to face it to save three lives from misery, whether he liked the outcome or not.

Luckily with the mothers present Steve was able to be pretty natural with Anni, and after the two older women had driven away in Diane's car, he helped her clear the dining room and stash the dishes in the dishwasher.

She said as she handed him a plate, 'My mother loves driving around in your mother's Cadillac.'

He placed the plate in a rack. 'I bet. But they seem to like one another as well.'

'They really get along. That's good.'

He wanted to say more but they'd said a lot of it before and it hadn't got them anywhere. So where did he start? He was going to have to think this out before leaping in. Although he saw his hesitation as fear. He didn't want to know what might happen when they made their final decision.

Instead he mentioned what he was supposed to have mentioned earlier. 'Rachel and Ben have invited us to dinner on Saturday evening. Now you have a Saturday evening.' He didn't want the last comment to sound sarcastic but he thought it did.

Anni, reaching up to put a glass away in a cupboard, made a face. 'Do we have to?'

He let his gaze follow her long slim dancer's legs and thought he noticed a slight thickening around her waist. His child. It was difficult to believe. He'd been through the children bit with Rachel and Ben and never thought it might happen to him. In those days it was the last thing he'd ever wanted to happen. Although he loved his two nephews. Life, it seemed, was full of contradictions. 'Yes, we have to,' he said, 'if we're to keep up the façade.' He sounded hoarse and had to clear his throat. 'We haven't been to Rachel and Ben's yet,' he added. 'He is my partner, after all, as well as my brother-in-law, and Rachel is your sister-in-law.'

She slammed the cupboard door. 'Of course, we can't forget about your position in the law practice, can we?'

He'd actually thought she had relaxed slightly. Anni was a great actor. Her blue eyes blazed purple now. She held in her anger well. He had to commend her for it.

He said, 'It's nothing to do with that. And what the hell, Anni? Now you haven't got your career, we depend on my money.'

'That's not true. I have plenty of savings and more coming from the rest of my contract. Ray owes me a percentage of the take. And the take was excellent, believe me. I'll probably get a cheque soon. And if you don't like supporting me, then I'll go into partnership with Joni as soon as possible. I can also sell my condo and move somewhere cheaper. I have loads of possibilities. I can support my baby.'

Steve felt his throat close up. 'It's *our* baby, Anni.'

'I know who the father is. But it's my body that will be out of shape. In a few months I might not be physically able to cope. I have to plan. I'll have someone else to look after.'

Her comments made him feel not angry, but futile, as if he weren't needed. He said, to stake his claim, 'Me too. I want to help.' He meant more than help but he saw that she took his comment the wrong way.

Anni turned away from him and busied herself with kitchen work. 'Then we have to work something out, Steve. But not tonight. I'm tired.'

Steve went to his study. But he didn't open the clasps of his briefcase. Instead, he stood with his hands in his pockets, staring at a group of early purple crocuses beneath a tree illuminated by an outside lamp. He didn't think. He couldn't think. Thinking made the unthinkable inevitable.

The dinner party with Rachel and Ben was unavoidable. Anni stood at the double door with Steve beside her. The house was huge and stood on a two-acre lot.

'How long have they lived in this house?' she whispered to Steve, shoving her hands into the pockets of her leather jacket which she wore over her new blue dress. Everything she'd worn for the past week or so seemed tight. This new dress was comfortable. She wished being with Steve were just as comfortable.

'About two years. Rachel sees it as moving up.'

'It is really big and it's a beautiful lot. All those trees. Did Ben build it?'

Steve kept his hands stuffed in his jacket pockets. 'No. He hired a builder. Ben's loaded. As well as having made a bundle himself, his dad owns a company that launched some computer software programs that took off.'

'Rachel married well,' Anni commented.

'That was her purpose in life. Getting Barbie married to the right Ken.'

Anni thought that might be a joke but there was no twinkle in his eyes, none of the old magic she'd experienced that night in Ray's garden in the misty musky heat when she had fallen so deeply in love with this man. She knew it all now. Knew every move that had brought her this far. She already loved her baby as passionately as she loved the father. Except he didn't seem to love her any more now his promotion was secure.

Steve rang the bell again and Rachel opened the door wearing a suitable *at home* jumpsuit of purple silk that Anni thought looked wonderful with her black hair.

Rachel ushered them inside. 'I thought Ben was getting the door. Come on in. It's still cool, isn't it? We'll get spring one day, I suppose.' She took their jackets.

Rachel hung up Steve's jacket with Anni's. 'How are you feeling, Anni?'

'Fine. If you mean the baby.' She wasn't sure why she added the last remark.

Rachel gave her a raised-eyebrow look. 'Yes. I mean the baby. Are you going to find out the sex?'

'No,' Anni said. 'I want a surprise.'

'Then you'll have to have two names handy. I longed for Jacqueline but Jack arrived.'

'Does Jack know that story?'

'Yes. We all have a giggle about it once in a while. Come on, Ben's down in the family room. He built a real log fire to take the chill off. The kids aren't here, they've gone to Gran Martin's for the weekend. You're definitely showing, Anni.'

Anni patted her slightly swollen belly. 'A little bit. I know it's there.'

The first time Anni had met Rachel at the barbecue she wouldn't have anticipated ever having a conversation like this with Steve's older sister.

Anni looked around as they followed Rachel to the family room. The rooms were well lit by arched windows gazing out over the treed lot and landscaped garden. The family room was cosy with Ben's blazing fire in the stone fireplace. For the first time Anni saw him out of a dress suit and braces. He wore jeans and a royal blue Toronto Blue Jays sweatshirt, looking like a man a woman could fall in love with.

'Hi, Anni,' he said warmly. 'How's it going?'

'Fine,' she told him, thinking she'd always be in awe of Ben Martin. Then she understood what all this easiness was about. She had become the right wife suddenly. She was pregnant and she wasn't dancing. At least she presumed that was why the Hunter family were suddenly completely on her side. Almost when it was too late, she mused sadly.

Rachel went to check on the meal and Ben to get the drinks. Anni had chosen orange juice.

While they were gone Anni perched on a footstool near the lovely heat with her skirt drawn down to her feet. Steve sat behind her, legs

stretched out and nudging her hipbone. She
longed to touch him but instead she turned to
appraise him. He wore jeans with a thick knit
cream sweater Anni had given him last Christmas.
His dark gold hair seemed longer again and
touched his neck. His skin was smooth, except
for a faint line of late-day stubble around his chin.
He often put off shaving closely on the weekend
just to relax and leave his routine. Anni had been
avoiding observing him at close quarters lately
and knew why in that moment. Each time she
looked at him, each time she was with him, she
fell in love with him again. She remembered the
first night when his masculine square jaw had
jumped with a fidgety nerve. She saw the nerve
flick now.

'Are you comfortable down there?' he asked.

She nodded. 'Yes. I'm fine. It's lovely and warm
by the fire.' She remembered another fire in
Cornwall and how she had loved him so completely when they first got married.

'I'm pleased you're taking so much care for the
baby,' he said.

'I wouldn't do anything to harm the little kid.
It's keeping me going.'

He shifted in the chair. 'In a way I couldn't.'

'It's different with us. Our love isn't so unconditional.' Anni spoke aloud things she had thought
about lately. 'When I had my father alive, his love
was unconditional. He loved me regardless. When
he died I lost that. My mother was never so
generous. Or at least never showed it in the
past. She expected more from me. I'm going to

try and be like my father with this child. And I hope the child's love is unconditional as well.'

'I'll have to be the same way with the baby,' he said.

'I'm aware of that.' She felt the tension like a taut wire between them. It was a pity they couldn't just capture what they had before without having to go through a post mortem, but she could see that would never happen. Damage had been done. Repairs needed to be made before they were up and running as a unit again. If ever.

On the way home in the car Steve said to Anni, 'They like you now.'

'Because I'm having a baby I've become respectable,' she said. 'That's the reason.'

'I don't believe that is the case, Anni. I believe they genuinely like you. Rachel isn't intentionally mean. She was likely just looking out for me.'

'Because I might not be the right woman for you. Well, that's true, isn't it? I wasn't. You took second choice.'

Steve ground his fingers around the steering wheel. 'That is not true. Lydia was lying. Don't you believe that?'

'I suppose,' she said, pushing her hair from her face. 'I don't know if I even care now.'

'Then what is going on between us?'

'I presume either we don't love one another and you married me for your partnership and I married you for the baby or we do love one another and we have to capture whatever it was that we had in the first place.'

'You speak as if you're detached.'

'I have to stay detached to stay sane. This isn't easy for me, Steve.'

'It's not damn easy for me either. I want us to take a vacation before the baby comes. I want us to spend an entire week talking this out, making decisions, whatever.'

'All right,' Anni said, knowing she sounded resigned. 'Make the arrangements, I'll be there.'

Before he decided where they would go for a week to hide away to talk, Steve first wanted his facts straight. He didn't want to bring the family into his affairs with Anni, but he knew he had to get something very clear, and Rachel was the answer. In the morning from the office he phoned his sister. 'I want to see you, Rach.'

'You saw me last night at dinner. Although I have to admit you were very quiet.'

'I want to see you alone.'

'All right. I'll put on the coffee-pot. It's a long time since my little brother wanted to ask my advice.'

'It's not exactly advice. It's a question. How about noon? I'll take a sandwich with that coffee and have my lunch with you.'

'Cool. See you, Steve.'

Steve hung up. He had to find out the exact truth. For the sake of his marriage, his child, his entire life. And then he had to make Anni believe him. Even if she didn't love him, he wanted her to know he loved her and his proposal had been honourable. He wanted honesty. If only for the sake of his child.

* * *

Anni walked through the doors of Ray's studio and felt strange, as if she had been gone a long time. Maybe she had. She'd performed most of her dancing at the Empire Theatre for the past few months. But still, she felt as if she didn't belong here any more. And she didn't. When she met Ray he would sign off her contract and she would be free of him. Was that what she wanted? Sort of. But cutting the chains was tough. A decade of her life snipped away. Another one beginning.

Two young women rehearsed in the rainbow room but Anni didn't recognize them. Joni kept in touch with Cassie and she'd heard Ray had had a few new dancers join the company. His successful run with *Wedding Bells* had enhanced his reputation. Mothers were eager to place their sons or daughters into his dance company. But Ray's requirements were stiff. Not many would make it.

Anni walked through to Ray's office and knocked on the open door.

He was sitting as his desk besieged with paperwork. Patty used to act as his secretary but Lucinda had her own full-time employment.

'Do you want a job as a part-time secretary?' Ray asked as Anni sat down opposite his desk and crossed her legs. She wore black leather ankle boots, thick socks and a long skirt. Over the top she wore a long sweater and her jacket. Beneath all that was her baby. She bubbled inside when she thought about the child.

'No, thank you,' Anni said. 'I'm going to have a full-time job as a mother in a few months. Plus I'm going in with Joni eventually.'

'I knew that would happen,' Ray said, sitting back in his chair.

His shirt-sleeves were rolled up. He looked strong of body but tired of mind. His face, Anni thought, was more lined than it had been last summer.

'You know you look good,' he said.

'Thanks.' She winced inwardly because she had been thinking the opposite about him. 'I've come to sever the ties.'

'Yep, I know.' Ray picked up a number of stapled sheets of paper. 'It states here, Anni, that your contract ends on June thirtieth, but if you terminate your contract before that date, or if the show or tour you are currently appearing in is extended beyond that date, which it is, then that date is no longer valid and your quitting date is the actual date you leave the company.'

Anni realized Ray had this thought out before she even arrived here. She frowned at him. 'What are you saying?'

'I'm saying, that's it, you're gone.'

'I know I'm gone. But I'm owed money.'

'No. You haven't fulfilled your contract.'

'I'm pregnant, Ray. I couldn't help that.'

'Yes. You could.'

Anni uncrossed her legs and stood up from the chair. No more time to be casual. Ray was doing something he'd done to a lot of dancers over the years by reneging on contractual arrangements. That was why Anni was here in person. You had to fight Ray all the way. When she'd first begun with him she had been malleable, not really wanting to fight, but she was older now, more insightful. He was looking for a loophole to squirm out of paying for her services and he thought he'd found one. 'I bet you scoured that damn contract backwards and forwards looking for that clause,' she said.

He sat forward in his chair and leaned on the desk. 'I always knew it was there. It's there for a reason. So. Bye, Anni. Have a good life.'

She placed her hands on her hips. 'I made you money, Ray. You're not doing half as good with Tanya.'

'That's what I mean. I'm losing now. The show will close in August and that will be it unless I can bring in another star to work with Moe. We're pressuring Janine. However, at this time, your contract is finished.'

'Look. I'm willing to forgo a certain percentage because I'm quitting a few months early, but I'm owed money from before now.'

Ray pushed back his chair and stood up as well. 'Anni, we've had a good run. Call it quits.'

'Like hell I will. I'm owed that money.' She picked up her bag from the floor by the chair she had been sitting on. 'I'll see you again, Ray.'

In court, she thought, as she drove through the city streets to her apartment. She still had her copy of the contract tucked away in a file there.

Steve leaned his hips on the counter-top and watched his sister efficiently prepare cheese, lettuce, and tomato sandwiches. She'd probably prepared dozens of such sandwiches for her family, Steve thought, but he wasn't here to be sentimental. He had a question. 'Have you seen Lydia lately?'

'Lydia.' Rachel, raising a sharp knife to slice one sandwich, gave him a curious look. 'No. I haven't. Not lately. I think the last time I saw her was at some do just after you got married. Why? Have you seen her?'

'No way. What I want to know is, what did she tell you when you did last see her?'

Rachel sliced the sandwich. She prepared the bread for the second one. 'Do you want mayonnaise?'

'Okay, if it's going.' She went to the refrigerator and took out a jar of mayo.

'Rachel. Tell me.'

'You obviously know,' Rachel said, unscrewing the cap of the jar of mayonnaise. 'She told me you asked her to marry you and she turned you down.'

'You believed that?'

'I'm not sure. Lydia has a habit of saving face. Lots of pride. She was abused as a child, you know, by an uncle.'

Steve hadn't known that. Actually, when he thought about it he hadn't known much about Lydia at all. Their conversations had always been business-orientated. In some ways he'd made a similar mistake with Anni. He didn't know much about her past, hadn't told Anni about his own, except for superficialities. 'Then you believe it's not true?' he asked, taking the plate Rachel offered and being urged to sit down at the table in the breakfast nook.

Rachel sat down opposite him and poured coffee into big mugs. 'To be honest I did think it might have been at first. Ben did too, but we didn't say anything.'

'No. Just acted disapproving of my marriage to Anni.'

'I admit we did disapprove but it wasn't because of Lydia or anything she told me. But it's not like that now, Steve. Anni isn't quite how I expected her to be. She's different and Mother loves her and I like her as well. Janet just says, "I told you she was cool".'

'So you don't believe Lydia?'

'If you say you didn't ask Lydia to marry you then I'll believe you, Stevie.'

'Thank you, but I do not appreciate you telling other people about my affairs. Especially Marie Firth. Craig was a pain in the ass over my promotion.'

Steve saw that Rachel had the grace to turn pale. Then the paleness turned red and crept up her face and flooded her neck.

'How did you know I told her?'

'Because Anni was in my private washroom on the night of my promotion and she overheard you.'

'I'm sure you explained to Anni and told her the truth.'

'I've tried, yes, but we've barely had time to breathe since then.' Steve leaned back and stared at the refrigerator door that was covered with magnets and kids' drawings. Would his refrigerator door ever look that way? He felt a hollow ache deep inside him where all his emotion coiled in a tight knot of pain.

Rachel shook her head. 'I'm sorry, Steve. I didn't know she was in the washroom. And I'd had a lot to drink so I wasn't really thinking and I always like to tell Marie a little gossip. She's that type. But Steve, I knew you wouldn't find it easy being married in the first place, let alone to a woman like Anni. You're really going to have to work at this marriage.'

'I realize that now,' he said. Rachel's explanation didn't really help but at least he had Rachel convinced Lydia hadn't told the truth. 'Has it ever been like this for you and Ben?'

'I presume you mean, by "this", a sort of lack of communication. That's the story of our relationship. Ben's a workaholic, you know that. He has tons of work at home all the time. He barely saw the boys when they were babies. It's only now he's taking a bit of time for them.'

Steve heard the hurt in his sister's voice and he knew that Rachel wasn't against him. She was on his side because she knew how difficult marriages could be. All along she had been trying to protect him. 'But you get along,' he said.

She tossed her long hair. 'Oh, yeah. I love the beast. I always have.' She laughed. 'And he loves me. I do know that. But I haven't had a demanding career like Anni. I've been with the kids and took time to work everything out with Ben. I've had to force him to talk to me and explain his feelings. He's not very good with that but he's getting better. But I don't believe you are like that, Steve. You're more forthright. Although you do tend to turn around and hide your head in the sand when the going gets tough.'

368

'I guess,' he said. 'Although I'm not sure how to handle the situation. I admit the Lydia thing didn't help but it wasn't the sole reason we've hit a wall.'

'You've both been independent a long time. It's difficult living with someone and accommodating another person when you've always done what you wanted.'

Steve began to eat the sandwich. 'You're wise.'

'Older,' Rachel said. 'I'm sure it will work out. You're going to have a baby now. It'll have to, won't it?'

Steve agreed it would but he wasn't sure how as he drove back to work. The temperature had zoomed down the thermometer since this morning and the warmer weather of the last few days was gone. He actually saw snowflakes in the air. During the afternoon, when he looked out of his window, he saw the snow had accumulated on the roads and the traffic was at a crawl. When he turned on the radio the weather forecast was predicting over a foot of snow, maybe more closer to the lake. More than they'd had at one stretch all winter long. But this snow was heavy, wet spring snow. It was affecting the entire Great Lakes area and the Eastern Seaboard of the USA.

There were accidents everywhere. The 401 north of Toronto was closed down to one lane. Downtown Yonge Street was chaos. Steve began to worry about Anni. He had left her in bed this morning, sleeping and tousled, so he didn't know her movements today. He phoned the house but Anni wasn't there. He left a message on the answering machine.

He phoned his mother and wished he hadn't. Diane panicked. Her parents had been killed on such a day in spring. A freak storm when they were on their way back from wintering in Florida.

'I'm not talking about an accident, Mother,' Steve said. 'I'm just checking to see where Anni is.'

'I haven't talked to her today.'

'All right. Fine. I'll call Marian.'

Marian hadn't seen her daughter either. He tried Anni's apartment but there was no answer there. She had disconnected her answering machine for some reason.

Hell, he was going to go home. By that time she might be there. Quickly, he packed up his brief-case, said goodnight to Alf, who seemed like the only person left in the office.

'Paul sent the women home,' Alf said. 'I'm leaving myself in a few moments. Take it easy. The roads are treacherous and everyone was getting into a spring-like mood so they weren't prepared for driving in snow again.'

'You take it easy as well,' Steve said, and went down to the parking lot for his car.

'I can't believe Ray would do that to you, Anni,' Joni said, trying to concentrate on Jonathan's crankiness and her friend waving her contract around before her eyes at the same time.

Anni had found Joni at home today and collapsed on to one of the big oversize sofas that Joni had in abundance around the two-storey brick city house. 'Well, he has. What am I going to do?'

Jonathan began to scream. 'That's what *he* recommends,' Joni laughed. 'Come on, honey. Don't cry. There's nothing to cry about. Go to Aunty Anni.'

Pointed at Anni, Jonathan noticed her silver pendant and immediately stopped crying and reached for the bright object. Joni handed her son to Anni and Jonathan was immediately quiet, laughing and gurgling.

'We might have to switch kids,' Joni said wryly. 'He likes you better than me. Lord, he's been cranky these last few days. Reminds me of his father when he gets like that.'

'Charles is cranky?' Anni forgot all her problems with Jonathan happy in her arms. She stroked his downy dark hair.

'Better believe it. Now. Do you want some tea?'

'I'm off caffeine. It'll have to be herbal.'

'You know me. Queen of Herbal. Keep him happy and I'll go get it.'

When Joni returned with a tray of tea and cookies Jonathan was dozing in Anni's arms.

'What a little baby,' Joni cooed. 'You know what I think, Anni. I think you should ask Steve about your contract.' She raised a dark eyebrow. 'After all, he is a lawyer. And he's not Ray's lawyer any more.' Steve had handed Ray's account over once he'd been promoted, in the general reshuffle of work.

'I've hardly spoken to Steve lately,' Anni admitted.

'Here's your chance. You're going to have to patch things up.' Joni put the tray on the black lacquered coffee table. 'Do you want me to pour?'

'Please.' Anni cuddled Jonathan. 'He's so warm and soft.'

'Isn't he just? Do you want him for a while, you know, for practice, while Charles and I get some sleep? Here, let's put him in his cot then we can have our tea in peace.'

Anni handed over the baby but every couple of minutes she couldn't stop peeking to see if he was all right. She knew she was going to be an anxiety-ridden mother. Just like her own. Now she understood Marian's hang-ups about herself. Especially with her mother's story about falling off the horse. She told Joni about that and they chuckled at the image of Marian Ross on top of a horse.

'Still, it's changed my opinion of my mother,' Anni said, sipping the hot, fragrant tea.

'You never wanted an opinion of your mother, Anni,' Joni said wisely. 'You wanted to fly away and not have anyone cut your wings. You're still doing that with Steve, I believe.'

Maybe she was, she thought. But Steve hadn't helped with his supposed reasons for marrying her.

The two women had been so engaged in their conversation they hadn't noticed the snow.

'Oh, my lord,' Joni said. 'Are you going to be okay, Anni?'

'Sure, I'm fine. It's not far.'

'But it's still coming down. It looks like feet. Here, let me help you clean off your car.'

The ride home was extra slow but Anni eventually made it and drove her car gratefully into the garage. Dash began meowing loudly as soon as he saw her. She fed him in the kitchen and then went into Steve's study to check the answering machine. Steve's machine was different from Anni's old one; it showed the number of messages in red. There were five. She played them.

'Anni, Steve. I'm wondering where you are with all this snow. Hope you get home safely.'

'Anni, Janet. I have a neat collar and leash for Dash so you can take him out in the back yard. I'll bring it over on the weekend.'

'Anni, Joni. You left your silk scarf here. The blue one. I'll keep it safe. Don't worry. 'Night.'

'Ann. Your mother. Steve phoned this afternoon. He was wondering where you were. Hope you are safe at home, dear. Phone me and let me know.'

'Anni. Diane. Call Rachel right away, as soon as you get in. It's urgent. Very urgent. And don't worry, honey. I'm at the hospital.'

CHAPTER 20

The phone rang once and Rachel picked it up.

'It's Anni, Rachel. What's the matter with Diane?'

'It's not Diane, Anni.' Rachel paused for a second. Then, breathlessly, her voice full of anxiety and tears, 'It's Steve. He's had a car accident.'

Anni heard a little yelp come from her throat. The receiver shook in her hand.

'Please be calm, Anni,' Rachel said, sounding none too calm herself. 'Ben and I will be over to drive you to the hospital.'

'All right,' Anni said, trying to get her mind around what Rachel had told her. 'Can you tell me anything about what happened?'

'No one will actually know until we talk to Steve himself, and he's in Emergency. We'll see when we get there. Mom and Dad and Janet are there already and so is our family doctor, Dr Stern. Everything's under control. Just wait for us, Anni.'

'I'll be here.' Anni hung up the phone and looked around Steve's study. All his stuff. What if . . .? *No*. It couldn't happen. He couldn't die. Not Steve. She loved him so much, so dearly. She hadn't realized how much until this moment. If she lost him . . . Automatically her fingers splayed over her stomach. If she lost him, life wouldn't be worth living.

They'd been so stupid. Wasted so much time. And she knew that Steve's driving became erratic when he was agitated or upset. Had he been upset about something today?

Dash jumped on Steve's desk and looked at the phone, then at Anni. He knew something was wrong. She scooped him up into her arms and hugged him. He sat by her side as she prepared to leave the house. She was wearing leggings and a sweater. She put on her leather jacket, a black beret, tucked a warm scarf around her neck and her feet into high boots because of the amount of snow outside. She turned on lights. Everything was done without much thought or feeling. She waited impatiently. As soon as she saw Ben's black van arrive in the driveway she left the house immediately and locked the door.

'All right, Anni?' Ben asked, jumping from the van into the accumulating snow to help her.

'I'm fine.' Anni stepped through mounds of snow. Usually Steve shovelled but Steve wasn't here. He was in hospital. She could barely believe it. 'I just want to see Steve.'

'We all do. Come on. Climb in.'

With Ben's strong hand helping her, Anni climbed in and sat on the bench seat behind Ben and Rachel. Behind, there was another seat. The van seated seven altogether, she believed. Jack and

Jason were both on hockey teams and Ben often had his turn at driving the boys and their friends to various arenas around the Province.

Rachel turned around and smiled at Anni. 'I've been trying to get through to Mother on Ben's cellphone.'

'You don't know anything, then?'

'No.'

Anni felt her throat close up. Although she couldn't cry. She didn't know what she was going to find or how she might cope. She remembered going to the hospital to see her father when he was taken ill. By the time she'd arrived he was dead.

'Anni,' Rachel said, 'Steve came for lunch with me today.'

Ben grunted. 'Rachel . . .' he said, as if he felt she was saying too much.

'Was he upset about anything?' Anni asked, leaning her arms on the back of Rachel's seat. 'When Steve gets distraught he drives more impatiently. It's noticeable because he's usually so careful.'

Rachel looked slightly sheepish. 'He came to question me about Lydia, his ex-girlfriend. Apparently you overheard me talking to Marie Firth.'

Anni felt heat flush her cheeks. 'I shouldn't have listened,' she said.

'More like it, I shouldn't have talked to Marie about my brother.'

'So what is the truth?' Anni asked.

'Steve didn't ask her.'

Anni wanted to be angry but she was so worried about Steve she didn't want to expend the energy. 'Then why spread the gossip?'

'Marie is that type of person. She likes to gossip and that was the most recent morsel. I'd had a bit to drink and at that time I truly didn't think you were right for Steve. But I've changed my mind.'

'You mean you like me now?' Anni said. *After you've nearly wrecked my marriage!*

'I do,' Rachel gave her a pained look. 'Forgive me.'

Anni patted Rachel's shoulder. 'I forgive you.' But inside she felt betrayed. Even though she knew the gossip she had heard was only a symptom of deeper problems with Steve. Problems she was now free to solve. *If he lived.*

Ben drove well through the snowy streets but it was a slow, monotonous trip. Anni wished she could jump from the van and run to the hospital. She was sure she would arrive sooner. But at last Ben dropped Rachel and Anni at the main door and went to park the vehicle.

Diane met them in the long corridor. She looked pale and harassed in a thick parka with a fur-lined hood. 'He's okay,' she said. 'He's okay.'

Relieved, Anni fell into her mother-in-law's arms. 'Can we see him?'

Diane still held Anni as she spoke. 'He's just getting cleaned up. He had a cut over his forehead that bled a great deal. But they tested and found no head injuries, thank goodness. His arm was also cut badly.' The older woman shuddered, obviously imagining what actually could have happened to her son. 'My mother and father were killed in a car crash, you know.'

'I know,' Anni said. 'Steve told me.'

'The weather was exactly like this. They were travelling back from Florida in springtime. A spring storm.'

Anni hugged Diane again, aware that a bond had formed over the past few months, a bond she hadn't really been aware of. A bond she was going to need when the baby came. 'Steve will be okay,' she soothed, even if she didn't really know it for sure. And yet she felt a contentment, as if she belonged in the Hunter family and would never be an outsider again. Even Rachel's confession hadn't marred the bonding. The black dress and red heels incident seemed so long ago, so far in the past, it might have been a different woman who dressed that way. It *had* been a different woman.

'Do you know what happened exactly?' Rachel asked as they walked to a sitting area where her father and her sister sat. 'Steve's such a safe driver usually.'

'It wasn't Steve's driving,' Diane said. 'Steve told Dr Stern that a little boy ran into the road in front of a garbage truck. Steve had to swerve across the road. Because of the icy streets, and because the road was full of parked cars he sideswiped two cars. He couldn't help it. There was nowhere for him to go. The Mercedes is scraped all along one side, I believe. And Steve's door was dented in. Steve's lucky.'

Imagining Steve inside his car crashing into other vehicles, Anni held her throat with her hand. Her stomach plunged even if inside she felt strung up, as if she were full of tight wires. Her chest ached from the effort of holding herself taut. 'I couldn't believe he'd have an accident that was his own fault.'

'I know,' Diane said, 'but it was either the cars at the side of the road or the child.'

'Typical Steve,' Janet said, and looked at Anni. Anni knew how much Janet loved her brother.

Ben arrived at that time, snow capping his hair and dark wool jacket. Anni wondered why she'd ever thought him stuffy. He had his lawyer persona the same as Steve, and the same way she had her dancer persona. But at this moment they were all merely family coping with what could have been a terrible tragedy for two families if Steve had hit the child. And if he'd died to save the child . . . well, Anni would expect that of Steve. He'd be a hero. He was certainly her hero. She felt her eyes well with tears. But she didn't want to break down. She needed action.

She said firmly, 'I've got to see him.' And she walked to the reception desk.

'I know you,' the nurse said. 'I saw you dance *Wedding Bells*.'

'That's me,' Anni said. 'My husband is Steve Hunter. He's in Emergency. I want to see him.'

'Just a moment.' The nurse picked up a phone and dialled an extension. When she hung up, she said, 'He's been fixed up. He's just resting for a while. Dr Stern will meet you at the third door along.'

'Thank you,' Anni said with a smile and returned to the family who were now sipping on coffee from foam cups. 'I'm going to see Steve.'

Diane jumped up. 'I'd like to . . .'

Her husband put his hand on his wife's arm. 'Let Anni go first,' Ray said. 'We know Steve is okay.'

'Give him my love, Anni,' Diane said.

'I will.' And mine, she thought as she hurried down the corridor to where a stout dark-haired man stood waiting.

Dr Stern seemed to know who she was. He beckoned her into the room. 'He's fine, Mrs Hunter. But he'll have a few nightmares, I'm sure.'

Steve was sitting in a chair dressed only in his suit pants. He had a plaster across his forehead and a bandage across his chest, and his left arm was bound. His hair was scraped back from his forehead and Anni thought he looked deathly pale.

As he looked at her, his usually bright eyes weary, she could feel the tension and restraint they had used in their dealings with one another over the past few months. Just because she loved him, wanted to love him and didn't want to lose him, it didn't change any of that.

But *she* was going to change it. He was her child's father and she wanted him alive and healthy so they could enjoy their family life. Not only that, she wanted him alive and healthy for his own sake, so he could have his life and enjoy it. And if they didn't make things better soon they were never going to achieve any of that.

'You gave me a shock, Steve,' she said, realizing the doctor had left them alone.

'I am a shock,' he said wryly. 'My shirt is wrecked. Mother brought along one of Dad's sweatshirts. Do you think you could help me with it.'

'Sure.' Anni put down her purse and picked up the extra large black sweatshirt. She helped Steve ease it over his head, trying to avoid the bandages. 'Do you hurt?'

'Real sore. Lots of blood. But the kid's okay?'

'Yes. The little boy is okay.'

'I'm sorry, Anni.'

She tucked the sweatshirt down around his waist. 'What for?'

'For dragging you into this mess with me.'

'What mess, Steve?'

'All this extra stuff in your life. My family, me, the baby, now this accident. Your dancing . . .'

'To hell with my dancing, Steve. Right now you're the most important thing in my life. And the baby, of course. I love you, Steve. I love you.'

She saw his face light up slightly, but he winced when he tried to smile.

'My head is pounding like a damn jackhammer,' he said, touching the plaster. 'Do you mean that, Anni?'

'I mean it. And I'd sit on your knee and prove it if you weren't so bashed up.'

'Sit on my knee anyway, honey. Come here.'

Anni perched gingerly on his knees. She cupped his face with her hands and kissed his mouth gently. 'If I lost you I'd die, Steve.'

He lifted the arm that wasn't bandaged and touched the silvery tendrils of her hair beneath her black beret. 'I love you as well, Anni. I did the first time I saw you. You know that, sweetheart.'

'I fought you, though, Steve.'

'Did you ever.' He brushed her cheek with the backs of his fingers.

Dr Stern entered the door followed by Diane, Ray, Ben, Rachel and Janet.

'Can't keep them all out,' the friendly family doctor said with a grin. 'Take him home and keep him quiet for a few days. There wasn't any concussion but we have to be careful. He'll be sore when the pain-killers wear off. I'll give you another package, Mrs Hunter. And some extra dressings for that arm wound.'

Anni lifted herself from Steve's knees and a little shyly began to fasten her jacket. 'Thank you.'

Dr Stern gave her a sideways look. 'I know you probably have your own doctor, but if you need to come by and see me as the baby develops, don't hesitate. I delivered Jack and Jason and I know the Hunter family well.'

'Thank you,' Anni said again, thinking she might just take the doctor up on his offer. Her own doctor wasn't her original doctor any more. He had retired a few years ago.

By the time Ben delivered him home, Steve's body felt as if it were a mass of aches. It helped, though, to have Anni at his side, so concerned. If it took a car accident to bring Anni back to him, then that was fine. He'd suffer. At least the pain was physical and would eventually heal.

'So tell us what exactly happened?' Ben asked from the front seat of the van. Although the snow had stopped, the traffic was still tied up.

Steve shook his head. 'Like any accident, it happened and now I'm making sense of it. I was driving home. The roads were plugged, so I turned up a side street for a short cut. There were cars parked on both sides in front of the houses. A garbage truck was blocking the way. So I put my foot on the gas to pass and just as I accelerated a little boy ran out into the road in front of the truck. Naturally I swerved to miss the boy and side-swiped a row of cars. It happened so quickly. I only reacted, I didn't think.'

'You didn't pass out?' Rachel said.

'No. But there was blood everywhere. I thought, this is it, I'm going to bleed to death. It looked worse than it was, I think. The boy's mother panicked. She called the police and the ambulance and came back to talk to me. She couldn't open the door but the other door was okay so she put a snow compress on my forehead. Otherwise maybe I would have passed out, maybe even lost more blood. Luckily Dr Stern was at the hospital and treated me right away and called the family.'

Steve put his good arm around Anni. 'Who called you, Anni?'

'Your mother,' she told him.

Ben helped Steve inside the house when they arrived. Anni made them all hot chocolate and sandwiches. Diane phoned as soon as they began eating and Steve talked to his mother on the phone to reassure her he was being taken care of.

Eventually Ben and Rachel left and Steve was alone with Anni. Despite their declarations of love at the hospital he wasn't sure how they would react to one another now they were alone.

But Anni said as soon as she had made him comfortable in the living room, 'You risked your life for that little boy's life, Steve. I find that admirable.'

'It was really nothing. I wasn't going to kill a child. That would be death to me, carrying around such a memory.'

Anni knelt at his feet by the sofa. 'I know. And I've been wrong to doubt anything about you but good. Steve. Forgive me.'

He touched her hair, her beautiful silky silvery hair. 'Forgive you for what? It's me who needs forgiving. I never told you things I should have told you. I suppose in a way we did rush our relationship and I had no time to tell you about my past girlfriends, or that I needed to be married for the promotion. I didn't want anything to get in the way. They didn't seem as important as loving you. I suppose it amounts to the fact that we didn't have enough time to forge a proper foundation and we wobbled.'

'I think that as well,' Anni said.

He stroked her hair. 'At least it was me who had the accident, not you. And you weren't with me. That's a relief.'

'You were coming home early, though?'

'Because of the storm. I called you and you weren't home and I was worried about you. If you had any problems I wanted to be there.' Steve forced a painful smile. 'I think those pills are wearing off, Anni. I'm feeling real bad.'

'You should go to bed. Can you make it upstairs?'

'Of course I can. But I might not be able to make anything else.'

'I'll put you down for a week from now,' Anni said. 'How's that?'

He gave her a lopsided grin. 'A week might be stretching it.'

'We'll see.'

The following morning Steve stayed in bed. Anni made phone calls to the insurance company and the body shop that had Steve's car. When that business was finished she went upstairs to see him. He was sleeping soundly with Dash beside him on the bed. She left them to sleep and went downstairs to call all the family, including her mother, who had been talking to Diane.

Steve revived the next day but he didn't go to work. The woman whose child had run into the road to cause the accident sent flowers and good wishes. In the card she said she would remember Steve forever. Everyone else visited bringing fruit, flowers and food until the house was packed. Anni's mother. His parents, Janet, Rachel, Ben, Alf and Sandy, Paul and Geraldine. Joni, Charles and baby Jonathan.

At the end of the week Anni drove Steve to the doctor to check his wounds. Dr Stern advised another week off for Steve to recover fully.

When they arrived home Anni cooked a meal for them both. They sat at the table over the succulent chicken and glasses of wine, both feeling the pressure and tension of the past months slip from them.

Steve began to tell Anni about Lydia, and how he had once suggested, because he'd never figured he'd ever meet anyone, that they marry for convenience. But it hadn't been a serious proposal. He figured she'd used it as such to save face.

'It wasn't really that, Steve,' Anni admitted. 'Oh, I was hurt at first, but when you told me you hadn't actually asked her, I believed you. I think I was more shaken up about the promotion stipulation.'

'They wanted me married but I wouldn't have married you solely for that.'

'You would have let it go if I hadn't said yes?'

'Truthfully, yes. When I heard I had the promotion it never felt as good as it did the day we got married. It still doesn't. It's just my job.'

Anni stared at her hands that were wound tightly together. 'I think I used the gossip I heard as an excuse to keep away from you so you wouldn't interfere with what I had to do. I wanted to escape dancing with Ray's company and it would have been so easy to leave without fulfilling my obligations so I had to keep driving myself. You were my vulnerable spot.'

'Now I've forced you to leave,' Steve said.

'No. I want the baby so much. I'm really happy about it, Steve. I don't care about Ray, about the show. Oh, yes, I'll want my career back again, but in a different form. I'll be with Joni.'

'And that's okay?'

'Wonderful.' She smiled.

Steve touched her clasped hands with both of his. 'I don't want to ever feel that I've dragged you

386

away from something you love. I also hope I can live up to your father.'

Anni frowned. 'What do you mean?'

'I don't know if I can live up to your ideal man.'

'I'm not sure he was my ideal.'

'But he was your male role model figure in your life.'

'Yes, and he did some silly things as well. He went and saved a huge sum for my wedding and all the while my mother had to scrape and save to get by.'

'So he had faults?'

'He certainly had faults, Steve. But he never ever told me I shouldn't dance. He always supported me. Although he didn't support my mother's horse-riding.'

Steve looked puzzled. 'Horse-riding?'

Their hands were firmly entwined now and Anni told Steve about her mother's riding and the accident.

'That's a strange image. Your mother on a horse.'

'I know.' Anni chuckled. 'Anyway, what all this is about, Steve. I love you.'

Steve squeezed her hands and said hoarsely. 'And I love you, Anni Ross.'

The following day Ray and Lucinda dropped by to see Steve. Ray brought a cheque for Anni.

'What was that for?' Steve asked when they were alone again at last.

'Oh. He was going to screw me on my contract. I was ready to hire my lawyer.'

'Me, I hope.'

'Yes, you. Since you're not *his* lawyer any more.'

'But he didn't?'

'No. Ray's bark is worse than his bite. Usually his threats brought me to my knees and I succumbed, but this time I couldn't succumb. I'm going to have a baby and I'll soon be literally in no shape to dance.'

'I can see that shape changing day by day.'

'Go on. I've hardly put on a few pounds.'

'Come here,' Steve said. 'I'm almost ready.'

Anni went into his waiting arms. His bandages had been reduced to small plasters now. The colour was back in his skin. She kissed him and pressed her body into his and whispered, 'You're more than ready by the feel of it.'

'Yes. Let's put that answering machine on one ring, lock the door and go upstairs to bed.'

They prepared for no interruptions and were soon upstairs in bed.

Steve's mouth possessed Anni's once again and his body covered hers. His pulse throbbed with her pulse, his need hard and demanding. From the core of her being, Anni began to respond, lifting her hips, shifting to allow him into the liquid heat inside her. His tongue flicked over her breasts and she closed her eyes and gave way to the gliding sensations of his warm mouth against her skin. It was like dancing and she was completely lost. Anni and Steve began the marriage dance to the fulfilment of their love.

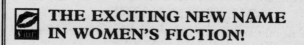

THE EXCITING NEW NAME
IN WOMEN'S FICTION!

PLEASE HELP ME TO HELP YOU!

Dear *Scarlet* Reader,

As Editor of *Scarlet* Books I want to make sure that the books I offer you every month are up to the high standards *Scarlet* readers expect. And to do that I need to know a little more about you and your reading likes and dislikes. So please spare a few minutes to fill in the short questionnaire on the following pages and send it to me.

Looking forward to hearing from you,

Sally Cooper

Editor-in-Chief, *Scarlet*

QUESTIONNAIRE

Please tick the appropriate boxes to indicate your answers

1 Where did you get this Scarlet title?
Bought in supermarket ☐
Bought at my local bookstore ☐ Bought at chain bookstore ☐
Bought at book exchange or used bookstore ☐
Borrowed from a friend ☐
Other (please indicate) _____

2 Did you enjoy reading it?
A lot ☐   A little ☐   Not at all ☐

3 What did you particularly like about this book?
Believable characters ☐   Easy to read ☐
Good value for money ☐   Enjoyable locations ☐
Interesting story ☐   Modern setting ☐
Other _____

4 What did you particularly dislike about this book?
_____

5 Would you buy another Scarlet book?
Yes ☐   No ☐

6 What other kinds of book do you enjoy reading?
Horror ☐   Puzzle books ☐   Historical fiction ☐
General fiction ☐   Crime/Detective ☐   Cookery ☐
Other (please indicate) _____

7 Which magazines do you enjoy reading?
1. _____
2. _____
3. _____

And now a little about you –
8 How old are you?
Under 25 ☐   25–34 ☐   35–44 ☐
45–54 ☐   55–64 ☐   over 65 ☐

cont.

9 What is your marital status?
   Single ☐   Married/living with partner ☐
   Widowed ☐   Separated/divorced ☐

10 What is your current occupation?
   Employed full-time ☐   Employed part-time ☐
   Student ☐   Housewife full-time ☐
   Unemployed ☐   Retired ☐

11 Do you have children? If so, how many and how old are they?
   _____
   _____

12 What is your annual household income?
   under $15,000   ☐   or   £10,000   ☐
   $15–25,000   ☐   or   £10–20,000   ☐
   $25–35,000   ☐   or   £20–30,000   ☐
   $35–50,000   ☐   or   £30–40,000   ☐
   over $50,000   ☐   or   £40,000   ☐

Miss/Mrs/Ms _____
Address _____
_____
_____ Postcode: _____

Thank you for completing this questionnaire. Now tear it out – put
it in an envelope and send it, before 31 July 1998, to:

Sally Cooper, Editor-in-Chief

USA/Can. address
SCARLET c/o London Bridge
85 River Rock Drive
Suite 202
Buffalo
NY 14207
USA

UK address/No stamp required
SCARLET
FREEPOST LON 3335
LONDON W8 4BR
Please use block capitals for
address

MADAN/1/98

***Scarlet* titles coming next month:**

THE MOST DANGEROUS GAME Mary Wibberley
Scarlet is delighted to announce the return to writing of this very popular author! 'Devlin' comes into Catherine's life when she is in need of protection and finds herself in that most clichéd of all situations – she's fallen in love with her bodyguard! The problem is that Devlin will leave when the job's over . . . won't he?

DANGEROUS DECEPTION Lisa Andrews
Luis Quevedo needs a fiancée in a hurry to please his grandfather. Emma fits the bill and desperately needs the money. Then she makes the mistake of falling in love with her 'fiancé' . . .

CRAVEN'S BRIDE Danielle Shaw
For ten years, Max Craven has blamed Alison for the death of his daughter. Now he returns home and finds his feelings for Alison have undergone a transformation. Surely he can't be in love with her?

BLUE SILK PROMISE Julia Wild
When Nick recovers consciousness after a serious accident, he finds himself married within days. Nick can't believe he's forgotten the woman he loves so passionately. Then, little by little, he begins to realize that his beloved Kayanne thinks he's his own brother!